Deadline

Douglas Keil

This story is a product of the author's imagination. Names, places, characters and incidents are intended to be fictional. However, the character Chuti Tiu was inspired by a real person. The CRISPR gene editing medical technology exists, as does the Sunway TaihuLight supercomputer.

Copyright 2019 Douglas Keil
All rights reserved
ISBN: 9781791341701

*Cover image created from original painting by
Bertrand Girard, owned by author.*

From the Author:

I receive all the accolades for planning and cooking Christmas dinner, but it's the chopper of dangling participles and cleanser of repetition who deserves equal credit for the feast – my beautiful, persnickety, brilliant and long-suffering editor and wife, Beverly. Hooray, and thank you.

There is the inspiring, and there is honesty. Stephen King's <u>On Writing</u> is both.

Chapter One

Seven-fifteen a.m. I've nicked myself shaving, and I'm late again for a job that has no starting or ending time. But my boss needs to exert his authority by gathering all the editors every morning at 7:30.

I walk down two flights of stairs to Parnell's Pub where Paddy is already working behind the bar.

"You look like hell," he greets me.

"Yeah, I know."

"What was all that noise in the middle of the night?" Paddy and his wife, Kathleen, live below my warehouse loft.

"Sorry, Riedell and I were rescuing Rowdy. He was caught in the rafters again, chasing birds. I really love this warehouse, but being up in the cathedral rafters in the middle of the night is kind of a pain."

Paddy shrugs. "You need to teach that cat to chase birds during the daytime."

"Got to go. See you later."

* * *

Dropping my satchel onto my desk, I see the red circle on my calendar. James Berk, the billionaire who just about ruined me ten years ago, is being released from prison today. A rapist and a murderer, the bastard was convicted only of tax evasion.

As I settle at my desk, my cell phone vibrates.

"We need to see you, now," she emphasizes in that rasping voice of hers. I recall her scent, as if she is only inches away. Lavender. How can I possibly remember that fragrance? How can I forget it?

Like James Berk, Gayfryd is a high point, and a low point of my past. "Not going to happen," I say, looking out my glass cubicle, eyeing my Managing Editor, Van Wie, at the far end of the City Room. He spots me looking at him and waves me to his office.

I shake my head, no, pointing to my phone, conveying that I'm busy. Maybe I should tell him his wife is texting me her new address.

* * *

I'm spent, wonderfully sated, unable to move. Actually I'm afraid to move. Gayfryd is panting like a panther. Her damp hair is on my chest. I'm her kill, draped in an acacia tree, knowing if I stir she'll pounce. I remember her volatility all too well. My ersatz lover is insane, and this was a mistake.

Why did I cave in to her? Gayfryd is my boss's wife, and my Publisher's niece. It ended a long time ago. My life is different now. But that intoxicating memory of lavender, and all that follows. I'm willing prey, and a complete fool. Gayfryd is the most vivacious, vicious, pretentious, dangerous, and sexiest woman I have ever known.

I need to leave, but she's pinning me down. I decide to risk it, lifting one leg off the bed. Too slow. Her panting changes to a growl. Her nails rake down my ribs.

A high caliber gunshot reverberates outside, off the Helmsley Hotel's reflecting towers, shaking the window glass.

Leaping from the bed, I trip, falling flat out. Slowly I get to my feet, hoping I didn't break it. Damn that hurt.

I press my face to the balcony window. "There's a cop car below," I shout. "The windshield is shattered. Splattered with blood. This balcony door won't open." I turn to Gayfryd. But she isn't there.

"Where'd you go?" I'm naked, and her lingering heat is leaving me quickly. I can't focus. Shivering, I grab my allotted towel, drop to my knees, and look under the sofa bed. God, the marble is cold and hard. "Where are you?"

Scanning her private hideaway, I see closed mahogany double doors, presumably leading to the adjoining residence. Gayfryd has warned me not to leave this room, but I have no choice. Clutching the towel, I push the double doors open and take a step inside.

"Are you in here?" I call for Gayfryd, but instantly realize this isn't her new apartment. I'm in a doctor's office of some kind. IV stands, a blinking AED, rows of glass cabinets filled with bandages, and vials of prescription drugs. A privacy curtain, partially drawn. I can see stirrups at the end of the examination table. This looks like an abortion clinic. The bitch set me up.

I can hear wailing sirens groaning to a halt below. There are emergency vehicles swarming, and I know in minutes the cops will be coming up, floor by floor. I can't be here.

"Get out now," I hear myself saying. Except I'm naked. Where are my clothes? I could drape myself in a sheet. *Excuse me? Could you direct me to the sauna?* I'd be cuffed in seconds.

The blaring bullhorns outside snap me back to reality. Backing out of the doctor's clinic, I instinctively wipe away my fingerprints. I've already decided the sheets are coming with me. DNA.

A gunshot and a bloody police car below the room where I am having sex with my boss's wife, all while I am investigating corruption in the NYPD. Too much of a coincidence. I need to get out of here.

I can't use the elevator. Twenty floors up, and the back stairs are my only option. I'll find my clothes, race down, and pray that the police haven't sealed off the exits. When I get back to the office, I'll tell my assistant, Gert, to cuff me to my desk if Gayfryd ever calls again.

Pulling the sheets off the bed, I hear a click behind me. Spinning around, I see Gayfryd's face, contorted and enraged. I notice something in her hands.

"Why?" I ask.

Chapter Two

It is the darkening side of afternoon, and growing cold quickly. The streets are unusually empty. I'm limping across East 46th Street, holding my Tasered right side through the pocket of my corduroy jacket. A patrol car whizzes past. Then two more. They could be going on another call, but I know better.

My cell vibrates. It's my assistant, Gert. She'll know what's going on, she always knows. Three more blaring cars whiz by. I turn up 1st Avenue and step into a quiet alley so I can hear. A drop of something hits my chin. I look up for a leaking a/c unit.

More cars scream by. "What?" I yell into the phone.

Gert responds in kind, yelling back, "Cop shot his partner dead in a squad car outside the Helmsley. Windows are covered with blood and brains. The shooter is sitting in the cruiser with his service pistol pressed in his eye, deciding."

"Damn," comes out as a honking firetruck blasts by. I wonder if these cops are targets of our corruption investigation. I put my cell down to my leg, thinking. I'm a reporter. I should go back for the story. But after what happened at Gayfryd's, I'm thinking I've already filled my dumb move quota for the day.

"You there?" Gert yells.

"Can't hear. Going to Parnell's. Call you back," I tell her as the emergency noises abruptly stop. I'm a New Yorker, the constant din is comforting. Quiet, that's disturbing.

Resuming my limping gait, I feel another drop on my nose. I swipe the spot and look at my sleeve. It isn't water or lucky bird crap, it's my blood.

* * *

Pushing through the revolving door into Parnell's Pub, I head straight to the men's room. Kathleen is behind the bar watching the TV. "Paddy's there," she hollers to me.

"Figures," I yell over my shoulder. Of course the Department would call Paddy. The Helmsley is in his old precinct. He still knows almost everyone there. They might use Paddy to talk down the cop with the gun in his eye.

The overhead fluorescent light is flickering, at least I think it's the light. Doesn't really matter. Whether it's the light or the throbbing behind my eyes, it's probably a blessing I can't get a clear look at myself in the mirror. Splashing water on my face helps. But it can't erase the images of the bloody windshield, or the insane rage on Gayfryd's face.

Tearing off a paper towel from the machine, I stand in the foggy little room wiping my hands until they are well past dry. What the hell has happened? Nothing this morning makes sense.

Returning to the bar, I take my regular spot, second stool from the end near the kitchen. There are only two other customers. Kathleen is glued to the muted TV screen, hoping to get a glimpse of her husband. Memory guides her hand to a glass on the center shelf. She scoops up ice and pours my Jack Daniels, never taking her eyes off the screen.

I can see the gawking crowd being pushed back by the police. I watch, mildly amused at confused cops aiming pistols toward one of their own who has his gun pressed in his eye. Who are they going to shoot?

Paddy must be inside the Command truck, which is idling no more than fifty feet from the bloody squad car. He'll be on-air soon, I can sense it. He is best face-to-face, the honesty in his eyes, and compassion in his voice. He connects.

I know I've lost my edge since Emma died. My priorities changed. I'm raising a young girl. But sitting here safely in Parnell's while my friend is on the scene feels wrong. I should be there. After all, I'm the reporter.

The police corruption series I'm working on has sparked my old ambitions. I'm enjoying the rush, but now it's not only me I'm endangering. Is there any way this shooting is related to my series? My gut says Gayfryd, and maybe Berk, are connected. I can't get a handle on it.

"Couple of cops are in the car. Could be Paddy's former boys from Midtown," Kathleen tells me what I already know. "Looks like one is dead. The other is holding his gun to his own head. It's as if he is waiting for someone to give him the okay to kill himself."

Putting my cellphone on the bar, I notice my right hand is trembling. Eyes still on the TV, Kathleen moves closer to me. I hide my hand and the phone in my side jacket pocket. My gut takes a twist. I manage to say, "Left my…in the restroom," as I rush back, reaching the toilet just in time.

Deep breaths. That helps. I sit under the flickering lights until my stomach settles. Then, I call the office and reach Gert. "I'm at Parnell's. Kathleen is glued to the television. We think Paddy is in the Command truck at the Helmsley. Do you have your scanner on?"

"Of course."

"Good. Listen for any mention of Paddy, okay? Check our source at the precinct. Find out which cops are in the car. You know where I was, don't you?"

"I can guess. The Helmsley."

"It was stupid of me," I admit.

"You're a guy," Gert replies.

"This wasn't like the old days. It was a set up. I don't know why, my gut says..." Just as I say the word, my gut announces it's not finished.

I can't get my cell in my pocket fast enough to cover up my retching. Once I'm done, sweating, gasping, I see my cell on the floor, still connected. "Sorry," I say to Gert. "Really done now," I tell her, hoping it's so. "These cops have got to be connected to our investigation."

"Feels that way to me too. You'll stay at Parnell's?"

"Yeah. Kathleen's working the bar."

"Have her mix you a Pepto."

"Will do," I say pressing my cell off. I grab a paper towel to open the door.

"Found it," I call out to Kathleen as I return to the bar. She is still fixed on the television. Doubt she noticed I was gone. She has the TV remote in one hand and her cell phone in the other.

"You hear from Paddy?" she asks, not looking.

It's an odd question. Paddy would certainly call his wife before me. "He'll call once he's got the situation under control," I say, wincing at the platitude.

"Course, I know," she says, still fixed on the screen as the camera shot widens. She feels her way to the Jack Daniels and a glass, and pours another until the precious liquid spills over her hand.

"Sorry," she apologizes, finally turning toward me. "Holy shite! What the hell happened to you? You okay?"

"Fine, I'm fine," I lie, trying to sound convincing.

"Oh no you're not." Kathleen reaches under the bar for a brown bottle of hydrogen peroxide and a handful of sterile pads. "Look at you," she scolds, her Irish brogue becoming more pronounced.

Having been the surrogate mother to a brood of brothers and a shiftless, sod father, Kathleen mastered first aid at an early age. Nursing was a natural progression.

"Ouch."

"Don't whine. Your lip is split. You'll be drinking through a straw for a while. And this eye, will you look at that shiner? I'll get some ice. You should get this checked out at the hospital. Look up. Side-to-side," she orders.

Holding my face in her hands, she observes, "The orbital rim is intact. Pupils are reactive, but there's possible damage to the zygoma, the bone beneath the eye. You really should get it looked at, but I know you won't until you're staggering like my dear ole Da."

I don't try to respond. Her worries are focused on what's happening at the Helmsley. She doesn't even ask how I got in this condition.

With her repairs complete, she cleans off a few smears from my chin, and tosses the bloodied waste. "That will hold you for a while." Rounding the bar, she scoops ice in a towel, spins it tight and slaps the compress on the bar, gesturing to my head.

I reach for it and flinch with pain. She notices.

"What's wrong? Off with your jacket," she orders, returning to my stool.

Kathleen's mothering feels awkward. My own mother was never the nurturing kind. And, Kathleen is my older friend's much younger wife.

As Kathleen pulls off my well-worn corduroy, I see a tight camera shot of the cop with his gun muzzle jammed in his eye. "This can wait." I tell her. She ignores me.

I make out the cop's uniform, but the TV shot is deliberately blurred, so positive identification is impossible. "Smart cameraman," I say, quickly correcting to "cameraperson." Gert and Kathleen enjoy educating me into the morass of political correctness.

My cell is vibrating on the bar. Gert is sending a steady stream of texts. At least one of us is on the job. I scroll through as Kathleen strips back my shirt.

"Ouch, damn it. That hurt."

"That's a bee sting, nothing compared to what's coming. Wait 'til your body starts showing you how pissed she is for what you did to her. She'll be reminding you to be more considerate for weeks."

"I'm a he, remember?"

"All bodies are female. You're just our fruit, with a little stem attached. So, what'd Gert say?"

Talking with Kathleen is like swatting at no-can-see-ums, gnats.

"Hang on, I've got some Dickenson's witch hazel in the kitchen."

"Witch hazel? I thought that is used for. . ?" I have no idea what it is used for. Doesn't matter. I am talking to myself.

Pulling my cell closer, I see Gert's text messages: *No suspected terrorist connection. Cop-to-cop murder. Ninety six point four percent of cops commit suicide using their service weapon. No property in the tax records under Gayfryd's name at the Helmsley address. Nothing on Paddy.*

Since Gert's nephew introduced her to the digital universe, Gert has become a techno freak. My word. Gert would probably prefer wizard. Already she has considered a possible terrorist attack, located the apartment/clinic, and tried to connect Gayfryd to the police shooting. All without leaving her desk. I used to be the one telling her the breaking news. Now she's telling me. And she's the assistant.

"Try our Midtown source again," I suggest. "He must know who the cops are."

With my jacket laying on the bar, and shirt pulled down around my waist, Kathleen splashes handfuls of the cold, peculiar-smelling liquid on me like she is washing a car.

"Ow," I yell, jumping back.

"Shawn, Baby. This isn't what hurts. This does," she says pressing a finger in my ribs, causing me to inhale sharply. "If your brain won't tell you it's dumb to sleep with another man's wife, your body will."

Once I resume breathing, I ask, "Would you not mention this to Paddy?"

"You think he's not going to notice your kisser?" she says, holding up a bar shaker as a mirror.

"I mean the ribs. Paddy will bang me around the racquetball court even more if he knows." In truth I'm embarrassed having him know Gayfryd did this to me.

"Get dressed," she says shaking her head, finished with her nursing. "Now, out with it. You were finally caught by her husband?" Kathleen smiles.

"No."

"One of her other lovers?" Kathleen says, dramatizing *lovers*. She despises Gayfryd, despite never having met her. "One of them caught you. Got his day confused."

I understand, and oddly appreciate, Kathleen's sarcasm. "I may have seen something I shouldn't have," I whisper.

She hesitates a moment, waiting to see if I'll explain further, then busies herself polishing the bar top, keeping an eye on the TV.

"Look, there's Paddy," she points, forgetting the polishing. "He's getting out of the Command truck. It's over," she declares and collapses onto the bar, sobbing with relief. Paddy is a lucky man.

"He did it," she says, wiping her face with her bare arms. Ready to buy someone a drink, she sees only a couple rummies down front, and two drinks still in front of me. So she pours herself a McCallum, downs it, and pounds the shot glass on the bar. "Paddy talked him down," she boasts, rightly so.

"He hasn't lost his touch," I agree.

My cellphone vibrates. *Call Me!!!!* Gert texts.

"Shawn?" Gert answers the first ring. I stand, sending a colossal spasm up my right side. I drop the phone, both hands gripping the bar rail trying to absorb the pain.

"Shawn?" Gert shouts again.

My cellphone is lying on the bar in front of me with Gert calling my name, but I can't move. I can't speak. A single tear rolls down my face, dropping to my shirt. I can't even lift my hand to stop the tear. All I can do is squeeze the bar.

It feels like minutes pass, I have no idea. Finally I open my eyes, blinking, forcing a smile back to my hideous reflection in the bar mirror. I see the self-portraits of Emma's mental patient friends hung around the wall surrounding the mirror. My reflection fits right in. All the paintings have been sold and resold, sponsored by Parnell's clientele, donated to the homeless. Not a drawing leaves its place on the wall. "Reminders," Paddy says, "that the line is thin."

"Hi, Honey," I say to Emma's self-portrait on the left. "You'd think I would learn."

I ease back down to my stool. "Shawn," Gert yells again.

Kathleen returns, slapping a finger of Vaseline on my lower lip. She sees me quivering. "What happened?"

"Phone," I whisper.

Kathleen picks up my cell just as Gert yells, "The dead cop, he's our *Ace of Spades.*"

"Holy Shit! The dead cop is our confidential informant?"

"What's she talking about?" Kathleen demands.

"The shooting. The location. Gayfryd. Paddy. It's a set up," Gert screams.

"Call Paddy, now!" I shout at Kathleen, blood flying off my lip. Kathleen panics. "I can't. Just tried. His phone is off."

"Again," I demand. The next spasm hits. I manage an urgent whisper. "Everyone you know. Call! Extreme danger!"

The TV camera person has been given the "all clear," and is moving in for the money shot. On the dashboard, an officer's cap. Scrambled eggs. The picture tightens.

"Still no answer," Kathleen yells, pushing the call button again.

We see the uniformed negotiator and Paddy leave the Command truck, hands in the air, moving toward the squad. The officer in the car appears stunned to see the phalanx of uniforms closing in behind them, ridiculously pointing their weapons.

I can see Paddy's eyes meeting those of the cop with the gun. Paddy reacts first, grabbing the shoulders of the leading uniforms, pulling them away.

"Get back!" I yell as the police car erupts in a two story ball of flames. Eight blocks away, we can hear the blast rumbling outside the Pub.

"Oh, my God," Kathleen screams. The TV flickers before going black. "Paddy." Kathleen turns to me. Her legs crumple.

I stand immobile, clutching the bar rail, as the TV comes back to life. Firetrucks that had passed me by earlier are spraying the incinerated squad car with foam. Paramedics are swarming to bloodied cops, shell-shocked gawkers, and reporters flattened on the pavement, clutching microphones to silent mouths.

A camera, lying on the ground, is aimed at the Helmsley's front entrance. The massive glass double doors are dangling from the hinges like the last autumn leaves hanging from a branch. A doorman's heavy coat is smoldering nearby.

Still nauseous from my spasms, I can offer little physical comfort to Kathleen. My phone rings again.

"I see him," Gert yells. "He's up, bloodied, staggering, but he's alive."

Chapter Three

Kathleen starts preparing for the after-work regulars. If anything, Kathleen is practical to the core.

I move to a quiet corner and call Gert. She answers on the first ring.

"Call Emergency at Eastside Mercy, Bellevue as well. Get the names of the staff and attending physicians. I want to know the heat, residue, fragmentation, everything. Do we have any housekeeping contacts at the Helmsley? Wouldn't hurt to make contact with the Parks Service. They have cameras scattered everywhere. When you get the cops' names, get the home phone numbers."

"Roger that."

"I'll call the wives direct once you get the identification. But this is going to be your story. I'll be your confidential source, your byline. Got it?"

"Yeah, but,"

"No buts. We are going to stay objective."

"Kathleen okay?" Gert asks.

"Think so, she's getting ready for the rush."

A pause. Gert's voice, a whisper. "It's Starch. He's had a stroke."

Cuthbert Storch is the esteemed Chronical owner, Publisher and Chair of the Board, affectionately known as Starch by Gert and me, and now most of the City Room. Starch has become a sort of protector for me ever since the James Berk treachery ten years ago. Though we are cut from opposite cloths, I admit I've become fond of the pedigreed, stiff-collared old fart.

Starch is the one who initiated the police corruption project and by-passed Van Wie to give me the opportunity, and the resources.

"Starch going to make it?" I ask.

"Who can tell? The nurse is in his office, and the ambulance hasn't arrived yet. All the hospitals are Code Black because of the bombing."

"I'd better get over there."

"There's nothing you can do for him. You won't get near his office. But here's the strange part: Van Wie doesn't care what's happening with Starch. He ordered Security to snatch Arlo's computer. Why do you think that was his first reaction?"

"Because he knows something we don't know."

"Like what?"

"That there might be a connection to our project and the bombing."

"Our dead informant?"

"Think about it. I get a call from Gayfryd after all this time; a cop kills another cop who happens to be our informant, while I am at the Helmsley. Then the bomb. I think Van Wie is trying to tie the pieces together. With Starch out of the picture, it's his chance to find out what we've been doing. He suspects Arlo is the connection to the secret project."

Arlo, the hacker Starch assigned to us, is sketchy at best. Gert and I don't trust Arlo for a second. Gert has been warning me for months. "Our files are not secure. And those flash drives you hide in Starch's safe, we'll both go to prison if they get discovered."

Starch has an everyday safe, and then the real one below. With him out of action, his lifelong secretary, Mrs. Wright, will invade his office. She knows about the second safe, but I don't think she has the combination. It's for his personal stuff. And our flash drives. She'll want to get in it just to protect him, not us.

The General Counsel will bury our remains if anyone gets their hands on those flash drives.

"Shit. You better pray Van Wie can't trace Arlo's hacks. And start shredding fast," I tell Gert.

* * *

I yell to Kathleen, "I've got to go." I take a few steps, and my right knee buckles, nearly sending me to the floor. "It's just..." I try to cover up. Kathleen isn't buying a word. Grabbing my arm, she steadies me against the end of the bar, checking my pulse. "One-o-six. Tachycardia. You aren't going anywhere."

"Wow, my head hurts," I say, remembering an article about a heavyweight boxer. Those were his last words. He never answered the bell. Died on the locker room floor.

"You are going to sit," she orders, checking my eyes again with the bar flashlight. "Responsive." Grabbing my ears, she pulls my head from side to side, staring in my eyes. "You eat?"

"Riedell forced a yogurt on me last night to keep Irksome happy," I say.

"Who's Irksome?"

' He's the Super who lives in your belly. Emma told Riedell about him. If you don't feed him, he won't put coal in the furnace. Your eyes won't open, you can't hear, smell, touch; the whole shebang. You are a zombie. So, you don't irk Irksome. Get it?"

Kathleen gives me a look like I'm losing my marbles. I should go upstairs and crash for a while until I can think straight, but Riedell's school is in session in our warehouse.

"Put this under your tongue," Kathleen says, replacing the Jack with a glass of water. I hold the bitter pill in my mouth as she drops a soft leather bag in front of me. "You'd better start pleasing your Irksome, or you are going to keep feeling like shit. Arm."

The bar empties as Kathleen pumps up the blood pressure cuff, listening with her stethoscope. "Put your head down on the bar. Breathe normally."

Doing as instructed, I close my eyes. My pulse is thudding in my ear. Another pumping on my arm. "Pressure's dropping," she says. "Don't move."

Manhattan clam chowder has an especially distinctive scent. The bowl is so hot I can feel it radiating. My stomach does a flip, evaluating which way to go, eventually settling in my favor.

"Sit up slowly. Open your eyes." Kathleen orders, nudging the bowl closer. "Now eat. You didn't have a heart attack, if that's what you are thinking."

Maybe not, but it's an excuse I could use for not being at work.

* * *

"I really need to get to the paper," I try again. "My gut says..."
"Your gut is probably hemorrhaging."
"I doubt..."
"You're concussed."
"But I'm..."
"You should be in a hospital. Except right now," she says pointing to the television, scanning the carnage from a respectful distance, "they're Code Black. You're better off here. Paddy lies like you do. He's probably got second or third degree burns, ringing ears, and ordering the EMT's to take him last. His boys will bring him here," she says taking a mallet to the ice bin. "Here's where you're staying. I've got one eye for each of you."

"I'm much better, really. The soup is working. My stomach isn't rumbling anymore. Headache gone. You know I can help all these people," I motion toward the screen. "Their families and friends are worried. I can give them information."

It's a good pitch, I think. No need to tell her about my Publisher's stroke, and the flash drives in the safe.

"Here, or Emergency. Those are your only two choices," Kathleen says, ending what I foolishly thought were negotiations.

An hour passes. Still no Paddy. No calls either. Kathleen has taken my cell. She says little boys shouldn't play with dangerous toys. I hate to admit she has a point; I seem to injure myself each time I answer the damn thing.

"What is so important Gert is flashing your cell every two seconds?" Kathleen wants to know.

"It's Starch," I decide to tell her, hoping my speech isn't slurred. I can't tell. It's like smelling your own breath. Someone else has to tell you.

Kathleen doesn't bite. She's got her nurse mentality working. Press her buzzer one more time and I'll get to sit on a cold bedpan.

"He's had a stroke. A bad one. That's what Gert is texting."

"Believe it or not the Chronicle has other reporters." she says.

"That's not it," I say, trying a new approach. "We're doing a major piece. Working with the Justice Department."

That catches Kathleen's interest. "You're looking into Jamie's case!" she shouts. Jamie, her imprisoned, drug dealing brother. I should have seen that coming.

"No, sorry, it's something else. I can't explain. There are other, let's just say factors." I'm pushing the envelope, knowing I have to be careful not to go too far. "There is a flash drive in Starch's safe. It's got confidential data on it: targets, informants, stuff that could hurt the wrong people if it gets out."

"And what's on this flash drive is not all legal, is it?"

I shake my head, agreeing. "Not even close. There's this Independent Prosecutor with Justice. She goes back a long way with Starch."

"What does she have to do with the paper?"

"We're investigating corruption. She's using Starch's connections. It's a joint project." My head is killing me.

"This about the NYPD?"

I nod, keeping my eyes low, anticipating the next question. "Paddy?"

"Not directly," I assure her.

"Why Paddy left the Department," she concludes.

Now we're getting way off line. I'm not answering. Every time I open my mouth Kathleen reaches for my back molars. Shut up.

"This shooting, the bomb. They connected?"

"I honestly don't know, but they could be. That's why I need to get to the office."

Kathleen eyes me. "What aren't you telling me?"

"The cop who was shot in the squad car. He was a confidential source we got from Paddy. He called himself the Ace of Spades. Everything we got from him is on the flash drives in Starch's safe. It wouldn't look good for Paddy. I need to cover some tracks."

"Here, take these," Kathleen says stuffing a couple more pills in my mouth. Percocet would have been nice, but I'm happy with extra strength Tylenol. "Get back to work. I'll call Gert, tell her you are on your way."

I always walk the ten blocks to the Chronicle for exercise, but my body is slamming on the breaks. I can barely get off the stool. I must look like the invalid I feel. Kathleen turns the revolving door, hails a cab and pre-pays the driver.

Chapter Four

"ID," the desk guard orders. I refuse to wear the plastic lanyard with photo identification like every other employee. The guards intend to break me. In turn, I intend to free them from their bureaucratic mindset. They all know me, they read my column. And, I've given them enough grief.

I have numerous wise cracks in mind. Instead, I mumble, "Of course." My split lip makes answering especially painful. I produce the laminated ID from my jacket pocket, and the officer does a thorough examination.

I slip unnoticed into the buzzing City Room. "What took you so long?" Gert demands as she continues to shred papers from my file cabinet, pretending to be straightening up our office. "By the way, you look like hell," she adds as she delivers the update. "Starch is incommunicado. Any ideas how you are going to get in that safe?"

"I'm okay. Thanks for asking," I say, emptying folders and removing staples so they don't jam our little shredder. "I've got an idea, but for the moment we're good. No one is getting into that safe."

"How's that?" she asks.

"Tell you later," I put her off. The safe is only one of our problems. There is enough evidence in my office and on Gert's desk to get us fired outright, and we know who's been waiting for this gift horse.

"Keep shredding," I say stepping outside my cubicle to her desk, keeping watch while crumbling all the Post-its, scribbled notes, and receipts in sight. Some of them might be important, but right now we are in survival mode.

Four of the beefiest guards in the building are surrounding Arlo, our project hacker, who is sitting at one end of the Editorial conference table, while half of the Chronicle's IT Department is attacking his laptop and sorting through the nearby stack of boxes.

The daytime staff are crammed around the far end glass conference area straining to hear details of Starch's stroke from our Managing Editor, Jonathan Van Wie.

"Is he coming back?" I hear one staffer call out. I don't mistake the question as concern. City Room is a misnomer, Viper Room is more appropriate.

The managing editor doesn't answer. He's spotted me, even though I'm as far away from the glass throne as possible without being in the freight elevator. Van Wie has been waiting years for this moment.

"Duel at dawn?" I loud whisper to Gert. She sees him coming, the horde trailing behind. There are no secrets in a City Room.

He's Ivy League, and bleeds blue. Me, state-schooled and just bleeding. That alone would be enough of a divide. But my lack of breeding too close to his home is another reason Van Wie hates me.

It's in the past, except for today, but some guys just can't let the past drop. The fact that his wife, Gayfryd, was the pursuer doesn't seem to matter. I didn't even know who she was until it was too late.

"Almost done?" I hurry Gert while I'm standing casually at her desk acting like Van Wie is bringing us tea and doughnuts. Gert doesn't answer. Hearing the whirring of the shredder, I can easily imagine her non-verbal response.

We've been careful, but not overly, because we've been protected by Starch.

"Van Wie is making his move before the body's even cold," Gert says.

"Fifty yards," I say. "Keep going, he's stopped to admire the intern who just walked over. Must like her outfit."

"She's blocking for us," Gert says.

"What?"

"Throw something for him to fetch. Your shoe. Distract him. I've still got a stack here. I'm never going to make it," Gert says.

"Not going to work. He's staring at me. Telling the intern he'll get back to her."

"Then throw him a kiss. That will confuse him."

"Or bring him running. Besides, my lip is split."

One sheet at a time is all the shredder will take. Gert keeps feeding it.

"Gotta hand it to the old man."

"What?" Gert asks.

"It's like he anticipated this. Nothing's coming or going from his office. There's a military team in place. Even battleax Wright and General Counsel Jackson can't get in. At least for now. So, don't bury Starch just yet," I warn. "He's always known what's been going on around him."

I can hear the shredder jam. "I'm not going to make it. What I've got left in my hands alone will get us ten years," Gert moans.

"Then come out. Bring what's left. You might as well have a front seat for the festivities."

"More like the Saint Valentine's Day massacre," Gert says coming, dropping the stack on her desk and taking her position at my side. We look like the Little Rascals preparing to lie about the broken window.

"I'm liking our odds," I say rubbing her shoulder.

"Grab my breast."

"What?"

"My right one," she whispers staring straight ahead. "Do it while you are still an employee, I can sue the living shit out of this place. Look at the witnesses. Come on, molest me. I can take it."

I slap her butt.

"Coward."

"You're not the first to call me that today."

The papers Gert dropped are a mess. But I see the top sheet is a dated transcript of a call from our source, the now deceased Ace of Spades. Wouldn't you know it?

"Quick, pretend you're throwing up in the waste basket," I tell her.

"What?"

I push the incriminating stack off the desk. Bullseye.

"Wait until he's close enough to hear you, then do it. And make a run to the Ladies with your head in the basket."

"You're nuts. Clever, but nuts."

"Dump everything in the women's napkin trash."

"The what?"

"Getting close. Almost time," I whisper.

Van Wie finally dismisses the intern with a flourish. She bought us time, just not enough.

"Do it," I say.

Gert ralphs into the wastebasket with uncomfortable conviction, drops to one knee and repeats the disgusting performance. I offer her a handkerchief. She waves it away, jumps up with the basket in her hands and continues retching into it, running past Van Wie as she makes her escape.

I stand, acting confused, holding my open handkerchief in hand. I don't know how she produced the smell, don't want to know, but the performance stops Van Wie in his tracks, along with much of the room. Van Wie recoils, brushing his suit with the backside of his hands like Gert must have splattered some vomitus on him.

"That was close," Gert says returning in an instant, acting as if nothing had happened. "What's up?" she asks wiping her hands and throwing a brown paper crumple on the floor where the waste basket had been. It hits Van Wie's shoes. "Oh, sorry Sir, didn't see you there," she apologizes.

"You okay?" I ask Gert, who has also managed to make herself look sickly pale. I roll her chair close urging her to sit.

"Better," she smiles, touching my hand in appreciation.

"Disgusting, the two of you," Van Wie growls, snatching a few tissues off the desk, wiping his shoe. "What happened to you?" he snarls. "You look like what she threw up."

I heard only a few snickers from the floor. It's a tough room, they expect better.

"Never mind," he says, changing tactics, clamping his hands on my shoulders. "A prayer for his recovery!"

"What the Hell," I say trying to get away, but Van Wie grips harder, lowering his head. The staff closest follow in kind, forcing the others to stand and dip their heads in silence.

"Jeez," I say, appreciating his act. "You have no shame."

Van Wie is actually drooling. Only a few bubbles, but Gert and I can see.

"You think we should hug for the sake of your sycophants?" I whisper.

"Hug me and I'll slam your balls up to your ears," Van Wie whispers back, wiping away a non-existent tear.

"Family," I announce loudly, putting my arms high in the air.

Gert's eyes pop at the double entendre. Gutsy, even for me, but what the hell.

Van Wie wipes away another missing tear with his middle finger. "Fuck you," he whispers before turning away.

Unwilling to let the bastard leave the winner, Gert says loudly, "Shawn was in the explosion."

"The Helmsley?" Van Wie demands.

"That's shrapnel from the cop car." Gert points to the blood coming through my shirt. "I tried to get him to go to the hospital, but he wouldn't have it. Not with the Boss and all."

Gert's BS so confuses Van Wie, he doesn't know how to react. "Horrible thing," he manages. "We used to live in that building. Why were you there?"

"Where?" Gert continues jerking him around.

He gives up. "Doesn't matter," Van Wie snarls. "If you were on the job, get yourself checked out."

"Maybe I should write up the story," Gert presses, "Shawn being a hero and all?"

Please stop, I beg her with my eyes, but Gert is swinging for the rafters. "Can't have him blowing his own horn," she smirks at Van Wie.

"Yeah, right," he dismisses me. "You do it," he tells Gert. "Get the copy on my desk in an hour. And you," he points at me, "give her your hero BS, then get down to the nurse. I'll personally be doing the piece on the Boss," he announces, letting the full weight of his loss be known. "All your files on Starch's Special Project with the Feds, on my desk, in an hour," he comes back and hisses in my face. "I'm in charge."

Realizing he may have announced his coronation prematurely, à la General Haig, he adds, "until the Old Man returns."

"That went well," Gert says loud enough for much of the City Room to hear.

"You know I was at Parnell's with Kathleen when the bomb went off."

"I know, the man infuriates me. I had to say something. I'll write about a mysterious person who saved a child – a collective person – the first responders – Van Wie will think I'm trying to keep you humble."

"One way or another, he'll bury your article."

"I know," Gert says. "I'm sorry."

Chapter Five

"You better get all those thumb drives," Gert warns. "Or we're doing time. And remember, orange is not my color. I'm a winter."

"A what?"

"I'll get you some coffee," she says, "one time only. You being blown-up and all," she grins.

I hate coffee, but the caffeine might help. I'm into migraine territory. "Whatever you make up for that hero story of yours, be sure Van Wie cuts it."

"Just how am I supposed to do that? I'm a professional, remember?"

"You got yourself into this one."

"Hey. Who yelled out 'family'? He can't be that much of an imbecile. I could smell the lavender on you from the Ladies. You reek of it," she says, holding her nose. "His wife bathe in the stuff?"

"They are separated, and I don't know."

"Well that smell helped me toss up last night's pizza on demand."

"Ha, nice job. What happened to the papers in the trash can?"

"Rat food. I'll make sure they are burned." Gert grabs my arm and turns me away from Van Wie's windows and his binoculars. "What happened at the Helmsley?"

"I'm not sure. What you suspect with Gayfryd of course," I say shaking my head.

"Hey, you're a guy. You're expected to do stupid stuff."

"Yeah," I say dropping my shoulders, "except this was beyond stupid. It was a set up. Planned and timed."

"How so?"

I move closer. "Round one – beyond incredible. I mean, this gal can. ."

"I get it." Gert says, gesturing for me to move on. "So she's good in the sack. Had to be for you to put up with that perfume. What else?" she demands, pointing her finger in front of my split lip.

"Gayfryd's got a new condo. Same building, different floor. I thought it was the same layout, like all the residential areas. Even her Matisse and Cezanne paintings were there."

"Except?"

"Except this gunshot erupts from below and bounces off the windows like a war zone. I fell out of bed, looked down, saw the bloody cop car window."

Gert jerks her thumb over her shoulder toward Van Wie. "You thought that jerk shot himself and fell from the balcony onto the cop car because he caught you with his wife?"

I shake my head no. "I didn't know what to think, but when I turned around she was gone."

"Panicked?"

"Well yeah, maybe, but not like you think. I opened the doors to the next room, strictly forbidden," I say holding my hands up like I was being arrested in a Woody Allen movie. "Turns out it's a clinic. Abortion, by the look of it."

"And that's when...?"

"Hello Mrs. Wright," I announce. She's standing behind Gert. I have never seen Starch's secretary outside of his offices. This can't be good. According to Gert, Mrs. Wright knows the name of every person employed by The Chronicle, alive or dead. Even more daunting, she knows everyone's job, and how well they do it.

"Eunice," Gert says gritting her teeth.

"Gertrude."

First name basis, there is obvious history between my assistant and the formidable Mrs. Wright. Wonder what that's about. Once the two she-wolves have finished exchanging pleasantries, Gert shifts her eyes behind Mrs. Wright in an obvious signal that the entire City Room is watching.

"He's in bad shape. Damn ambulance took him to Eastside. Idiots. Place was a shambles, this bombing and all. You'd think the capital of the world could... Anyway, we'll know in twenty-four hours. He can use your prayers," she all but orders, efficient to the core.

I'm worried Mrs. Wright is planning one of those knees-on-the-floor prayer circles. Neither my knees, nor my soul, can take that kind of stress, but like always, Gert is in my head.

"I'll pray for him," Gert says, faking a knee dip just to cover.

"I'll hoist a drink to Starch, a bit later," I say.

Mrs. Wright seems to have experience with catastrophe, and is keeping the stalwart flag held high. I hate to admit it, but there is much to be admired in her stiff upper lip demeanor. Having a teary, babbling emissary come down to the City Room would create panic.

As much as I rail against colloquialisms, ink being in her veins is a blessing.

Mrs. Wright takes charge, moving us into my cubicle and closing the door. We all remain standing. "You should be aware," she says holding an armful of files.

"Is this about our NYPD investigation?" I ask pointing to the folders.

"Of course not, you ninny," Mrs. Wright snaps at me. "This is Company business."

I think Mrs. Wright considers everyone who isn't on the top floor to be a ninny, but just in case, I retreat to my *Unflawed* columnist, wise-ass persona. There is some protection in the Pulitzer, I've learned.

"Ninny?" I ask Gert, acting mortified.

"She really speaks that way," Gert interprets the expression as if Mrs. Wright isn't standing inches from us. "Eunice also insists on saying wire, for telephone," Gert adds for good measure.

I step back, in mock horror. "Really? I heard a rumor there is running water out back in the privy. That true?"

"I'm right here," Mrs. Wright harrumphs. "Are you two about done? This is serious. I warned Cuthbert he was making a mistake with you." She drops her folders on my desk, reaching for a Kleenex.

Dabbing her eyes as if composing herself, she is making me feel guilty, until I notice the tissue is dry. Gert gives me a glance. Mrs. Wright, deciding she has properly chastised us, stuffs the tissue up her sleeve and grunts.

"Your attendance is expected at an emergency Board Meeting," she says leaning near me, assuming a conspiratorial air. "Today. Four o'clock sharp. With Cuthbert down, that bitch is going to push her inheritance claim. We think she's going after everything. And, we're going to need your *special* knowledge to stop her."

I look to Gert.

"Gayfryd is trying to take over the Chronicle," Gert interprets for me. "And I bet your balls, Van Wie is in the thick of it."

Mrs. Wright gives Gert a withering look. She notices the clear bags of shredded papers on the floor. I'm not sure, but I've got the distinct feeling Mrs. Wright understands we are covering our asses, and maybe Starch's as well.

"If these," Mrs. Wright kicks a bag with her laced widow's shoe, "have anything we can use against that creature, paste it all back together and get it upstairs. You may have to do your duty on this one," she says touching my sleeve, as if confirming I'll do the right thing. Give me a leather helmet, I'm supposed to take one for the team.

"When you are done cleaning-up," she says kicking another bag, "call upstairs. Request a meeting with Mr. Jackson. He'll give you the guidance you need," Mrs. Wright orders, opens the door, makes a military left turn, scowls at the staring reporters, then marches off the floor.

Hello? Is it me you're looking for? My desk phone sings out the Lionel Richie song. The vintage black phone with personal ringtone is Gert's gift. The ringtone is clever, but only once.

"Shawn Shaw's office," Gert answers pretending to be a secretary.

"Tell Shaw she will destroy him."

Gert holds back the phone looking at it before dropping the hand piece back onto the cradle.

"Wrong number?" I ask.

"Apparently not," Gert says acting concerned.

"Apparently not what?"

"You, she was looking for," Gert sings out.

"Very good," I admit. "One for you."

The phone starts to sing again. Gert snatches it up before 'me'.

"It's her," Gert whispers with her hand over the mouthpiece.

"Fool me once…"

"It's Gayfryd," Gert says, dead serious. Before I can decide, Gert motions she's hung up.

Now Gert's cell rings. "Ten minutes. I'll try and locate him," she assures the caller and hangs up.

"Are you going to tell me?

"That was Eunice. She's made your appointment with Jackson, the General Counsel. He's also the Acting Chairman."

"Why do I have the feeling…"

"Listen," Gert says moving closer. "Don't be taken in by Walter Jackson. Full head of white hair, roundish, friendly, easy smile, and sharp as tacks. He's Starch's pal since prep school."

"Good to know."

"He also takes his annual month-long vacation with his wife and Mrs. Wright."

"Great."

"Better," Gert grins, "Mrs. Wright and Walter Jackson are lovers."

"Aww. I don't even know the guy, and I'm feeling sorry for him. His wife…?"

"A magazine editor. Want to see her picture?" Gert offers pointing to a fashion magazine in a pile on the floor.

I shake my head no.

"Look at this," Gert says picking up Mrs. Wright's "forgotten" folders. "Should we look?" She doesn't wait for an answer. She opens the top folder and there is Gayfryd's picture clipped to an investigator's cover sheet.

"These weren't left by accident," Gert says.

"I need to get out of here," I say. I drop my office cell in my right pocket and search for the old clamshell in the top desk drawer. I drop it in my left pocket. Gert is the only person who has that number. She understands.

"So are you going to see the company nurse?" Gert grins.

"Good idea. Try to get the exact time of Starch's stroke while I'm out."

Gert nods. "You never explained this," she says waving her finger around my face, "but I can guess. You think Gayfryd heard about Starch during your 'appointment'?"

"You have no idea how prophetic that could be. I'm going to get lost looking for the nurse's office."

"Be well."

* * *

I put a jam in the back door behind the executive garage and disappear. When I return, I find the nurse's office, wait for the x-rays and examination. I've taken just the right amount of too much time. I've missed my appointment with General Counsel Jackson.

I ease my way through the rear door of the City Room, trying to attract little attention. "Looks like I'll live," I whisper to Gert.

"Board meeting delayed until tomorrow morning. Flight problems. Jackson called himself this time. Wants you upstairs, ASAP."

"Damn."

"I've got the numbers of dead and wounded. Names of the two police officers. Hospital information. A few quotes from the attendants for *my article*. Any hero stuff you want me to add?" Gert smirks.

I'd completely forgotten about Gert's ruse to deflect Van Wie. "Stick with the first responders. Leave me out of it."

"Done," Gert says waving her printout. "I don't suppose you want me to mention the dead Lieutenant was our informant?"

I bite my cheek, "No."

"Then I'll be finished in ten."

"Send it to Van Wie. I don't need to see it," I say anticipating her courtesy.

Gert twirls her finger, warning. I sense movement behind me. A scent, female. Someone sent the cute blonde intern from Columbia University to check on me and find out what Mrs. Wright wanted. "Still no word on Starch," I tell her, remembering my own intern summer and how they played me. Lots of eyes in the City Room are on their sacrificial lamb, hoping for a big blowup. But I don't take the bait.

"I got this," I say to Gert, standing tall, easily crowning over our visitor's head to address the whole City Room. "An emergency Board Meeting is called for tomorrow. First thing," I say loudly. "I'll tell Ms. Columbia here what I learn right after." Quietly, I say to her, "Meet you in the stairwell in the morning."

"Thanks," she gets it, I think.

"And thank you for the block you threw earlier," I say heading for the stairs.

Chapter Six

Greeting me outside the secure maze of anterooms is the goddess Aphrodite wearing a crisp white suit. A nice change from the sour Mrs. Wright.

"Shawn Shaw. I have an appointment with Mr. Jackson," I say putting out my hand.

"Athena," she introduces herself.

"I was only one goddess off," I say. She doesn't shake my hand, but indicates I'm to follow her.

This wing of the Executive floor is for Business and Legal Departments, unfamiliar to me. It's not as intimidating as the gothic hall leading to Starch's office, displaying the portraits of lineage. Athena leads me past a cadre of Brooks Brothers-decorated intellectuals studiously examining spreadsheets as we walk through the main area.

"Mr. Jackson," I say when Athena ushers me into his sedate office, "nice to meet you. Request a continuance."

"Granted," he grins. "And its Walt," he says, eyes smiling. A chubby Walt Disney. "I should have made the effort at your first Board Meeting," he apologizes, "but I wasn't certain you'd survive."

"Me either," I admit. It's been nearly eight years since I was elected to the Company Board – well, placed there by Starch - and the esteemed General Counsel has never spoken a word in my direction. My Chronicle stock came to me from James Berk when my comrade in arms, the brilliant Ms. Tiu, disabled his conspiracy to take over the Chronicle. It's in a trust for my daughter, Riedell.

Walt extends a hand indicating I should sit. There are three chairs, although Athena remains standing at the door. Apparently the number of chairs isn't a sign she will be joining us.

Gert warned me before I left, "Don't forget. Walter Jackson has Mrs. Wright's folder on you, as well. Be careful."

"You did a decent job on the James Berk assault," Walt admits as he navigates toward his preferred seat. That was a decade before, and this is Jackson's first mention. He's really reaching, I think.

"I had considerable help from..."

"Of course you did," Walt cuts me off. On to business. "Sit," he orders, motioning me to one of the tufted leather armchairs. I glance toward Athena, but she has faded into the law journals.

"What can I do for you?" I jump in. There is no hiding the damage to my face, so I lean forward all but forcing him to ask. He doesn't.

"I don't think Cuthbert would mind if we refer to him as Starch?"

"Okay," I agree.

"He likes the name, you know," Walt laughs, "says it came from you."

Walt's office has a smoking room ambiance, much like Starch's. Except with Walt there are family photos everywhere; kids on horses, kids looping about gymnastic equipment, young adults graduating from prestigious colleges. Starch has only one photo of someone I assume is his wife.

"Anyway, should Starch not make it through," Walt pauses to pluck what I'm certain is cat fur from his suit sleeve, "he has, of course, anticipated this possibility and made certain arrangements with Mrs. Wright and myself. You understand?"

I nod carefully. Here it comes – promise or threat? Walt hasn't ordered me up to the Executive floor for tea.

"The Chronicle stock in your name? There is a reason Starch gave you the loan."

"I couldn't afford to pay the taxes," I say.

"Of course, but there is more to it. Starch wanted you to have a stake in the Chronicle's future."

"You're speaking in the past tense. Is Starch dead?" I rise from my chair.

"No, no, dear boy," Walt assures me, pressing me back onto the chair with calming hands. "Although he might wish he were if we don't protect the company from, um ..."

He's apparently referring to Gayfryd, but he's leaving it for me to answer. I wait him out.

Eventually, Walt leans back in his chair, rubbing his chin. "Clever as my friend says you are," he mumbles, praying his fingers as if signaling he is contemplating his next move. I toss out the ball.

"As always, Starch has my proxy. I'm guessing you have his while he's sidelined. I assure you, nothing has changed in my book." I don't wait for an answer as I stand to leave.

Walt stays in his chair. "Good. That's what I want to hear." He looks away, sitting back tapping his pinkie signet ring on the carved wood arm of his chair. I haven't been dismissed yet.

"I believe you know Gayfryd Van Wie?"

"Yes, I know her." Gert and Kathleen would love that description.

"If Starch doesn't return to The Chronicle, for whatever reason, there is going to be a war for control of the Corporation." Walt leans forward, lowering his voice. "It's going to get very messy. No holds barred."

A cloud blocks the sunlight at that precise moment. Though I am not crediting the venerable General Counsel, Cecil DeMille could not have timed the imagery for greater effect. The room becomes ominously dark. The portent of the passing cloud better be coincidence, otherwise I'm sitting with Lucifer, because avuncular Walt is again referring to his life-long pal in the past tense.

As if the skies are actually under his control, a stray ray of sunlight catches the glass obelisk on Walt's desk, and cuts a murderous triangle across the carpet, ending at my feet. Normally, I'd say something smart, but given the collection of today's events, wisecracks feel cheap and disrespectful.

"So, we can count on your support?" he pushes.

"Yes."

"Good." Walt moves to the edge of his chair. "Now this may be entirely preemptive, but it has come to our attention the woman in question has been involved in certain improprieties, and shall we say, possible illegal activities."

Walter notices me shifting at the reference to Gayfryd, except this time the stabbing pain in my back hasn't come directly from her.

"We may need to draw on your intimate knowledge of this woman to pursue a particular line of questioning, should we end up in court."

Don't bring a knife to a gun fight, Sean Connery's line comes to mind. "Then you know about my past relationship with her?" I ask.

"Of course. Gayfryd Van Wie, if that's even her name. Dubious claims. A mere scoundrel willing to use her sexual charms to achieve her objectives. And I, as Starch's lifetime friend and confidant, am unwilling to stand by and watch a media empire, and the man behind its creation, be besmirched. Especially while my friend is un-well and incapable of defending himself, and this great institution."

I pray I'm never in a courtroom with this man.

"Loyalty," Walt continues. "I recall you writing that it's a virtue you consider sacrosanct."

"You read my column?"

Walt reaches to his desk, turning his "General Counsel" nameplate towards me. "It's mandatory. I have to be prepared when your victims sue."

"Thanks."

A nod.

"You don't believe Starch will come back?" I surmise.

"It's a distinct possibility. That's why we have to be prepared. So are you with us?"

"Are you planning to take control of the Company?"

"Taking control is not my intention. Safeguarding would be the appropriate term. You'll understand more after the Board meeting."

"You are certain there is going to be a fight with Gayfryd for control of The Chronicle?" I try to absorb the reality of that scenario.

"No question," Walt assures me. "And not just the newspaper," he cautions. "The whole Chronicle Company; TV stations, radio, cable, the whole shebang." Walt sits back in his leather chair waiting for the enormity of the business to sink in.

"I took the liberty..." he begins his closing argument while removing a thin, blue wrapped document from his inside breast pocket. I can guess what's coming.

"For the sake of our outside investment firms," he apologizes handing me his gold Cross pen. "I'm afraid we are going to need their support. They like all the "i's" dotted. You know the type," he commiserates our mutual dislike for those people.

"Sure, I understand," I say folding the document in thirds and stuffing it in my back pocket. Walt's eyes bulge.

"You being a lawyer, you would want my lawyer to read an agreement of this importance before signing, wouldn't you?" I ask him.

The smile stays frozen on Walt's face. A flicker of his left hand at the side of his chair. I see the reflection of one of his buttoned-down types slipping out the door. I'm guessing a notary.

"And perfectly right you should," Walt agrees, abruptly standing, leaving no doubt of his disappointment. "I'll just say we have an agreement in principle, if that's alright with you?"

Walt doesn't wait for an answer. An open hand suggests the exit door is available.

I feel a chill as Mrs. Wright emerges outside Walt's office. "The Board meeting. Eight a.m. tomorrow. Be on time," she informs me, then adds more warmly, "Walt is a good man. You'd do well to be on his side."

Chapter Seven

"That coffee helping?" Gert asks as if it's a medicinal brew because her fingers pushed the buttons.

"A little," I thank her. I am improving, although half my head feels like it's stuffed with puffed wheat. Adrenaline is amazing stuff, and Walter gave me an injection straight to the heart. It's only late afternoon and I've been sated, castrated, berated, and deflated. What next?

"Let's walk and talk," I say.

"She came back for the files," Gert tells me the instant we hit the street.

"Figured. What else did you see of interest?"

"Besides Gayfryd, I saw an empty file labeled Destiny Foundation." * The elusive organization James Berk supposedly represents. The people pursuing Emma and her sister, Ms. Tiu.

"Warnings then," I understand.

"That's the way Eunice works. Leaves crumbs, keeps her hands clean. So, what happened with Jackson?" she asks.

"I don't think Mrs. Wright or Walter Jackson had anything to do with Starch's office being sealed and guarded. Walt's main concern is protecting the company from a takeover by Gayfryd and Van Wie. I was either being groomed for battle, or prepared for the stockade."

"You're out now."

"Released on my own recognizance."

Gert gives me a flicker of appreciation while evading a bicycle messenger and increasing her pace.

I do my best to keep up, even though my recently acquired sciatica resists. "It just occurred to me, maybe Starch has had private

---

   * The Destiny Foundation is the scientific portion of a fictional Destiny Society. References to each will appear throughout this story. Thousands of secret societies exist throughout the world, and across history, although their existence isn't all that secret.
   Take "Skull and Crossbones", the sinister sounding Yale organization. Is it, in fact, sinister? Members boast about their inclusion in the society; yet not one will disclose its purpose.

security all along, automatically putting his office on lockdown when he's out."

"Actually that would be pretty smart on Starch's part," Gert admits. "Especially if the Feds are involved in our corruption series. Keeps the flash drives and whatever else he's got in the safe secure."

"A safeguard to keep out his private secretary and school chum?"

Gert hugs my arm. "That's more like your suspicious self. You think Starch is that devious?"

"Sure."

"He's getting up there in years. He might have been planning to clean house. He's taken a liking to you."

"No way."

"Jackson mention your loan?"

I nod. "That was just a way for Starch to put me on the Board. I'm a token. I know it, Walt knows it."

We walk in silence for a block.

"There was a blonde upstairs waiting for me," I tell Gert. "I thought she was one of Walt's staff. Except she came into his office, stayed in the background. Walt never addressed her. Maybe she's Starch's personal lawyer. She might have authority to lock up his office."

"And, at some point, have access to the safe," Gert reminds.

"So until Starch recovers, or is declared whatever, the flash drives seem safe."

"You believe that?" Gert asks.

"No."

We continue walking the ten blocks up 1st Avenue to Parnell's. At 6'2" I have a decent stride, but I can't adjust well to Gert's tempo. She generally wears sneakers, moves quickly in spurts, and rarely follows a straight line. I feel like I'm chasing a squirrel.

"How soon did Battleax Wright come back for the files?"

"About ten minutes after she left."

"And you're certain she didn't leave them by mistake?"

"Last time Eunice made a mistake, Germany lost the War," Gert says, changing walking lanes.

"But you did get a decent look?"

"Sure," she says, waving her cellphone in the air in answer.

"You copied her files," I realize.

"Buy me a drink and I'll show you."

"Out with it Gert, I'm not in the mood for games."

"Okay," she says slamming on the brakes. "Your girlfriend..."

"She's not my girlfriend. Today was a..."

"Mistake. I know." Gert starts again. "Remember when Starch asked you to stop screwing his niece?"

A wise man would keep his mouth shut at this juncture. "He didn't exactly say..."

"Looks like she's not his niece, but his daughter."

"What the... Our comatose leader fathered Gayfryd?"

"There was some good stuff in that investigator's report."

It's a crisp fifty degree day, and I'm sweating keeping up with Gert. Physically and intellectually.

"Explain?" I demand when we reach Parnell's front door.

"Cuthbert? Gayfryd? How many people do you know with names like that? None," she answers herself. "Cuthbert is Starch's mother's family name. Good ole Southern family name. Who would have guessed?" Gert says doing a Scarlet O'Hara, hand-to-her-forehead exaggerated sigh. "Want to guess the family name of your girlfriend's mother?"

"Gayfryd," I say closing my eyes.

Gert taps the tip of my nose. "You should be an investigative reporter. Think Parnell's has any stew left over from lunch? I'm starved."

"Starch's daughter?" I repeat like a ninny.

"No birth certificate of record. Mrs. Wright's investigator tracked down Gayfryd's mother," Gert says pushing through Parnell's revolving front door, not giving me a chance to start it moving. "Mother's dead. Suicide. I'm guessing Starch had to tell his wife somewhere along the line."

"So, you think she drank herself into that Long Island nursing home?"

"I buy it. Speaking of which, pony up that drink you owe me. And I'm hungry."

Chapter Eight

Gert hurries over to the bar, giving Paddy a squeeze. "Something decadent," she orders. "Surprise me."

"Thought you were hungry," I say, coming up to my regular seat.

"And what the hell happened to you?" Paddy demands, his baritone echoing through the empty bar.

"Gert," I blame. Gert raises her fancy concoction, accepting the honor.

Paddy changes the subject. "How's Starch?"

"Not good. Twenty-four hours. You know, the standard wait and see. So how are you holding up?" Gert asks sipping the odd drink through a straw like she's a dilettante with her first cocktail.

The cop shooting and the bombing seem like days ago, even though the silent TV continues to show the carnage.

"You look better than I expected," I tell Paddy.

"Three SWATs cut around me as I was rounding the Command truck. They saved my ass. Never knew what hit them. Can't tell you how many are dead. I was ordered out," he says.

"How early did they call you in?"

"Right after the report of a suicide in progress. I've never seen a situation like that," he says quietly, keeping an eye on Kathleen who is polishing the bar top at the far end.

"Gert, what'll it be next?" Paddy asks, holding up his red bartender's guide. He is challenging Gert and himself.

"Gimlet," Gert decides.

No idea how her constitution can take a lime drink atop that chocolate creamy mixture she finished sucking through a straw. Tossing the guide back under the bar as if a gimlet is far too easy, Paddy puts on a good face. "Bombay? Straight up?"

"Yes to both. Looks ever so elegant that way," Gert says sitting tall in her bar stool, happy to be the center of attention. "Want to hear what happened to our boy?"

"I was about to ask," Paddy encourages her, reaching back to the premium shelf for the Bombay. It takes him two tries before his hand clamps on the blue bottle. He notices, so do I. He flips the bottle in the air and catches it behind his back, as if to say *get off my case.*

Kathleen joins us, not wanting to miss a good story. Paddy leans back, towel in hand, polishing shot glasses. Gert clears her throat, rotates her head over her shoulders, arching her back in preparation. My hang-dog plea for mercy is ignored.

"Okay." She sticks out her arm pointing a finger at me. "His girlfriend kicked his bare ass right out into the hallway of the Helmsley this morning. There he was, naked as the day he was born. My hero, my boss," she proclaims, "getting his ass kicked by a ninety pound bitch. And I mean kicked. Curled up in a ball, protecting his privates. She threw his clothes out after him and slammed the door. Leaving him there on the carpet crying for his mommy."

Gert grins at me. "Went too far with the 'mommy', didn't I?"

"A smidge," I agree, kissing her cheek. "And where did you get this wild fabrication?"

Credibility challenged, Gert gives up her source without hesitation. "The Helmsley floor maid saw it all, told the bellman, who lives two doors down from my Aunt in Brooklyn. His wife told…"

I put up my hand in surrender. "I get it. Convicted with irrefutable evidence."

"You didn't give me that version!" Kathleen howls, reaching over the bar smacking my arm.

"Facts, clear and simple," Gert says toasting Paddy while playfully poking my bruised ribs.

"Ow."

"Sorry," she apologizes, patting my arm when she sees me touching the spot and wincing. Gert turns serious. "It's all true, isn't it?"

Paddy tries covering for me. "You'll never get the full story out of him. Reporter's code, or some such nonsense."

"On the plus side, you all get your wish," I say. "Gayfryd is out of my life. I've taken my vows. I'm a celibate monk from this day forward. This corduroy jacket is my frock. Gert, you can shave my head. I'm done with women."

"Just little boys in long pants," Kathleen commiserates with Gert, clinking the gimlet glass with her wedding ring.

* * *

The commuter rush hits Parnell's early. Knowing Paddy is still rocky, Gert fills in at the beer taps as if she were born to it.

"What do you know about the bombing?" the first Suit asks Paddy, joined by several others eager for information. Kathleen gets their drinks and nudges Paddy to tell them. I've heard Kathleen harping at Paddy to promote his police experience, draw more business into Parnell's with his insider knowledge. As much as I love Kathleen, that nudge brings out her worst.

But Paddy doesn't need her prodding today. The Suits are regulars, and Paddy knows his role; start with the truth. The exaggerations will follow.

"Five police officers dead at the scene, sixteen uniforms injured, five life threatening. Plenty of minor injuries. The civilian count is still coming in. But the last number I heard is upwards of another five dead, sixty injured, probably more."

"Terrorists?" "Anyone claim responsibility? Any arrests?" "What kind of explosive?" "Who were the cops in the squad car? Why were they at the Helmsley?" The questions keep flying.

I know the Commissioner has already scheduled a press conference. Paddy has first-hand information, so all he's really doing is giving his customers a ten minute advance. But he pulls back, he's done.

Gert notices and cuts in front, spinning cork coasters like they are miniature Frisbees. "Okay Boys, you've got a real live hero in your midst. Tell your friends and family you had a drink with Paddy. What'll it be?"

Gert works her end of the bar while Kathleen works hers, a bottle of Bushmills never leaving her hand.

I stay on my side of the bar where I belong, keeping an eye on Paddy who has withdrawn and is polishing glasses in the background.

"Let me take a look at Gert's cellphone," Paddy suggests once the customers quiet. They're seeing the Police Commissioner on TV repeat what Paddy told them.

"You already know about the files?"

"Sure. Gert called about twenty minutes earlier, asking if we got in any fresh shrimp." Paddy says as busboy Mandell puts her prawns and sauce on the bar.

"The files are a setup," I warn Paddy. "Mrs. Wright didn't leave the information by accident."

Paddy holds the cell out at arm's length, waiting for me to decide. "Yes or no?"

"What I mean," I try to explain, "is, this could get legal real fast. I'm not sure if you …"

Paddy sets Gert's cellphone on the bar. "Forget it. I'll refresh her gimlet." Paddy isn't easily offended. I chalk up his brusqueness to a rough day.

"We could use your old cop's eyes to find the gaps in these files," I apologize.

He picks up Gert's cell. "If one of you will turn up the lights, I'll just see if my *old cop* eyes are still working," Paddy says scrolling through the files. "I won't try to comprehend."

"Drama queens," Gert calls us under her breath.

Paddy continues to scroll through the pages, stopping, expanding and straining to read particular items before passing the cell back to Gert. "Maybe we should print this out." He lifts his chin meaning I should send the file to the printer upstairs in my home.

"Your private daycare school," Gert drops a not so subtle hint.

"Turned into something more lately," I tell her. Gert hasn't been inside my home in years. I know she is curious. Emma used to invite her upstairs all the time. I've covered the two of them with blankets for the night - passed out snoring on the sofas.

"I understand," Gert says rubbing my arm. She doesn't.

"So do you want to come upstairs, or not?" I cave.

"First you get a gal drunk, and then sweet talk her." She gulps down her gimlet, "Well, okay. But don't think I'm easy," she says slinging her purse over her shoulder. "I take tea in the morning, in case I forget to mention it," she says just loud enough to get the attention of the Suit next to her. "Come on, Big Boy. Saddle up," she announces patting my butt.

The Suit stands. Gert doesn't notice, just like she didn't notice his interest when she insisted he try one of her prawns. Poor guy. Gert runs at high speed, subtle doesn't get her attention.

I have some extraordinary women in my life. Gert is one of them.

* * *

"We'll have to be quiet. I'm almost never home during school hours, so we might be intruding."

"Come on," Gert says noting the infrared security cameras in our bunker-like, re-enforced concrete stairwell. "I'm sure kids' schools look a little different since my day."

"Kathleen is disappointed in what the school has become."

"Why?"

"When Emma died, it was Kathleen's idea to turn the warehouse into my home and a daycare center for infant Riedell and the children of her nursing friends. The nurses would take shifts watching the children and teaching them. No costs, and Riedell is the built-in beneficiary."

"Great idea."

"Wonderful in the beginning," I admit.

"What went wrong?"

"Riedell. Tiu. Both. By age three Riedell was reading Latin. The other kids were sucking Legos. Tiu would teach Riedell mathematics and science on the computer screen while the nurses' children were crying because Sesame Street wasn't on TV."

"Intellectual discrimination," Gert says.

"Funny, but in a strange way, yeah. Tiu didn't understand. Instead, she continued to have people install bigger computers, larger video screens, and inter-active teaching mechanisms. Eventually, most of the other kids faded away. "

"Until?"

"Until we evolved."

We arrive at the top landing. "Wadjet. Visitor," I say.

"This is a new twist."

"Hello, retired Det. Gert," Wadjet says, her electronic voice echoing off the concrete. "Please place all weapons, sprays and explosive devices in the metal tray, if you'd be so kind?"

"You're shitting me," Gert says, eyeing me as the drawer extends.

"Tough school," I shrug.

"Thank you," Wadjet says when Gert puts a holstered .38 snub nose from her purse on the tray, followed by a retractable knife, and a pepper spray."

It's my turn to give her the stare.

"Tough neighborhood," she shrugs in turn.

"Hands on the outlines, and face forward for retinal scan," Wadjet requests.

Gert complies, and is cleared with a smiling Egyptian goddess emoji. "And why am I not surprised you have a vault access to your home?"

"The security was a gift from Chuti Tiu after Emma died," I explain. "We live over a bar in case you haven't noticed. Tiu might have gone overboard in protecting her niece."

"Does Tiu spend time with Riedell? I thought she vanished after you two put Berk in jail."

"She has a presence," I say with a twist of mirth.

Hearing the air locks release and titanium rods slide back, Gert shakes her head entering. "School in session?"

"Riedell might be teaching a class."

"Isn't she like ten or something?"

"You know kids these days," I evade the question.

Gert isn't buying it. "Where is she? I haven't seen Riedell since forever."

"Over there, I think," I say waving my hand in the distance. There is a collection of kids and adults kneeling on ergonomic chairs listening to a lanky, fawn of a girl who is twirling in circles on roller skates while explaining a mathematical equation projected in the air.

"She looks tall."

"It's the skates," I say, not mentioning Riedell was crawling the last time Gert saw her. "Riedell wears Emma's skates - her way of channeling her mother. This might be one of her Dimensions classes." I watch the tapes, some nights. "Typically the discussion begins with an equation describing some aspect of nature, like gravity, and evolves from there. The Universe, accident or design? God or Science? Riedell is the logic coordinator."

"These are kids?"

"Sometimes."

"Oh, hello you," Gert says, surprised to see the three foot tall Impet appearing at her side. The Impet is wearing enormous black glasses, functional if you are Galileo.

"Tiu," I say looking toward the ceiling.

"What?" Gert asks.

"Oh nothing. House humor, that's all."

Gert knows something is up, but she shakes it off.

The Impet's red and black polka dot sundress, and large patent leather shoes are over-the-top, but Gert has had just the right amount of libation to miss Tiu's joke. No sense spoiling it, for either of them.

"We're picking up some printouts," I tell the Impet. "Are they ready?"

"Yes, Headmaster," the squeaky little voice answers. We get a follow-me wave from the Impet. My cat, Yeti, sleeping over the Impet's shoulder, opens an eye in my direction.

"Is that Riedell or a projection?" I ask the Impet knowing full well I'm talking to Chuti Tiu. Gert hasn't caught on. If I told Gert what is happening she'd think I was the one drinking Paddy's concoctions.

"Projection," the Impet says. "Riedell's having her tests done. I'd be exhausted if it were me, but not her. She thinks it is fun. Riedell's nice. She's a four dimension processor," the Impet adds. "Only she and Aunt Chuti are fours. Are you Aunt Chuti's father?"

"If I were, I would send her to her room immediately," I say. Chuti Tiu is having too much fun.

"Is she a robot?" Gert finally asks after trying to touch the Impet who stays just out of reach.

"What's a GERT?" the Impet asks. "An acronym for what?"

"Generally Edgy, Resourceful and Trustworthy. A backronym," I say. "When you're a level four, you'll see the value of a GERT." In my best W.C. Fields voice I say, "Get away little girl, I'm processing."

"You're funny," she says running off.

"Oh Headmaster," Gert mimics the Impet's voice, seeming to get the joke. "Isn't she adorable? Right out of Disney."

"My exact thought," I agree. "Tiu is learning humor."

"Is she here?" Gert asks. "I haven't seen Tiu since…well, you know."

' Believe me, Tiu is everywhere," I say waving my arms.

"And you think I drink too much," Gert says, tiring of my non-answers as she begins to explore. "I've forgotten how huge this place is, like Grand Central."

"Not quite. But it's big. Better than half the floor was filled with machinery and crates the last time you were here. We've gone through a lot of changes."

"I'll say. I didn't even notice those skylights before," Gert says pointing up, moving her finger across the roof line.

Chuti Tiu took our acceptance of the security upgrades as permission to transform the entire building into a clandestine techno-center. Parnell's patrons have no idea what surrounds them.

"What's that shimmering coating over the brick walls? You can see through it, but..."

"Those are ultra-high definition screens," I explain. "There are forty or so. Thin as paper, membranes, actually. The screens are in rest mode now, but when school is in full session they will be all over, joining together, arching, and sometimes enclosing the entire roof, transforming this space into anything and everything."

"What are you talking about?"

"It feels like you are an eagle soaring through it all. I wish I could show you, but..." I say, hoping Chuti understands I'm asking her not to, but the translucent membranes begin gliding further up the walls until they are arching over us.

"They're enormous. Football stadium size."

I understand, Tiu is waiting for me to choose. "You couldn't be satisfied with your little Minnie Mouse, could you?" I say to her.

"Are you talking to me?" Gert asks

"Part of the reason I haven't had you here before..."

"Spit it out."

"Okay. Humpback whales migrating the Maui Coast," I yell. Immediately a 300,000 pound humpback soars fifty feet over our heads, sending Gert crashing to the floor. We are standing in the Pacific Ocean, feeling the concussion of its tonnage crashing into the sea, the singing all around us from the surrounding pod. A calf leaps above.

"We are among them," I say as Gert clutches my leg.

"No shit," she manages to eke out. She stays on the floor, in the middle of the ocean, unable to stand, clinging to my leg. Once she gets a grip on what's happened, she stands, shaking me hard with both hands. "Why have you kept this from me?"

"This is only a teaser. There is so much more. Data pour in here from everywhere, and I mean everywhere — the latest Hubble Space images, emerging brain stem research in China, meetings of the Russian Federation Council. Twenty-four seven. You have no idea."

"CIA," Gert leaps ahead.

"Maybe, who knows? You've only seen a slice of what Tiu can do," I admit lifting my arms in frustration. "CIA, KGB, NIH, World

Health Organization, and whomever else you've got involved," I yell in the air.

"Who are you yelling at?"

"No one. Venting. Isn't it obvious?" I say calming down.

"What is Chuti Tiu doing?" Gert asks, her tone serious. "Because this feels more like a War Room than a school. Where's the mainframe? The computer running all this?" she spits out her questions in rapid fire.

"Here. Everything you are looking at, but can't see," I say as a 2,000 feet high tsunami wave crashes over us. "Oh-h-h shit-t-t!"

"Your Chuti Tiu has a strange sense of humor," Gert says getting up.

"I think that was her way of saying we've worn out our welcome."

"Okay, back to the Pub?"

"Your print-outs are at the door," the Impet says before prancing away

"I get that you're trying to protect me. Ignorance is bliss and all that B.S. But I'm the one who protects your ass. And that cute little girl?"

"The little girl isn't real. She's a hologram."

"Come on. I was talking with her, she…"

"You were talking to a computer generated program. Designed by Chuti Tiu. The Impet is part of Tiu's security system."

Gert looks gut shot.

"Showing all this to me wasn't your idea, was it?"

Shaking my head no. "Tiu decided."

"Why?"

"I think she feels I need your help for what is coming."

"Because of the Helmsley?"

"I don't know how Tiu thinks. But Gayfryd, the shooting, Starch, the bombing – all of it," I say. "There's a connection. This is Tiu's way of telling us more hell is on the way."

"Like what?"

"Riedell. What's coming involves Riedell."

Chapter Nine

"The Lieutenant in the squad car this morning, he was your NYPD informant," Paddy says, holding up the file.

"Ace of Spades," Gert says. "Code name he chose. Ace contacted us. Said he reads Shawn's column. That should have been a warning." She accepts a hot tea from Paddy who brewed a pot of his own blend behind the bar.

"You knew this Ace was a cop right away, didn't you?" Kathleen asks Gert.

"He used the right words," Gert answers.

I sense Gert growing cautious with Kathleen's questions. Despite being friends, I've learned to do the same. Gert's cell phone buzzes, a text. Gert holds up her phone to me. *Gertrude, have him call me. We are in great distress. G.*

"Show them," I say.

"Who's 'we'?" Kathleen asks.

I take a sip of Gert's tea, and give Paddy the eye. His special brew is laced with Sambuca. "Gayfryd. She talks that way," I explain.

"Maybe she wants to confess to the Press." Paddy suggests.

"Not likely," Gert says.

"Might be an apology," Kathleen offers, indicating my split lip. "Call her."

I shake my head, "I'm sure it's not." But they keep looking at me so I hit the call return.

"She'll be a moment," Gayfryd's secretary answers. "Ms. Van Wie asks that I inform you she's speaking with her father's doctors. Please hold." I'm listening to classical music. If she was planning on apologizing, it would be 'ran-over-your-dog' country.

"Stay on the line," Gayfryd's secretary reminds me. "They are close to resolution."

"Resolution of what?" I ask. Debussy's Suite bergamasque is my answer.

"So why would Starch's secretary have a file on your Ace of Spades?" Paddy wonders, holding up one of the printouts.

"Only Gert and I knew who Ace was," I say.

"Not Starch?"

"He didn't want to know."

"Yet here is a file with Ace's personal information, work history, and an investigator's report on his finances," Paddy says, dropping the folder on the bar top. "Your Chronicle bosses want you to know they made the connection. Why?"

"Ace gave us uncorroborated NYPD dirt," Gert explains. "He liked telling us stories of corruption; evidence gone missing, witnesses losing their memories or disappearing before trial, that sort of thing. But never proof. He said we had to get that ourselves."

"Testing you."

"Exactly. Then he'd call demanding to know when the stories he gave us would be published. Acting superior and irritated, like 'if you can't show some initiative on your part, then how can I trust you to follow through on the big stuff?' That sort of thing."

"Stringing you along before setting up the trade," Paddy recognizes the tactic.

"Exactly. We were ready to dump him altogether, when Shawn came up with his ID. You never said how," Gert looks at me as if maybe I'd like to explain.

"Never reveal my…"

"Yeah, yeah," Gert waves me off. "In no time we've got the goods on Ace's wife, druggie kid, debt – the works. My guess, it came from Arlo."

"Who's that?" Kathleen asks.

"Starch assigned him to our team, said he was a computer hacker on loan from the Feds," I say over the music playing in one ear. I decide to hang up on Gayfryd. She can call back.

"I investigated him," Gert brags. "Really didn't take much work. The kid is a criminal computer wizard the Feds nailed for 1,000 years in solitary unless he flipped."

"What agency flipped him?" Paddy asks.

"CIA, NSA, MI, FBI, DIA. Take your pick. Could be anyone, or everyone."

"I think the kid was used to take down a major cartel," I say. "After that the Agencies put him out for sale to the other spooks. Starch told us DOJ has him for the moment. According to Starch, drug lords and arms dealers would kill Arlo on the spot, so DOJ uses him to infiltrate fraudulent businesses where he wouldn't be known."

"And Starch didn't think he was a target?"

"Honestly, I don't think the idea ever occurred to him. Starch believes he is helping the Feds clean-up the NYPD, like it's his civic duty. He's an anachronism."

"Wow!" Paddy says pulling out his unabridged. "Belongs in the past."

"We think the NYPD corruption series was a smoke screen."

"For what?"

We shrug, "Don't know."

"Arlo is good, but he's as dirty as they come. Starch gave him a cover job at the paper," Gert says. "Except Arlo used our computers to hack the Governor, the Mayor and the Commissioner on his first day. Showing off. He searched the bank accounts of the entire Police force!"

"You read his hacks?" Paddy asks.

"Hell no. Once we saw what they were, not only couldn't we use any of it, we didn't want to know. We figured the DOJ, or whoever really planted Arlo, was setting us up."

"Very likely," Paddy agrees.

"Arlo was like a kid with his hand in the cookie jar," Gert continues. "With the Chronicle computer at his disposal, and no Big Brother looking over his shoulder, Arlo started hacking all those three letter federal agencies that were treating him like a dog."

"A chance to 'out' his handlers?"

"Or prove his abilities?"

"Anyway, Arlo starts dropping off flash drives on my desk like they are peppermints. 'Wait 'til you see this. Really cool.' Like he was giving me pirated Xbox games. The operational names alone were enough to give me a rash. That's why we started using Starch's safe. Figured no one would ever see we had top secret files. What Judge is going to grant access to a media mogul's private safe, protection of sources and all...?"

"Except."

"Yeah, except here we are feeling like the Rosenbergs awaiting trial, and our only defense is a criminal hacker."

"Coincidence?"

* * *

"Do you believe in coincidences?" Paddy asked me one afternoon long ago.

"Sometimes," I answered. "Then I think it might be fate. But I don't believe in predestination. So maybe I sleep on it, try to calculate probabilities. I usually conclude the coincidence was actually a set up. Like this Christmas party." I told Paddy about the woman who was drunk and mistook me for someone else in a dark bedroom. Turns out she is my boss's wife.

Paddy nodded and told me he didn't believe it was a coincidence that he met Kathleen when he had a knife wound stitched at the hospital. Turns out Paddy and his partner had been responsible for nailing Kathleen's younger brother Jamie on the 3rd strike charges that led to his lifetime sentence.

We concluded both of these coincidences were carefully planned. The difference is that Kathleen came to love her husband, and will crack a bottle of Guinness over the head of any fool who tries to harm him. Me, I've got a split lip and cracked ribs.

In addition to her love of Paddy, Kathleen holds a maternal kind of love for her brother, Jamie. Kathleen visits Jamie in Fishkill once a month. She returns in an emotional state ranging from sadness to rage. I've overheard her verbal assaults against Paddy, and I've received the cold shoulder. It usually takes her several days to recover from the visits.

My sin is I promised to write a Chronicle story pressing for a re-hearing. My lackluster effort never got past Van Wie. But truthfully I was never committed to Jamie's plight after Gert's research showed he has been dealing almost his entire time inside. Jamie would not make a good poster boy for a rant against the three-strike law.

* * *

"Charlie," Paddy greets the detective while sliding the copies of Mrs. Wright's files under the bar. It isn't an effusive greeting, more like I give my dentist.

"Paddy. Gert," Det. Charlie Stone returns Paddy's greeting in kind. "Too recent for one of you, and too long for the other."

Gert lifts her glass, but doesn't turn around. Their eyes meet in the mirror behind the bar.

"Came by to check on my old Sergeant, and what do I find? A squad room legend," he says referring to Gert, "boozing it up with a material witness. Imagine that," Stone approaches me. "Five of NYPD's finest, murdered, sixteen injured, twelve civilians dead and still counting, hundreds more injured, and an eye witness sneaking out the service entrance. Big time reporter doesn't think to call the

Police? Now what do you make of that, Mr. Flawed?" Stone is so close I can smell his breakfast: whiskey.

"Who told you I was there?" I ask, pretending to be calm even though my socks are sliding down.

"Your own Goddamn newspaper reported you were at the scene," Stone says, his breath so foul my split lip burns. He pushes the late edition Chronicle in front of me. Gert's story. How could I have been so stupid? "What were you doing at the Helmsley?"

I can imagine my Managing Editor explaining my whereabouts to Stone. "I believe at the time in question, Mr. Shaw was at the Helmsley having a go at my wife."

"Personal business," I answer.

"What kind of personal business?" Stone demands.

"The kind that remains personal," I answer a bit too quickly.

"I want you at the precinct now," Det. Stone orders.

"Are you arresting me?"

I'm certain he knows how bad his breath is, because he exhales like a dragon. "One hour. Midtown. Have your smart ass there, or I'll haul you in through central booking. Got it Mr. Flawed?"

I stand, feeling the damage from an earlier spasm. "You know the Press is always happy to cooperate with the NYPD," I say, taking in his fetid breath as if it is lavender perfume.

Det. Stone keeps up the stare while I reach for the mug of tea Paddy has put in front of me.

"I'll take mine neat in one of those fancy mugs, Sarge," Stone orders, quickly downing the rail whiskey Paddy pours for him.

"One hour," Det. Stone points at me. "Don't keep the Lieutenant waiting." Gert recoils from the hand he puts on her shoulder. "Like old home week around here," Stone says to her before he pushes his way out the door.

Paddy slides over a fresh gimlet to Gert. She sighs, looking me in the eye. "I was lonely and horny," she confesses. "He said all the right things." I nod, who am I to judge?

"Stone's boss," Paddy explains, "is Lt. Garcelli, my former trainee turned partner, and in the end, my boss."

"The one who closed the door on your career?"

My phone buzzes; it's Gayfryd so I take the call.

"We were not amused by this morning's incident," she says. "We were quite startled. Thankfully our self-defense training activated. You are forgiven."

I hold out my cell so the others can hear. "What's she..?" Gert starts whispering, until I raise my hand to quiet her.

"You may respond," Gayfryd says.

"I, I..." is all that comes out, as I'm realizing how incredibly idiotic she sounds.

"We are quite busy today, especially with Daddy and all, but there is a misconception on your part that must be clarified. Are you prepared?"

"Gayfryd, I saw..."

"A Family Care Center. We do not brag about charity, but there it is. A few of my friends and I provide care and support for the less fortunate. While we don't condone murder, those two despicable policemen were ever so deserving."

"You knew them?"

"Certainly not in a social way, they were, after all, villains, disgusting blackmailers."

"And you had nothing to do with the shootings or explosion?"

"Certainly not. As you may recall, at the time of the incident we were quite engaged."

"Engaged?" Gert mouths. "Like," she pantomimes thrusting her hips.

I have to look away to keep my attention on Gayfryd's logic. "The bombing happened after you attacked me and left me in the hallway."

"We have explained that unfortunate incident to our satisfaction. We'll discuss it no further."

"Unbelievable," I say covering the receiver.

"And with all that commotion afterward, we have had quite an unsettling day. But we will persevere. Now to the point. The Chronicle. We will be assuming control, and will expect your support. Naturally, our trysts must be put on hold until we have solidified the full allegiance of the Board. So there you have it. Questions? Good. Must dash."

"I can't believe that woman," Kathleen says.

"He sleeps with her," Gert points at me, almost in tears laughing.

Chapter Ten

"Assume these two know everything," Paddy says as we start walking to the Midtown Precinct on West 54th & Eighth. Paddy's decision to come with me is more than moral support. He is telling me this is serious.

"They know about our NYPD corruption series?"

"Of course."

"The Feds involvement?"

"Likely," Paddy says without breaking stride. "Stone didn't order you over for a little chat. He's looking to put you in jail."

"For what?"

"How about hacking into the personal accounts of 40,000 of New York's finest?" Paddy says as he keeps walking. "In case you haven't caught on, your ass is swinging in the wind."

"For running from the Helmsley?"

"That doesn't help, but think. Every time we come up with a name connected to the suicide/bombing, you are the common denominator. I wouldn't count on the police missing that for very long. And didn't it strike you strange that the Feds loaned you a criminal hacker?"

"Of course. I knew we couldn't trust the guy, but Starch was impressed. Starch's Independent Prosecutor friend told him she's ready to crack the NYPD wide open. Got a stack of warrants ready to be served."

"With Starch out of action, I suggest you make sure this Prosecutor has your back."

"Meaning?"

"Deniability. The Feds propose a joint task force with the Chronicle. Starch likes the idea and gives it to you, his rebel investigative reporter. You get a Chronicle exclusive: cleaning-up the NYPD, right?"

"That's the idea."

"Except it's you who is running an illegal hacker, not the Feds. Your information is compromised with hacks of secret FBI and CIA operations. And, just to nail down your coffin, your proof is locked in a safe to which you have no access."

"Not sounding good."

"Oh, it gets better. Remember, Arlo works for you, which means you are the one who conducted the illegal searches. Your boy even used your Company's computer. The Feds aren't even involved. And this Independent Prosecutor you don't even know, is where?"

"Washington, DC."

"Probably getting a warrant for your arrest. Without Starch to back up your story, files locked in his safe, and an unstable ex-lover angling to take over the Chronicle, guess who is disposable? So when you asked me, why am I coming along? It's too see how you look in your grey jumpsuit."

"Shit." I say slowing my pace.

"Listen," Paddy stops. "I've got no power here. In fact Garcelli doesn't like me very much. So when you walk through those doors, you act smart or pull that 'protecting your source' routine, he'll drop you in a dark hole. And no one will know. No one. Understand?"

I nod. At least Paddy will know if I go missing.

"When I started this NYPD piece, I asked you to put me in touch with a cop you knew was dirty."

"You wanted a source."

"Right. So why Ace?"

"I knew his life was in the dumpster, and he was looking for an out. One that didn't jeopardize his wife and kid. I hinted there was a remote possibility you could get him into witness protection."

"I never said."

"I know." Paddy's voice rises a notch. "He knew I was pushing the envelope, but desperate people hear what they want."

"Talking to me didn't get Ace killed," I say, as much to convince myself as Paddy.

"Maybe," Paddy allows.

"So, what do you think happened?"

"Can't guess yet. I didn't know for sure he was your source, just assumed so since you never asked me for another lead. You'd better figure Garcelli and Stone know your connection to Ace." Paddy clamps a mitt on my shoulder. "Don't get too clever. If Garcelli gives you an out, run."

* * *

I've been waiting 30 minutes in the small room. The late edition Chronicle is on the table along with coffee. I haven't touched either.

Det. Stone bursts through the door, accompanied by Lt. Garcelli, Assistant Chief of Detectives. No formalities, he throws out his opening question. "Exactly where were you at the Helmsley today?"

"I was inside the building," I say turning to face him. "I heard a gunshot and went to the window. I saw the slick-top, blood splattered on the windshield."

"Exactly where was this window? Lobby? Restaurant?" Garcelli asks, plopping down his paperwork at the end of the table. What a pair. Garcelli is square chested, big stomach, looks like he has a foil-wrapped calzone in his desk drawer at all times. In stark contrast, Stone is sickly thin with a yellow complexion, leaving little doubt what is in his drawer. Geez Gert, I understand lonely, but him?

"No, higher up," I say.

"How much higher?" Stone demands, his eyes fixed on me like I'm prey, while Lt. Garcelli checks that the cameras and mics are working. They're setting the stage.

"Twenty-second floor."

"That's a private residence floor. What were you doing there?" Garcelli asks, forcing me to turn back and forth between the two of them.

"An interview. I'm a reporter. You may have seen my column *Unflawed.*"

"Still running, is it?" Garcelli snipes. "I thought your readership collapsed when you went on that year-long tirade against the NYPD."

"I had no choice," I explain. "NYPD sat on their collective fat asses refusing to investigate James Berk who raped and killed my friend, Emma."

Stone takes off his plaid sport jacket, exposing his gun. I'm supposed to react to the obvious threat. But guns in holsters don't scare me. He takes the Chronicle off the table, places it on his chair and sits on it. Subtle.

"What was the interview about?"

"Confidential," I say despite Paddy's warning.

"You think you're going to hide behind that fuckin' privilege crap while I've got five police officers dead and near a hundred civilians lying in the hospital?" Det. Stone rages.

I don't answer. Knowing Paddy is wandering around somewhere in the building helps.

"Who were you *interviewing*?" Garcelli asks, grinning at the euphemism.

No one is kidding anyone. I know they have the Helmsley security footage. Garcelli, Stone and the squad all watched me naked, bleeding and curled in a ball taking everything Gayfryd could dish out. Stone is salivating cheap whiskey waiting to produce the footage. Paddy did warn me.

"I was *interviewing* the hell out of my Editor's wife," I confess. "We were in bed when I heard the gunshot ricocheting off the windows. Sounded like a cannon."

Stone shrinks at my blatant admission. I've taken his leverage off the table. He's lost his rhythm. Worse for him, he needs a drink.

"Okay," Garcelli mutters, regrouping. He tosses a gum tablet in his mouth, sliding the packet to me.

"I'm good," I say flicking the packet back across the table to Stone. "Little sugar might help the shakes."

Garcelli tries to hide his smirk at Stone being called out. Stone notices and sweeps the gum packet into the wall.

"Coffee? Coke?" Lt. Garcelli asks me, unfazed by his detective's anger, picking up his packet of gum from the floor.

I shake my head no. My stomach growls for all to hear. I grab to stop the grumbling but hit my side, wincing as my ribs scream silently. There would be little satisfaction in besting Stone if I'm in that hole Paddy warned me about, praying for a cockroach as company.

"Suit yourself, I need a jolt of caffeine," Garcelli says pressing a buzzer screwed to the table. Moments later there is a knock on the door.

"Coffee," says a voice we all recognize.

"Come on in, Sergeant," Garcelli says. He's not surprised as Paddy swings the door wide, kicking the stopper down to the floor, while Stone grabs the files and takes a position leaning against the wall behind me.

"Sorry to interrupt," Paddy says. "I just got a call from Mr. Shaw's office." He holds up his cell as confirmation. "His presence is requested in Washington, DC."

"I haven't completed my interview," Lt. Garcelli says. "Your reporter pal is telling me how he spotted a vehicle outside the

Helmsley while he was banging his boss's wife. Even used cop slang, like he is one of us. Is he one of us, Sergeant?"

Paddy doesn't answer. Garcelli has made his point.

"You're aware the deceased Captain and Lieutenant were being investigated," Lt. Garcelli says sitting on the table.

"Internal Affairs?" Paddy asks.

"No. My team," Garcelli nods toward Det. Stone. "Commissioner's directive. He didn't tell you?"

Paddy remains silent, Garcelli's comment is an obvious jab.

"The Commissioner brings in this tech wizard one night, very hush hush. Kid had these tiny cameras, actually looked like flying bugs."

"Drones," I say.

"Yeah right," Garcelli turns pointing at me. "Almost forgot you know all about that shit, don't you?"

"What do you want?" I ask now that I know Lt. Garcelli and Det. Stone didn't bring me in for questioning. They are letting me know Arlo is also working for them.

Cards on the table.

"We've got the hotel's surveillance tapes. When the uniforms started opening doors on the private floors, what do you think they found?" Stone continues without my answer. "A medical facility. No luxury suites with marble floors and crystal chandeliers, but a wing of medical offices. We saw evidence of cameras where you were *interviewing* Mrs. Van Wie. We want those tapes and everything else you have on those two officers."

"Why do you think I have any of that?"

"Because you instructed your hacker boy to surveil my cops and Mrs. Van Wie."

I did no such thing. That means Arlo has been working on his own. So he's playing the cops, Starch and the Chronicle, me, probably Gayfryd, and maybe Berk. That little Bastard.

"I want it all, every micro-chip of data that kid hacked."

So, at least Garcelli doesn't know Ace was my source. I didn't want to see Arlo's flash drives before, I guess thinking I'd get the information I needed legitimately. That ethical ship has sailed. I need to see those drives.

"The hacker's name is Arlo," I volunteer.

"Yeah. That's the kid," Garcelli nods at me as if appreciating my cooperation.

"In his world, he's anything but a kid. So if you're asking for…"

"I don't care if the kid is Grandma Moses," Stone yells. "Cut the bullshit, Shaw. We've got you. Dead Lieutenant from our precinct, and a Borough Captain, outside the building where you are doing some poor schmuck's wife, recording it all. That makes you a direct link, got it?"

"I'm a reporter. The only thing I did was sleep with a beautiful woman. So cuff me," I take a chance, putting out my hands.

Stone moves closer, I avoid inhaling. "Nice try. You knew Mrs. Van Wie was running an illegal clinic. You knew about it just like you knew the brass in the squad car were taking protection money."

"Crooked cops?"

Stone slams the table. "Don't play innocent."

I look to Paddy. So they just confirmed that Arlo was working for Gayfryd. He gives me a slight nod.

"I think you confronted Mrs. Van Wie with a sample tape. Told her you could make her problem go away, didn't you? Maybe a roll in the sack as thanks. A little sexual quid pro quo?" Stone suggests circling around. "This morning was a reunion visit. She dumped you once, didn't she? Kinda been gnawing at you. Big man about town, rejected."

As I start to respond, Paddy's mitt presses down hard on my shoulder.

"Who else was in her apartment this morning?" Det. Stone demands.

"No one," I say sounding unsure. I really don't know if anyone was there. Stone keeps throwing every idea that pops into his head, and I'm reacting. I should know better. "I only saw Gayfryd in the apartment. Mrs. Van Wie, that is," I correct her name for their recording.

"She trigger the bomb?" Lt. Garcelli asks easily.

"I have no idea."

"You know what I find interesting?" Garcelli wonders.

I shake my head, no.

"My boys went through that entire suite of offices, and they didn't find a single medical file, not a name on a folder, no flash drives, laptops, no computers, nada. Only loose cables. Except a fortune in imaging equipment, operating theaters, and supplies were left behind. Doesn't that strike you as curious?"

"Suggests someone left in a hurry. And don't hospitals keep all their information in the Cloud these days?" I suggest.

"Your boy Arlo would know more about that than me," Det. Stone says with a lupine grin.

Always back to Arlo. Arlo's cover at the Chronicle as the Gadgets Editor working down in the basement was inspired. The dreadlocks, pot, and bizarre language keep the other IT geeks away, leaving him to do whatever he likes, using the Chronicle's computer.

"Let me try and help you here," Lt. Garcelli suggests, twirling his gum package in his fingers. "Let's pretend you never told your boy to plant illegal devices. And let's also pretend your cell phone was left behind after your interview." Garcelli leans in closer. "And, maybe that cell phone, with an extraordinary battery life, was left on record. Follow me?"

I nod. Clearly my cell phone is his euphemism for Arlo's flash drives.

"So if you come across that cell phone again, like real soon, it might help us identify who is behind the bombing. Isn't that possible?"

"I'm planning to see her," I lie, trying to buy some time.

"Mrs. Gayfryd Van Wie?" Garcelli says surprised. "When are you making contact? We'd like to talk with her as well."

"When I get back from D.C."

"How about we talk to her now," Garcelli orders, pushing a pad across the table. "Write down her contact information."

"She contacts me. Always has," I say pushing the pad back. "I'm guessing she doesn't actually live at the Helmsley. It's been a few years, but her husband had an office party at the Trump Towers. Have you tried there?"

Stone glares at me. "I spoke to your boss this morning. He said he and his wife are separated. Have been for over a year."

"I didn't know."

"Do you know who has the lease on the medical suites?" Lt. Garcelli asks.

"I didn't know there were medical offices in the Helmsley. This morning, I thought I was going to Mrs. Van Wie's in-town residence."

Lt. Garcelli shakes his head as if I'm not listening. "The entire floor is leased by a Mnemosyne Corporation. Sound familiar?"

I nod.

"Isn't that owned by James Berk, the man you helped put in prison?" Garcelli asks. "The man you say murdered Emma."

* * *

The swinging doors from Parnell's kitchen burst open. Emma is on roller skates, the infant Riedell is in her arms, held out as if she is on forklift blades. Emma tosses Riedell to me as she glides past. Emma's face is elaborately made-up in a curious version of the Lion King. Her hair, ratted out, has a single braided tail down her back. She's wearing black plastic garbage bags duct taped to her wrists and ankles. She is a cat-bat. This is reminiscent of the creative, crazy pre-Berk Emma I loved.

But instead of gaining loft, Emma sweeps several tables clean of their meals with her garbage bag wings. Unfazed by the crashing noise, she skates through the food and broken plates, spreading her wings.

"Engulf us," Emma screams, swirling on her skates, an avenging arch-angel, knocking over chairs, tables. "Trash abounds, gulls flapping, dive-bombing the streets, rats scurrying in joy. Disease, pestilence and blessed death." She continues twirling around the room, cawing, screeching and flapping.

The customers in the room are silent, still. Baby Riedell cries.

Emma brakes. Stretches out her arms for her daughter, grasping but strangely held back. She flutters to a knee, her head drops, wings flop to her sides. She falls to earth, whirling helplessly, writhing in agony.

The customers are stunned to inertia. Uncertain whether Emma's performance is finished, a few random hands clap. Emma stops moving. Silence.

Riedell still in my arms, Kathleen gets to Emma first, opening her eyes. They are filled with blood; more is dripping from her ears. Kathleen rolls Emma on her left side, a nurse in charge. "Paddy call 9-1-1," she orders.

Moments later, the paramedics charge through the door. Pulse, oxygen. I catch the no-chance look they give Kathleen, and bury Riedell in my arms.

Berk turned Emma into a circus act, although his real intention was much worse.

* * *

"You tried to get Berk indicted for Emma's murder," Garcelli says, opening the wounds.

"Of course I did. As if raping a mental patient wasn't heinous enough, he had her brain surgically destroyed, which led to her death. That's murder."

"The murder charge never really had a chance. You know that."

"The District Attorney made that call, not me."

"You made out just fine with that hospital settlement. From what I hear, that Emma School of yours looks like the NY Athletic Club; an Olympic pool, running track, surround sound, and enough big screen TVs to open a nightclub," Stone says.

I begin to protest, until Paddy shakes his head, *don't argue.*

"You know Berk is out of prison," Garcelli says, returning to his chair. "He's going to get a full pardon, Medal of Freedom, maybe even a Nobel Prize. Some fantastic medical discovery called CRISPR.* Imagine doing that while you are in prison."

"It's BS. The CRISPR discovery is a byproduct of someone else's work."

"Whatever..." says Stone. "Fucking Jonas Salk is what he is. I hear CRISPR can cure cancer. Gave those inmates who volunteered for his research a million dollars each."

I shake my head in disbelief. I know CRISPR is Chuti Tiu's work.

"Tom," Paddy says calling Garcelli by his first name. "Shawn is trying to help."

"How? By investigating *our* Department, with *your* help? You didn't think I knew?" Garcelli snaps, directing his anger at Paddy before turning back to me.

"We need to go," Paddy says moving towards the door. "Washington said ASAP."

Garcelli wants to hold firm, but Paddy knows cops' triggers better than most. Washington is synonymous with Federal, which trumps

---

* Stepping aside from this story for a moment, it is worth mentioning that CRISPR is absolutely real. The complex acronym refers to an injection that seeks out undesirable genetic code, DNA. The target, perhaps cancer, is snipped out and replaced with a healthy substitute.

CRISPR offers the promise to eliminate all genetic diseases, and much more. As you might expect, CRISPR has already created serious medical and ethical debates.

Garcelli's authority. The NYPD cannot be seen as obstructing. Especially if the bombing is declared a terrorist attack.

"We need to speak with Mrs. Van Wie," Garcelli makes his final pitch, without threats. "Any help from you goes a long way with me," he says. "This is your chance to set the record straight, before Mrs. Van Wie gives her version of what happened at the Helmsley."

I stand to leave. "Remember that cellphone you might have misplaced," Garcelli reminds me. "Give me everything you can get your hands on, and I'll keep you and yours in the clear. Or, take your chances."

"Always happy to stand a good cop for a drink or two. You know where. I'll be in touch," I say, leaving with Paddy.

* * *

"I like him," I say as we exit the stone fortress on West 54th.

"Sure," Paddy says pushing past the gathering media. The Midtown station was designated Bomb Command Central.

"I thought you are cop savvy. The gum, coffee. Garcelli was trying to get your prints and DNA," Paddy says.

"I've got nothing to hide."

Paddy gives me that *you're an idiot* look. "And when he stops by for that drink you promised him, don't invite Garcelli upstairs. It's an invitation to search."

"I've got nothing to…" I stop.

"Maybe you don't," Paddy shakes his head, "but I'll bet Chuti Tiu does. In case you haven't noticed, your floor has become much more than a children's day school these past few years. Midnight deliveries. People in blue jumpsuits coming up the back freight entrance. Always at night?"

"You're right. I'll be careful."

"Good, because Garcelli and Stone have been looking for a chance to take you down. They'd be the heroes of NYPD for burying the Chronicle's *Mr. Unflawed* once and for all."

"I'll leave Tiu a message. She'll be ready for Garcelli," I say as we part ways.

"Tonight," Paddy decides.

"What about tonight?"

"We need to make a late social call after you get back from DC. Arlo. Garcelli wants us to do his dirty work, which isn't a bad move. We need to get ahead of this game fast."

"I thought you made that up about Washington."

"Nope. You need to find out where you stand with Starch's Prosecutor friend. Too bad your resident genius hasn't been around."

"Tiu?"

"We're going to need her help."

* * *

"Damn it's cold," I say to no one. I stuff my satchel inside my jacket, like the street people use the newspaper to add a layer of insulation. I pull up my collar and lower my head as I leave Paddy and head to the office.

"Dollah Mister, dollah?" an old beggar woman pleads to me. She is fully cloaked in what looks to be one of Kathleen's army blankets.

It used to be spare change, now dollahs. Even if I have a dollah, it's inside my satchel which is keeping me warm. But it's freezing for her; I cave, opening my jacket as the human blanket keeps moving closer, witch's hand stretched out for the donation.

"You are a good man Shaw," says a voice I recognize from under the blanket. "Continue to get the dollah and pretend to give me directions to a shelter," she says making pantomimes of hunger, rubbing her belly for anyone watching.

"What the hell are you doing?" I ask Chuti Tiu, showing more anger than I feel. Why does she have to be so mysterious?

I never know when Tiu will appear. I hear her voice, mostly when she is talking to Riedell, through images on the screen, teaching, training, always encouraging her niece to explore. Occasionally I see and speak with Tiu when she appears in holographic form. I've learned when she might be in the city by the speed of her voice transmission. The speed of sound is one of Tiu's great frustrations.

"Mimic me. Rub your stomach and point west," she orders. I obey.

"It's time," Tiu says. "Berk is shrewder than I expected."

I like hearing the sound of her real voice, rather than the electronic version. Listening to the rhythm of her breathing reminds me she is human.

"Berk allowed us to send him to prison," Tiu tells me.

"Allowed us?"

"He crossed the line with Emma, and had to pay a penitence, or be expelled from Destiny."

Hearing Tiu's clear, precise voice coming from this disguise is confusing, like having a meaningful conversation with a heap of garbage.

"Ten years at Berk's age, that's a hell of an act of contrition," I say.

"It wasn't all punishment. The Destiny Foundation does not squander time. There is a purpose to every action."

"CRISPR," I realize.

"Good, you know. Prison was an ideal laboratory. Lose a few prisoners, no one will care. Now wave your hands at me, act angry," she says.

I do as she orders, though it makes me look heartless to the lingering media. She extends her hand, bowing, pleading, but her voice is strong.

"What's happening?" I ask. "Is Destiny still after you?"

"Oh, they are after me. But they have redirected their Pit Bull, James Berk."

"What do you mean?" I ask, trying to get what she is saying.

"Berk is after Riedell."

"Over my dead body."

"And Berk understands that. He would be more than happy to kill you, but he can't."

"That's comforting."

"Killing you would make you a martyr in Riedell's eyes. Berk is too clever for that. Riedell would be useless to The Destiny Society if she was forced to join them."

"Like you," I say.

"Berk plans to eliminate you by destroying everything you care about: your friends, your job, your city, your purpose. He will make you a pariah in Riedell's eyes."

"The bombing? Killing and maiming all those people?"

"What makes sense to Destiny is incomprehensible to others."

Tiu waves her arm anxiously, keeping up the beggar charade. "Berk is coming after our girl. Fix that firmly in your mind, and prepare to lose everything to save her from him."

"Who wants Riedell? Berk? Destiny?"

"Right now they are one and the same."

"Then help me."

"Give me the dollah, and point north. Then pick up what I leave under the blanket and go."

Turning away to point her toward the pretend shelter, I feel the bill snatched from my hand. Looking back, I find her blanket on the ground.

I retrieve the papers beneath. A marriage certificate. Apparently Tiu has become my wife. And they say romance is dead.

Chapter Eleven

On the shuttle flight to Washington I study the copies of Mrs. Wright's files. The private investigator has laid out a scenario that ties Starch to Gayfryd's mother. Just when I think this day can't get any worse.

Gayfryd, born under another name in Ashville, North Carolina on the wrong side of town. Mother, a looker with lots of men around. Seems the mother decides her daughter deserves better. Maybe she figures Starch is the father, or maybe she chooses Starch as the patsy because his family has serious money. No evidence of paternity tests. Checks start coming regularly from Starch's parents to an account in an Ashville bank. Mother commits suicide when daughter is about ten. Daughter goes to live with an uncle who abuses her. Daughter comes of age, the checks stop, the uncle tosses her out.

At this point Gayfryd seems to have reinvented herself. Always imaginative, ambitious and bright enough, she gets a job at a city newspaper editing the society pages. Learns to mix with some of the right people. Following the smell of new money, moves to Silicon Valley where she creates a plausible past and plots a brighter future.

She targets a brilliant software entrepreneur, James Berk, who has been dethroned by his backers. Conspiring with her new partner, she helps him regain his Company. As a reward, he backs her to return to New York where she attempts to claim her place in her father's media empire.

Starch remembers her mother, and realizes it is possible, but not likely, that he is her father. Denying paternity but unable to shake a sense of guilt, he gives her a job. She bides her time. Sensing an opportunity, she marries Van Wie, then an assistant Managing Editor. She has secured her place.

Where and when have Gayfryd and Berk come together again? And why does Berk have the lease for Gayfryd's charity medical clinic? There is nothing charitable about Berk, or Gayfryd. What are they up to?

Paddy's warnings about coincidence come to mind.

* * *

I've been summoned to meet Starch's clandestine Federal Prosecutor. About time.

The Jefferson Hotel in Washington, DC is her idea. The main entrance is a portico over two layers of brass double doors. Familiar, yet very different. I can't quite spot what it is.

A uniformed bellman recognizes my unfamiliarity with the setting before I can ask directions.

"You're here for the Independent Prosecutor. If you'll follow me," he says leading me to the guest library. "Ms. Kasey," he says rolling a white gloved hand in her direction as he withdraws.

So that's who it is, Diane Kasey. The ADA in NY who wouldn't prosecute Berk for murder. Tiu and I handed her the conspiracy case that finally sent him to prison. So a Federal appointment, Independent Prosecutor, was her reward. That explains why Starch kept her identity from me.

Hearing her name, she folds The Washington Post, removing her glasses. Oak bookcases line two walls of the room, a wood-burning fire overcomes the evening chill, and a Winslow sea painting across from a Jefferson oil all lend to a comfortable, patriotic aura. I feel out of place. I've moved from money and influence to the seat of power.

"Shawn Shaw," I introduce myself, perhaps a bit too loudly for the cluster of browsing dignitaries.

She stands, meeting me eye-to-eye. "Diane Kasey. I remember you." A full handshake.

I must have left the Jefferson's front doors open to bring in that much of a chill, but I give her my full smile anyway. Gert loves telling me, "You're not all that much to look at, but you got lucky with that smile."

I remember Kasey as young, athletic, ambitious. Now she seems battle-scarred and wary. Still long and lean, her brunette hair has dulled, and her mouth is unaccustomed to smiling. Not unattractive, I decide, in a refined, well-maintained sort of way. No head turner by any means, but well-packaged. I sense the mien of a woman who has endured a bitter divorce she never saw coming.

A waiter appears. "May I bring you a fresh Blue Mountain, Ms. Kasey?"

She raises an eyebrow, giving permission.

"Earl Grey," I answer the waiter's questioning eye. I remember the brand Paddy favors.

"How's Mr. Storch doing?" Ms. Kasey asks once the waiter leaves.

"Fine." I'm hesitant to volunteer any further information. NYC politicians I understand: greed, revenge, control. Washington, not so simple: influence, connections, power. This feels like a town where honesty is a sin.

"I plan to see him tomorrow."

"Good," she says as if "planning" is ambitious thinking in Washington-speak, and she is wishing me good luck on an actual visit.

She closes her legal-sized notebook, wanting me to know she's been busy. Flipping her Cross pen, she signals, 'Get on with it'.

Happy to, if I had a clue. So, I take a shot. "We plan to run the first part of our NYPD Corruption series this weekend. Do you have a comment for the record?" *Fast enough for you?*

"And why would I?"

Not the response I was hoping for. So I try again.

"You would be sending the message," I say flipping open my pad. "Let them know there is a new Marshal in town," I suggest.

Independent Prosecutor Kasey swirls her glasses by the arm, giving me a studied gaze. It's actually a deciding gaze.

"You know, I have no illusions why the AG asked me to take this job. I know the territory. Every US Attorney General needs a major cleanup on his resume."

"So you're not the first IP to get the NYPD clean-up assignment, I take it?"

Diane Kasey smiles.

I have no idea what that means, but I give her my best crinkle-eyed Robert Redford grin, indicating our common understanding of whatever the hell she is talking about. She simply stares.

Okay. No charm. No humor. I drop the smile and lower my eyebrows. Whatever I did, works. She settles down, and I do my best to disguise my relief.

"I'll do my bit, of course. Lop off a few NYPD heads. Prompt a few resignations," she says matter-of-factly, as if the decapitations are collateral damage.

"You want me to use that?"

"You do, and I'll instruct Joseph," she nods toward the arriving waiter, "to use your ball sac for a tea strainer."

"Then off the record it is." I open my hands, waiting to learn why I am here.

Again, nothing. She drinks her coffee and sits back.

What the hell. I'm down to my last chip. "There never was a joint investigation, was there?" I toss out.

"The Federal government doesn't need help from a City newspaper to take down crooked cops."

"Okay. I take it, no quote for my series?"

Independent Prosecutor Kasey smiles, no. "While you are here, perhaps you can explain why my office received a call from a person named Gayfryd?"

"Ah," I say, finally understanding. Her contact and backer, Starch, is down, and she wants to know who is stepping in. She probably has the same report I read on the plane.

I wait to see if she will answer; instead she busies herself with the coffee, summoning the waiter, Joseph. Seems I'm better at saying nothing, than something. Gert would be proud.

"Well, if that settles it," I say getting up, "I've got a police suicide story to finish for the weekend edition."

"What suicide?"

"We were investigating the two NYPD brass you read about." I tap the front page of her newspaper. "Turns out their car was also rigged with a bomb."

"Terrorists?"

"Not sure yet. You can read about it in the Chronicle tomorrow. So thanks for the tea. I've got to get back."

* * *

Gert calls as I'm boarding the plane. "Gayfryd got a judge to grant her custody of Starch," she tells me the news. "They took him from the hospital and moved him into *Bethesda House."* Starch's Connecticut mansion.

"They?"

"Mrs. Wright says Gayfryd arrived with a full ambulance crew and, I quote, the man who made the front page of the Chronicle when he was released from prison."

"James Berk," I understand. "What does the witch expect us to do?"

"Walter Jackson is in Court right now, requesting independent supervision of Starch. He's also seeking a pre-emptive injunction."

"Against what?" I ask.

"Attempt to take over the Chronicle. Mrs. Wright says our acting Chairman wants to invoke his power of attorney."

My skin grows cold.

"She wants us to get information. Investigate the hell out of your girlfriend."

* * *

What a day. Morning coffee was eye-popping sex with my boss's wife. Not all bad, except the smear on my bagel was being beaten and thrown naked into the hallway. There was a police suicide outside the window, followed by a bombing killing five, injuring hundreds and nearly incinerating my best friend.

For lunch, my Publisher has a massive stroke, and for cocktail hour I'm interrogated, accused, and threatened by New York's finest. Next, I'm summoned to Washington, DC where I am intimidated by a Prosecutor from the Federal Department of Justice.

Now my nemesis, James Berk, is partnering with Gayfryd to manipulate my Publisher and take control of the Company. Why did I bother to wake up this morning?

Oh yeah, and I got married!

I grab an airline pillow, and take a window seat, closing my eyes.

Chapter Twelve

"I think that stretch over there is for you," Paddy says the instant I push through Parnell's door a bit past 10:00 p.m. He inclines his head towards the corner at First and 53rd. "It's been there forty minutes."

I'd like to call it a night, though the nap on the plane, and this thirty degree temperature have done their best to refresh me.

* * *

"Give us a chance to explain," she begs from the half-opened window of the stretch limo.

I'm itching to attack, but remorse from Gayfryd means there is a deal forthcoming. Never hurts to listen. What does she want to 'explain:' the beating; the bomb; snatching Starch; trying to take over the Chronicle? Does she know about my meeting with the Independent Prosecutor?

On cue, the uniformed driver opens the rear door. I get inside, warm, taking the seat across from her. I resist the whiff of lavender. Not this time. "And what part of today's disasters didn't involve you?" I ask.

"The gunshot. We panicked. We rushed downstairs, then returning you surprised us. We thought you were an intruder. Defending us was our first instinct."

"Intruder? Nice try. And you can cut the royal 'we' crap."

She doesn't blink, so I reach for the door handle. Instead of protesting, she sits back in her white fur motioning toward the champagne in the silver ice bucket. "Won't you do the honors?"

"I'll pass. Paddy says the anti-venom just arrived. Kathleen needs to give me the shot before I get another snake bite and the toxin gets to a vital organ."

"Hiss," she mocks cobra-like, flickering her tongue, holding out her glass. "We hear the Chronicle's henchman, Walter Jackson, tried to poison you against us with those scandalous files."

"Walter and I had a nice chat," I lie. "He is worried you are going to soil the Chronicle's reputation. Any truth to the rumor you are planning to rape and pillage Starch, now that he's incapacitated?"

"Aren't you the clever one?" Gayfryd pushes her still empty glass at me. "Now we are a source of information," she says twirling her index finger. "Pour," she orders as the limo slips into the Midtown traffic like a trout released back into the stream.

"Oh that's so much better," she says empting half of her fluted glass, holding it out for a re-fill and writhing in the luxury of her fur. "We don't like drinking alone."

I pour myself a glass. I hate champagne, but I sip it anyway thinking the alcohol will smart my split lip and keep me alert in the warm limo.

"You know, we can do this without your support," she says, looking at me, pressing the rim of her glass to her lower lip. "Although having you on our side would provide a little wiggle room," she accentuates the offer with a slight shift of her hips and a pat on the seat next to her. "We needn't be at odds," she coos reaching over, touching my knee. Her hand moves higher. I steel my leg, but I can't hide the reaction.

"The attraction is still there, isn't it," she confirms, settling back into her fur, sipping her drink. "We were particularly naughty this morning, weren't we?"

"I said you can drop the Majesty routine," I tell her, dumping my champagne in the bucket and helping myself to what looks like JD from the bar. For the moment, pain is my friend, but why suffer unduly. "I only put up with your royal act to get laid."

"Oh, aren't we being ever so manly," she says, scratching her nails on the leather seat, never breaking her composure.

Think cold I tell myself. Blizzard. "Obviously you aren't kidnapping me to apologize, so what exactly do you want?" Despite knowing better, I seem to let Gayfryd unnerve me. And she knows it.

"I want the stock you stole from my partner, James Berk, returned to us. Clear enough for you?"

I'm numbing my lip on the ice in the JD glass. "No wonder the Chronicle Board is fortifying the castle. They will never let you take over the Chronicle, even with Berk's billions."

"Of course we will. Jimmy promised. He's even got his Destiny Foundation medical team fixing Daddy."

"Daddy, a dubious claim at best."

She shrugs. "He'll be healthy enough to sign the papers in a few days. Maybe we'll get the President of the United States to witness the signature after he gives Jimmy his Medal of Freedom." She toasts Berk.

The JD isn't stinging enough. I drive an elbow into my ribs. "You are a wonder," I say, never letting the searing pain affect my Redford smile. "And the Judge is satisfied with you caring for a man of Starch's age at home?"

"Of course. We are his daughter. Who could be more qualified? Jimmy even hired a staff with an ambulance. The Judge practically insisted for Daddy to come with us."

When does delusion cross into insanity? Emma managed, until it was impossible. Does Gayfryd know she is bordering on the edge?

"Walter Jackson is desperate for me to sign over the voting rights to him," I tell her.

"Blood is blood," Gayfryd says, widening her eyes and angling her head as if some people just don't get it.

"I get it," I assure her. It's senseless to argue. Let her think she's won.

"Walter and that horrible Mrs. Wright will have to go, of course. We'll keep paying the dividend equivalent to keep your school running. And you'll keep your job," Gayfryd assures me reaching forward tapping the privacy window. The limo reverses direction so easily I don't even feel the movement. For her, the deal is done.

"I told that Washington, DC Prosecutor we'd continue cooperating with her investigation. Women can talk to each other, you know, in a way men can't possibly understand. Naturally, I'll keep you in the loop. Another Pulitzer coming your way, we can smell it," she says touching her nose.

I look the other way.

"And don't feel too badly," Gayfryd comforts. "Once all this is settled, you'll see it's for the better. The newspaper side of the Company is failing. I have ideas. And who knows? Maybe you'll even get to have sex with the Boss once in a while?" she smiles, patting my knee. "I'll have Jeffrey drop you off a block early. Give you time to think up your story for your friend. Sound good?"

"Sure."

"There is one thing," Gayfryd says as we slow to the curb. "Daddy seems to like you."

"We've always gotten along," I say, pressing my elbow into my rib, the defeated look frozen on my face.

"You could facilitate the transition and make it easier on Daddy if you'd tell him about our decision."

"Of course," I lie.

"Excellent. We've all moved into *Bethesda House*. Daddy feels most comfortable there, and the environment suits the medical staff."

"When would you like me to see him?"

"Tomorrow," she says as Jeffrey opens the door. The rush of cold air brings up her fur and helps numb my pain. "You'll hear from me."

Jeffrey closes the door and tips his cap to me, before the limo slips back into the stream.

* * *

Paddy shakes his head when I come back inside Parnell's. "You look like hell."

"It's a fashion statement. I've got a lot to tell you, but I need to go upstairs and check on Riedell first."

"Mandell," Paddy yells back to the kitchen. "Upstairs. Any dinner?"

Mandell holds two fingers over the swinging door.

"I think you have a house guest."

Tiu. "Oh, I almost forgot, Tiu and I got married this morning on the street near the Precinct." I tell Paddy. Tiu probably told Riedell before she gave me the happy news. No matter. My daughter has a mother again, and I'm on my honeymoon.

"Not enough hours in the day for you, are there? Congratulations," Paddy offers.

"I've got jaywalking tickets that were more memorable. She disguised herself as a street person this time. Got a dollah off me. I'd better get up there."

Paddy holds up a hand to wait. "I'll close in an hour. Doc said I have to stay awake anyway because of the possible concussion."

"Sorry, I didn't even ask…" The explosion seems like years ago.

Paddy waves off my thoughtlessness. "If you've still got some fire left in you, it might be a good idea to get those flash drives."

"Break into Starch's safe?"

"No, Arlo. Come back in an hour, you'll see."

I'll be lucky to make an hour. Right now, I'm running on pain energy. Hope Paddy has a good plan.

* * *

"Riedell. Wife Chuti. Hologram Chuti. Any of you home?" I announce my arrival, as though they haven't been watching.

"Very funny," Chuti Tiu says, coming from the kitchen with her tea. Cup and saucer, as always. "Riedell is asleep."

"Which one are you? Real you, or see-through you?"

"Cute."

"About your wardrobe this morning. You fulfilled a dream – I always wanted to marry a bag lady. There is so much upside."

"Glad I could satisfy your fantasy. It will be the last you'll get for quite a while."

The bloom is off the lily, as they say. Tiu knows about this morning with Gayfryd.

"I know, it was a mistake," I apologize. I haven't looked in a mirror, but I seriously doubt if my face has improved. Interesting that Prosecutor Kasey didn't mention my lip, or what I suspect are purple bruises. Either no interest, or she already knew.

"Your sex memories were triggered," Tiu says with the detached disposition of a clinician.

"That's what it was," I readily agree. "Pheromones. They always get me."

No reaction, Tiu is in no mood for wit. "You're aware Berk has been released from prison?" I ask.

"One of the reasons I'm here. Sit." She gestures.

I do as instructed. Golden fur Yeti jumps onto my lap already purring mid-air. I could sleep a thousand years listening to that motor. I notice there is a mug of tea and a JD option sitting on the table beside me.

"It has always bothered me that Berk didn't fight," Tiu says still standing, sipping her tea. "There was another way he would have got my ataxia cure."

I don't ask. She is referring to the bad history we share. Berk raping Emma, passing on his genetic condition, giving brilliant Tiu a reason to discover a cure for Friedrich's ataxia: to save her niece. In the process, she managed to turn his algorithm against him and set him up for conspiracy and tax evasion.

"In fact, I was certain Destiny would pull Berk out of the country. I never thought he'd get before a judge, much less imprisoned,' she says.

"You are telling me Berk arranged going to prison? I find that tough to believe."

Tiu shakes her head, not so much disagreeing, as thinking. "I suspect at the time, prison was a simple solution."

"For what?"

"To decide if he was going to claim Riedell," she says.

"That will never happen."

"Don't be too sure. Look at this little slice of the Universe we have created," Tiu says waving her hand to encompass the warehouse. "Over here," she opens her right hand, "we have the infamous *Unflawed* columnist living with a ten-year-old girl who is neither legally nor biologically his daughter."

She opens her left hand. "And on this side we have a self-made billionaire, falsely imprisoned, now freed, cleared of all charges, about to receive the Medal of Freedom. A man who also happens to be Riedell's biological father."

"A product of rape."

"Unproven," Tiu puts up a finger. "Also, when viewed without bias, Berk is an unbroken genius who, despite his wrongful incarceration, persisted to give the world the greatest medical discovery of the century."

"CRISPR?"

"Exactly. Berk is Jonas Salk magnified 6,000 times."

"Six thousand?" Tiu doesn't use numbers for hyperbole.

"Think. Salk only cured polio. There are 6,000 genetic diseases; Alzheimer's for starters."

"I follow. So Berk can do whatever he wants. Are you saying we don't have a prayer keeping Riedell away from him?"

"We are married, that's our prayer of a chance."

"Smart move," I admit. Pretending our marriage is anything more than a ploy stretches even my fertile imagination.

"But it won't be enough," Tiu says.

"You're saying we can't stop him?"

"First he'll get visitation rights. Then he'll fight for custody."

"I still don't understand why Berk would want to raise a young girl."

"Riedell isn't just any young girl. And, he doesn't. He's bringing Riedell to Destiny."

Chapter Thirteen

Arlo's neighborhood at 2:45 a.m. is alive with junkies and vermin. The City that never sleeps — not exactly what the song intended to convey.

Driving the well-known Parnell's soup kitchen van into Arlo's neighborhood gives us safe access. A hot meal, a blanket, socks are pure gold, especially at this hour of the morning. Surgical blasts of frigid gusts whip through the streets, narrower than Midtown, driving destitute beings to huddle around smoldering 55-gallon drums, filled with broken wood pallets, cardboard, and yesterday's Chronicle.

I'm a New Yorker, yet I've never had the desire, or nerve, to venture into this part of my world. Now, with my brain exhausted, and body hurt, I feel gritty and tired, beat up and sore. I almost fit in. Except with my signature corduroy jacket, I'm a bit overdressed.

I can't imagine Kathleen coming out here alone in the food truck. If she were my wife, I would have to come along with a sawed-off shot gun across my knees. Someday I'll ask Paddy how he deals with her mercy trips. Not now.

Getting out of the van, I help Paddy haul two twenty-gallon canisters onto the elongated rear bumper.

"You," Paddy picks out a wino from the crowd, handing him a sleeve of red plastic cups. "We'll be back in ten minutes. You are in charge of the soup and coffee. Can you handle it?"

Giving the derelict the responsibility for passing out cups of warm sustenance is equal to a million dollars' worth of pride. No doubt how Paddy worked the streets back in his day.

"You and Kathleen are crazy," I say.

"I know." He understands.

I check Arlo's address on my cell. "Calling him first?" Paddy asks.

"No fun in that," I say leading the way inside the only building in sight that isn't a barbed wired warehouse or collapsing tenement.

"Yeah?" Arlo answers moments after my fist pounds on his metal door.

"Shawn," I announce, glancing at Paddy for his reaction to Arlo being awake.

"His ears must have been burning."

A series of locks, slides and crossbars start moving, then stop. A pause "Shawn?" Arlo checks again.

"And Paddy," I tell him.

"Gentlemen, an unexpected pleasure," Arlo deadpans, welcoming us inside, bolting the metal door behind. I expect him to be pissed, or at least anxious. He's acting like we've been invited.

Arlo is wearing a black silk robe and sandals. He smells freshly shaved, and his hair is slicked back and secured with a ribbon like he's a 16th century British naval officer. So much for the Rasta *don't worry, be happy* kid in the Chronicle's basement. I don't look at Paddy for his reaction.

Stepping inside, I expect a futon on the floor, books and newspapers stacked against the walls, and a plywood sawhorse holding his computer. I can't be more wrong.

Arlo lives in a fashion designer's showcase. The furniture is custom, straight out of Restoration Hardware. Acid washed brick walls, vaulted coffered ceilings, and expensively framed original art works adorn the apartment. The kid is a pure enigma.

"To what do I owe this honor?" Arlo asks me.

"It's been a long day," I grumble. "The Police want the recordings you made of Gayfryd's offices at the Helmsley."

"What are you talking about?"

"The cops saw evidence you compromised Gayfryd's security cameras. Did you hack the cops as well?"

"A third grader could hack cops. Those guys are walking cell towers. Scanners, phones, walkies, pagers, computers. What a joke."

I look at Paddy for confirmation. "Not surprised," he says. "Even Kathleen has a scanner."

"Why would I waste my time planting bugs in your girlfriend's cameras when I can hack any computer on the planet, every cell phone, smart watch, refrigerator, TV, street camera? I can get inside every Credit Card Company, sports arena, tele-communications giant. I can tell you when someone on the international space station scratches his ass, or when the captain of the Russian nuclear ballistic submarine, *Severodvinsk*, farts."

Paddy just sits, spreading his arms across the back of the expensive pearl-grey sofa like this is all my idea and my play. But I notice he has his gun in his hand, draped behind.

"Give me everything you hacked. Now!" I yell, feeling impatient and unwilling to let this low life play me.

Arlo moans and crumbles to the inlayed wood floor, as if his backbone has been extracted in a single pull, leaving him spineless as a boned fish. He begins wailing as Paddy and I watch the display, unsure how to respond. His silk robe opens, exposing his upper legs and mid-section which are covered with scarring from burns, and much worse. Torture marks, I think. His groin is swaddled in some kind of linen cloth.

Arlo sees me staring. "I worked for Silk Road."

"You worked for a clothing company?" I ask.

"Drugs, arms, human trafficking," Paddy explains, unmoved by Arlo's bizarre behavior.

"I ran the counter-insurgency section. Best on the planet. Confuse, hit and destroy."

"You were in charge of eliminating threats," Paddy understands, "competitors and authorities."

"Every one of the fuckers," Arlo snarls, no longer playing injured. "Tracked them right into their snug little picket-fenced gingerbread homes. Killed their dogs, took out their children, and their children's children. Nobody messes with me."

Arlo's pupils constrict as his upper lip curls. "Interpol, Royal Canadians, KGB, DEA, CIA, FBI, Europol, Frontex, CCIC, CARICC, LEA, you name it, I screwed them good." Arlo's speaking pace keeps accelerating; spittle is flying from his lips. "And I never left my keyboard," he finishes his litany of terror, standing erect, smug in his accomplishments.

"Until?" Paddy asks.

"I got snatched."

Arlo is good. No doubt his accounting and computer skills would be in demand. His problem: he can't stop bragging.

"Now, I'm based at Langley, confined at their condo, River Tower; one side has a view of the Washington Monument, the other, Arlington National Cemetery. Subtle, don't you think? I'm chipped, monitored, and reminded often that they can do what they want with me."

"You are a criminal, illegally spying on U.S. citizens," I tell him.

Arlo laughs.

"Who sent you to the Chronicle?" I press.

"Does it matter? One of the acronyms tells my handler, I've got a gig in NYC. Hey, why not? I go, figure I'll find out who the buyer is, and who the seller is, when I get there. It's part of the game."

Arlo looks to Paddy who he senses is a kindred soul. He's researched us both. "One day while I'm working this Chronicle gig," Arlo nods towards me, "I'm listening to those two cops stroking their balls. All of a sudden it strikes me, I know this voice. It's Ace, our stoolie. I've connected a dirty NYPD cop to a shakedown of the daughter of the Chronicle publisher. I figure it all out."

"Whatever agency you're working for must have started popping champagne," Paddy guesses.

Arlo shakes his head, no. "That's what I thought, except my handler disappears. This guy was black ops, big time. He doesn't scare."

"So the Government Agency you are working for replaced your handler?"

"And my protection as well. I'm out here naked," Arlo grins at me. "All I have is an electronic voice, and a thirty-four number string. Everything I record or hack goes to the number; anything else I tell the voice."

"Whatever Lt. Ace and his Cap got themselves into is way bigger than a shake-down of an abortion clinic," Paddy realizes.

"Any ideas?" I ask.

Arlo smirks. "Tell you the truth, it was a relief to answer the door and see it was only you."

"Okay. Time to wrap this up," Paddy says putting his pistol away, and picking up a baseball-sized geode from the coffee table. He stands, tossing the expensive decoration from hand-to-hand.

"That's an extremely rare piece," Arlo says, focused on Paddy's hands.

"Get all your back-up flash drives. Now, before I start making some holes in your walls."

"Chill, man. I'll do you a solid, no need to…"

Arlo loses his color when Paddy pulls an electronic wand from his belt, and holds up the geode. "Neat or messy?" Paddy asks, indicating how he intends to find the drives.

"I'll get them," Arlo jumps. "Let you both clear the air with your friends at NYPD on this bombing thing. Honest. I like Mr. Shaw," he says to Paddy as if I'm not in the room. "I wouldn't try to frame him."

Paddy starts passing his wand from one painting to the next. The wand light goes to the top several times. Paddy taps the wall with the geode. "In here," he orders Arlo.

"Your wand hit a stud or something," Arlo insists. "My safe, it's in the bedroom." He leads the way.

For being such a large man, Paddy moves with surprising speed. He follows Arlo, stopping at the doorway, putting his hand on the pistol under the back of his jacket.

Arlo is kneeling next to the bed, opening a wood panel intended to camouflage the safe concealed as an end table.

Arlo opens the safe and selects a leather pouch. "This is all you need for your detective," he says, offering it to Paddy who nods okay before kicking back a rug exposing a safe camouflaged in the wood flooring.

"Everything," Paddy orders, snapping open a large plastic evidence bag.

"I have my passport, money..." Arlo protests.

"Keep the money and jewelry. I want all the drives, your password list, and the ID's."

"My passwords are in my head."

"Good for you. But give me the list anyway. I'm not as smart as you."

"You won't be able to..." Arlo stops arguing when he sees Paddy's face. Paddy's heard it all, and he's not negotiating.

"Passport."

Arlo drops it in the bag.

Paddy sticks his hand in the safe. "Bottom compartment," he orders. "I won't ask again."

Arlo pulls out a velvet sack.

"What's this? Pretty heavy," Paddy says shaking the bag and pulling out a stainless steel egg.

"That's my nest egg."

"Diamonds?" Paddy asks.

"Good guess. Open the container, take one for your wife."

"I'm not a thief," Paddy shuts him down. "You'll get these back when we verify the drives. Hand over the wallet, keys," Paddy says.

"That's it, I swear," Arlo begs.

"Get some rest, son. You look like Hell."

"You'll need my help finding what they want on those drives," Arlo says, thinking he still has an advantage. "You've got better than

1,000 terabytes of data. Even the Feds can't sort through that in a year."

"What did they offer you?" Paddy asks, passing me the bags.

"I don't know what you mean," Arlo lies.

"You've admitted to being a thief, liar and informer. Playing everyone you think you can con. And now you are trying to play us," Paddy says picking up a Lalique figurine by the head. "I don't believe you."

"You have to. I'm telling you the truth," Arlo says, cringing.

"Give me all the flash drives."

"You have them all," Arlo insists.

"I want what's in here," Paddy demands, waving the glass figurine toward the wall of paintings.

"Do you have any idea what that costs?" Arlo yells.

Paddy responds by picking up the geode, tapping the two together.

"Okay, okay," Arlo pleads. He retrieves an MRI disc and chill box, passing them to Paddy.

"What do I have here?" Paddy asks.

"My life," Arlo puts his hands together begging Paddy to be careful.

Paddy jams the MRI in his jacket pocket. The chill box clinks a bit in Paddy's hand.

"Please," Arlo pleads.

"Tell me."

"This," Arlo stands opening his robe and lowering his loin cover. "I'm in trans. I just gave myself a hormone shot before you got here. Can I please have the box back? The hormone vials are of no value to you."

"They are now. I'll be in touch."

* * *

"Trans?" Paddy says as we head back to the van. The coffee and soup canisters are empty. The blankets, all gone, but the lead beggar Paddy appointed is waiting.

"To tell you the truth I can't tell which direction Arlo's headed, guy or gal?" I say.

"An early grave is where he's headed," Paddy says handing the bum $10.

"What do you think about his snatch and torture story?" I ask. "You believe him?"

"There are no rules for some," Paddy says. "If he was held by one of those Middle Eastern torture cells, anything could happen. They may have even started his transition. He's lucky to be alive."

"What do you mean?" I ask, not quite connecting the dots.

"I think the torture included castration."

I think about that for a minute.

"I'll have Tiu copy the data you should give to Lt. Garcelli. I'll keep everything else in my office safe at the Chronicle until I can get it into Starch's private safe. No sense getting you exposed."

Pulling away from Arlo's neighborhood, I feel energized by the recent adrenalin rush. I'm starting to make some connections. Arlo is under medical treatment. He's surveilling an illegal clinic. He knows who Gayfryd is, and probably knows of Berk. I need to find out how they are all connected. But first, some sleep.

Chapter Fourteen

"You have a Chronicle Board meeting in one hour," Wadjet wakes me.

Looks like Riedell has already fed the cats because they are curled up sleeping in the skylight sun, instead of badgering me for breakfast.

"You are starting to keep my hours," Chuti Tiu says, coming from the kitchen carrying a bowl of something. "It's all I can do to keep up with her," she raises her chin toward Riedell who is speed skating around the entire warehouse. The pigtail. I can't make out Riedell's face in the distance, but the legs are her, and the pigtail is a sign that Aunt Chuti is here.

"These are from Arlo," I say passing her the flash drives. "I'm hoping there is enough surveillance of the two cops and Gayfryd's clinic to make all the connections. He said there are 1,000 terabytes on these, whatever that means."

"Means I'll have it sorted by the time you finish brushing your teeth. But do it fast because there is a big blonde coming in downstairs. I'd say she is looking for you," Tiu says pointing to a screen monitoring the bar. Not only is my wife here, but she is on high alert. We don't normally have all building cameras on display. At least, I don't think so.

"Athena," I say recognizing the goddess who escorted me to General Counsel Walter Jackson's office at the Chronicle.

Tiu punches the air and projects a massive collage of images, mostly academic ceremonies. "Accomplished," she concludes, giving no indication if her assessment is positive or not. "I'll notify Paddy while you change. By the way, her driver is outside. He was in Parnell's twice last night, late."

* * *

"Here to fire me, or give me a ride?" I ask when I meet Athena downstairs in the Pub.

"Neither," she says handing me an envelope. "Loan extension, three years, 0% interest rate. Non-reversible. No conditions."

Pretending to understand the legalese, I scan the two pages as she watches. "It will be tough for me to find a sober lawyer at this hour."

"Give me a dollar," Athena says.

"Last dollar cost me my freedom," I say, knowing Tiu is watching.

"Well this dollar will give some of it back. I wrote the contract. It's valid. No wiggle room, and severe penalties should the Chronicle renege." She points to the $10,000,000 notation.

I give her my dollar.

"You just hired me."

"For a dollar?"

"I'll be brief," she says.

Nothing like attorney humor at the crack of dawn.

"What's wrong with this place? It's empty," she says.

"Not too much of a breakfast crowd," I say loudly enough for Paddy to hear. "The place isn't really open yet. Just deliveries."

"What can I get for you?" Paddy asks rising from the cellar trapdoor behind the bar.

"I'm good for..."

Towering over all of us, Paddy sets four cases of Bushmills on the bar as if they are mere Kleenex boxes. Athena isn't quite Emma's stature, but she is a big girl, especially in her heels. Trying to cover her surprise, she says, "Coffee."

"I'm Paddy," he says, offering his hand. "Welcome to Parnell's."

Paddy shakes Athena's hand with the delicacy of my cat Yeti patting my nose when I'm asleep, vying for attention.

"This is my attorney, Athena," I say handing Paddy the agreement.

"I take it Paddy is your confidant?"

"Friend," I clarify.

"Good. Now we all know one another." Athena sets her briefcase on a stool, accepting the coffee Paddy slides in front of her.

"I'll need a dollar from you as well," she tells Paddy.

"You have to be the cheapest lawyer in town," he says not looking up from the papers, slapping a bill from the tip jar onto the bar.

"Said she'd be brief," I say.

"How long does your morning commuter rush last?" she asks Paddy, surprising us that she knows about pubs like Parnell's.

"Twenty minutes," he says glancing at the Train clock behind him.

"Then for the next twenty-one minutes I'm your lawyer," she says collecting the dollar. "That means attorney/client confidentiality.

Ask what you want. Say what you want. I cannot repeat a word. Understand?"

We nod, yes.

"Are you working for Starch or the Chronicle?" I ask her.

"Both. I am Mr. Scorch's…"

"Starch," Paddy and I say.

"Right. He likes that you call him that," Athena says keeping her attention on each of us. "As I was saying, Mr. Starch…"

"Just Starch."

"Okay, Starch hired me as his Estate Attorney. I am also the Executor of his will. Twenty minutes remaining."

"The Chronicle?"

"Consultant to the Chairman."

"Paid by?"

"Starch."

"You work for the Acting Chairman Walter Jackson, or his mistress?"

"Not for Jackson or Mrs. Wright."

"You don't seemed shocked about the mistress information."

"Starch told me."

"What else did he tell you?"

"Too general. Be specific, and don't waste your time trying to violate my status with Starch. Nineteen minutes."

"Gayfryd or James Berk, any involvement there?"

'Berk no. Gayfryd, yes, but not directly."

' Is she really Starch's daughter?"

' I don't have that information. Eighteen minutes."

' Is this loan agreement intended to keep me on the Chronicle Board?"

'Yes."

'Why?"

"No idea."

"Sambuca?" Paddy suggests holding the bottle over her black coffee. "Takes the chill off."

Athena pauses a second before pushing her mug closer. "Thanks."

Paddy is doing more than serving a customer, he's backing me off. He returns the agreement to me.

"Satisfied?" Athena asks.

"For now."

"Good. Healthy skepticism," she says taking the loan agreement back, signing it and passing me the pen to sign and have Paddy witness. "I'll send you a copy. You still have some time. Anything else?"

"Yes. Why are you doing this?"

"These are the wishes of my client."

"You could have waited until after this morning's Board Meeting. They are planning to vote me off. Even with the Trust's stock, I'll never be asked back without Starch."

"Both true."

"So why?"

"There is the letter, and there is the intent. Starch wants your irreverence and your passion to inspire the Chronicle. Also, for reasons I cannot and will not explain, he wants Gayfryd to have that opportunity as well."

"She doesn't give a damn about the Chronicle or the people who work there. It's the money and the deference she wants. Queen Gayfryd."

"He knows. I think that's his other reason for wanting you to stay with the Chronicle."

"Not because of the Pulitzer prestige?"

"No, of course not. That's business. What he admires about you is not the award, but the series itself that won the Pulitzer. You and Emma."

"What do you know about Emma?"

"I read your series. You didn't just write an exposé, you wrote about a person. You wrote about abandoning people who do not meet certain standards. You wrote, 'Leaving her was never an option for me.'"

"Did I write that?"

"Emma," Paddy says. "She brought out who you are."

I shake my head in embarrassment.

"Even with his wealth and power, Starch never made a commitment like you did to anyone. That's why he respects you so much."

"So again, why are you doing this?"

"Helping you? Because believe it or not, being a lawyer makes me a member of the Court."

"Ouch. Did that hurt you as much as it did me?" I say.

"Sorry, I'm trying to do the right thing here. I'm in a bit of…" she stops, takes a sip of her coffee. "Starch brought me to the Chronicle for a specific purpose. But that was…" she sips again. "I ran into a roadblock."

I'm starting to get it. "So, did Starch recruit you to the Chronicle to get rid of his old pal Walter Jackson?" I ask.

"That question is beyond the scope of our agreement, but what I can tell you is Mr. Scorch…"

"When did you last speak to Starch?" Paddy asks.

"Not since his stroke," Athena admits. "Now I have a question. As your twenty-one minute attorney, client privilege still in effect, are either of you involved in the bombing?"

"No," we say vehemently. "Of course not," I add.

"Good. Because it would have saved me a ton of work if you were."

Paddy and I glance at each other.

"You sure you two don't want to turn yourselves in? I don't do criminal, but I have a good contact," she presses.

"Hey, we're the good guys here. Case closed."

"Okay, okay," Athena shakes her head, sadly. "If you are going to stick to that," she looks up, serious, waiting, before finally smiling. "I'm going to recommend to the Board they hold off on their vote until Starch can address the Board himself."

"And if you, his attorney, haven't spoken with him, how do you know. ." I look at Paddy. He gets it too.

"We know what you're getting at. You want us to break into Starch's estate and see what condition he's in before you have to make your next move."

Chapter Fifteen

I stop by my office before heading upstairs to the Board Room. Our Intern is already at work.

"We had a nice visit with our snitch, Arlo, last night," I tell her. "Here's some stuff we collected besides the thumb drives. Have Gert stow this in my office safe, will you? I've got to go upstairs."

* * *

Mrs. Wright is passing out thick folders to the other eight Board members when I take my chair. Starch's long-time buddy, Walter Jackson, is running the meeting. Athena is nowhere in sight.

"And one for our late arrival," Mrs. Wright makes her point as she sets a folder on the table in front of me. "I need this back at the end of the meeting."

"And what is in this?" I ask. After only two hours sleep, I'm in no mood for her snipes.

"Mr. Shaw, abide by the rules of order," a bow-tied octogenarian says.

"Excuse me, Sir, am I not allowed to ask a question before the meeting begins?"

The harrumphs of annoyance are almost deafening. Walt calms his brethren with two hands, lowering the volume to silence.

"Kindly inform this impudent young man, I am not a Sir, Mr. Jackson."

"Shawn," Walter preempts me from answering. "Now, would everyone please open your folder?"

I do, and the first page is a legal document addressed to me. It's the proxy agreement Jackson asked me to sign when I met with him. I flip it over and begin to read the forty page legal filing. Glancing up, I notice none of the others are reading.

"Walt, this will take some time. Unlike the others, I wasn't given an advance copy. Any reason for that?"

Mrs. Wright turns scarlet, darting her eyes to Walt.

"And, Walt, are you still General Counsel? Because I'm sure I'll have some legal questions." I add.

"Let me help you with the short version, Mr. Shaw," Walter Jackson says, rising. "We have been advised that our beloved

Chairman, Cuthbert Storch, has been ruled 'incapacitated' by a Federal Judge this morning. His daughter, Gayfryd Van Wie, has filed for control of the Chronicle Company. She has asked me to continue on as Acting Chairman until this matter is resolved in the Courts. Is that clear enough for you, Mr. Shaw?"

"For the first time, crystal," I say getting up. I buy some time walking to Walt at the head of the long table. "You're not here to prevent a takeover. You want her to take control. You've been paid off. I notice some of Starch's paintings are missing from these walls. The Matisse? Who got that?" I scan the faces around the table. "The Chagall? Hanging in your bedroom?" I ask touching the shoulder of the gender-confused octogenarian.

"Mr. Shaw!" Walter Jackson yells, pounding the table. "You're out of order. This Board has convened to facilitate a smooth ownership transition of the Chronicle Company."

"You've got to be kidding me." I pull a folder from my satchel, waving it at Walter. "I expanded on your investigation of the lovely Ms. Van Wie."

"Mr. Shaw. I authorized no such investigation."

"Exactly right. Which got me to wondering, why didn't you? Because investigating is something I'm pretty good at," I say dropping another eight folders on the table. "By the way, I investigated all of you as well."

Jackson charges on. "This board recognizes Gayfryd Van Wie as Cuthbert Storch's legal heir. I call for the nomination of Mrs. Van Wie.."

Chairs begin sliding back, there is plenty of muttering.

"You can all sit down," I tell them. "Remember, no one ever gets hard time after they hit eighty. Just looks bad, don't you think? Beating up on old folks and all." I give them my best Cheshire cat grin.

No one smiles in return, but no one leaves either.

Walter Jackson is losing at the intimidation game. I'm dead tired but feeling euphoric. I have nothing in my folders but scrap papers. It's amazing what people will tell you without saying a word. I didn't hear a single denial.

I wave a pamphlet in the air. "Remember this?" I ask Walter, making sure the three letter acronym can be seen by everyone. "You sent this to me years back, when Starch first asked me to join this Board. Well, I read it. Pretty boring, but I remembered this part:

according to SEC rules, you need a quorum to have one of these meetings. But you know that legal stuff, right Walt?"

Silence.

"Now, here's a wrinkle I found when Walter here told me to sign this," I say flapping the proxy agreement. "You all represent a considerable number of shares, but you have abdicated your voting rights to Starch, in exchange for...let's just say 'special privileges.' Everything legal, maybe a bit suspicious, but nothing felonious. Is that another correct word, Walter?"

"I don't have to stand for this," the octogenarian says, trying to push away from the table.

"No, ma'am," I say picking one of my investigation folders, "you don't, unless..." Her chair stops.

"Good. You'll note, I haven't signed this 'rights conveyance'. Right term again, Walt?"

"It will do," Walter Jackson shrugs as he drops down onto his chair.

"Because, I believe I'm the only person in this room with actual voting privileges. That's correct, isn't it Walter?" I ask tossing the SEC folder on the table in front of him.

"And what do you intend to do, Mr. Shaw?" Walter says.

"Thank you, Walter, for asking. This sellout to Gayfryd Van Wie is blocked," I tell them.

Walter stands, apologetic, but not to me. "Members of the Board, your indulgence please. Mr. Shaw, your loan from the Company is recalled effective immediately." He takes a moment to let that sink in, then presses on. "Do you have payment in full now?"

"Of course not."

"Then we will have a court order within the hour," he nods to Mrs. Wright to make the call. "Your Trust will be notified of the adjustment in their holdings. As for you, herewith you are removed from your seat on the Board. The guards will escort you out of the building. You are twice fired. And that will be all."

I reach for my folders. Walter slams a hand down. "These stay. Company property. Guards!"

Two hefty men grab me under my arms. I don't resist as they hoist me in the air and drag me to the door.

"Just one problem," my warrior goddess, Athena, appears in the doorway, holding up some papers. "The loan from Mr. Storch was re-negotiated. Mr. Shaw retains full control of the Trust's Chronicle stock. No one here has the power to dismiss Mr. Shaw from his job, or the Board."

An uncomfortable silence follows.

"Well, it seems that you are in control for the moment, Mr. Shaw. What is your plan?" Walt asks, gritting his teeth.

"I appoint my Assistant Gert, as Acting Chairperson until Starch returns," I say as the guard releases me. "Vote?" I raise my hand. "Yea. Good. It's unanimous."

No one moves.

"Mrs. Wright, as Secretary, please notify the Press of our decision," I say waving goodbye as I leave them wanting more.

Chapter Sixteen

I board the train from Grand Central to Greenwich, Connecticut, home of exclusive country clubs and stately mansions buried among lush trees. Home to Starch's beloved *Bethesda House*.

A cab brings me to the entrance of the Gothic stone, glass and steel chateauesque structure dominating the richest waterfront landscape in the region. The majestic leaded glass doors direct your eyes to the elaborate spires standing as stoic guardians, rising from steeply pitched slate roofs.

Four corners of the eight sections are adorned with towering glass turrets. Any one, a magnificent home in itself. To the left is a twelve unit carriage house, and an adjoining maintenance garage. Stables are off in the back, complete with exercise paddocks. I can hear whinnying in the distance.

There is a transport ambulance parked in the driveway, but there are no ramps to the entrance. Not a good sign.

"Wait," Gayfryd barks through the intercom.

That's interesting, no haughty, "One moment please." Maybe this is her 'country relaxed' persona - jeans, tee-shirt and bare feet? Not likely.

"You simply show up," she says, opening the massive door so quietly all I notice is the in-draft. "Presumptuous, but acceptable," she decides. Now there is the pompous attitude I so love and despise.

I avoid looking directly at her by plan, because this is the point where I've historically lost control. I rehearsed my presentation in my mind on the train so many times, that I'm nervous. I force myself to relax and feel that I'm in control as I ignore her lavender scent.

"Beautiful home," comes out of me as I raise my eyes to the ceiling. It's not as high as my warehouse home, although the fresco is every bit as magnificent as my skylights.

"Mmm," is all she says, closing the door as my cab pulls away. She's wearing a kimono robe, making me think of Chuti Tiu. I'm sure James Berk is somewhere in the house, since they are joined in some type of pact I can't rationalize.

Without the Christmas ornaments, *Bethesda House* is returned to old money luxury. Agaria white marble floors fan out to glass-walled hallways, and a distant dining theater. An amber glow bathes the leather-bound volumes that fill the two-story library behind the double curved staircases leading to the rampart balcony. The entire house is a testament to great wealth, and a bygone era.

I tap my cell to vibrate, leaving it in my bag. I need something in my hands. Searching my satchel as I stand in the cathedral foyer, I find a pencil. Perfect.

My plan is to demand Gayfryd take me to Starch before I even discuss the stock I control. That's my plan, but like Mike Tyson said, "everyone's got a plan until you get punched in the nose."

Dropping the robe to surround her bare feet, Gayfryd destroys mine. She is wearing a diaphanous Grecian silk toga, white, embossed with gold Romanesque hash marks at the hem. Beneath, she appears naked.

She steps back, ignoring my bewilderment. For the moment, she is allowing herself only to be admired, while my thoughts race back to the seconds before a gunshot echoed up the Helmsley walls.

"We are serving tea in the salon," Gayfryd says, leading the way with one arm lifted at the elbow, hand tipped at her wrist. Her posture is perfect. I feel the crippling desire. Everything about her is a calculated sham, but she presents with such self-assurance. That's a big part of the appeal. I poke the blunt end of the pencil into my bruised ribs, bringing me back to the moment. I conjure up the half-woman/half-snake creature of myth.

"I came here to see Starch," I demand. I know I'm running on adrenaline, with nothing more than a cat nap on the train, but I need to stay in control. I'm seeing small details, and exploding their significance in my mind. The toga alone took me to mythology. And now I'm thinking she'll ravish me on the marble floor, killing me as a sacrifice.

"I know you met with the Board," she says. "They've rejected you, haven't they? No more *Mr. Unflawed*. Simply plain Shawn Shaw. How does it feel, poor dear?"

"Like the teenager watching from the outside."

Gayfryd stops, turns and comes in fast, grabbing me. "Have you decided to join us, or is it just this talking?"

I twitch but don't move. "I'm here to make a deal." Part of me wants to push her hand away, but not the strong part. "Walter Jackson and his Board of sycophants are planning to strip the company before they let you take control," I say, receiving an extra squeeze and a grin before she releases me.

Uncertain if I should thank her or not, I push on. "I don't have the resources to fight them, but you do."

"Meaning?"

"Meaning I know you've got Berk behind you. That's the money you need. Starch has already admitted to being your father, which takes care of the paternity issue. With my help, I don't see how the Board can stop you."

"Those crooked old parasites! I floated a few of the paintings their way and they wet themselves."

"I knew they couldn't fool you," I offer.

"Then tell me!" she insists in her deep, demanding voice.

"The number of shares in my trust is small, but significant because they are uncommitted. I heard the Board, and I've heard you. The mere fact that you have brought Starch home means a lot to me, and to him. I know it's a leap of faith, but I choose you."

"'Course you do. You're not going to get this from Mrs. Wright," she grins, doing a twirl. " I can't believe her gall. "You know they can't beat me in Court," she says kissing her finger and pressing it to my lip.

"You know, they are planning to loot you personally as well. They don't care about the Chronicle. One by one they will come to you, pledge their allegiance, and secure their payoff. This house, the art collection, everything will be gone."

I'm certain James Berk is in *Bethesda House* somewhere, listening.

Gayfryd steps into a pair of black, red-soled Louboutin heels and picks up her kimono from the floor, dragging it along. I can't shake the feeling Gayfryd has rehearsed this scene. Her performance is choreographed, like her entire adult life.

She circles around the floor a few times, acting as if she is considering my offer, weighing her options. Then she faces me. "I raised myself from dirt. Dear ole Daddy didn't even acknowledge my existence until my mother committed suicide."

I know bringing up Berk is a risk. But I'm betting Gayfryd is at a crossroad she never really believed was possible. I also know Berk. He will never allow Gayfryd to become independent. I don't know what she thinks Berk owes her, but loyalty is not in his character. Gayfryd needs me more than she knows.

"You always knew Starch was your father?" I ask.

"Of course. I was about the same age as Riedell when he came back, sniffing around my mother like a rutting pig. I heard him say he missed her. Not so much that he didn't send his friends by, but we knew."

"How do you know about Riedell?"

Shaking her head she moans, "You really can be dense. Pour me a vodka," she says pointing to a bar in the salon. "And get something for yourself."

I bring the glasses, well filled.

She holds up her glass for a toast. "Partners," she laughs and downs the drink immediately. "Well, not really partners, but it sounds good right?" She holds out her glass for a refill.

She doesn't gulp this one down, but takes a healthy swallow nevertheless. I'm realizing she's nervous, surprising me really, until I put it all in context. Gayfryd is at the door of realizing her wildest dreams. She has Berk backing her with money, Starch guilty as charged, a blue blood husband waiting to be called up, and her lover, begging to return. Gayfryd is going to savor her moment.

"I know all about you, Saint Shaw. Better than all the rest of us. Savior of the sinners. Saving darling Emma," she says dragging out her name until it lands on the floor. "Raising her child."

"What is your relationship with Berk?" I ask, hoping the vodka has loosened her lips.

"Jimmy? An old flame. I helped him reclaim his company. He remembers my sacrifices; now he wants to help me. A fair trade." She takes another long swallow.

"I take it Starch doesn't know about Berk and you?"

"No way. No need. You and me?" she giggles. "You are going to be working for me. Morning meetings right on Daddy's leather couch. Maybe I'll get a white bear rug for the floor. Come on," she says.

"Where are we going?"

"To see Daddy, of course. Kiss the ring. Isn't that the plan? You'll report to Walter Jackson and the Board on his declining condition. And before they can say juris prudence, I'll be in control of the Chronicle Empire. Come on. He's in his tower," Gayfryd says over her shoulder, moving down a hallway, her regal bearing slightly compromised from the drinks. Yet she leads, confidant I'm salivating after her and my future at the Chronicle.

* * *

It's a butterfly sanctuary. Knowing nothing about butterflies, other than their rarity in my City, I feel like I'm in a Disney castle. Harp and chime sounds, not exactly music, are piped in faintly, almost imagined. "When I'm near the end, bring me here," I say.

"Search him. Take his cell," Gayfryd orders a grey-faced orderly in a white institutional uniform. The green-eyed snake has returned.

The rat-faced orderly jumps at Gayfryd's command. A second orderly, much larger, muscled, delicately handsome, steps up behind. Unlike the orderlies Emma dealt with at the hospitals, these men seem like career criminals. Of course, I understand. They're fresh from Fishkill Penitentiary, Berk would have recruited them.

For no obvious reason, a well-worn bathrobe draped over the back of a leather club chair captures Gayfryd's complete attention. The robe has hanging threads and permanent stains. My guess, it belongs to Starch. Nothing he'd wear meeting people, but the kind of robe you cannot discard.

Gayfryd seems confused. The abandoned robe has some curious meaning to her, as she sniffs and smooths the sleeve, bringing it to her cheek. It's as if she's regressed to a young girl, triggering memories real or imagined. There is an uncanny beauty to this scene, despite the instability it projects.

"Ma'am?" the smaller orderly asks, needing direction.

"Oh, whatever. Take him there," she says motioning with her hand, not looking up or caring. I think Gayfryd may very well be insane. It's a conclusion I don't reach casually, particularly because if true, it doesn't cast me in the most favorable light.

The thugs turned orderlies wave me to follow. They aren't giving me any trouble. And ten years in prison will not have improved James Berk's physical condition, even if his Friedreich's ataxia is cured. So unless Berk has brought along extra muscle, I'm not in any danger. I'll confirm Starch is safe, and call for help.

My guides lead me to the backside turret of *Bethesda House* where they push through the air-lock doors, oblivious to the spectacular setting. "Amazing," I can't help myself. I close my eyes, feeling the gossamer caresses of the whisper light butterflies. This is absolute tranquility.

"Where is he?" I come back to my senses.

"There," the larger one points.

My corduroy jacket is a living garland. Hundreds of white, yellow, and black wings alit on my arms and shoulders, tasting, fluttering. I swear I hear a gentle purring, like my Himalayan cat, Yeti, napping next to my ear.

"He's asleep," Gayfryd says from the door. Her voice is calm, as if she has made a discovery of her own.

I move toward Starch, quietly. I don't want to startle him, if he can be startled.

He, too, is covered like a fairy king in a bouquet of trembling wings. Spanish moss hangs from a cypress tree, almost touching his shoulder where he is sitting in his forest, chin resting on his chest. I cross the stone floor to Starch's wheelchair, and kneel down close enough to hear him breathing.

"I don't want to wake him," I absurdly apologize, because, of course, I do.

In a perfect world, a cadre of renowned physicians will confer over Starch after conducting an exhaustive battery of tests, and make a concerted decision. In this real world, a white coat with an unpronounceable name looks at a clipboard, not the patient, and directs the orderly to insert the feeding tube commensurate with the insurance coverage.

Right now, I'm the last line of defense Starch has, or he's on his way to being strapped down to a gurney for the next decade.

"Just catching a minute, Mrs. Wright," Starch says, eyes closed. "Wake me when he arrives."

"Your severely flawed, pain-in-the-ass reporter is here," I whisper.

He doesn't answer.

"Starch?" I say taking his hand. Putting my index finger to the inside of his wrist, I press twice. Emma created the code. It's worth a try. Gayfryd is watching closely. Too closely.

Starch's right eye opens a crack. I feel his finger poke my wrist, twice. The same eye blinks awake. He's got the code, faster than I picked it up.

His head twitches, searching for direction. His mouth, guppy-popping as he forces himself awake. His grip is not releasing. I feel the index finger press again.

"Are you getting through to him?" Gayfryd asks.

Starch growls to no one in particular. Even his growl is slurred. I can see there is no movement in the left side of his face.

"Mr. Shaw has come here because I brought him, Daddy," Gayfryd says coming nearer, poking a straw in his mouth. He sucks the cup dry, which sends Gayfryd for a re-fill.

A dribble falls from his lip. I touch it dry with the sleeve of my jacket. Starch responds by giving me a snickering look like it is the first time a pedestrian fabric has touched his face. Another poke of the finger. Starch is warning me.

I tap his wrist.

"Thanks," he grunts turning his head in the direction of Gayfryd.

"Don't talk," I whisper. "Just use your finger."

I can see drool on the collar of his silk pajamas. Such would have been intolerable before the stroke, but Starch is adjusting. At least mentally, Starch is better than he's letting on.

"The Board needs to make a decision," I say loud enough for Gayfryd to hear me. Gayfryd might be insane, but she is not stupid. Feeling a finger slide on my wrist. Starch is signaling he doesn't understand.

"Your friend, Walter Jackson, is deciding on the disposition of the Chronicle," I tell him.

The finger swishes twice. *No.*

I decide to change subjects to see if Starch can follow. "Counsel is advising," I say hoping I'm not being too obscure, "that since your Prosecutor isn't following through on her deal, we should drop the NYPD series."

I feel a slow slide of his finger in apology.

"Also, our confidential source was killed in a bombing," I tell him. His eyes widen. That's good.

"Now you've seen Daddy's condition," Gayfryd says moving between us, pulling up the folded sheet at Starch's waist, effectively ending our conversation. She strokes Starch's face with the sleeve of the robe she is wearing.

His eyes close in pleasure the same way my cat Yeti closes hers when I scratch her ears.

"Daddy tires quickly," Gayfryd says, kissing him on the forehead. "You could bring on another stroke. Time you go. You've seen him, and spoken to him. So you can testify he's being kept in good care. And you can also see the effects of the stroke. He's drooling on himself." Gayfryd shakes her head, pulling me away. "It's sad, but a home is the best place for him."

"I can see that," I agree, dabbing at an invisible tear, à la Mrs. Wright, accepting Gayfryd's condolences as she hugs me. Turning back to Starch while pushing me away with her butt, she tucks him tightly into his chair with the sheet, until he is fully restrained. Not a newly acquired talent, I notice. "I believe it's in Daddy's best interest."

I nod agreement, moving several yards away, dropping my head, waiting for Gayfryd to escort me out. Gayfryd takes my arm. I pull away and return to Starch, hugging him goodbye.

He whispers, "Don't let them take me."

"Sad, very sad," I say breaking away, putting my hand on Gayfryd's shoulder as we leave the old man. "One minute…and then." I feign another Mrs. Wright tear for good measure. "I'll just call a cab," I tell her, reaching in my satchel.

"No need," Gayfryd brightens. "We were going to have tea. And, I need our arrangement in writing," she says.

The situation is clear to me. Gayfryd is Starch's daughter. True or not, it doesn't matter. He declared her so, she accepted, and a judge agreed. Done deal. She's living inside the house. With possession being nine tenths of the law, *Bethesda House* is hers, and the Chronicle will soon follow. So unless Starch gets up and walks to the door, he's going to spend the rest of his days dreaming of butterflies.

I turn back to Starch, reluctant to leave, but knowing Gayfryd has won. "I'll let the Board know you are doing well," I say loud enough for Starch to hear, hoping to offer some encouragement. "We all want you back."

"I'm afraid that won't be possible." The voice comes from behind a large cluster of Miltonia orchids. "The old man will be having a relapse soon. Stress from your visit and all. He is not nearly as well as you might think, but then there is no reason a reporter should be expected to understand."

"Good to see prison hasn't dampened your ego, Berk. And a Doctor now, I understand."

"It was thoughtless of you to mention the bombing," he counters. "I noticed he reacted poorly, didn't you?"

"No. Not at all. I think Starch prefers to hear the straight truth."

"Where he's going, life will be all deception and illusion," Berk says making a needle motion into his arm.

I notice Gayfryd tightening Starch's stained robe around her, receiving Berk's snarl of disgust in response.

"Kind of you to bring the dregs of Fishkill along for an outing," I say hearing the phony orderlies nearby.

"The boys are licensed nurses," Berk grins. "There is a wonderful education program in prison, if you know the right people," he informs me twirling his cane, proud to display his new mobility.

"Prison. The misunderstood man's Harvard. Appears incarceration suits you."

The niceties are over. Berk smiles, the misaligned, yellowed teeth I remember have turned Hollywood. "I almost hated to leave Fishkill," he says dancing on the stone floor. He isn't Fred Astaire, but remembering how the crippling ataxia had invaded his body, Berk is astonishing.

"Ever think if you had made a right turn instead of a left that night in the mental ward, we would never have met. No Emma, no genius sister, Tiu, and no brilliant young Riedell either?" Berk eggs me on.

"And still, I think all rapists should be castrated on a public chopping block." I counter.

Berk's spine does a hitch, but his face remains impassive.

"I'm indebted to only one person, Gayfryd, and one entity, The Destiny Foundation. No one, and nothing else. Although, in a way, I do owe you," he says pointing at me with his cane. "Your Pulitzer-winning story about that slut Emma gave me the chance to repay my debt to The Destiny Society." *

I don't care if he's infirmed or healthy as an ox; Berk calling Emma a slut sends me charging at the bastard. Berk doesn't move. I take two steps, and the large orderly hits me in the spine with a crippling jolt from his cattle prod, sending me to the stone floor. A second shot to my injured back and I'm rigid. My rage competes for

---

* "The soul that sees beauty may sometimes walk alone." Goethe.

Since the Golden Age of Greece, philosophers, polymaths, scientists were often considered heretics by the body politic and organized religion. Few in number and rarely having contemporaries, at death lifetimes of brilliant work were lost or destroyed.

The specifics are unknown, but the secret Destiny Society evolved, creating a method of preserving genius from one intellectual generation to the next. In effect, the modern day Cloud.

The Destiny Foundation emerged as the Society's scientific research division.

control of the pain, but my legs are cycling uncontrollably as Berk sticks his cane in my gut, bearing down hard.

"I so love futile bravado," Berk says, leaning into the cane while I wretch in agony. "It is so fleeting, isn't it? Like fame."

I can't manage a word. Berk eases off the cane. "You see, The Destiny Foundation had lost track of the sister, Emma. They didn't really care if she existed. They had no use for her. She was defective, and an embarrassment."

Trying to focus, I reach for my one leg that has stopped pedaling, although still twitching.

"The retarded sister," he says, nudging me with the cane. "I informed Destiny of my plan to use the poor wretch as bait."

"You fucker," I creak out.

"If I could find the sister from your articles, I knew Chuti Tiu could as well. But it turned out she already knew where the retard was, and decided to leave her with you anyway. After that, all I had to do was put you out there on display. Show Tiu how you were abusing her sister with those mind-numbing electroshocks. Burning into her flesh with your barbaric torture. I was surprised Tiu didn't incinerate you herself. But you know the saying, "too smart for your own good, right?"

Berk flips up his cane and takes a swing to my ribs. The eruption of pain rolls up my spine, into my brain, and seeps out my ears.

When I return to whatever form of consciousness such agony allows, Berk is sitting in a chair beside me like we are having a grandfatherly talk. A butterfly lands on his arm.

I focus on that delicate butterfly, pulling the soothing rhythm of those fluttering wings inside me as a hypnotizing metronome. I've withdrawn from my physical self.

Berk sees the butterfly in my eyes, lets the creature gently step into his hand, smiles appreciating its beauty, and then crushes it, dropping the remains on my face.

"I really don't need that small amount of Chronicle stock you and Tiu stole from me. Especially when that video showed me how Gayfryd thanked you. She's an amazing gal, isn't she? And then I thought, maybe I should do something for you as well. You know, show some personal appreciation for you raising my daughter."

Still on the floor, I shudder.

Berk applauds my spasmodic antics with the glee of a child. "You know, oddly enough, my incarceration worked out quite well; gave my little girl time to mature, gave Destiny and me time to develop Tiu's genetic algorithm to its full potential. Cured me completely, by the way."

My back and groin are competing for sympathy, so I pass on the chance to give Berk my congratulations.

"Call it coincidence, call it opportunity, either way during those ten years we made enormous scientific breakthroughs at Fishkill. I almost hated to leave."

Hated to leave? What's Berk talking about?

Berk grins. "I lived very well inside. But you wouldn't know." He waves his head as if apologizing. "Of course not. The Destiny Society has interests in prisons. It's the ideal human laboratory, much better than the looney bins. Come on. Your new wife, Ms. Tiu must have told you."

I make no reply.

"Get him up," Berk orders.

I am unable to rise without the help of the orderlies.

"You know, you can still come out of this with your head held high." He snickers at his own joke. "I'll let you continue to live in that warehouse, maybe even keep your job. I might permit an occasional supervised visit with Riedell. Consider this little skirmish just settling the score," he says, tapping my chest with his cane.

"Over my dead body will you ever get Riedell."

"That can be arranged. Just say the word."

Managing to get to my feet, I turn and play my final card. "To keep you away from Riedell, Tiu would return to Destiny. Of course, she would demand that you are out."

Berk laughs. "Once again, Son, you are a day late and a dollar short. Tiu has been working with The Destiny Society all along."

"You're lying."

"Am I? Ask her."

I have nothing left.

"And by the way, that newspaper of yours turned out to be a goldmine. I was planning on giving it to Gayfryd just for thanks for standing by me, including those conjugal visits at Fishkill."

"You deserve each other. What goldmine?"

"My boy Arlo is one clever little hacker. While he was getting me the information I needed, he also unearthed a treasure in Chronicle research. All those stories reporters of yours have been doing over the years, all the dirt never printed because of your high and mighty

Chronicle ethics. Now I've got every grimy detail. Enough to bring J. Edgar clawing out of his grave to get his hands on what I have. I can even reach into the White House."

One orderly already has a full-face oxygen mask on Starch, and a restraining strap across his chest. Starch is being moved. Gayfryd takes my arm, trying to get me to walk.

I don't budge.

"Get him moving."

"Where are you taking Starch?" I manage to ask as I'm being hauled by the back of my belt.

"Our doctors will be taking charge," Berk says, ordering Starch's departure.

The second orderly comes hurrying down the hall. "You call for a van?" he asks Berk.

"No," he says, suddenly suspicious. "You check the cameras?"

"Something's not right. They're frozen."

"Doesn't matter. It's probably only the linen delivery. We are moving. Give them the towels and get rid of them. And tell our driver our guests are ready to leave." Berk turns to me. "I'd say our business is concluded. Gayfryd's man will get you to the train. The Lump," Berk waves his cane toward Starch, "will be well-taken care of in…"

"A Destiny Foundation medical facility," I finish.

Berk smiles. "You are catching on."

Hurrying her way around us, Gayfryd gets to the front door first. When she opens it, I see Mandell, Tiu's security expert, who masquerades as Parnell's busboy, is on the other side holding a stack of towels, a gun underneath.

Chapter Seventeen

My Manhattan contingent have come to my rescue, accompanied by Connecticut Marshals Paddy arranged. The Marshals move inside *Bethesda House* behind Mandell. They cuff the orderlies and lead them away.

Paddy holds Gayfryd's driver, Jeffrey, against the limo by sheer intimidation. "He told me he has an expired license, and a weapon under the front seat," Paddy tells the nearest Marshal.

"Place all your personal items in these bags," the officer in charge orders Gayfryd and James Berk. "Jewelry, cell phones, electronic devices, wallets, credit cards, currency. You may retain one form of personal identification."

"My cane?" Berk asks.

"Sir, please place the weapon on the ground in front of you, and step back."

"I only have my father's ring," Gayfryd shows the officer the ring on her hand. Gayfryd's robe has mysteriously fallen open.

"The ring and the robe will need to go in the bag as well. I will get you a transport gown," the Marshal tells her as his deputy returns with a shapeless blue jumpsuit from the trunk of his cruiser. The Marshal suggests changing in the privacy of the house, but Gayfryd removes Daddy's robe and passes it to the dumbfounded Deputy.

Standing in her heels on the pebble-stone drive, in her sheer toga, Gayfryd extends her hand to the Deputy, requesting assistance.

"Alright, enough, you perverts," Gert shouts stepping through the mesmerized men, throwing the jumpsuit at Gayfryd. "Skinny-assed Bitch. Get in your duds."

Gert breaks Gayfryd's spell. Kathleen, wearing her hospital scrubs, marches past them into the mansion, taking charge of Starch.

"This is Mrs. Van Wie's residence," Berk says, either bluffing or deluded into thinking he still has authority. "We are caring for her gravely ill father."

"Our Judge says otherwise," Athena announces coming from her limo, legal documents in hand. It feels like a reunion of the women in my life.

"Let me see those," Berk says, trying to grab the papers.

"Stand down, Sir," the Marshal orders, stepping forward.

"Starch has been mildly sedated," Kathleen says as she returns, shaking a plastic bottle. "Looks like sleeping pills."

"I've got the driver on possession, for starters," the Marshal tells Paddy. "Weapons and parole violations on the other two."

The deputies load the three men into a transport vehicle.

"But I've got nothing on these two," the Marshal whispers to Paddy, indicating Berk and Gayfryd.

"Understand," Paddy acknowledges.

"I'd like to get Mr. Storch to the nearest hospital for a thorough examination," Kathleen reports to the Marshal. "With your permission, we can transport him in the Parnell's van."

"I appreciate you helping us out," the Marshal thanks Kathleen, turning her away from Berk and Gayfryd. "This is a fine man you've got here," he says, nodding toward Paddy." I'll never forget what he did for my son." The Marshal wipes an eye, unembarrassed. "Nothing I wouldn't do for your man."

Kathleen nods her appreciation to the Marshal, while giving Paddy an admiring gaze.

Mandell is putting down a wheelchair access ramp to the *Bethesda House* entrance, as Gert reaches the front door with Starch in his wheel chair.

"I'll make one more quick check," Kathleen says, holding up the plastic container. "Don't want to miss something." She dashes back inside.

"You the caretaker?" the Marshal asks a man in overalls who has emerged from the nearby garages.

"Them thugs," the caretaker points at the men in the back seat of a squad car, "told me to stay in the barn if I didn't want to get hurt."

"You are safe now. You have keys to lock up?" the Marshal asks.

The caretaker shakes his head. "They threw the keys away."

"I'll stay and call a locksmith. Give me a chance to clean up, get the place ready for Starch coming back to *his* home," Gert offers loud enough for Berk and Gayfryd to hear, before marching back inside the house. The sound of a door closing and deadbolts slamming into place preempts any protest.

"My cell phone and wallet?" Berk asks as the assemblage begins to disperse.

"They'll be at the County Courthouse," the Marshal says handing them his card. "My Deputy will provide you with transportation."

Berk steps back in reaction to the offer. "How far away is the nearest town?" he asks.

"Greenwich? About 2.5 miles as the crow flies," the Marshal says, pointing east.

"We'll walk," Berk decides.

Too bad. My cell was ready for the picture of Berk in the back seat of a police cruiser.

Walking does not suit Gayfryd. She hurries to our limo where Paddy is holding the door for Athena. "Any chance a poor girl could hitch a ride into the Big Ole City with you?"

The Marshal pulls his squad near Berk, slides down the window, "Last chance," he says pointing a thumb to the back.

Berk shakes his head, no, and is left in a cloud of dust.

The instant the limo moves, Gayfryd unloads on Athena. "It seems unnecessarily harsh to leave a crippled man out here, alone in the wilderness," she says, giving one last look at Berk while settling in the back-facing seat of the stretch limo, looking for the bar, ignoring Paddy and me.

"Based on what I know of Mr. Berk, he'll work that cane to his advantage," Athena dismisses the idea of returning for Berk. "Besides, this gives us a chance to talk. Isn't that why you arranged this whole charade in the first place?"

I won't give Gayfryd that much credit, but my body is sending out strong signals to be quiet as I shift, trying to find a comfortable position. Paddy gives me a large glass of something brown, and passes out bottled waters to the others.

Gayfryd wastes a pout on Paddy before returning her attention to Athena. "What are you offering?"

Athena removes a paper from her burgundy briefcase. The polished leather with gold initials and shiny brass clasp barely looks broken in. I hope my lawyer has more experience than her legal accessory suggests.

"I have been authorized to offer you $5,000,000, tax-free, to abandon any and all claims of paternity," Athena tells Gayfryd.

"*Bethesda House* alone is worth $300 million, excluding the art," Gayfryd says.

Athena smiles. They have agreed on what Gayfryd is; now they're negotiating the price.

"I'll bring the total to ten million. Offer expires in one minute," she says, handing Gayfryd a pen.

"Jimmy has guaranteed me I'll get the newspaper. That's worth a billion, easy," Gayfryd counters.

I have to give Gayfryd credit. Accustomed to her armor of luxury, here she is working the deal of her lifetime in a police-issued jumpsuit.

Athena, sitting opposite, leans forward. "Ma'am, I have affidavits from Berk's former partners in Silicon Valley, whom you seduced and photographed. I have copies of the videos you gave their wives to use in their divorce proceedings, along with cancelled checks they gave you for the evidence."

Athena tugs on the knee of Gayfryd's jumpsuit. "I have notarized affidavits from the women you blackmailed at the clinic, and I have your DNA. You want to grow old in prison?"

Gayfryd signs the paper.

"Good. Witness, please," Athena says indicating the correct line for me "Notarize please," she says slipping the paper through the pass-through window to the front seat. "Just write down your account number, she tells Gayfryd. You will receive a wire transfer when the flight you are on leaves the country."

Gayfryd sighs.

"Now, Jeffrey, pull over if you would, I need to exchange seats."

"Jeffrey?" Gayfryd asks surprised. "My driver was..." she turns her head toward the driver. Athena allows herself the faintest of grins as the limo eases to the side of the road. "Jeffrey came with me from Harvard. He's one of my graduate students and, as you know, he is an excellent driver."

Turning to the pass-through window, Jeffrey tips two fingers to his cap, and slides the divider closed.

Athena is almost finished. As she exchanges her seat with the notary, she stops to address Gayfryd. "Mr. Storch is abundantly aware of the folly of his youth. Even before this stroke, he began making restitution. Regarding you, Mr. Storch asked me to be especially generous, I believe in respect for his deceased wife. However, my investigation regarding your lineage is inconclusive. I do not believe you are his daughter."

"My mother told me..."

"Others have made the same allegation. However, based on the timetable we constructed," Athena says, "I'd say, doubtful, very doubtful."

"Do you know who my father is?" Gayfryd asks. The child-like question comes out so genuine, I feel a twinge of sympathy.

Athena shakes her head no. "And just so we are clear, should Mr. Storch suffer further harm or embarrassment from you, I'll consider our agreement void, and make it my personal mission to destroy you. That is, if Dr. Berk leaves any remains once he realizes you have betrayed him. Are we clear?"

A strangled "yes" escapes Gayfryd's throat.

"Thank you. Now sit back and enjoy Jeffrey's exceptional driving one last time."

Chapter Eighteen

I wake with mind-numbing leg cramps that send my cats flying off the bed. Other than the felines, I am home alone. "Wadjet, where are Chuti Tiu and Riedell?"

Wadjet may know but apparently isn't permitted to tell me. She shows me pictures of Mars.

The long hot shower helps, along with a handful of Tylenol, but it is still dark and cold outside. Too early for coffee with Paddy downstairs. Even the morning deliveries are hours away. But I know where life will be up and running.

* * *

"Thank goodness. You all right? You look like hell," our City Room Intern says when I come in the Chronicle's back entrance to my cubicle.

"Quiet day so far," I say, hand on my door. "How's it going for you?" I swear she is wearing the same outfit she had on yesterday.

"Gert called last night to tell me she'll stay behind to manage things at *Bethesda House* until Starch gets settled. I'll be filling in here in the meantime. Okay?"

"Sure, but it might not be the best career move for you," I warn her, glancing at Van Wie's office.

"I'll take my chances. Besides, you lead an interesting life. The rest," she says waving a pencil at the City Room, "only write about interesting lives. Might as well cut out the middle man." She hands me a stack of messages.

"Well, my friend Paddy can always use a bar back when you get bored here."

"Good to know." She stands, waiting to ask a question.

I look up. "What?"

"Before you left, you named your assistant as Acting Board Chairman. Does that mean...?" she lifts an eyebrow.

"Sure," I grin, dropping the messages, and retrieving a pamphlet from my satchel. "You might need this," I pass her the SEC leaflet.

"What's this?"

"A gift from a guardian angel. I doubt it will work twice, but it was good to know we've got a friend watching over us."

"So there is an 'us'?"

"Temporarily, so I'd get Chairperson on your resume fast, I doubt it will last the morning."

"Oh well," she says. "Fame is fleeting."

"Tell me about it. And sorry I didn't fill you in after the Board meeting, like I promised. It was very short."

"No problem. Besides, I could hear Mrs. Wright cursing you from down here."

"Good. So how much has Gert told you?"

"I'm up to speed," she assures me.

"What's going on up there?" I ask without looking in the direction of my Managing Editor's glass office at the far end of the City Room.

"I believe that is Mrs. Van Wie in her husband's office staring at you," the intern says. "She's really quite beautiful."

She knows. I keep my head down, cleaning out my satchel. "Are you Gert's daughter, niece, relation of some kind? I ask because she doesn't usually allow anyone in her space."

"Nope. Just awesome, like her."

"Good. Awesome beats blood every time. It's Amy, right?" I say, congratulating myself on pulling that out of the air. "Welcome aboard."

I am wondering why Gayfryd is in Van Wie's office, and not on a plane. Maybe she needs a quickie divorce. I know she isn't about to give Van Wie half of her bribe. Who cares, that's their problem. My priority is getting into Starch's safe. I need to get whatever is in there to Chuti, so we can see how exposed we are.

"I left a message with your service yesterday while you were rescuing the boss." Amy holds out a formal notice. "According to this paper, you were notified electronically that you are due in court this morning. Did you get the message?"

"No idea what you are talking about. If I am being sued again, all summonses go directly to the General Counsel's office."

"No, this is Family Court. A preliminary custody hearing about your daughter Riedell," she says trying to make it sound less threatening. "And you need to get moving, like now. You want me to call Judge Rytrynowicz and say you are sick?"

"Judge who? I don't know anything about this. No wonder Berk looked so smug yesterday when we left him standing in the driveway at Starch's house. Where do I have to be?"

"Three blocks away. I lined up a couple of lawyers," she says holding up a list. "They are not the best, but on short notice…"

Now I know why Tiu and Riedell are missing, and Wadjet was covering for them. Knowing Tiu, she could be on a jet for Singapore, or making a deal with her contacts at The Destiny Society. For whatever reason, she's leaving me hanging.

"I'll go alone. I don't want to get saddled with an idiot until I find out what this is about. I'll request a continuance. That's what they always do on TV. No sense in wasting money."

"Good thinking. And I'll ask building maintenance to edit your column this week," she says crumbling her list of attorneys and tossing it in the trash.

"Not a good idea?"

"You mean having janitorial proof your column?"

I stare at her.

"Going to court without a lawyer is dumb."

"Okay." I motion toward the trash. "Pick one."

"I can help you," Arlo says, appearing from nowhere.

"I'm sorry. I neglected to mention Bob Marley here has been pestering me every ten minutes," Amy says, not hiding her distaste for Arlo.

"Why are you up here? Selling weed to the Staff?" I ask Arlo.

"Enlightening, that's all, man." Arlo holds up a thumb drive. "Missed this," he says.

"What is it?" I ask, moving closer.

"This is the hospital video of Berk raping Emma before your girlfriend's brain was…" Arlo finishes by slashing his finger across his forehead.

"Why are you giving this to me?"

"The only way I can get out of this life I'm living is to come clean. You have everything else. This is the last of it."

Amy says, "Don't trust this guy."

"Right now I don't have much choice."

Arlo holds up the drive. "Take this. Berk's proof he is the daddy, but a criminal act." Arlo grins.

"Proving no consent. Okay. You are coming to Court with me," I decide.

"Just take the drive. The last place I need to be is in a courtroom."

"You're coming."

* * *

"Judge Rytrynowicz," the take-charge bald man announces himself, raising his bushy eyebrows expecting a reaction. "First one to pronounce that baby correct gets the baby." The Judge waits for a reaction.

Beware self-deprecating humor from a person in power, I remember a former editor's advice.

"You should call me Judge R. Now sit," the Judge waves the group in his courtroom down. The place is a converted cafeteria with the business section featuring a grey metal Steelcase desk, set perpendicular to a twenty-foot wooden collapsible table. An assortment of molded plastic chairs surrounds the table, and a thick Webster's Unabridged Dictionary sits at the intersection for balance.

Arlo and I take seats just inside the reception door, while Berk and his associates, five in all plus a stenographer, fill the entire opposition side. Yesterday Berk was pummeling me with a cane, and dancing like Fred Astaire. Now he is in a wheelchair. What a manipulator. This is well beyond a preliminary hearing. I'm outgunned and being set up.

"Judge R, I call for a continuance," I say, not sure what to expect.

"Sit down Son, we haven't even started. For the record, I recognize two faces right away, and one name," the Judge says. "Of course, the distinguished Senator from the great State of Tennessee."

The highly recognizable Southern lawyer, actor, and former politician gives the Judge a well-rehearsed bow of humble appreciation. I'm seeing the Senator as Foghorn Leghorn, the pompous cartoon rooster.

"Returning to my roots," the Senator says before taking a deep breath to elaborate. He catches a disapproving eye from the Judge and stops the oratory, opting only to clear his throat.

"And to my right," the Judge continues, "I recognize an esteemed Pulitzer Prize winner and Chronicle columnist, Shawn Shaw. Also retreating from the limelight of late, no?"

"On assignment," I reply, sensing a trap.

"And I recognize the name, Dr. James Berk. CRISPR, I believe it's called. Absolutely astounding, if what I read is true; a cure for Alzheimer's. I never expected to witness such a significant discovery in my lifetime. This Court is in awe, and in a quandary."

A quandary? That's interesting, although with a veil of suspicion. I'm not going to ask.

Berk is sitting in the middle of his attorneys. He's keeping his head down, not engaging the searching eyes of the Judge who is expecting some indication of acknowledgement for his homage. None is given.

"My client is a humble man, Your Honor," the Senator explains Berk's peculiar behavior and demeanor. "All this celebrity over his earth-shattering work is frankly quite overwhelming, In addition, you may be aware, my client has just been released from a ten-year prison term where he was unjustly implicated by this self-serving newspaper reporter." He gestures toward me.

I know Berk for the conniving and deceptive bastard he is. But there is no way I can convey to this Judge our history. My eyes are batting like an owl's in a lightning storm. I want to put up a defense, but I'm lost. Yesterday I defeated Berk, leaving him helpless in Connecticut. Now the arrogant bastard of yesterday has transformed himself into a sympathetic, Einstein-like character, complete with lace-less tennis shoes, a Chi Rivera tee-shirt, and stained cargo pants.

Berk never lost his focus. He's here to get my daughter.

"May I offer the services of our stenographer?" the Senator asks the judge, seeing no such official present.

Even I see reason to object, but I stay quiet.

"You may," Judge R says.

My naïve legal strategy was to ask for a continuance. Maybe I should try that again. Seems like Judge R's court isn't ready for the hearing anyway.

Before I get the words out, the Judge says, "Thanks for the offer, but we'll be relying on this little baby." He pulls up a mini-tripod and camera from the floor. "Take special notice of my second baby reference," he adds, pointing to the laser-etched wood plaque leaning against a cardboard box: *Family Court*.

"Each party will get their very own personal copy of my recorded transcript at the conclusion of today's festivities, available in the lobby, along with my CD of Country/Western favorites. Okay? Good."

No one laughs.

"I'll just set up the Judge Judy Jury here on my desk, and we can let the battle ensue. Damn," he says giving the JJJ a tap, then another. "Mrs. R, my JJJ seems to be…"

"Let me help, Your Holiness," Arlo says. He's wearing his Rasta knit cap, which given the peculiar nature of the Judge, may work in my favor. "I wrote a review of the JJJ 45 C. The battery is suspect." Arlo pops off the back, setting the lithium batteries on the table. "This little switch here," he says showing the Judge, "DC to AC. Plug this in here, and we're in business."

"Thank you, young man," the Judge says, appraising Arlo.

"Your Honor?" the Senator stands, casting a dubious eye toward Arlo.

"Judge R, or this," the Judge says twirling his eleven-letter name plate.

"Yes, Judge R," the Senator says, realizing his star power isn't working.

"I've read the petition, so let's get to it," Judge R orders.

"Where is the child in question?" one of Berk's associate counsel asks, alerting like the hyena he is, smelling blood.

"Mr. Shaw," Judge R says, "although a courtroom may not be your typical venue, I'm certain a man of your experience understands the importance of being represented by counsel."

"So I've been told."

"And yet here you sit virtually unarmed in the face of a substantial force," he motions towards the Senator and his co-counsels, "An army, if you will, unprecedented in my courtroom."

"Judge R, I was only made aware of this hearing thirty minutes ago."

"That argument doesn't fly. Coming into my courtroom unprepared is no excuse. However, this is Family Court. We try to be as informal as possible, but make no mistake, my authority is absolute and I will adjudicate in the best interest of the child. Is that clear?"

"Abundantly."

"And you still plan to represent yourself?"

"At this time, yes, Your Honor. Is it okay if I request my continuance now?"

"You are out of order, Mr. Shaw," the judge denies my request.

"I never received a single notice until this morning at the office," I try again.

"I have verification of three separate electronic transmissions initiated three weeks prior to this date to Mr. Shaw and to Ms. Chuti Tiu, as co-litigants. Re-transmitted again this morning to Mrs. Shaw. Reputedly the defendant's wife," Berk's associate says.

These guys are prepared; this isn't a preliminary anything. I just found out yesterday I have a wife, and he already knows. I really did come to a gunfight with a knife. Hopefully, Chuti has my back. If all I have is Arlo, I'm standing here with my pants down.

"Judge R?"

"Mr. Shaw, you may go ahead."

"Sorry, Judge R. I've had my share of unpleasant history with our esteemed felon," I say pointing at Berk. Before Senator Foghorn can object, I add, "I believe my wife has taken our daughter away for safekeeping. Riedell is afraid to be near that man," I say pointing again at Berk who, at the nudge of the associate, looks up from his hand-held device, and scowls on cue.

"Well, no need for the young lady to be afraid in my courtroom," Judge R says. "Mrs. R? Come here, Dear," he calls. "Mrs. R is also the bailiff," he explains to us.

Straight out of Mayberry RFD, a kindly looking woman appears from the back of the room wearing a gingham print dress, button sweater, and sensible shoes.

"Show them, Dear," Judge R says, reclining in his tufted leather high back, fingers interlaced across his chest, proud as punch.

Mrs. R turns, throwing out a hip displaying a .45 Colt revolver nestled into a tooled leather holster strapped to her side. Her sparkling smile, gone.

I stop myself from laughing out loud.

"Be respectful, Mr. Shaw," Judge R orders.

"Sorry Judge R, very sorry." I take a deep breath. "My wife," I say, surprising myself at how easily those words come out, "took our daughter to visit her Godfather, Cuthbert Storch. He was abducted by…"

"Liar," Berk barks.

"Something to say?" Judge R demands.

Berk shakes his head no without looking at the Judge.

Judge R holds his stare on Berk as Senator Foghorn begins to rise, and is silenced by a raised hand. For my part, I receive a look of concern. "How is Mr. Storch doing?"

"He isn't doing very well," I tell him. "But he's in good care now."

"Sorry to hear. Send him my concern and prayers," Judge R says.

I sigh, head down, tightening my lips in silent appreciation. One for the good guys.

"Judge R," the Senator says, taking his time as he draws himself to his full height, "I object to this poor attempt to elicit sympathy."

In response, Judge R spins around in his chair, snatching the *Family Court* wood placard, slamming it on the table. "Lest we forget!" The Senator sits so fast it looks like he was shot dead.

"Now Mr. Shaw," Judge R returns to me with a softness to his voice. "Perceived threats noted. But you must produce the child at this time tomorrow, or I'll hold you in contempt. And just so you understand, that's not a fine. It's jail. For you. Not the child. Got it?"

"Your Holiness," Arlo says, holding up his laptop.

"Funny once, young man, not twice. Remove that hat. What have you got?"

"Clarification and edification of the lineage regarding the predisposed child in question, your Judgeship," Arlo blurts out.

"Cut to the chase, son. What is it?"

"The actual footage of the child in question being conceived."

"You have the video of James Berk raping my friend, Emma?" I ask.

"Where did you get this evidence, young man?" Judge R intercedes.

Arlo points a finger at James Berk, who is playing with an electronic device. He doesn't care how his indifference comes across.

"Mr. James Berk," Judge R asks Arlo, "gave you this video to bring to this court?"

"That's Dr. Berk," the Senator corrects, receiving a withering look from the Judge.

"I find that curious and suspicious," Judge R says. "Are you sitting on the correct side of the table?"

Arlo starts to answer, but settles on a two-fingered Peace symbol as his response.

"You okay with this?" Judge R asks me.

Another spasm travels up my back. "If my lawyer were present, would she object?" I squeak out.

Judge R nods yes, giving me a puzzled look.

"Let's just get on with it," I whisper, exhausted from the effort.

As instructed, Arlo sets his laptop on the table, points his finger toward a white wall, and starts running the video.

We see Emma strapped to a gurney, her legs spread wide, cruelly exposed. A tongue guard I recognize from her electroshock therapy is in her mouth. Her hospital gown is bunched up around her neck under her arms. I can see her beautiful blue eyes searching in panic. Her nostrils are flared. There is no sound.

"Stop this," Judge R orders immediately. "Relevance?"

"We have no objection, Judge R," Berk's lawyer declares.

"I didn't ask you," Judge R answers. Pointing at Arlo, he demands, "How did you obtain this vulgarity? Be very careful with your answer."

"I work as a freelance information detective."

"You're a computer hacker and a spy," Judge R says.

"Yes."

"For whom?"

"Anyone who pays."

"And this," Judge R points to the image on the wall.

"I was working for Dr. Berk on another project when he made this recording available to me."

"Dr. Berk sent it to you?"

"Not exactly sent it. Made it available, yes."

"Still no objections?" the Judge asks, looking at each side of the table.

I wave my hand to get on with it. The spasms are starting to merge into a laser show behind my eyes.

The white shirt and pants of an orderly come onto the scene. This isn't security footage from the hospital, I realize. This is James Berk acting in his own docudrama. Berk comes into the camera's range wearing a patient gown. It's the one he was wearing when I saw him in the hospital getting treated for his ataxia.

Moving the orderly aside, Berk caresses Emma's face. Berk is wearing surgical gloves. Emma doesn't struggle. The orderly binds her head down with a leather strap, the same kind I've seen used in executions. The orderly lowers the gurney, and Berk mounts her.

"Judge R?" the Senator jumps to his feet, "Inadmissible. We have no…"

"Stop the video," Judge R demands.

"This is footage of an alleged event, some nine or ten years ago, a deceased litigant, no chain, no case," the Senator persists.

Judge R taps his *Family Court* plaque with his pen. "We are arguing a petition for the right to visitation, lest you have forgotten, Senator. Your client provided this video to his employee, with the apparent intention of having it presented at this hearing. Is that correct?"

"Judge R?" the Senator opens his arms as if saying he's been put in an impossible situation.

"If it's your strategy to have the opposition present this video, because you think this depravity will appear less prejudicial to your client, you haven't succeeded," Judge R. says. "I will see the video."

Berk never so much as lifts his head as Arlo restarts the file.

My memory of Emma is now almost entirely through my daughter, Riedell. As much as I don't want to damage that impression, I need to see what Berk did to her.

I remember the first time I saw Emma in the mental ward, the orderlies attacking. Emma was a robust woman; even strapped to a gurney, she was spitting at them, and biting at any piece of flesh she could reach. Berk would never have succeeded assaulting that Emma. I saw him only an hour earlier in his hospital bed on that day and he seemed weak, although raging at the nurses.

Yet in this video, Emma's face is calm. She is neither willing, nor compliant. She's exhausted. I recognize the look. When Kathleen and I would take Emma home after her electroshock touch-ups, it was all we could do to get her into a cab. She would sleep for twenty-four hours straight afterwards.

That's how Berk raped her; he electroshocked Emma.

In the video Berk takes his time raping Emma. The Senator flails his arms, "Preposterous, defamatory."

Judge R motions Arlo to stop the video as Berk gets on top of Emma a second time. The Judge is no longer watching the video, he is looking at Berk in disbelief. Berk is still focused on his electronic device. He simply doesn't care what's happening around him.

Even with the projection stopped, the Senator continues to make unheard protests until Judge R takes his eyes off Berk.

What am I missing? I can see Judge R is equally confused. Why would a man seeking visitation rights allow himself to be portrayed as a rapist?

Judge R bangs the table. "Okay, Senator, what were you saying?"

"Judge R, Mr. Shaw is taking considerable liberty identifying the young lady, Riedell, as his daughter, when in fact he has no legal basis for that claim," the Senator says.

Judge R turns to me.

"I was legal guardian to Riedell's mother, Emma, who died when Riedell was an infant. I have cared for and raised Riedell these past 10 years. I am also married to Riedell's aunt, her only living blood relative," I say sliding the papers to the Judge. "Mr. Berk's only claim to parentage is that," I pause for emphasis, "he raped Riedell's mother."

"Mr. Berk, if you can tear yourself away from your computer game, what say you? Feel free to seek advice of counsel before you reply."

"No need. Consensual," Berk says not looking up as he continues fiddling with the device in his lap.

"That statement will require some explanation in light of the video, Mr. Berk."

"It's Dr. Berk," he answers looking at the Judge for the first time.

"Duly noted," Judge R says, waving for Arlo to turn the JJJ 45 C back on. "You are aware, I can see the restraining straps on the woman with whom you claim to have had consensual sexual congress."

Berk nods.

"I'm sure you are also aware I'm not empowered to send you back to prison, even if you admit to raping this poor woman," Judge R says putting up his hand. "I'm sure it doesn't come as a great surprise, but I find you a reprehensible person."

Berk shrugs his indifference.

Judge R is openly accusing James Berk of rape, and Berk doesn't care. Even I know the statute of limitations has kicked in, or Senator Foghorn would be screaming his indignation.

I'm lost. Why would Berk spend ten years in prison, apparently without protest? A seventh of his life. And now return, claiming to be Riedell's father.

"Judge R, we plan to continue with our application," the Senator says.

"In that case, Mr. Shaw. I have no choice in this matter. I'm ordering an in-home evaluation of the child. Expect to see Mrs. R at your residence this week."

"I will make sure my daughter is available," I say, hoping I can deliver on that promise.

Judge R says, "No excuses this time. Should you fail to comply, Child Services will be notified and Riedell will be placed in foster care. The bailiff will notify you all of the next hearing. Any questions?"

Chapter Nineteen

"Court?" Paddy asks as soon as I return to Parnell's.

"I can't make any sense of it," I tell him. "Compared to the Family Court when I petitioned for guardianship of Emma, this was like Disneyland. And, can you imagine Berk meeting Riedell? *I'm your father because I raped your mother. Come here and give me a hug.* Riedell would skate stomp him into kitty litter."

"This is all for leverage over your wife. Berk would be in a nursing home if Chuti Tiu hadn't created the cure for his ataxia, and now he's back to his original mission. I think he's still fixed on delivering Tiu to The Destiny Society."

"Tiu only worked out the cure because Berk gave the ataxia gene to Riedell. Cost him ten years of his life. I'd have let the bastard…"

I hoped bringing Arlo to Family Court would expose Berk as a rapist. Which it did. But I hadn't thought through the implications.

"Behind you," Paddy stops me. I see Arlo in the bar mirror. He's coming in the front door with Det. Stone right behind. Stone seems to be shoving him forward.

"Dry out there today," Stone says tapping the bar, having pushed Arlo across the room and onto a stool. Paddy pours the detective a shot that's quickly downed, then a second.

"That's better," the detective says.

"Well Detective, you here for the Irish stew?" I ask taking my white mug from Paddy. I'm over-tired, I know. I need to be careful, but Stone's invading my territory.

"Just my pound of flesh," Stone growls in Arlo's face, forcing me to look away or laugh. The guy's a joke. But Paddy isn't laughing.

Paddy gives Arlo a raised eyebrow, "What can I get for you?"

"Same as Mr. Shaw," Arlo says, pleased he's being treated like a customer and not the kicked dog. But Stone intervenes.

"Come over here kid, let me get a good look at you," Stone says, acting like he's just noticed Arlo's dreadlocks and Rastafarian outfit.

Arlo knows he's smarter than everyone in the room. In my experience, keeping that advantage to yourself is wise, but Arlo can't control his mouth.

"So what's it to you copper man," Arlo eggs Stone. "Dimba? Nah, I peg you for a dipper?"

I recognize the language. Arlo is baiting Det. Stone with West African slang, asking if he is a pot or crack user. Paddy shakes his head, he's done with this conversation. He moves down the bar.

"Just this," Stone threatens, pulling out his cuffs, forcing Arlo to the bar rail, kicking his legs spread wide. He pulls out his wand and roughly scans Arlo up and down his sides and between his legs, creating enough whoops and buzzes to wake the dead. "Empty your pockets now!" Stone orders.

I'm figuring Arlo is wearing a bug. But out comes a Marine combat knife, Mace spray, and a Taser. "Almost forgot," Arlo brags sliding a collapsible baton out from a slot in the leg of his cargo pants. So much for the laidback, ganja-smoking Rasta.

Det. Stone isn't nearly as surprised as I am. Paddy scrapes Arlo's arsenal into a plastic bag as Stone hits Arlo with the wand again. "Wonk."

Stone uses the wand to push off Arlo's skull cap, dropping it to the floor. Stone's boot comes down hard on the cap crushing what must be a mic hidden inside a bag of weed.

"You know where this wand is going next?" Stone suggests, giving Arlo full disclosure. To my amazement Arlo opens his mouth, removes a molar, and sets it on the bar.

"Looks custom," Stone says, picking up his shot glass.

Arlo winces.

"Agent Greene," Det. Stone says to the tooth, "got your boy here with me. He's going to give NYPD some info. I'll send him back in a few." Stone raises his glass, makes a fake swing, and then sets the shot glass down with a slam beside the tooth.

Even a smartass like Arlo knows he's pushed too far. Four felony items on display, and an angry cop in his face, Arlo starts begging, Arlo style.

"Thank you. Really man. Took me a month to get that tooth. FBI bastards are too cheap to use Novocain."

"I'll keep this chilled for you," Paddy says picking up the tooth with a bar napkin, dropping it in a shot glass, and stowing it in the mini-fridge.

"Now you," Det. Stone turns to me, "I've got enough to drop your boy in a deep hole right here," he says twirling the plastic bag filled with Arlo's weapons. "But I'm all about cooperation," he says, dry washing his hands. "I could use an invite upstairs. Maybe meet that genius wife I've heard about, and get a look at this special school. Brother's kid could use some *special ed*. Whattya think?"

"And why would you need to meet my wife?"

"Lt. Garcelli and I thought she might want to help the NYPD get through these flash drives. Your source is for shit," he says leveling a gaze on Arlo. "There are thousands of hours of video alone. We want the bombers now. We could use some citizen cooperation."

The NYPD's IT Department would have given Lt. Garcelli the bad news. Arlo had pulled a classic lawyer trick: give the required information while burying the gems in an ocean of flotsam. What information Arlo had on the dirty cops, Mob, and bombing is sunken treasure.

"I doubt if my wife, Chuti, is home. She doesn't keep what you'd call regular office hours," I tell Stone while Wadjet is notifying my very resourceful wife of the situation. I imagine Chuti sending a little Impet hologram downstairs with a list of questions for Stone; or, she might have something more disciplinary in mind. "And school is probably in session," I add.

"Why don't you give me an upstairs tour anyway, seeing as I'm here," Det. Stone insists. "I won't disturb the kids. Paddy, one for the road?"

Paddy gives me the raised eyebrow as he pours another shot for Stone. Neither of us wants Stone around, but if I've learned anything from Paddy, it's to deal with the issue at hand. Delaying only allows the problem to mushroom out of control.

I spot a flicker of a roller skate in the bottom corner of the TV behind Paddy's head. That is my signal Chuti is watching, and has come to the same conclusion.

"Then come on up," I decide. "Arlo?" I ask Stone.

"He'll come with us," Stone decides, hoisting Arlo upright by the belt of his cargo pants.

I am actually asking Tiu, not Stone, but my question serves the same purpose. Chuti displays a second skate on the TV in answer.

"Well the three of us it is," I say confirming for Chuti.

"Confession time," I lean over and whisper to Arlo. At this point being anywhere around Stone is the last thing Arlo wants, but he's caught.

"Wadjet, two guests," I say putting my eye to the security reader as Arlo and I wait at the top of the concrete stairs. Stone is clutching the rail half-way up, sweat gathering on his forehead. The third floor in a turn-of-the-century conversion building is more like an eight flight walk-up in a normal building. And this building is anything but normal.

"Wadjet?" Stone asks, trying to hide his panting with a cough. Booze and cigarettes clearly have taken their toll.

"Egyptian Goddess," I say. "We're big on Goddesses at the Chronicle. Wadjet is Goddess of Protection."

Arlo jogs in place as we wait for Stone. Wouldn't bother me if Stone collapsed on the stairs, but Stone accidentally shooting Arlo in the process would really piss off Tiu.

"Up yours, Kid. I'll break your leg if you don't cut the shit." Det. Stone orders.

Arlo stops. The metal bank teller drawer slides from the wall. "All weapons please," Wadjet commands.

"They will be secure," I assure Det. Stone.

Stone grunts, but doesn't actually complain as he puts the wand, his primary pistol, and his ankle weapon in the tray. He pulls a sap from his belt, slapping it on the wall in front of Arlo's face, before dropping it in the tray.

"I already gave downstairs," Arlo says holding up his arms.

"Thank you," Wadjet responds with airport politeness, retracting the tray. A massive four foot deadbolt slides into the reinforced frame before the door swings open with an airlock gasp.

"Children," I explain answering Stone's questioning look. "Always forgetting to close the door. Problem solved."

Stone grunts.

* * *

"Cozy," Arlo says hurrying inside pushing past Stone before dramatically crumpling to the floor. "Heaven." Arlo spreads out on his back, looking up, making snow angels with his arms and legs.

In a city that inherently confines personal living space, expanses like Grand Central or Carnegie Hall accentuate the senses. "It's over a hundred feet up to the peak," I tell him. "Some of those skylights are stained glass from Italy, brought here for *safe keeping* during the War. Of course we also have the inevitable sparrow or two." I'm sure the exquisite glass is lost on Stone, but Arlo may appreciate it.

"Never imagined this place existed," Arlo says, awed by the unexpected grandeur. He grabs his heels and lifts his legs in the air spiraling on his butt.

It took me nearly a year to stop having a similar reaction. The last thing I want to do is encourage the little bastard to enjoy my home, yet I cannot help admire his incredible *joie de vivre*.

"This is a..." Stone seems lost for words.

"Former munitions factory. Cannon balls were made here initially. Later torpedoes," I tell Stone. "That's why this place is built like a fortress," I stomp the floor. "You could line up a dozen Sherman tanks in here without bowing this floor a centimeter."

"I'm not Housing," Stone growls. "But I'll bet I know some folks who'd like to run another code check. Can't say you made a ton of friends in that Department, the way you trashed their Inspectors."

Ignoring Stone's threat, I move past him. My first rant against the Department of Housing was about extortion and prejudice. Black and Hispanic families struggled to buy homes, only to have the dreams shattered with fines for senseless code violations. No inspectors were fired when I exposed their practice, only relocated. A Pyrrhic victory.

"Still old machinery back in some corners," I say, waving off in the distance. "We've carved out a little corner of the place for a kitchen, couple of bedrooms," I point at what looks like an old Hollywood sound stage.

Stone makes a kick at Arlo, but misses. Arlo easily evades the foot, sliding out of reach on the inch-thick, high-gloss polyurethane coating we poured over the rough-hewn wood beam floor. There are some things about Arlo I can't help liking, but it's almost time to be done with him. One more contribution, then he's out of my life for good.

"Where are your little geniuses? No teachers? Not even a table, a chair. Whatever this place is, it ain't no school. A fucking write off is what it is. No wonder you keep it under wraps." Stone laughs.

"You are a moron," Arlo says to Stone. "I suspect Wadjet activated the security protocol. Same deal down at Langley. Nothing and no one is seen."

To show there is a school here, I activate a small version of one of the membrane screens.

"What's that? Just a big screen TV?" Stone slurs.

"This is a live image of Yellowstone Park," I tell him. "Wadjet, sound." The entire warehouse fills with the natural peacefulness of nature, the grunts and squeals of elks coming from miles away.

"Cows. Big deal," Stone says turning away, focusing on a big table. He can't imagine what this therapy table becomes when fully activated. Emma frequently snorkeled there in her private Great Barrier Reef. The table is no longer used, but it's my last memory of Emma being happy.

"That's Emma's therapy table. The kids don't have the patience to use it," I explain.

"That nut case you took in," Stone says.

My cell vibrates in my pocket. It's Paddy.

"Bailiff Mrs. R from Family Court is here," he says, "She is requesting a spot check. What should I tell her?"

* * *

"Well that's quite some Irish Pub you have downstairs," Bailiff Mrs. R exclaims in her high-pitched but soothing voice. "And that darling Wadjet, isn't she a stitch?" she says putting down her hobo bag and shaking my hand.

"Oh, am I intruding? 'Course I am. Reason it's called a spot check. Inspection - detection," she explains.

While I was meeting Bailiff Mrs. R at the door, Tiu called out the living room setting for us, and diverted Stone and Arlo into a labyrinth of caves, one of many holographic teaching aids, at a far end of the warehouse.

I invite Bailiff Mrs. R to sit, and she chooses Emma's old secretary's chair.

I keep one eye watching for Arlo or Stone as the living room section of the warehouse is morphing into an Olive Garden restaurant. Philodendrons are growing, cascading over the mezzanine tiers. The membrane screens have turned the industrial stone walls into warm red brick. Bailiff Mrs. R doesn't seem to notice the gradual transition, and I swear I can smell bread baking in the oven.

"So this is a spot inspection?" I say, sounding like a game show host, and feeling as if the stage is about to collapse.

"Mrs. R, so happy to meet you," Riedell says, skating out from her bedroom.

"Riedell!" I say far too loudly.

She zips behind the secretary's chair and takes Bailiff Mrs. R on a ride, bringing her all the way into the kitchen. "I'll bet you could use a nice cup of Golden Yunnan tea," I can hear her chatting. "We get it right across the street at D'Agostino's."

"You should teach that kid some manners," Stone tells me, suddenly appearing inches away. "Nearly ran me down. Who's that woman?"

"The decorator," I say as the living room setting glides back into its wall, leaving the three of us men alone in the enormous, empty warehouse. Plants and red brick walls have disappeared, along with the teaching aids. And they don't even seem to notice.

"You need a decorator," Det. Stone says, lighting a cigar. "This dump looks like hell. But I'd get someone a few decades younger, unless you want to live in an old folks' home. You offering a drink? Those caves parched my throat. They almost looked real."

"Rowdy and Yeti would welcome a treat," Wadjet suggests over the sound system.

"Drinks coming right up. Treats first. Kittens always a priority in this house," I excuse myself, feeling the temperature in the room dropping as I am summoned to the kitchen. Tiu is ready. Rowdy and Yeti, sensing the change, have already disappeared. Tiu has declared war.

"Little woman hiding somewhere?" Stone calls after me. "She another disappearing act, like that furniture?" He stamps his feet as if he's looking for a hidden trapdoor in the floor.

"She's on her way," I call back before turning into the kitchen, out of Stone's sight. "Thought I'd join you," I say to Mrs. R, who is comfortable in the breakfast nook. "A couple of building department guys just finishing another spot check. You know, inspection – detection," I smile.

"Find anything?"

"Not yet. How about some more tea?"

"Lovely," she accepts.

"The inspectors' last test can be a bit noisy," I warn her. "I'll turn on the sound masking system."

"Chuti, you're on," I whisper, tucking in my ear piece. Pouring the tea, and a hot chocolate for Riedell, I take a seat with them, glancing at the muted monitor above Mrs. R's head.

Stone's "Shi-i-i-t!" starts the action, coupled with arm waving whooping screams from Arlo.

"That's nice," I say sipping my tea. Mrs. R and Riedell agree.

* * *

Excluding our little breakfast nook, Chuti has turned the entire warehouse into dead-of-winter Antarctica. No ceiling. No floor. No former munitions factory.

Stone and Arlo clutch together, standing waist deep in snow. Their heads jerk down, then up, realizing they are on top of a two-thousand-foot glacier, peering at hundreds of miles of sea and ice. An earth-shattering explosion shudders the ice mass. A crack, followed by a massive cannon shot emanating from nowhere, echoing everywhere.

They see the fissure lightening across the ice field, before hearing a deep bowel-jarring rumble. A thunderous eruption cracks as the skyscraper mass of glacier gives way at their feet. Panic. Legs drop off at their waists. Screams. Arms flying. Hips, stomach, chest, are yanked below following the stretched feet and legs as their eyes widen, searching into the azure cauldron below.

Over the exploding glacial calving, I catch distinctly different screams. There's a hard thump to the floor. Stone. More yells and hollering as they plunge straight into the frigid depths of the Antarctica Ocean. Weighted by tons of ice, they sink down, twisting, tossing. White, blue, green, an ethereal helix of millions of iridescent plankton appear twirling around them as they are scooped up in the maw of a grey whale breaching two hundred feet in the air before expelling them out onto the snow.

Their universe goes black. The spectral image of Chuti Tiu moves forward. Stone is lying on the floor shivering, fearing for his life.

"You are intruding where you do not belong," Chuti Tiu's image says.

Arlo, lying on his side, tingling like a struck tuning fork, attempts to speak, but she hushes him with a swipe of her hand.

"You are being played," Tiu says floating closer, calm, relaxed. She stands between them. Bending over Det. Stone, she says, "The person you are after is James Berk."

"Who?" Stone manages to ask.

Tiu doesn't repeat herself. Her hologram disappears through a brick wall, ending the conversation.

Twenty seconds have elapsed, my cue. "Thought you could use some refreshment while we wait for my wife to arrive," I announce coming out from the kitchen. A bottle of water in one hand and whiskey neat in the other, I stop, acting surprised that Stone and Arlo are on the floor gasping.

"I was gone only a few minutes. What happened? You two get in a fight?"

Stone, ghostly and pale, gets to his feet, grabbing the whiskey. He gulps the drink and staggers toward the door.

"Wadjet, they're leaving," I say, grabbing Arlo by his shirt. I give him the water and usher him to the door. "There won't be a next time, you understand?"

* * *

"Sorry for the interruption," I say, returning to Riedell and Mrs. R in the kitchen.

'Okay, let's get to it," Mrs. R says, getting up from the breakfast nook. "Unusual home, Mr. Shaw, even for NYC. Certainly secure and well maintained, from what I've seen. Now why don't you show me around?"

As I look at our home through Mrs. R's eyes, I see little evidence of domesticity. The floors are polished, but bare. Even the stained-glass skylights against the exposed rafters give no suggestion of hominess. The furniture retracting into the walls lacks permanence. Only the soft presence of Yeti and Rowdy suggest people actually live here.

Mrs. R watches in amazement as Wadjet reshapes the enormous screens into Riedell's favorite setting, transforming the entire warehouse into Yellowstone National Park. It is so vivid the cats take swings at the wolves who don't know Rowdy and Yeti exist.

Riedell kills the white noise system and brings in nature's clamors: dins, breezes and absolute peace. The snores, grunts and mating squeals of elk can be heard in the distance. We listen to streams gurgle, Gray jays raspy calls, dusky grouse rustling in the underbrush, and mountain chickadees flittering through the lodge pole pines. Mrs. R is in awe. "Wonderful!" she exclaims.

She reaches into her bag and hands me papers. "These are financial forms you need to complete. Approximations are fine for assets, although we do require verification of income, bank accounts, and outstanding debt. Keep it simple. My goodness, the other litigant gave us a printed annual report."

Diet, exercise and schooling are the subjects of the next ten minutes of questions, primarily answered by Riedell. Questions about her studies follow.

"Interesting," Mrs. R. concludes, trying to be non-committal as Riedell rattles off her study areas, including reading fluency in Greek and Latin. "I can also speak some Latin," my daughter says, "*Loquerisne Latine?*"

"Not enough to be useful," Mrs. R answers.

Riedell may be the smartest person in the room, but she is playing someone else's game. I lean close to her and whisper, "*Superbia et ante ruinam exaltatur.*" Pride comes before the fall.

Despite the intellectual litany, Riedell on roller skates is simply a young girl. I don't want to dissuade that image.

"Okie dokie then," Mrs. R decides, not giving anything away. She stops to admire a brown bear swagger across a meadow. "Amazing what nature shows us. Judge R will be in touch. I'll let myself out."

"Just give me a second," I hurry ahead to make certain Det. Stone and Arlo are down the stairs.

"Let me show you my bedroom before you go," Riedell says to Mrs. R.

Chapter Twenty

"You take care of that flu bug," Paddy calls out after Det. Stone. "What happened? He looks like death warmed over," he tells me.

"Forgot his gun and shield," I say, passing them in a bag to Paddy.

"I'll call a friend," he says putting the bag below the bar.

"He never left the flash drives you gave Garcelli this morning."

"I don't think Stone ever wanted Tiu's help. The flash drives were only his excuse. He wanted to get inside your place for a look around. More evidence tying you to the Helmsley bombing would be my guess."

"He's got the hallway video, what more does he need?"

"Tying you into the clinic. He wants you dirty."

"Great."

"Did Stone meet Tiu upstairs?"

"Not really. She sent him on a short vacation, and then dropped the hammer on him. Hard."

Paddy nods and smiles.

"You saw all that?"

"Enough." Paddy punches the remote, pointing to the TV. "Wadjet apparently thought I'd enjoy seeing them leaping around and falling on the floor. No sound, but the terror was obvious."

"Tiu dropped them in Antarctica on the edge of a calving glacier. Not so subtle way of showing Stone he was out of his depth," I say. "He'll be having iceberg nightmares for a while. And I think Wadjet was alerting you, not trying to entertain."

"Have it your way, but I owe Wadjet an extra amp or two for dinner."

I can hear Riedell's skates on the concrete stairs escorting Mrs. R. "Riedell is bringing the Bailiff down now. Arlo gone?"

"Restroom," Paddy says tipping his head toward the side door. "Stone wasn't the only one who got the crap scared out of him."

"So who is this Agent Greene Stone mentioned?" I ask, lifting my chin toward the mini-fridge with Arlo's wireless tooth inside.

"Don't know, but I'm thinking, FBI. If I'm right, that explains how Arlo has been able to operate so freely."

"He's riding on the FBI's horse while taking a few side gigs for Berk, the Chronicle, and anyone else willing to pay," I say accepting my mug, spinning it on the bar. The tea doesn't have the near term restorative power of JD.

"I'm surprised the kid has lasted this long," Paddy says.

"So kind of you to assist me," Bailiff Mrs. R says to Riedell, waving goodbye as my daughter skates through the pub and out the front door. It's freezing outside. Riedell is wearing a ski racing one-piece, and doesn't seem bothered.

"Beautiful girl," Mrs. R tells me. "And, your wife reminds me of myself," she laughs. "Behind the scenes. Ever so mysterious, don't you think?"

"You two are spitting images," I say, having no idea what she means.

"Paddy, a nice scotch for the three of us please," Bailiff Mrs. R says sitting down at the near empty bar, making sure we notice the .45 under her sweater. "Special permit," she says, holding up her badge. Child Safety Act. Your lovely Wadjet knew."

Paddy passes out the special crystal glasses. I don't need to ask: Macallan 36. The bottle hasn't been touched since James Berk was sentenced to Fishkill Penitentiary.

"Lovely," Mrs. R says, sipping the scotch. "Perfect preparation for the Grand Event," she tells us.

Before I can ask, she summarizes her investigation. "Kitchen, sleeping areas, hygiene – exceptional. Fire and safety are world class. Lovely home. Beautiful child. But I wouldn't want to get on the bad side of that darling wife of yours. Although I have to admit, I didn't take well to that Det. Stone, either. Not much better than that creep Berk. Shame he invented this CRISPR. Seems like Hitler finding the cure for cancer."

"Glad you understand," I agree, not missing the fact she knows Stone is a detective, not a building inspector.

"Well I do, sure enough. Judge R though, he's a stickler for the law. He'd sooner whip that man raw for what he did to that poor woman, but if Berk's the father, he's got rights. That's the law. Too bad your wife couldn't send that man somewhere cold. Really cold."

Don't underestimate the kindly woman in the gingham, I tell myself.

"Nothing out of school. You'll hear from Judge R for yourself. And by the way, I appreciate the heads up with that CI of yours. Where is that little stoner, anyway? I wanted to ask him how he finagled the JJJ 45 C this morning."

"Restroom. So you know him?"

"Oh, yeah. I just can't place him. Anyway, we have the closed-circuit. I don't miss much," she says touching the corner of her eye. "Tell you this," she warns with a finger. "That boy is gonna be sporting a blow-hole of his own, real soon, if he doesn't find a new line of work, like becoming a monk in Tibet."

"With some there is no other way," Paddy understands.

"I hear ya," she says taking down a good-sized swallow. "Also, suspect that cop, Stone, is going to take early retirement real soon. Either he finds God, or becomes one of those," she says gesturing toward the regulars at the end of the bar.

"It won't be in here. That much I can guarantee," Paddy says, topping off her drink.

"You saw everything upstairs?" I realize.

"Of course," Mrs. R clinks my glass, "reflected in the glassware behind your head. You know a good hand never sits with her back to the door," she grins.

Paddy holds up his hand when she reaches for her money. "Stone is an old problem, for more than a few of us. I hope he sees the light."

"God bless him if he does, but my bet favors the other direction," she says, finishing her thirty-six year old scotch and waving goodbye over her shoulder.

* * *

"Wow! Man. Cool. I was Jonah," Arlo comes out of the rest room all keyed up. "I've tried those VR goggles a few times, always got sick. But that was total immersion. Dude, I was standing on a glacier, experiencing global warming to the ultimate."

It's no coincidence Arlo emerges from the rest room only after Mrs. R is gone.

"Not scared? A little nauseous?" Paddy asks. I don't have to look at Paddy to know he's working Arlo.

"No way, man. That was awesome. Anytime, man. Take me to the galaxies far, far away."

"You done?" I ask.

"Mint tea, Captain Spock?" Paddy asks pushing a mug forward.

"Interesting coincidence you coming in with Det. Stone. How'd he know who you were?" I ask, giving his dreadlocks a flick.

"Man. You don't dig Rastafari?"

"Answer the question."

"How would I know, Dude? Maybe he saw my ID," he says holding up the Chronicle lanyard, "and made the connection."

"I'm sure that's it," I say. "You came here to tell me something?"

"Oh yeah. Seems like decades ago now. Get it. Ice Age?"

Paddy and I don't respond.

"Yeah, well," Arlo takes the mug. "I came to apologize, man. I didn't know what that Family Court deal was all about. With that CRISPR shit, Berk's got some extra juice these days."

"So you do whatever Berk wants, like showing him raping Emma to a Judge?"

Arlo shrugs. "I mean, really, sorry man, you had to see that."

"That video was proof Berk is my daughter's real father," I explain. "Gives Berk the right to see Riedell. And in time convince her to…"

"What?"

"Never mind. You're in Berk's pocket, always have been."

"You knew?"

"Sure. I smelled a rat the minute you were assigned to me," I say leaning on the bar. "Starch never planned to run anything more than the standard once-a-year NYPD corruption investigation. The Chronicle looks like a reform crusader, and the Commissioner gets to clean out some dirt."

"Smart, Dudes."

"Got that right. Starch knew you were a plant from the get go. My job was to find out why."

"You were playing me," Arlo says, acting amazed at my admission. His eyes light up. "Your wife, Chuti Tiu, she knows who I am, doesn't she? I should have guessed," he says grinning at his oversight. "Those Government alphabet agencies spend so much time backstabbing each other they can't believe Indies like Berk, me and your wife are working them."

Arlo sits straighter. He's been revealed, so he might as well try for a play. "I'll help you for real, if you give me some face time with your wife. I'm good," he says without bragging, "but Chuti Tiu, if that's even her real name, you cannot imagine. In my world, someone like her only comes along once in fifty years."

"More like 500," I correct.

"What?"

"Never mind. So you'd risk losing access to Berk's special medical resources?" I ask.

"Maybe your wife will help me."

"Do you think sending you to Antarctica was a sign of compassion?" I ask.

"CRISPR?" I heard that word a few times today," Paddy says. "How big a deal is this thing anyway?"

"All I know is whatever part of CRISPR* Tiu developed, it cured Berk and Riedell's ataxia. It cured a genetic disease that was already rampant in Berk's body, and not yet developed in Riedell. Totally gone," I say.

"Gene editing. That's monstrous big, Dude. Ending Alzheimer's alone. Three million cases in the U.S. Forty-four million world-wide. Can you imagine the bucks there? What would you pay to have your brain back? They'll be throwing money at Berk. He's already a billionaire, he'll be a gazillionaire."

"Destiny is never going to let that happen," I say, realizing why Tiu has lived in the shadows all these years. "Isn't Lt. Garcelli coming here?" I ask Paddy.

Arlo jumps at my mention of the Lieutenant. "I have to book it, man. Don't forget this," he says, tossing me a flash drive. "This is the hospital video I hacked for Berk. This one has sound. It might help you. Remember our deal," he gives us the Vulcan split fingers as he rushes to the door. "Live long and prosper."

"There's no meeting with Garcelli," Paddy says after Arlo goes out the door.

"I know, I couldn't explain with Arlo here. I just realized why Tiu is letting Berk take credit for CRISPR. She's forcing Destiny public."

"I don't understand."

"You don't have to. It's the way Tiu works. She and Destiny are polar opposites."

The commuter customers start arriving. Paddy pours drinks, calling to me, "Don't go yet."

---

* This is representative of actual applications of CRISPR technology. In October 2018 UC Berkley doctors used CRISPR-Cas9, as it is now known, to genetically repair Delaney R, age 19, who had a rare disorder, Charcot-Marie-Tooth disease, which would have caused her to lose control of her skeletal muscles.

Shooting by, he asks, "This grand event the Bailiff mentioned. Any idea what it is?"

Before I can answer, he is at the other end of the bar. Back again.

"Do you need a hand?" I ask, realizing Kathleen isn't there.

"No," he says. "Mandell will be here in a sec to handle the beers."

Off he goes, and back again. "Kath didn't come home last night. She called to say she was staying at Starch's with Gert."

"Yep, Gert told me."

"Kath said Starch is like a kid again. New lease on life stuff. He had a bunch of ideas, something about a Coming Out party."

"This isn't good," I mumble reading a text from Intern Amy. *Mrs. Wright says Berk is calling for a Special Board Meeting at the Chronicle. One hour.*

I tell Amy I'm on my way. "Gotta go," I yell to Paddy.

"What's up?"

"Berk's still going after the Chronicle."

Chapter Twenty-One

"Retaliation, plain and simple," the reinstated Acting Chairman of the Chronicle, Walter Jackson, says, standing behind his formicable desk when I walk into his office. "Berk's still coming at us."

I get the distinct feeling Starch's old prep school buddy is taking a new approach.

"Starch is much improved," I say as if that was the question he should have asked.

"Good. Good. So I've heard. I was notified this morning by his Trust attorney that his state of incompetency was declared null and void."

"You were notified by yourself?" I ask.

"Not that it is any of your business, but it seems my dear friend failed to inform me of certain changes he'd made in his legal affairs." Walter looks across the room and I see Athena sitting in a corner reading documents.

"I will remain acting Chairman until so notified by Mr. Storch himself. The reason I ordered you here," Walter says, taking his seat behind his desk, "is because you are the cause. You and your band of hellions ejected Dr. Berk and Gayfryd Van Wie from *Bethesda House*. Storch was in their care. And your interference so infuriated Dr. Berk, he is going to take over the entire Chronicle Company in retaliation," Walter says as if the connection is obvious. "Your action sparked his reaction." Walter holds up a legal notice. "Your intrusion could cost the Company millions, or worse."

"You wanted your old chum stuffed away in a nursing home." I realize. "It cost you nothing to give up the family estate to Gayfryd. You and your cronies are settling for the Monet's and Matisse's, right? Not a bad tradeoff."

"My responsibility is to provide safe passage for the Company and its employees," Walter actually harrumphs.

Shaking my head I lean in toward the man. "You're an amazing piece of work, Walter. The Chronicle employees have no idea of all the personal sacrifice you've made on their behalf. I say we should erect a statue of you in the lobby for the grateful employees to admire."

"You're fired, you insolent bastard," Walter rages from behind his desk.

"Mrs. Wright," I call out, knowing she is hovering just out of sight. "Wally just called me a bad word. He needs to be disciplined."

Walter Jackson shudders. "I'm under contract," I remind him. "I can't be fired for insolence. That's precisely what the Boss pays me for."

Walter turns crimson.

"Look," I say, backing off slightly. "My priority is making certain Starch is safe. I can't worry about what happens to the Chronicle. That's your responsibility."

As I turn to leave it occurs to Walter Jackson to ask. "You are not reneging on our agreement, are you?"

"No. I will keep my word. The Emma School Trust will vote against a takeover."

"Good. In that case, you are dismissed."

"Not quite so fast," I say. "Quid pro quo. Isn't that the right phrase? No sense being in your company without learning something."

"I'm glad to have taught you a bit of Latin," Walter says, dismissing me as he begins reading from a document on his desk.

"That's not quite what I meant, Walt," I say, moving a few family photos so I can sit on a corner of his desk. "I gave you something you want, right? In return I want a new contract."

"I intend to review what we have in effect the moment you leave."

"Not for me Walt. Mine is brand new, and iron-clad. I want a new column for the Chronicle. Something that will draw a younger set of readers. A different point of view," I say enunciating every word. "But educated, opinionated. And I have a few other changes for the Chronicle in mind as well."

"What do you mean?"

"My new assistant is good. She deserves a weekly column when Gert returns from helping Starch. A three-year contract should give her time to establish her worth."

"Ten graphs, one year. No more."

"Twenty, and one year."

"Done. Her name?"

"Amy. I'll have to get back to you with the surname."

"It's Grant," Athena says, "Amy Grant." She approaches us, giving me a slip of paper. "I'll have the contract ready by day's end."

"Thank you, ah, Ms.?"

"Athena," she says shaking my hand as though we've never met.

"Then Athena it is. And I'll be off. Cheer up, Walt, you've got a new thoroughbred in your stable."

Outside I read Athena's note. *Gayfryd did not take the money.*

* * *

"Hang up," intern Amy says, hurrying inside my cubicle.

"I'm on with…"

"Don't care. Hang up," she orders, pushing her cell phone toward me.

"Tell Ms. Kasey I'll have to call her back," I say. It has taken six tries to get her assistant to accept my call.

"There's been another explosion. In SoHo. Emma's old hideaway. The apartment's still in your name, isn't it?" Amy says tapping the picture of a pile of rubble. The building looks like the Las Vegas casinos after they have been imploded for the television cameras.

"Initial word is gas leak," Amy says. "And I just got off the phone with a Lt. Garcelli. He wants you in his office, like yesterday."

"Does he know I lease a space in the building? Of course he does. See if you can find Gert," I tell her, grabbing my jacket. "And if a woman by the name of Athena brings a contract, look it over and tell me what you think when I get back, will you?"

"I'm not a lawyer."

"Me neither, but I just got a lesson in *quid pro quo,* so I'm down with the basics. I'm sure you can do better."

* * *

Paddy is pointing at the fire trucks on the news when I get to Parnell's.

"Lt. Garcelli wants me to surrender myself," I tell him.

"Really?"

I shrug, "Who knows? He wants me in his office ASAP."

"Remember, Garcelli is no fool. He'll know if you're being set up, but he still needs to cover his ass."

"Got it."

"Two explosions with connections to you. What's Garcelli supposed to think? Someone is working hard to pin these on you. Means, opportunity…"

"And my motive was to blow away the cops because I am infatuated with Gayfryd?"

"She might have told you about two cops who were shaking her down. Maybe even forcing themselves on her."

"Ha, more likely the other way around," I say.

"Whatever. And, you have a relationship with a former Silk Road mastermind, Arlo, who would know how to get the Semtex, even how to make the bomb."

"Okay, I can see that."

"Especially if you've got a guy like Stone feeding his boss a story."

"You think Arlo could have blown up Emma's building?"

"Arlo being Arlo," Paddy says, "anything's possible."

"But he just gave me the flash drive to nail Berk."

"He's still Arlo. Scorpion and the Frog."

"Yeah, it's his nature."

"Depending on how my old partner Garcelli wants to look at this, he could also make a case against Gayfryd and Berk," Paddy says, trying to cheer me up.

"I'd better get over there," I say, "before Stone has me convicted and strapped in the chair."

* * *

"Took your time getting here," Lt. Garcelli barks, slamming his phone down hard into the receiver.

"I walked. Needed time to think," I say, taking a chair, even though it wasn't offered.

"You write this?" Garcelli snarls, throwing the latest Chronicle headline at me.

"No."

"Is it true?"

"Could be," I answer.

Lt. Garcelli remains standing behind his desk. He's eyeing me, but some poor chump out in the bullpen catches his fury, "I'll shove that goddamn doughnut up your ass, Henderson," Garcelli yells.

I don't need to turn to know Henderson threw the powdered jelly in the trash and grabbed a phone.

"You know what detectives call a coincidence?" Garcelli says, slapping the photo of Emma's demolished building on the desk.

I don't answer.

"Bad luck. That's what we call a fucking coincidence," he laughs, sticking a used cigar in the corner of his mouth. The plastic holder is labeled "Dad."

"Why do you lease space in SoHo?"

"It was Emma's. I co-signed as her legal guardian."

"She's been deceased for years," he dismisses my explanation.

"Murdered. Emma was murdered, by the man you released from prison."

"I didn't release anyone. My job is putting perps in the can, not getting them out. Now explain SoHo."

"Goes back to when Emma was released from Bellevue."

"So you rented her a storage loft?"

"Emma was bi-polar. She needed a safe place."

"So you found her a closet in a slum building as a safe place?"

"All we could afford."

"Any of her wacko pals from the insane asylums still using her safe place?"

"No."

"Then why keep it?"

"Paddy and Kathleen use the place for storage; food cans, water, Swiss Army knives, and blankets," I say.

"That homeless stuff they do," Lt. Garcelli understands.

"Exactly," I agree, remembering Ockham's razor - simple solutions. "I took all of their storage space above the Pub to create the school, so it seemed only fair to give Paddy and Kathleen use of the SoHo place." That is close to the truth.

The real reason I still pay the rent is for Chuti Tiu. When she was working all hours stopping Berk's virus from taking over the Chronicle, Tiu needed periodic recharging. I know she still uses the place as her Shibari safe house, where she finds release practicing the Japanese bondage art form.

"Why the Swiss army knives?" Garcelli asks, stretching, shaking out a leg. The squatness of the man gives me the impression of a battered fighter. But Paddy warned me, "Don't be fooled by his appearance. Assistant Chief of D's is not a token job. Think Capone shrewd, but on the right side, most of the time."

"The knives are Gert's contribution. Said they are the best tool the homeless can have. TSA at LaGuardia has them by the boatload for free," I explain.

"Gert's a smart woman."

"Made me what I am today," I grin.

"Thought she'd be able to do better," Garcelli deadpans. "So why'd you name my dead Lieutenant the Ace of Spades?"

"He came up with the code name himself. Said no one would believe a left-wing rag like the Chronicle would call a black man by that name."

"You know your Ace wore a wire. His own. I mean he wore it all the time. From the first day at the Academy. Never knew then." Lt. Garcelli growls, throwing the unlit, chewed up cigar in the trash. "Promised my wife I'd quit."

"I'm not surprised about the wire. Guys like him need insurance."

"Still stinks," Lt. Garcelli says, fishing the Dad plastic holder from the old coffee cups in the garbage. "Bastard was a double agent."

"What does that mean?"

"Your Ace was wearing a wire for me as well. What do you think it means? My undercover rat Lieutenant was helping me clean up the Police Department, while at the same time using The Chronicle to nail this command to the wall."

Garcelli pauses, looking for another cigar he can't smoke. "His ass was so wired he couldn't take a shit."

I wonder how much of this Arlo knows.

"Were you and Paddy anywhere near the SoHo loft last night?"

"Where do you think the flash drives came from? We were out in the early hours."

"And you rigged the building to blow?"

"Not a chance."

"Then who would?"

"I don't have a clue. We done here?"

Lt. Garcelli keeps staring at me. "Ten dead so far, three amputations, and hundreds maimed. Last night, two, maybe three dozen homeless injured. And that's just what we found. Who knows what's under the rubble. The Chronicle's attempts to connect the two explosions will only bring in the Feds. Help I don't need right now."

"I don't control what the Chronicle prints."

"Yeah, right." Garcelli squeezes past his desk to my side. "Your wife find anything on those drives of yours?"

"They aren't my flash drives," I say.

Garcelli slaps his hand on the metal desk. "Let's quit dancing around here. I don't think you, your wife, or Paddy had anything to do with the SoHo explosion. Our IT folks loaded up those drives Paddy gave me and dumped the data. They don't have a prayer of sorting through any of this within the next century. I need your wife's help." He slaps a bag of flash drives on the desk. "But you don't really need these, do you? You have your own set."

I nod. "I'll see what she can do. You get any demands from terrorists?" I ask, ever the reporter.

"Don't be printing another inciting story," Garcelli warns.

Chapter Twenty-Two

Riedell and I play a game of unspoken conversation at breakfast, communicating while not actually speaking. She insists we play. I point to a story in my stack of newspapers. Riedell twitches an eyebrow of recognition, then waits for me to find a topic she has circled. I'm supposed to connect the circles to understand the bigger picture. Occasionally, I do.

Chuti Tiu has joined our breakfast ritual, in the flesh, since our nuptials, although it's generally not breakfast for her. She's probably returning from Singapore or Chennai, India. I had become accustomed to the holograms; seeing her live always startles me. We each get a kiss on the head before Chuti opens her kimchi, and Riedell dips into her granola mix, both courtesy of Mandell. And neither the least bit tempting to me.

Chuti is a beautiful Santa Claus no one ever sees. Her gifts to scientists around the world are what Riedell circles in my newspapers for our odd breakfast game. Tiu doesn't explain the complexity; she shows the simplicity. That is her elegance.

I occasionally get a head butt from Rowdy or Yeti as they climb over me, hurrying to capture the sunny spot in the nook beside my daughter. Domestic tranquility I never knew I wanted. Do I really have to go to work?

***

"You look like..." Gert doesn't finish.

"I know. What the cat dragged in."

Gert shakes her head. "I wouldn't be so trite. Remember, I work at a big city newspaper. I was going to say, like a sack of rusty doorknobs," she says handing me an envelope.

I am feeling more rusty than knobby. "Riedell told me this morning I was eating the cats' food again."

"Trying to keep your coat soft, are you?" Gert says stroking my corduroy.

I know I'm running on empty, but I'm pretty sure I would have noticed if I was eating cat food. Yet my instant oatmeal was in their bowls.

"What's in the envelope?" I ask Gert.

"Went out electronically last evening. This is the formal version."

"The Grand Event?" I guess opening the invitation; embossed Crane stationary, *Bethesda House* at the top. Nice. "And what do we owe this to?"

"He's calling it a Grand Event, nothing else. All a mystery, designed to keep his friends confused. Starch has seen the light since he got his second chance."

"Might have to change his nickname."

"Which brings me to why I'm back here in the office," Gert says. "I know the timing's not great, with Stone, Berk, bombs and all the rest, but I'm running this extravaganza for Starch. Which means, poor you will have to get by with Amy."

"She gets her own tea most mornings," I say, raising my eyebrows, offering a salacious grin.

"I'll put a stop to that," Gert says lowering her eye. "Don't start back-flushing on me," she warns. "And I didn't receive my wedding invitation from you."

"Me either," I admit.

"So that's how it is?"

"Kidding aside, I have no idea how it is. Except our Destiny alert is at DEFCON 1. Stone pushed his way into our home, and Tiu almost annihilated him."

"That's not good."

"She took him down, big time. He was so confused, he left without his gun and shield."

"I need to get a copy of that video," Gert grins. And by the way, Van Wie came over earlier screaming for you. And I mean that literally," Gert says pointing at the empty Managing Editor's glass office at the far end of the City Room. "Seems his wife is moving back into his home, along with her new partner Berk."

"Wait until they see this," I say tapping the invitation in my hands.

"Every shaker in the City, and more than a few from DC are invited. I asked Riedell not to tell you."

"She didn't. And when do you talk to Riedell?"

"Every nanosecond or two. We're on SuperLink together."

"I don't even want to ask."

"Good. Because it is not for you."

Amy runs up and kisses me on the cheek.

"Well, looks like the two of you are getting along," Gert grins. "I only stopped by for a minute to give you the invite."

"I heard Starch is improving?" Amy asks, trying to play cool, but she clearly has just come down from Athena's on high and can barely contain her excitement.

"Improving? That's an understatement!" Gert laughs. "Our nurse friend, Kathleen, had to stay with him or he'd be booking a ride on the Space Shuttle. Got an interesting bucket list. Got to run. Come down and look. I'm being chauffeured around town in a Rolls, meeting with Kings and Princes."

"Sounds grand," Amy says, still wired, beaming at Gert who obviously knows about her column and contract.

"I told you he's not always a self-centered ass. Now, both of you, cancel any other plans. Sunday is the Grand Event. I've already been to Starch's Club and put that place in an uproar. The Governor and Mayor are locked. Tiu is bringing Riedell and the entire school. There is more. Don't ask. Be surprised. I've got to run."

Gert hugs Amy. "That's for you as well," she says tapping the envelope. "You walk me down?" Gert asks taking my arm as Amy rushes to the phone.

"You did a good thing there," Gert says jerking her head back at Amy as we push through the doors to the stairwell. "Starch has improved big time, but he knows his body is temporarily disguising the truth."

"How long?"

"No one can tell. But he knows he is on borrowed time. He told us, Kath and me, it's his Faustian bargain. That, no one can know. Especially," she says, eyes going up toward the Executive floor.

"I understand."

"He believes in you. He wants you to stay on the Board. Not because he thinks you are the person to run the Chronicle Company. He wants you to keep reminding the others of their responsibility. That's what Shawn does, he said. A good soul and an asshole is a rare combination. That's a quote," she says, poking my chest.

"I thought you and Kath flushed the drugs out of him."

Gert shrugs. "Now, here's the biggie," she says. "Gayfryd is not Starch's daughter."

"He is disowning her? Can't say I blame him after this last stunt."

"I said, listen. And keep this to yourself. Gayfryd never was Starch's daughter. Starch did sleep with the mother, often it seems. He was young and was doing what young men do with certain women. The problem came when Starch needed to marry a proper woman, arranged by his parents."

"Old money, that's the way they work"

"Right. But the woman he was using got pregnant. She knows Starch is from old money and goes straight to the parents. They buy her off."

I nod. "Nothing new in that story."

"Except Starch had a very thorough medical examination yesterday. In addition to the high probability of a recurring stroke, they found he had childhood measles. Starch is sterile."

"You mean all these years Starch has been believing Gayfryd is his daughter?"

"Seems so."

"But old money gets blackmailed all the time. They would have checked out her claim long ago."

"Maybe, maybe not. They probably told Starch they would handle his indiscretion so it wouldn't jeopardize his marriage," Gert says shaking her head.

"Clever on their part, really. The parents get leverage over their son. They pay hush money to the mother, but never child support, so no admission. First rule: protect the gold. And the gold is their boy."

"The wrinkle," Gert says, "is the woman tells her daughter that Starch is her father."

"Makes sense. And the proof is the checks, which will only come if they keep silent."

"After Starch's parents die, his old friend Walter Jackson takes over paying the money. Naturally, he needs to find out why. So he hires an investigator. That's where the files came from."

"And Starch knows he's sterile?"

"He does now. I read him the report."

"Walter know as well?"

"My bet, that part was left out of the files Mrs. Wright left on your desk. But I have the feeling Sunday is clean slate day."

We round the corner to the ground floor. "Want a lift?" Gert offers.

"Thanks, but I'll walk. I have a few things to absorb."

Gert turns around, jumps up and kisses me on the cheek. "Sexual harassment," she says and jumps in the waiting limo.

"Keep her safe, Jeffrey," I wave to her driver.

Chapter Twenty-Three

Paddy is slammed. I head up the back stairs, hoping Tiu has returned and found some evidence linking Berk to the bombings. Not likely Berk would leave himself unprotected, but Tiu is Tiu, and I bet on her.

"Hey Rowdy, where is everyone?" I ask our Maine Coon who greets me at the door. Rowdy replies by butting my legs. Hearing Riedell's skates, I turn.

"I ran all the drives," Tiu says startling me.

"Any luck?"

"You don't want everything going to the police, so I'll give you a version that will satisfy Lt. Garcelli. Riedell is having a little trouble with the print-out, but it will be ready in a few." Tiu says

"Any surprises?" I ask.

"That's for later. Berk still tops the list. But that's as far as I can go right now. We're going to need Garcelli to run some forensics".

"I don't like the sound of this. I have Garcelli primed and loaded to put Berk back in the slammer. So, what aren't you telling me?"

"I don't want to guess. I need facts for Sunway* first, and I don't have enough from Arlo's drives."

Tiu puts a hot mug of dark English Breakfast Tea on the table beside a banana, and a small blueberry yogurt. "Eat and listen. You have to be in Family Court in two hours. You're taking Riedell with you."

"Hi Shawn," Riedell skates into the kitchen.

"Hey there, I missed you," I say pushing my yogurt over to her.

---

* The Sunway TaihuLight is one of ten supercomputers in the world, and it is a colossus.

Built between June 2016 and June 2018 in China, at peak performance she is capable of 125,000 trillion calculations per second using 10.6 million cores.

This is a major comparison stretch, but a typical home computer uses four cores, capable of around 12 million calculations per second. Not bad, but the Sunway is 2.65 million times faster.

In this story, Chuti Tiu developed core algorithms for the Sunway, one of the reasons she was given her own system.

"Make sure you call him Daddy in front of the Judge," Tiu tells Riedell as she puts a finger full of Vaseline on my lip, and sweeps a safety razor over my face, catching the spots I've missed.

"Court is your focus for now. Kathleen…"

"Something go wrong with Starch?"

"No, he's good. He's on a mission. Kathleen is going to be your medical expert for Court," Tiu says. "I prepared her. Don't worry about Starch or anyone else, you need to stay focused."

"Okay."

"I've got Mandell's men standing by. You will have an invisible escort to the Court. If the Judge makes a ruling against us, Mandell's team is authorized to kidnap Riedell."

"Kidnap? Authorized?"

"Yes, by me," Tiu says. "Don't put it past Berk to try." Tiu puts her hand up, stopping my concern. "It's worth the risk taking Riedell to Court, but Berk can't so much as touch her, you understand?"

I nod, yes.

"If it goes wrong, I'll disappear as well. I'll be with Riedell. You can't come with us. Don't even try looking. We need you here. Understand?"

"I get it."

"Good. Now eat. Your body needs fuel."

"Don't irk Irksome," Riedell warns me.

* * *

Stuffing the folder Tiu prepared for me into my satchel, I locate my ever disappearing glasses, and grab my jacket. "Riedell, we have to go," I yell into the warehouse.

"Your daughter is ready," Tiu says from behind me. I turn and stop.

"You look different," I say.

Riedell smiles. "Aunt Chuti did my hair. It's a French braid," she says turning to show me the elaborate weaving.

"Nice, it suits you," I say. But there's more. Riedell's soulful eyes seem more alert than usual. She has her mother's high cheekbones, a little fuller, and a bit rosier. Where's that freckle I like to touch in the mornings to let her know I'm there. And that brilliant white smile looks even brighter. Is she wearing some makeup?

"We got Riedell a new wardrobe," ever elegant Tiu says. A crisp white blouse, short jacquard jacket, and creased wool slacks. Perfect. And then I notice, Riedell is wearing shoes.

"So I see. Just the right look," I say, turning away as emotions well up. My little girl is no longer my little girl.

* * *

Judge R is in full judicial dress waiting with his wife, Bailiff Mrs. R, at the court house door.

"Young lady, I'm Judge R," he introduces himself to Riedell, offering his hand. "My wife will be your escort. Anything you need, please ask. Okay?"

"I'll be fine Judge R," Riedell says. "No need to be concerned on my account."

Judge R smiles at his wife. "Thank you. Glad one of us is cool."

"Mrs. R was a guest in my house, now I'm a guest in hers. Don't worry," Riedell tells Judge R, putting a comforting hand on his arm, "we'll get along just fine."

When did this little girl become so cunning, I wonder, as my daughter glides up to Mrs. R, taking her hand. "My mother had soft hands like yours. The kind with strength below the surface."

Mrs. R almost melts. "Well, what do you know, what do you know," she manages. "How about a hot chocolate for a chilly morning like this?" She hurries them away as the Senator, his entourage, and Berk approach through the revolving doors.

"I'm primarily a tea person myself," I hear Riedell charming the poor woman as they leave, "But a cocoa with you sounds perfect. See you soon, Daddy," she waves.

"Try not to be too perfect," I say waving back, fairly certain no one but me notices the gesture she gives me.

"Morning Judge R," the Senator booms. "If I may Judge R, this is Dr. Darieux who has flown in just this morning, from Geneva. She is Dr. Berk's mentor. The guiding light behind CRISPR. I asked her here so she can provide this Court with crucial information."

"Doctor, an honor," Judge R shakes her hand as if he's touching royalty. "And why am I not surprised to learn a woman is behind such a brilliant medical discovery?"

"You're too kind," she says. "The discovery of CRISPR was a collaborative effort, but we are a long way from the cures the media has heaped upon us. They know so little of science and medicine," she says, conspiratorially, touching the Judge's arm.

"Of course," Judge R says as if he understands.

The doctor is a stunning woman, exquisitely dressed in a designer suit. Her hand and wrist are bejeweled in what I am certain is a small fortune. If the Senator really needs a medical expert, he's gone overboard, suspiciously so.

"Mr. Shaw's expert is already upstairs waiting," Judge R tells a surprised Senator Foghorn.

That's good for me. Whether passing out soup in the Bowery, inserting an IV in a hospital patient, or testifying in court, Kathleen is rock solid. Foghorn's prima donna belongs in The Hague, not Judge R's bizarre Family Court.

"Please excuse the informality," Judge R says to Dr. Darieux. "Mrs. R and I try to keep our Family Court comfortable and secure for the children involved in these troubling proceedings."

"Understandable," Dr. Darieux agrees. Her accent is subtle, her tone confident.

"Everyone," Judge R raises his voice, "follow me. We will be using the rear entrance to the courtroom."

Judge R waves 'Good Morning' with his Chronicle in hand to a roomful of children as we pass through. "Our day care center," he tells Dr. Darieux, who walks regally beside Judge R as if she is inspecting the facility.

"I hope to see your daycare school someday soon as well," Judge R says to me.

"Anytime," I say, hoping he doesn't take me up on that offer.

"Here we are," Judge R says as we enter the rear of the converted cafeteria. "The outer office is taken at the moment so Doctor, I'm going to ask you to take a seat away from the table until the Senator introduces you to the proceedings." He gestures to an orange plastic chair in the corner.

"Before we begin," Judge R holds up the Chronicle. "I have a feeling you had something to do with this," he says to me, shaking out the paper enthusiastically. The headline boasts: *Publisher Donates $3 Billion to Children.*

"Inadmissible. Grand standing," Senator Foghorn booms over Judge R's shoulder.

"A three-billion-dollar donation is inadmissible?" Judge R asks. "I haven't brought court to session yet, and you are objecting?"

"Mr. Storch is trying to influence the Judge prior to complete examination of the evidence. I humbly suggest presiding judge recuse himself from these proceedings."

"Sit down Senator, and humbly blow your recusal out your ass," Judge R says before banging his wooden name plaque on the table, calling the court to order.

Berk is sitting at the table in the middle of his legal entourage. He doesn't look me in the eye, while taking in the gathering in general, Kathleen in particular.

"I'll be damned," I say sliding the Chronicle in front of Kathleen. "Did you know about this?"

"Tiu didn't want you to know unless the Judge brought it up," Kathleen whispers an apology. "Starch is on a mission. He and that big blonde attorney were locked in the butterfly room for hours."

"Butterfly room?" Judge R overhears.

"One of Starch's hobbies," I explain.

"Starch?"

"A Chronicle endearment," I reply quickly moving on. "Judge R? Now that my medical expert is here," I say indicating Kathleen, "I ask that the video of the rape of my legal ward, Emma, be replayed."

"This is not a rape trial as this newspaper reporter is trying to claim," the Senator adds.

"He does have a point, explain," Judge R presses me.

"I happened to be at Eastside Mercy visiting a patient on the day of Emma's rape," I say.

"Sit," Judge R orders Foghorn before he gets the words out.

"By coincidence, I saw Mr. Berk in a hospital bed being treated for his ataxia condition. He was abusive toward me and the staff, excessively so, as if he wanted me to remember that particular occasion."

"Speculative, Judge," Foghorn tries again, and is ignored.

"Berk was medicated, and relied on crutches to walk. Here is a copy of my signature, dated on a sign-in sheet as proof I was at the hospital. I have sworn statements from three nurses who vividly remember Mr. Berk's condition, and verbal abuse. Also, there is a record that Security was summoned," I pull the documents from the folder Tiu gave me. I knew I could count on her.

"And the reason you are requesting a replay of the video?"

"I believe that a second review will show Mr. Berk's true purpose. An item we overlooked, Judge R, due to the violent and disgusting nature of the scene we witnessed."

"Judge R, really?"

"I'm inclined to agree with the Senator."

"Let him play it," Berk yells out. "I don't mind."

"I'm sure you don't," I say. "However, I'm not making the request for your pleasure. I would like the Court to hear a medical expert's opinion on Mr. Berk's condition, and the likelihood he could maintain an erection necessary to impregnate his victim, Emma."

"Dr. Darieux, does this topic fall into your area of expertise?"

"Your Honor, I am a medical doctor with a PhD in genetics and psychology. Insemination is a familiar subject," she says without the slightest hesitation.

Judge R motions for me to load the JJJ 45 C projection with the flash drive. Kathleen reaches into her medical valise and places a plastic bag on the table. The attorneys at Berk's table immediately confer.

The Senator jumps to his feet. "Judge R, at this time Mr. Berk would like to withdraw his visitation application."

"What's the problem?" the Judge asks.

"No problem, Judge R," the Senator says. "There will be no need to re-play the recording."

"Judge, I think my expert's opinion will clarify Mr. Berk's change of heart," I suggest.

"The petition for visitation is withdrawn, Mr. Shaw. There is no need…"

"Judge R. Reviewing the video will preclude a future petition," I tell him. "Why not resolve the issue now, rather than waste the court's valuable time in the future."

"Objection."

"Noted. Roll the video," Judge R orders.

The video is just as offensive as the last showing.

"Stop," Kathleen orders. "Back up. Stop. Enhance right there," Kathleen points using her finger shadow as a marker. "Judge," she says taking the syringe from the bag. "In Mr. Berk's hand is a syringe. As the Doctor can attest, it's an insemination syringe."

Berk isn't Riedell's biological father, I realize.

"Here is the list of medications, from Eastside Mercy's records, administered to Mr. Berk that day." Kathleen points to the bottom of the page, "Side effects; erectile dysfunction, along with various other problems. I would have had a better chance of impregnating my friend, Emma, myself that horrible day. Unless I used this device filled with another man's sperm."

Eyes of disgust turn on Berk, quieting the room.

Dr. Darieux breaks the silence. "The child's mother, Emma, was my daughter."

The Senator leaps to his feet. "We are amending our petition. We now request full custody of said child to Dr. Darieux." His assistant passes a prepared legal document to the Judge.

"Well, this looks to be an interesting morning," Judge R decides.

Dr. Darieux stands. "My youngest daughter, who goes by the name Chuti Tiu, created a sham marriage to this self-described *Unflawed* character," she says opening a hand in my direction, "for the sole purpose of keeping me from the legal, and I might add, moral responsibility of raising my granddaughter."

"Have you made your desires known to a court, or to your daughter, previously?" Judge R asks.

"I have, as Dr. Berk can testify," she gestures toward him. "While in my employ at The Destiny Foundation, he was charged with locating my eldest daughter, Emma."

"You lost touch with your own daughter?" Judge R asks.

"Emma suffered horribly from bi-polar disorder. I had no choice but to commit her to an institution. When she became of legal age, dear Emma bounced from one institution to another, as Dr. Berk discovered. She had several abortions, lived like a vagabond on and off the streets. In the end, she became enslaved to this person," Dr. Darieux points at me. "Under his control, reconciliation with her became hopeless."

"And you are now petitioning this court for full custody of your granddaughter, Riedell?" Judge R asks.

"Your Honor, I have no alternative. When Dr. Berk informed me of the marriage between my youngest daughter, Chuti, and this man," she points at me again, "I knew their intention was to continue depriving the child of her true heritage, and the considerable benefits of my Foundation."

"You've made attempts," Foghorn prompts.

"Oh, yes. Of course. I've made numerous entreaties over the years for a reconciliation, and was summarily rebuffed. It's seems I'm left with no alternative, other than legal adjudication."

"Yet you allowed Riedell to live in Mr. Shaw's home for almost nine years since your daughter, Emma's passing. This is the first time you have taken any legal action. Why is that?" Judge R asks. He's smelling a rat, the same as I am.

Dr. Darieux shows the first blush of irritation, a slight head quiver. But her obsequious smile returns so fast, I'm not sure Judge R notices the tremor.

"Judge R," Foghorn protests.

Judge R's flash of anger is enough to quiet the Senator, allowing Dr. Darieux the freedom to advocate on her own.

"My daughter, Chuti Tiu, is intellectually gifted, profoundly so," Dr. Darieux begins explaining as she circles the converted cafeteria table, moving closer to Judge R, taking command of the room. "I and my late husband," Dr. Darieux stops, pausing reverently to his memory. "We devoted our professional lives to nourishing Chuti's talents." Looking down, she shakes her head, as if conveying her failure. "Our reward: extraordinary brilliance squandered to debauchery and vindictiveness."

I know it's an act, but Dr. Darieux's presence is mesmerizing. Her elegance, aristocratic bearing and beauty, captivating.

Judge R stands as Dr. Darieux nears. She puts her hand on his shoulder. Seductive for him, while appearing distraught to the rest of us. "True, in retrospect, I may not have been the most compassionate mother. However, once I accepted my daughters were lost to me, I have taken refuge in my work with The Destiny Foundation."

Senator Foghorn slides Judge R a leather bound folder. I can see Destiny Society embossed in gold lettering at the top, with Destiny Foundation below.

"At the Foundation, we are dedicated to curing debilitating conditions like Dr. Berk's ataxia," she says nodding in his direction. "I can tell you the elimination of MS, and quite possibly Alzheimer's is within our grasp." Dr. Darieux stops speaking, touching the tome while allowing the magnitude of her disclosure to sink in. "My granddaughter will receive every advantage the Society can offer."

Judge R opens the portfolio.

"As you can see, The Destiny Society enables many corporations, research institutes and humanitarian projects throughout the world. We are 100% privately endowed, and enjoy the generosity of some recognizable names."

"Recognizable!" Judge R blurts. Embarrassed, he waves his hand for the room to ignore his comment, nodding for Dr. Darieux to continue.

"My granddaughter, Riedell, has been evaluated. She possesses an exceptional intellectual capacity. Possibly even beyond that of my daughter, Chuti." Dr. Darieux gestures toward me. "Can you imagine a child of yours, born with an intellectual gift that can affect the world for generations, and squandering that gift?"

Dr. Darieux pauses for effect. "It should be obvious why I cannot allow a child with such potential as Riedell, to waste another moment in the company of a worthless libertine such as this," she says giving me a baleful stare.

I give her a wide smile.

She turns away in disgust.

"This pitiful man is a muckraker who coerced my only remaining daughter into a sham marriage for the sole purpose of extorting me and The Destiny Foundation. Using a child, no less. Shameful," she finishes, returning to her plastic chair.

"Anything to say in your defense, Mr. Shaw, or would you like to leave it there?" Judge R asks with a wicked glint in his eye. "And I must say, for the record, a Pulitzer prize-winning reporter is more than a muckraker, my dear," he looks toward Dr. Darieux.

I hold up a flash drive. "I've brought this from my wife, Chuti Tiu."

"I most vehemently protest," the Senator blusters.

"Of course you do," Judge R says.

"How am I to question the veracity of this mystery person if she cannot even bless us with her presence?"

Judge R has been flip with the Senator's objections so far, but this time Foghorn has made a valid point. I see Judge R hesitating to dismiss the objection this time.

"Judge," I say passing him an envelope. "Confidential, for you only."

Judge R closes his eyes and spins the envelope on the table deciding. He opens it, reads, flips to the next page and the next, slowly standing. Without a word, he returns the three sheets of paper into the envelope and slides it back to me. "Whatever objection you have Senator, consider it overruled."

"But…"

Judge R points to the JJJ 45 C. "Let's see what she has to say."

"Objection, Judge R."

"Noted. Prepare your questions while Ms. Tiu has her say. I'll get answers for you. Good enough?"

"Well…"

"Good. Roll it."

"Good morning," my wife appears on the screen. "My name is Chuti Tiu. I am sister to Emma, Aunt to Riedell, wife of Shawn Shaw, and daughter of Professor Darieux. Also I am the subject of the best-selling novel *The Girl in the Freezer,* which details some of Professor Darieux's scientific experiments on children."

I slide the book in front of Judge R. He nods his thanks.

"May I suggest you ask Dr. Darieux for her passport to verify her identity?"

The screen stops, displaying a pause symbol.

"Good point," Judge R agrees. "My bailiff usually checks identities. Dr. Darieux, may I?" he asks holding out his hand.

Slightly miffed at being questioned, Dr. Darieux hands her passport to one of the Senator's associates.

"Pay particular attention to the birthdate," Chuti Tiu says from the screen. The pause symbol returns.

Judge R does as instructed, makes a mental calculation and rechecks the date. "Forgive this indelicacy, Dr. Darieux, but according to your passport, you are seventy-six years of age?"

"That's correct," Dr. Darieux answers, allowing a mild smile of satisfaction, knowing every eye in the room is looking at her in wonder.

The on/off sequencing gives the impression Tiu has timed her presentation for discussion, but no one has questions. The pause symbol flashes as the video returns to play, although no one has touched the JJJ 45 C or the remote.

"*The Girl in the Freezer* book is an account of Emma's and my childhood," Tiu continues. "It is not quite the advantaged upbringing our mother would have you believe. Emma was tested, declared unusable and sent to an institution. Perhaps a blessing in disguise. I was deemed acceptable, and raised in the castle's meat locker as the prime subject of The Destiny Foundation's central research: enhancing brain function while living in frigid temperatures. For ten years I lived in a 400 square foot dungeon, fed only as rewards when I solved advanced mathematical puzzles, and warmed only when I was being molested by my father."

"Preposterous," Dr. Darieux protests.

"The Destiny Foundation bought the rights to my book so they could bury any reference to their research. Also The Destiny Foundation does not want it known that Emma and I were sired by semen purchased from a sperm bank, the so-called Genius Repository."

"Hearsay based on a novel? Judge R, please. This woman," Senator Foghorn waves to the projection, "is turning this proceeding into a farce."

"Dr. Darieux, do you recognize this book?" I ask holding it up per Chuti's instruction.

"Drivel."

"I'll take that as a yes. Thank you, Dr. Darieux."

The JJJ 45 C restarts before Foghorn can object.

"CRISPR," Tiu says. "Your Foundation actually made the gene-editing discovery, isn't that right?"

"It's not my Foundation," Dr. Darieux corrects. "We are part of The Destiny Society, a private organization."

"But you run the Foundation, isn't that right?"

"I have that privilege, yes."

"And James Berk works for you, isn't that correct?"

"In a sense, yes."

"So, in short, you direct a scientific research center funded by very wealthy individuals. Do you intend to make this cure for genetic diseases like Multiple Sclerosis and Alzheimer's available to the public?"

"Dr. Berk's results have already been published. In fact, he is about to be…"

"That's not what I am asking," Tiu interrupts. "Does your Foundation intend to offer your genetic cure for Alzheimer's to the world at large? A simple yes or no will do."

As the room turns its focus on Dr. Darieux, Senator Foghorn begins to rise, drawing the attention of Judge R. who warns him, "Don't even try."

The Judge instructs Dr. Darieux to answer the question.

"That is far too complicated a question to answer with a yes or no. There are…"

"Yes or no works for me," Judge R says.

"Then I'm afraid the answer must be no." Dr. Darieux smooths her skirt before continuing. "Obviously my daughter is trying to impugn my integrity, and cast me as an unfit guardian for my granddaughter, Riedell."

"Is that what you and Ms. Tiu are attempting, Mr. Shaw?"

"I'm not a lawyer, Judge R. I wouldn't know how to *impugn* a witness. Besides, I only heard about the good doctor's legal maneuverings a moment ago."

Judge R smiles. "I have the distinct feeling you came prepared. Lawyer or not," Judge R says.

"Prepared with a video that cannot be questioned," the Senator adds.

"You will have that opportunity," Judge R assures the Senator. Chuti Tiu's screen turns black.

"Okay then," Judge R says. "Dr. Berk, since you have concluded your business with this court, I see no reason to enjoy your presence any longer. Find yourself a very good criminal defense attorney. Be assured I'll be passing on the relevant transcripts to the District Attorney."

Berk says nothing as he leaves.

Judge R resumes control. "As you are all aware, this case has taken an entirely new direction; from visitation to full custody. These instructions are to both parties. In three days I will expect to see detailed financial statements, living and educational plans for Riedell, verification of lineage, and contingency arrangements. This last requirement may sound harsh, Dr. Darieux, but as you are, according to this," Judge R holds up her passport, "a senior citizen, it is a considerable factor."

"Riedell is my granddaughter," Dr. Darieux sputters her indignity to Judge R.

"Any further arguments, presentations, histrionics or discussion? Good. You will be notified. In the interim, Riedell will continue to stay with Mr. Shaw and his wife, Chuti Tiu. Normally I would require you to keep the child in this jurisdiction. However, according to this invitation," he waves his envelope," Riedell is to be the Guest of Honor at Mr. Storch's ceremonies in Connecticut this afternoon. Full disclosure, Mrs. R and I will be attending."

"Judge R," the Senator objects.

"Every Family Court judge in New York, New Jersey and Connecticut is invited. This donation goes to the heart of our Association's charter. If you can show the Chronicle Publisher arranged his stroke, recovery, and very generous bequest to influence me, I'll ask any Judge you desire to conduct a new hearing."

"We are pleased to be in your impartial Court, Judge R," the Senator decides, raising his hand.

"I thought so."

"Your Honor," Dr. Darieux addresses Judge R. "I understand my granddaughter is in the adjacent chambers. I'd like to meet her. Introduce myself, and let her see I'm not the wicked witch, as I've no doubt been portrayed," she says raising a cuffed hand to her bosom at the foolishness of the representation.

"I'm sorry, Dr. Darieux, that won't be possible right now." Judge R concludes pounding his wooden *Family Court* plaque twice on the table.

"We need to get to Connecticut," Kathleen tells me holding up her cell phone. "Tiu is downstairs in the limo ready to take us."

"You go. I've got to stop at the paper. Amy has been texting me. I'll meet you at Starch's."

Chapter Twenty-Four

Van Wie, surrounded by staff, spots me returning to the City Room. Gayfryd sees me as well. Long, slender, and radiant, as if she has just returned from a spa week, she casts me a look that screams *'I warned you.'*

"Quiet down please," Van Wie orders, tapping his pen on the temporary lectern. "I have the privilege and honor to introduce my wife, Gayfryd Van Wie, daughter of our beloved Chairman, and his heir and successor," he says as she rises. Dressed in creamy white, she resembles an angel from this distance. The angel of death, I think to myself.

"My dear father will not be returning," she announces. "Although Daddy has improved, he is not expected to make a full recovery. This morning I was granted guardianship. I have assumed his duties at the Chronicle Company."

The City Room is eerily quiet. The staff is listening to Gayfryd, keeping their heads down, not giving away their feelings.

I don't need to hear the rest.

* * *

"This came from Athena," Amy says handing me a note. *Do not give up.*

"How'd it go in Family Court?" Amy asks.

"No decision. Met my mother-in-law, though. Unusual woman," I understate, flipping through my messages, keeping an eye on Van Wie. He's acting particularly odd. The front page about Starch's donation is taped to his office glass facing towards us with a heavy black "X" from corner-to-corner.

"Sending me a message?" I ask Amy.

Amy looks up. "Looks like 'go to Hell' from where I'm sitting. Word is Walter Jackson and staff are in every court that will listen. Lt. Garcelli called," Amy mentions. "Says he'll see you in Rikers if you're not in his office with his information, now. You might need to see this first." Amy hands me a folder.

"What is it?"

"The other Chairman sent it with Mrs. Wright."

"Walter Jackson is recalling my loan," I say reading the first paragraph. "Apparently forgiving my loan was more proof of Starch's inability to handle his finances, even before the stroke."

"Is he just getting back at you?"

"It's more than that. Looks like Jackson and the Board are backing Gayfryd," I say looking across the City Room. "They're trying to prove incompetency."

"Might be worth a quick stop upstairs, see what he has to say."

"He's probably already on his way to Starch's *Bethesda House*. I'm sure he wants a ringside seat. Whatever Starch does, Walter plans to have overturned through the courts. He won't miss a chance to see his old school chum make a fool of himself."

"My bet is on Starch. Gert says the old man is running at hyper-speed, like he's reborn. Gert has caterers trucking in food from half the restaurants in town, bought out all the Greenwich liquor stores. Gert's in her glory."

Amy shows me a photo Gert sent. There must be thirty catering tents on the front lawn.

"It starts at four," Amy says. "You should have left an hour ago, unless you have a helicopter."

"I have to get to Garcelli's first. I don't think I'm going to make the party. What about you?"

Amy lifts her chin toward the front of the room. "I think the story's here. Do you know the NYPD ransacked Van Wie's apartment?"

"Didn't hear about that," I smile. "I think you're right. Good call. When you wrap up your exclusive, stop at Parnell's. The owner is my friend, Paddy. He'll have Starch's ceremony on TV and can point out the players. A decent cup of chowder comes with."

"I'll meet you there."

* * *

"Garcelli is on a rampage," Paddy says, picking up my call before I hear a ring.

"Heading there now," I say.

"Make it fast," Paddy suggests. "Kathleen filled me in on the Court proceedings. Sounds slightly leaning your way. Tiu has Riedell, and is already gone, but…"

"I know. Speaking of Tiu, met her mother today. Kathleen tell you?"

"Yeah. Phenomenal was all she said. What's she like?"

"Seventy-six. Looks like a young forty-five. Stylish, impeccably dressed. Smart as a whip. Worked Judge R over like he was her slave. Dripping in money. Dazzling."

"H-m-m, who would have known. Better get your ass in gear. See you when I see you."

* * *

"Kath?" I answer my cell phone, misreading the caller ID.

"Garcelli," the grumbly voice answers, not amused. "There is a car waiting outside for you."

I look out Parnell's to see the NYPD cruiser idling at the curb. There's no way I am getting inside.

"I can get to your office on my own."

"I hear it's shit-on-a-shingle day at Rikers."

"Ten minutes, one stop."

"Don't keep me waiting."

"Should I bring a paper cup for Det. Stone?" I say as he hangs up.

* * *

"Gimme," Lt. Garcelli orders the instant my escort pushes me into his office where a techie is waiting to make copies of Tiu's report.

"The Sunway computer analyzed the Helmsley explosion for intensity and concentration. Using over ten thousand data points," I explain from Riedell's hand-written note, "with a very high degree of certainty, the explosive was placed on the concrete beneath the squad, not attached or integrated into the vehicle." I stop to let it sink in. "A detailed explanation of how the Sunway made this analysis is on the thumb drive."

"That's enough for now," Lt. Garcelli decides. "Someone shoved or rolled the bomb under the squad after it was parked outside the Helmsley?"

"Correct. The computer assembled facial recognition scans from the fixed cameras in the area, and tourist photographs uploaded into the Cloud * during that period."

"I didn't know that was possible."

"It gets better," I tell Garcelli, checking Riedell's note. "The computer crossed the facials of every person passing or in the building who has any association with the two police officers within the past ten years. That includes arrests, financial transactions, family, business and personal relationships. Even waiter's names on restaurant receipts. If they passed through the area, within the one hour the car was there, they are on this list of 346 names. I'm one of them," I add.

"Then my bomber is on this list," Lt. Garcelli decides.

"Likely, but not certain."

"Why not?"

"The attack might have been purely random; a cop hater, gripe against the Helmsley, or someone intent on creating terror in our fine City. Or the bomber used an unsuspecting surrogate. But this list is a good start, until the next."

"SoHo?"

"If that explosion is the next. It may actually be an accident. Regardless, there is only one street camera near that location. The resolution margin makes correlating facials near impossible."

"Cell phones?"

I shake my head, "no luck."

Lt. Garcelli grimaces in agreement. "Unless Paddy or you were the intended victim. You wired?" he asks me.

"No."

---

* The Cloud is purposefully named to sound mysterious, even ethereal. It is comprised of numerous enormous data storage and retrieval units similar to the mass IBM data centers of the 1970's. Back then these centers were located away from the main buildings as separate structures, often surrounded by barbed-wire fences. Data was transferred and stored on magnetic tape.

Fifty years later, the Cloud is mega-times faster, far more complex, and considerably more reliable, but doesn't look much different from the Vietnam era data centers, other than being scattered around the world.

The centers are linked together by various methods, so that an interruption in one facility is instantly supplanted by another. Hence the singular name, the Cloud.

"Mind if we check?"

I put my hands in the air as Stone's whiskey breath wafts over my shoulder. He scans me with the wand, pressing extra hard at the sore spot on my lower back. Obviously the hallway video has become general entertainment throughout the station.

"Enjoy Antarctica?" I ask turning around.

"Fuck you, Shaw," Stone says, tapping the wand on my ribs before leaving.

Between my cracked ribs and split lip, my body has managed to camouflage the pointy-toed kick Gayfryd landed next to my spine. Now thanks to Stone, I have a reminder of that deep ache.

"Good luck," I call out after him.

"That man did you a favor," Garcelli says.

"Yeah, right."

"He talked his way into your place. Didn't tear up a thing, and gave you a clean bill. You owe Stone. I was planning on getting a search warrant. Sending in a wrecking crew. Stone saved you that."

"Cut the crap," I say, taking the manila folder from my satchel. "Stone came to my house looking for something like this. This is a list of all the connections to your two dead cops. Mob, other cops, politicians, you name it. They are sorted, identified, time stamped, key worded and cross checked by subject. This is the last two months. If you like I can get you two years, five years, more."

"Shit. How did you?" Lt. Garcelli stops. "I don't want to know, do I?"

"You already do."

"What are you getting at?"

"This place wired?" I ask him.

"No."

"Do I need to have Stone come back with his wand?"

"You have my word. The place is clean."

"I can't, and won't use any of this," I tell him. "Almost all of this was illegally obtained. You might have the same problem, or worse, with your internal investigation."

"How worse?"

"Generations of cops for starters. It's a Pandora's Box. Corruption that has been passed on from father to son, uncle to nephew. Enough for a Federal Prosecutor to wipe out the entire Force. Every pension, every arrest, every conviction."

"Shit."

"Oh yeah. And I think Arlo already tried to sell you his info on the NYPD."

"Why would this Arlo person do that?"

"Because he was offering you a deal. I think he wants out from under the Feds thumb. And what better place than NYC with his own personal protection squad of 40,000 police officers?"

Garcelli stands, shaking Tiu's folder in his hands, considering his options.

"I'm not saying anything of what you said is true, but why would you think that?"

"Because the bum passing out soup from the van that night at Arlo's was one of yours."

"How'd you know?"

"I didn't. Paddy did. Good cop, remember."

"I do," Garcelli says.

"Arlo gave you a sample of what he's got on NYPD corruption, so you put a watch on Arlo. You need to decide. You going to take a chance with Arlo or trust me? Either way, you have a fox in the hen house."

Lt. Garcelli shifts but doesn't flip any switches or press any buttons. He knows I'm telling the truth.

"I also figure you have been investigating me ever since Arlo told you about the NYPD corruption piece I am working on."

"We handle our own dirty laundry."

"Unless you are the dirty laundry."

"Fuck you, Shaw."

"Seems like I've already been royally fucked," I say. "You found out Arlo works for the Feds. Maybe the Feds were running a sting. If so, that means Arlo is protected. Can he be handled? Or was he setting you up, hoping you'd bite and incriminate yourself? The Assistant Chief of Detectives? Good place to start, if the Feds really are trying to clean out the Department."

"Bastard is working for you," Garcelli throws in.

"That's how it appears," I agree. "Except the information he's giving me, I can't use; medical records, military information, bank records."

"Because?"

"Because it's illegally obtained, that's why," I say knowing Lt. Garcelli is testing me. "Plus what he was giving me was more than criminal activity, it was dirt. The kind used for blackmail, not jail."

"So who else was he working for?" Garcelli asks.

"That's what's got me worried, same as you. You had Stone watching him, but you couldn't roust him or break into his place yourself, so you jacked Paddy and me into doing your dirty work. How am I doing so far?"

"Keep talking."

"You need to know what he had, except Arlo was waiting for us. Played the victim, amazingly well. He gave us 850 million pages he knew you couldn't digest, especially because you didn't know who would be incriminated. So there we are."

"Where?"

"Right where Arlo wanted to be, inside my home."

"Why?"

"He wanted to see what my wife can do, and the resources she has."

"You're saying this kid knew we were watching him, knew you and Paddy would hassle him for some flash drives no one could use, and knew Stone would push to get inside your home?"

"Exactly. Arlo played all of us."

"The Helmsley? Where does blowing up two high ranking NYPD officers fit?"

"I don't know. I'm married to the smartest person on the planet, and live inside a supercomputer, and all I know for certain is…"

"What?"

"That I know nothing."

* * *

I walk back from Lt. Garcelli's headquarters, letting the crisp afternoon anesthetize my aches, and clear my thoughts. Inconsistencies begin making sense. I call Paddy.

"I can't make Greenwich in time for Starch's ceremony. It will be a zoo anyway."

"Just as good. I can use the help. Kath is going bat shit crazy. She heard the Vice President is coming."

"I wouldn't be surprised if she corners him to ask for a Presidential Pardon for her brother."

"Tiu and Riedell are already there with Mandell and the rest of the kitchen staff. Should be interesting when they cross paths with the Secret Service."

"My vote is on Tiu and Mandell."

"Plenty of Congress coming as well," Paddy says. "Kids, education, Starch handing out billions, no one wants to miss this one."

"Jackals smelling blood."

"Your peace offering to Garcelli accepted?"

"He's suspicious."

"Good. That means he took your information seriously. It will give Garcelli bargaining power with the FBI. Word is they are taking over. You tell him a 10-year-old girl did the work?" Paddy laughs.

"It was tempting, especially when Stone came in the room."

"A kid running background on bombing suspects and crooked cops. If that gets out, Garcelli and Stone will be guarding garbage barges for the rest of their careers."

"Garcelli figures the analysis came from Tiu."

"I'd keep it that way," Paddy warns. "I don't think Stone will come nosing around anymore, but Garcelli, he's another story. He won't scare."

"I hear you. I'll check in with Gert, and be home in ten."

Gert picks up on her burner cell. "You're not coming, are you? Figures." Gert answers herself before I can explain. "Doesn't matter. You'd just get in the way. But you're going to like this."

"Try me."

"A statue arrived this morning, draped for a grand unveiling, which means Starch has had this idea in the works for a while. You don't get a bronze statue of yourself made in a few days, even if you own Italy."

"How's Starch doing?"

"Better than I expected. He's not firing on all cylinders, and he knows it. Kathleen is a Godsend. She doesn't mince words with him. Even kind of rough with him physically. Just her way, I guess. She's been keeping him out of my way. The two of them have been practically living in his butterfly tower. She hates the little buggers, mainly because they love her hair."

"Good. I owe Kath, big time."

"The effects of the stroke will show. I'll try to keep his camera time to a minimum."

"Smart. Paddy and I will catch everything here. Tiu has all of Starch's home surveillance cameras linked to Wadjet and the Sunway. Kind of scary just saying that," I admit.

"Especially from a guy who thinks phone booths still exist," Gert laughs. "Tiu brought Mandell's entire crew. They are surrounding Riedell. Kid can barely move. Add Chronicle guards, State Troopers and the Secret Service, we've got enough security here to hold Palestinian/Israeli peace talks. You don't need to worry."

"Just some jitters. Tiu's mother showed up in Court this morning."

"Her mother? I thought she was only one of those filaments of her imagination?"

Gert's humor. "I'll tell Tiu you said that. But the mother is the real deal. Imagine Catherine Deneuve combined with Germany's Merkel, and you've got Tiu's mother."

"Elegance, brains and tough as nails, hmm. What's her play?"

"The good doctor wants full custody of Riedell."

"That's insane. No one in their right mind would give her Riedell."

"Believe me, if you saw the mother in person, you might change your mind. The woman is awesome, and connected past God. Tiu's not going to take any chances. Me either. So I need another favor."

"Shoot."

"Judge R from Family Court is coming to your affair."

"Send me a photo, and he'll be putty in my hands."

Chapter Twenty-Five

"I'm Chairwoman today, and I demand some respect," Amy announces coming inside a 'train-wrecked' Parnell's. The commuters going north hit fast and furious, leaving only a few stragglers in their wake.

"Madam Chairwoman," I say coming from the store room with a broom, offering her my stool. "Paddy this is Chairwoman Amy."

"Good to put a face with the name," Paddy says. "You've apparently impressed Shawn. What will you have?"

"Beer, and a broom," she smiles at me, taking the one I brought out.

I fetch another and we sweep the floor, keeping an eye on the TV. Starch's *Bethesda House* is swarming with dignitaries.

"Does Lt. Garcelli believe you are involved with both the Helmsley and SoHo explosions?" Amy asks, pulling a heavy stool out from under a table.

"What?"

"Van Wie ordered one of his guys who works the police beat to get a statement about you from Det. Stone. I overheard SoHo. I guess Van Wie didn't mention that."

"Nope."

"Jeez Paddy, we're sweeping Coolidge campaign buttons out from under these tables," Amy says, taking to the broom and Parnell's like she was raised in a pub.

"Save them. He may be running again," Paddy says.

"The cops know the SoHo explosion is just a coincidence, right? I mean gas leaks happen."

I don't hear suspicion in her voice. She's on my side. But she has a point.

"Cops don't believe in coincidences, do they?" I say, looking at Paddy.

I stop cleaning, dropping my wet towel on the table top. Amy is making a point. We just don't want to go there.

Amy sees she's hit a sensitive area and hesitates.

"Go ahead," I tell her. "Better to hear it from you than the cops."

"From what you said, Paddy was at the Helmsley. Were you at the SoHo apartment as well?" she asks him.

"I go there often enough." Paddy says, understanding what she's suggesting.

"SoHo has to be a coincidence," I decide for the both of us, tossing my wet towel in the laundry bin.

"Okay." Amy drops it. Unfortunately we are all recognizing the same possibility.

Paddy walks over, spreads his arms, and in one swoop moves four chairs and the table back where they were before my clean-up effort. "Much better," I say, handing him the brooms.

Amy sips tea from my mug. "Whew," she says feigning exhaustion. "Amazing what you can uncover with a little clean up, don't you think?"

* * *

"It's P.T. Barnum, but elegant," Amy says, appreciating how the massive red and white striped tents mimic the design of *Bethesda House* - six towers connecting to the majestic main building. And in the center, drawing the attention of arriving dignitaries, is the draped statue.

"He has full coverage," Paddy says, pointing at the wall mounted televisions throughout Parnell's playing every channel.

"Someone is broadcasting cell phone pictures of Starch. He's surrounded by kids," Amy shows us on her cell.

"Look at the river. There are some huge cruisers coming in down there. You'd think it was Fleet Week with all those blue blazers and white shoes."

"There are even more people inside the mansion," Paddy says, pointing to another screen. "I'll bet helicopters are shuttling back and forth from Starch's Country Club and the Westchester Airport."

"Starch doesn't look so good," Amy notices. "His hands are trembling."

"Jitters, that's all. I used to get them when I was on the talk show circuit," I say, dismissing her concerns.

Inside, Starch takes center stage in the Great Room. "I'm dedicating *Bethesda House*, home of my father and his father, to our children," Starch says, waving his brass buttoned arm expansively. "This will become a teaching center unlike any other in the country, where special-needs and exceptional children learn together."

Cheering erupts from everyone.

"He's good," Amy admits as we watch Starch work his crowd.

"My family's art collection," Starch says into the microphone, "no less than twenty Masters, will go up for auction. Take a good look around, my friends. I'm told by Sotheby's, there are a number of paintings that have never been publically displayed."

"Jacking up the prices, nice going," Paddy grins.

"He is good," I agree.

"Every penny, well not pennies," Starch jokes, "is going to our charity." Starch places a hand on Riedell's shoulder. She's standing directly in front of him, dressed in a school-girl blazer and grey wool skirt straight out of preppie-land.

"Look at my daughter," I say, bragging to Paddy.

Amy sees more. "Poor thing is petrified by all the attention."

"There's a lot of Emma in her," Paddy says.

"More and more every day," I agree. On Emma's face, the bold features were competing for attention. Riedell has inherited the best of Emma, though the final outcome is still seeking harmony.

We see a figure with auburn hair coming out of the mansion's front doors. Even at a distance, Kathleen is easily distinguishable. "That's Paddy's wife, Kathleen," I say to Amy who has already become one of us.

"She's beautiful," Amy says. Paddy swells in acknowledgment.

Starch moves outside and steps up to the podium. Several hundred guests mingle, champagne glasses held high. Children are swarming around Starch, almost carrying him to the microphone.

"You don't get a chance to steal this line too many times before it becomes true. The rumors of my death have been greatly exaggerated," Starch begins. He talks about inspiration and humanity, then moves up to pull the silk cover with great flourish, unveiling the massive bronze sculpture.

"I'll be damned," I say, near spilling my hot tea. "It's Emma!"

The statue is a huge roller-skating Emma with Lion King teased-hair flying in the wind. She is slam dunking a handful of rubbish into a wire-mesh trash can. The beloved litter queen of Central Park.

"That sly old dog," I whisper, wiping away a tear.

Kids, teachers, and Starch's Country Club pals erupt in applause, along with more than a few confused police officers, senators and congresspersons.

Starch grabs Riedell's shoulder for support, waving high in the air to everyone.

"Hold on Starch, you're almost there," I encourage him.

"Here stands Emma's legacy," Starch announces proudly, turning Riedell forward for all to see. Chuti Tiu steps out of the crowd and joins them. Starch puts his arm around her shoulder. "To our children's future," Starch calls proudly, waving his hand across one of the most magnificent estates in the world.

"I never thought she'd show herself," Paddy whispers.

"That's Chuti Tiu," I say pointing her out for Amy.

"She's so tiny. Somehow I expected such a genius to have a big head," Amy laughs. "She's magnificent."

A Lmo pulls onto the gravel entrance. The driver, impeccably dressed in a pearl grey uniform, leaps out to open the rear door, only to have it pushed into his face.

"You have no right," Gayfryd screams, emerging from the limo, grabbing for the driver as she falls hard on a knee in the gravel. Starch's microphone broadcasts her shriek to a silent crowd.

"This is a charade. Null and void," Gayfryd shouts, trying to regain her balance and waving a sheaf of legal papers.

"She's drunk," Amy says.

"Insane," I offer my opinion.

"And ten million dollars poorer," Paddy adds, remembering the deal Gayfryd accepted from Athena, but has now violated. "Doubt if our one-dollar lawyer will forget."

"By Federal Court order, the whole damn Chronicle Company and this fucking estate are mine," Gayfryd yells as her heels sink into the gravel.

"That's really going to piss her off," Amy says, "Those shoes are Christian Louboutin."

Gayfryd struggles forward, pointing at Starch. "I'm the legal heir, and he is going to an institution. He is not in his right mind," she shouts to everyone, no one.

Silence.

Gayfryd points her court order at the U.S. Marshal. "Do your damn job. Arrest that man."

"I don't think there will be any need for that, Officer," Walter Jackson says, stepping from the Country Club crowd behind Starch. I am Chairman of the Chronicle Company."

"Oh no you're not," Amy says, pointing a finger at herself, laughing.

"As you can see, Officer," Walter Jackson continues as if he's heard Amy from Parnell's. "My childhood friend is fully in charge of his faculties, thereby making this so-called Court order invalid."

"You told me your father is incapacitated. Is this your father or not," the U.S. Marshal demands of Gayfryd.

Jackson moves closer to the Marshal, taking his arm as if trying to move him aside. The microphone picks up his words. "I apologize for what this woman may have told you, but as you can see..."

Gayfryd slashes at a nearby Deputy. "Shoot the bastard," she screams, trying to grab his gun. "He's stealing my money."

"Look!" Amy points to another TV screen, "who's that woman?"

"That's Dr. Darieux, Emma and Chuti Tiu's mother. The one who showed up in Family Court this morning." I feel a knot in my stomach and search the television screens for Riedell.

The camera zeroes in on Dr. Darieux. Even in Starch's crowd of elites, she commands attention. We watch as the lady doctor makes her way forward.

"Is she trying to stop Gayfryd?"

"No, she's walking right past her," Amy says, "I think she's trying to get to your wife."

Tiu puts a protective hand on Riedell. As Dr. Darieux approaches, their eyes lock. Tiu is shaking her head defiantly, no.

"That poor woman is begging," Amy says, looking at the elegant Doctor's outstretched arms.

I see Mandell move to shield my daughter, who is still holding Starch's hand. The old man's head is down, dropped to his chest.

Berk comes out of Gayfryd's limo. Riedell is within ten feet. Tiu sees how close he is, just as Riedell disappears from our sight. The TV cameras are being pushed and shoved.

One steady cellphone stays on Gayfryd, who swirls backward catching Berk in the leg with her high heel. Both fall back to the stones, as Starch staggers.

Quickly to his feet, Berk tries to corral Gayfryd, pushing her back into the limo, but she is having none of it; fighting tooth and nail, clawing at his face.

"I'm his daughter," Gayfryd gets in one last cry as Starch collapses.

Starch's old school chum, Walter Jackson, freezes, staring, listening to Starch's groans being broadcast from the microphone in his hand. I see Gert calling for help on her cellphone.

Like an apparition, Kathleen appears at Starch's side, checking his pulse and breathing. The live microphone is still clutched in his hand.

"I'm a Doctor" Tiu's mother announces to Kathleen who has loosened Starch's tie and is taking his carotid pulse. "Nearest hospital?" Doctor Darieux asks Kathleen.

Riedell, Tiu and Mandell have disappeared.

The lead U.S. Marshal directs a standby ambulance to Starch.

"Oh shit," I whisper to Paddy. "They've got him."

As we see Starch being lifted onto a stretcher, we hear a blast erupt in the background. One of the television screens shows glass cascading like an avalanche from Starch's butterfly tower.

* * *

"What happened? Where's Riedell?" I ask Gert, finally making a phone connection

"With Mandell and your wife," Gert says. "I saw them running towards a helicopter. Can she fly one of those?"

"Maybe. Probably. If Tiu can't, Mandell can."

"Seems like the explosion was limited to the tower. Gayfryd is going crazy, screaming, attacking people. Berk's limo is spinning its rear wheels in mud, blocking the way for the ambulance." Gert is speaking in a hurried whisper, like an on-the-scene news reporter. "The ambulance is coming through now. A police cruiser just pushed the stretch away."

"Starch?"

"He's in bad shape. They are loading him now. Kathleen just jumped into the ambulance." I repeat Gert's words for Paddy and Amy.

"Good girl," Paddy says.

All the screens go black. "Gert, we lost all the cameras. What's going on?"

"The Internet is overloaded," Amy realizes.

"The explosion blew the hell out of the butterfly room. Glass everywhere. Butterflies sort of got lifted up in the air like balloons. Probably scrambled their radar some. But there are tons of them floating around. Some of the batty guests are trying to catch them. They think the explosion was part of the celebration."

"Gert? Gert? Damn, I lost her," I say.

"Another explosion," Amy says. "There's no way Garcelli will buy this is a coincidence."

* * *

"Get to work," Paddy says, tossing us aprons as a steady stream of customers pours into Parnell's. "Beer," he points to me. "Amy and I will handle the rest until Kathleen gets back. No food, got it?"

It's been the better part of an hour since we've had contact with anyone near the *Bethesda House* explosion, but we barely notice. We're working our asses off.

During a pause, Paddy makes contact with his Connecticut Marshal. The TV's are repeating video of the Helmsley, interviewing law enforcement and politicians in NY and Connecticut, while playing footage of 9/11, lest anyone forget.

My cellphone begins dancing around on the bar. "Fill us in," I tell Gert. "I've got you on speaker. Paddy and Amy are here."

"Tiu and Riedell are long gone. I think between the bombing, Gayfryd's hysterics, and her mother lunging for Riedell, Tiu panicked."

"Chuti Tiu doesn't panic," I remind Gert. "I can guarantee you, she has three avenues of escape at all times. What happened to the school kids?"

"Mandell's security force impersonating the waiters, stripped off their white jackets, revealing their uniforms, flipped camo-backed tablecloths, wrapped the kids in them, and vanished into the woods like deer. It was a crack military operation."

"How many people were killed or injured from the explosion? Starch's surveillance cameras are still down at our end."

"This was nothing on the order of the Helmsley. In fact, at first it seemed like a propane tank exploded. Except for the shattering glass everywhere. No one was hurt."

"Then why the black out on the broadcasting?"

"My guess is since 9/11 that's protocol. No sense inciting panic."

"The Chronicle has turned into a tabloid," I tell Gert. "They are connecting the Helmsley and the *Bethesda House* explosions like there is a people's revolt against the wealthy. This is Van Wie's doing, and the local stations are picking up on his theory because they don't have anything else. And no one is taking charge."

"Paddy's marshal buddy is in control here, thankfully," Gert says.

"The Chronicle had a backstory linking all three explosions, but it is buried. So far, neither local TV nor social media has made the SoHo connection to us. Otherwise we'd have NYPD breaking down the door."

"What's the word on Starch? Have you heard from Kathleen?" Paddy asks.

"No update on Starch, but it doesn't look good. Kathleen wasn't at the hospital with Starch," Gert says. "I thought she might be with you."

"No, we haven't seen or heard from her."

"You still have any of Mandell's security out there with you?"

"Two next to me."

"It's time you come home, okay?"

"You sound worried. Should I be worried?"

"Maybe a little. Tiu always has an exit strategy, so I'm sure she and Riedell are safe. Kathleen is the concern right now."

"The doctor who got in the ambulance didn't arrive at the hospital with Starch either," Gert says.

"You saying Kathleen is missing?" Paddy asks.

"Her cell probably died. Wouldn't hurt to call your Marshal friend, just in case."

"Yeah, it's probably nothing."

* * *

"Commissioner," Paddy says almost saluting the man coming in the door with Lt. Garcelli, They are accompanied by Independent Prosecutor Diane Kasey, Starch's supposed friend I met in Washington, and another woman I don't know. Ten uniforms clear the Pub and stand guard at the door.

"Shit," I whisper. Paddy pushes my tea away and quickly moves around the bar giving me a concealed double-tap on my back, the submission sign in martial arts. He's telling me to keep my mouth shut.

"Paddy," the Commissioner says shaking his hand. "There's been a call of a bomb threat."

"Here?" Paddy asks, caught off guard. Then he realizes a Police Commissioner would not be a first responder to an explosion.

"No. I got the call a few minutes ago from that woman. You know, the one who saved the government computers. Chuti Tiu, she calls herself. Gave me this address. Parnell's. Told me she has vital information connecting the Helmsley bombing, the Starch estate, and bombs that are imminent. The City is under siege."

"Damn," I whisper edging toward the swinging kitchen doors and back stairway. Mandell is waiting, blocking my way. "They are safe upstairs," he assures me through the louvers.

"I brought Lt. Garcelli," the Commissioner tells Paddy, dipping his head toward the Assistant Chief of Detectives.

Garcelli shakes Paddy's hand as if they haven't seen each other in years. Garcelli doesn't miss that the Commissioner is on a first name basis with his old training officer, Paddy.

"This is FBI Special Agent-in-Charge Greene," the Commissioner says to Paddy. "She's in the loop. Special Agent Greene, Paddy is retired, but remains close family."

I know there is a subtle message passed between the three cops; the common enemy, the Feds, has taken charge.

But Greene is not about to be handled. She walks past the Commissioner and Lt. Garcelli as if they aren't in the room. She's played the power game before.

"SAC Greene. Now we've met," she says grabbing Paddy's 'mitt' and giving it a good hard pump. "How about buzzing us in upstairs? She's up there, right? Bad times, yeah? Gonna get worse. Let's go."

Paddy points at me.

Chapter Twenty-Six

"Gert?"

"You call me, or did I call you?" she says, not waiting for an answer. "I'm still in Greenwich. The FBI is swarming all over the place."

"Same here. That's why I'm calling you."

"Has the FBI connected you to the *Bethesda House* bombing?" Gert asks surprised.

"I hadn't thought of it that way," I admit. "No. At least not… no. Why would you even ask that?" I stop talking, noticing Agent Greene eyeing me, curious that I'm suddenly on my cell. Even I have to admit it looks suspicious.

"I do not intend to re-new my subscription at this time," I say loud enough for her to hear me, pointing at the phone and shaking my head at the ridiculous solicitation.

Greene doesn't buy a word of it. She points upstairs.

"I'm being invited into my own home," I lower my voice to Gert while pretending to Greene that I cannot end the persistent salesperson's questions.

"You can't talk, got it," Gert says. "If you have the FBI there, good chance they are trying to connect you to at least one of the explosions."

"I'm not going to renew," I say, looking at Greene.

"Of course you aren't, but the FBI doesn't know that. You'd better start unravelling this story real fast, or you are going to be scratching out copy on cinder-block."

* * *

"Hand and retinal scan please," Wadjet directs us, forcing my visitors to line up one-by-one on the steep, re-enforced concrete staircase.

"This gets me into the White House," Independent Prosecutor Kasey says, slapping her ID in front of the retinal scan.

FBI Special Agent Greene did not introduce Kasey, and is seemingly indifferent to her presence. Maybe they have some history, or maybe it's just Greene assuming FBI top authority. It was only two days ago that I met with Kasey at the Jefferson, yet she doesn't acknowledge me. No need to press further. Besides, upstairs I have the advantage. I have Tiu, and her Supercomputer.

"Please position your actual eye," Wadjet orders more insistently, proving that machines can express feelings. The others grumble at Kasey's attitude.

I am on the lowest stair with Garcelli behind me, boxing me in. Not that I was planning to make a run for it.

"You know what this is about?" Garcelli grumbles in my ear as we move up a step.

I shake my head, no.

I hear Wadjet say, "Proceed." The vault-like bolts on the security door slide back. The air-lock releases. So what is waiting behind Door Number One today? The Commissioner enters first. One step and he freezes, causing the others to pile into him.

I'm prepared for the unexpected whenever I enter my home. I'm sure Garcelli knows about Det. Stone's excursion to Antarctica, probably the other reason he is staying behind me. This time Tiu has outdone herself.

We enter deep space. Nothing and everything; we are but specks in the Universe. No floor, no walls, no magnificent Italian skylights; no up, no down. The six of us are hovering in the cosmos. It's like we have stepped into a complete void, buffeted only by galactic breezes.

"What the hell?" our self-designated leader, the Commissioner, gasps, teetering to find his balance.

"You are in a white hole," FBI Agent Greene explains. No one else understands.

A distant star explodes, oddly encouraging the group to move further into the light-years * of dimensionless Space.

There is no way to prepare for Tiu. She is enigmatic, as always, in her greeting. Never a glimmer of normal behavior. This time she appears as Riedell, my 10-year-old daughter. She is shrouded in a celestial cone of light, suspended in deep space, holding our Maine Coon, Rowdy, on her shoulder, while twirling on skates.

---

* Being human, we think the universe revolves around us. Unlikely as that is, we still measure the cosmos that way. A light-year is the distance light travels in one Earth year, about six trillion miles. The nearest star in the Milky Way, aside from our Sun, is Alfa Centauri. It is 4.24 light-years away.

Independent Prosecutor Kasey is first to protest. "Excuse me! I didn't come here for some science fiction fun house. Is there an adult in charge?" she demands.

"Quiet," Agent Greene orders. "Listen and learn."

Riedell flips up her control tablet. "My Aunt Chuti wants you here so you can understand the forces behind the explosions. Auntcie up," she says her password to the Sunway TaihuLight Supercomputer.

"Everything you see is real; the stars, the galaxies, even that pinprick over there," Riedell points with her finger. "That is Earth. And if we increase the magnification, you will see the squad cars outside Parnell's on First and 53rd."

"How is this possible?" FBI Special Agent-in-Charge Greene asks no one in particular.

"I will explain when you are ready."

Riedell just told the FBI to shut up. Out of the mouth of babes. If I had spoken that way, Agent Greene would have me in cuffs, dragging my sorry ass down the concrete stairs.

Riedell glides in front of the group. "Right now you are using the Sunway's eyes," Riedell explains. Her young voice is hushed, as if coming to us by way of a breeze.

"The Sunway Supercomputer's eyes have a hundred million more facets than a bee, and a million times greater acuity than the Golden Eagle."

Lt. Garcelli is slowly rotating, taking in the Universe.

"Millions are difficult to comprehend. Imagine looking at a distant mountain first with your eyes, then using binoculars, through a telescope, and lastly through a microscope, capable of resolution to ½ the width of a hydrogen atom." My ten-year-old daughter explains. "The Sunway looks at a hundred million mountains simultaneously, calculating their contraction, expansion, rotation, and gravitational attraction, all in nanoseconds. * That's a massive amount of data only she can analyze."

---

* Time and speed are often confused. A nanosecond is a unit of time, one billionth of a second. Light, the fastest particle/wave in existence, travels about one foot in a nanosecond. The blink of an eye is a measurement of speed. One blink takes about 1/3 of a second.

I've been living with this Sunway, Tiu and Riedell for years. I've seen the magic, without really understanding, and I am still awed. The others must be overwhelmed.

"We can access every CCTV cam, building security video, wildlife and aerial drone cameras, and over 3,000 surveillance satellites. Around the entire world."

Before the group can process what Riedell has described, she disengages from our location in Space, returning us to a more comprehensible sphere, our home. I hear several sighs as the warehouse floor and soaring ceiling appear. The Commissioner stamps his foot on the hewn beam floor, confirming he's returned to Earth.

Only FBI Special Agent Greene has moved past the spectacular, and is concentrating on the potential of this resource.

"And now you are standing inside the Sunway's physical being," Riedell continues. "She is the most powerful supercomputer in existence. In addition to what she can see, Sunway can also hear." My daughter moves a finger on her tablet, placing us inside the Kremlin's War Room. Even Prosecutor Kasey is silent as we listen to Putin giving orders to steely-faced generals.

"Sunway can analyze the maps on the walls, locate military operations, infiltrate their computers, and," Riedell zooms in on one General, "provide a detailed background of their Command staff."

Riedell returns us to the warehouse which, compared to the Universe and Russia's War Room, has lost some of its grandeur. She summons up an amorphous screen the size of a supermoon.

The group watches enormous membrane screens form around and above us, creating a canopied amphitheater. "This was sent to us twenty-three minutes ago," Riedell announces. "She knows the Sunway is tracking her, and every possible avenue of escape."

"Enough already." Prosecutor Kasey says. "Why are we here?"

Agent Greene shoots her a look that could kill, as Riedell rolls up next to me. "Maybe Paddy shouldn't be here for this," she whispers. I shake my head. "Whatever you've got us into, you'd better run with it," I tell her.

Riedell touches her tablet. It's Kathleen. She is waiting, freeze-framed, sitting at the bar of a pub, clearly somewhere in Ireland. I glimpse at Paddy. He shows no emotion.

"My darling husband, you might as well hear this direct from the source," Kathleen begins. "I married you for one reason: to get my son, Jamie, released from prison."

"Son?" I repeat. It's not Kathleen's brother Paddy sent to prison. Jamie is her son?

Paddy wobbles slightly. Only I notice.

Tiu is anything but subtle; she has super-imposed behind Kathleen a live image of Fishkill Prison.

Paddy stands erect, as if he's facing a firing squad. Shoot straight for the heart.

"This is ridiculous. I don't need to waste my time with family squabbles," Prosecutor Kasey declares turning away, with nowhere to go. I catch the expression in her eyes; she knows exactly who Jamie is.

"Shush," Special Agent Greene quiets Kasey.

"Dear Husband," Kathleen continues, "I gave you every opportunity."

Focusing on Kathleen's eyes, I see resolve. And fear.

"You and Shawn," she says, "all I got was your promises to help Jamie. Nothing but talk. Some time ago, Jamie asked me to meet with a friend of his, another prisoner. I was reluctant, but once I realized he could help, I listened. It was the same guy you sent to Fishkill. James Berk. Small world, isn't it?"

Berk, my nemesis. I am on high alert.

"Premeditation," Prosecutor Kasey establishes. Greene gives her a warning stare.

Kathleen continues. "Berk said he could put Jamie on the front page of the Chronicle."

"By killing innocent people?" Garcelli asks.

"We did what you didn't have the guts to do. Blowing up a couple of dirty peelers, who cares?" yells a voice in the pub behind Kathleen.

Kathleen glances over her shoulder. "I never meant for anyone to get hurt."

The camera pulls back, revealing Kathleen's cohorts.

"The lads and I represent the **32CSM**, the true Ireland. We demand the return of our brother-in-arms, Jamie."

Kathleen cuts off the interruption, moving closer to the camera. "Tell your Commissioner, in exchange for Jamie I will surrender myself and stand trial."

A mother's love. Incredible. I look toward Paddy.

"Shawn, I'll give you the exclusive," she half-smiles. "Who knows, maybe another Pulitzer?"

"Thanks," I mumble.

"Send my boy home. Keep your promise," Kathleen ends. There is more, but the words don't transmit.

"If she thinks she is going to cut a deal," Independent Prosecutor Kasey fumes.

"You put him in there, Kasey," the Commissioner turns on the Prosecutor. "Is her kid already dead?"

They all seem to know about Kathleen's son. I move closer to Paddy. "What do you know?" I whisper.

"Not enough," he says, refusing to look at me.

I'm just realizing these people all have a history. Including Paddy. Maybe Paddy's abrupt retirement had something to do with Jamie and the three strike law.

The video continues.

"**32CSM** demands sovereignty. You will send $3.2 billion to our cause of freedom. Cash, just like you did for Iran. We'd better see some good Irish lads boarding a plane carrying sacks of cash," the man who spoke earlier orders. The voice is older, male, and somehow familiar.

"You have until ten a.m. tomorrow, your time. When we call, have proof our demands are being met, or we continue taking you down. We are prepared."

The screen goes dark.

Agent Greene says to the Commissioner, "You need to clear the civilians out of this facility."

"Oh no, you're not throwing me out of my home. We invited you here," I protest.

"No way are we allowing a reporter access to this situation," Kasey declares.

"You lose me, you lose access to resources you can't imagine. Including one of the most powerful computers in the world, and the genius who makes it work."

Greene thinks about that. "Here's my non-negotiable deal. You stay in my sight at all times, and everything you see or hear is off the record. Agree?"

I hold out my hand. "You've got a deal. Now, what is **32CSM**," I ask.

"It's the remaining radical arm of the IRA," Special Agent Greene explains. "I want that video sent to my people, ASAP, before some lunatic gets hold of it and it goes viral," she orders me, mistakenly assuming I am capable of such a task.

"You'd better let me do it," Riedell tells the Special Agent, holding out her hand to take the FBI cell phone.

Agent Greene hesitates. She looks at me as if asking permission. Riedell keeps her hand extended. I cough a plea, "Tiu." I know she's watching and listening. Why is Tiu making ten-year-old Riedell relay a terrorist threat to the FBI?

"What was that?" Greene demands.

"Something in my throat," I lie.

Prosecutor Kasey jumps in. "DOJ has supercomputer Watson. We can analyze..." she offers.

Greene sparks, flashing Kasey her credentials. "FBI, remember?"

Kasey huffs but keeps silent. Riedell is immune to their bickering. Her hand is still out, waiting. She's just like her mother, not intimidated by anything, or anyone.

"Should any of you care, my Aunt Chuti wrote the core algorithms for the Sunway, and most of the other supercomputers in existence. The same algorithms * that will help stop **32CSM** from detonating more explosives. Interested or not?"

Special Agent-in-Charge Greene gives Riedell her cell phone. Even I know, in FBI land that's tantamount to a cop surrendering a service weapon. I imagine Greene testifying in front of Congress that she surrendered her Federally-issued communication device to a young girl wearing roller skates, because... Greene's problem, not mine.

---

* Algorithms. You have been bumping up against these creatures all your life, but may never have noticed. They are the logic roadmaps to how everything operates.

Algorithms tell the speedometer how fast you are going; calculate the number on your thermometer; flip the billions of microchips on and off so you can stream movies, or chat with the grandkids. They sequence the intercontinental missiles when POTUS goes to Defcon 2, and signal Alexa to wake you to Rock Around the Clock at six a.m.

Those are all human-made algorithms. Your DNA sequencing is a major algorithm that came with the original equipment.

The Commissioner starts digging in his suit pocket for his cell phone, but Lt. Garcelli has already passed his to Riedell. "Mine will do the job for both of us. Sir," Garcelli tells his boss.

Clever. Garcelli may look like an over-weight cop waiting on his pension, but he's no fool.

Riedell floats the two cell phones over her tablet, taps twice, syncing the phones.

"Here," Riedell skates to FBI Agent Greene and Lt. Garcelli, returning their phones as she whirls around them all, looking at the hundreds of images suddenly filling the warehouse screens.

For me, Riedell twirling around on her mother's skates is normal. It's how she concentrates. Not so for this quasi-military group. They expect order and deference. Using Riedell as spokesperson, Tiu has disrupted their natural order. Why, I wonder.

"Can you locate the pub from where this message was broadcast?" Agent Greene asks Riedell.

Now I understand. Tiu enjoys having the Feds report to a child. My wife's humor.

"I just sent you the coordinates," Riedell says, waving her tablet in the air. "The algorithms will keep searching for anything related to the video. You have to know what information to discard," she explains. "The algorithms will search corned beef recipes because the Sunway pulled up the food menu she saw at Kathleen's pub. Sunway will learn real fast to filter out data that's not relevant."

"Then send in a missile if you know where they are, and blow that bar off the face of the Earth," Prosecutor Kasey says.

"Tempting," Paddy mutters at the idiotic comment, walking away from the group, not suggesting whom he'd like to have bombed.

"All you know is where the message was recorded," Riedell corrects Prosecutor Kasey.

"I doubt they stayed at that pub, waiting around," Paddy says.

"I guess you'd know," Kasey responds, her tone laden with suspicion.

"If you want to arrest me, make your move," Paddy shouts in disgust.

"You could buy some goodwill by sending Kathleen a live shot of her son," Riedell suggests.

The Commissioner and Agent Greene turn to each other.

Independent Prosecutor Kasey attacks Riedell. "You know where they are? If you are withholding information, I'll personally see you spend your next eight birthdays in Fishkill."

In an instant, I'm face-to-face with the Prosecutor. "Talk that way to my daughter again, and I'll…"

Riedell slides forward. "Don't worry about her Daddy. I think she irked Irksome."

"What?" Kasey sputters.

The Commissioner puts a calming hand on my shoulder. "We're all on the same side here."

Unfazed, Riedell taps her tablet. "This is Kathleen's son," she says, showing a live cam of the prison hospital. "He's been less than a model prisoner," Riedell says displaying his history of infractions on another screen.

"Medically, his primary condition is liver failure, with significant secondary issues. Jamie is dying," Riedell tells us.

"How does a kid get access to that kind of information?" Prosecutor Kasey demands from her fellow law enforcement associates. They stare at Kasey, bewildered that she still views Riedell as a mere child.

I know people like her. The less they know, the louder they get. Even politicians know better than to attack children. Especially this child.

My thoughts to Riedell's ears. My young daughter whizzes up to Kasey's nose, examining the woman as if she is an oddity in a sideshow. "So how goes it inside there?" Riedell taps Kasey's head.

"Get away from me, you little pest," Kasey shouts, flaying her arms in the air as Riedell easily escapes the swings, skating away.

"Paddy," the Commissioner says "you know these people. Do you believe they are capable of more destruction?"

"Kathleen's father and brothers are a bunch of drunks. Stupid sods. Hot heads. Never met them, but Kathleen has told me about their IRA activities. They would have access to explosive materials. Maybe some high level connections within the old IRA."

"And your wife?" the Commissioner asks. "How does she fit in to all this?"

"I believe a mother could do almost anything for her child."

Kasey leaps forward. "His wife is their spokesperson. She's the brains behind this. Isn't that obvious?"

"I don't think so," I offer my opinion. "I think she's being used by James Berk. He's on a personal mission, he's powerful and ruthless. He would think nothing of blowing up the whole city to get what he's after."

"If he thinks he's getting independence for Ireland, and three billion dollars to boot, he's barking up the wrong tree," Kasey says. "His demands should be directed at Washington, DC."

"Berk doesn't give a shit about Ireland," I mumble to myself, dismissing Kasey. The fact Greene isn't questioning further makes me think she knows more about Berk than she's letting on.

Getting no support from Greene, Prosecutor Kasey announces, "I need to fill in the Attorney General, now." She turns away from the group to make her call.

In a minor act of payback, Riedell points to where she has displayed Kasey's call on screen. There are no messages other than her assistant, who has called in sick. We watch as Kasey talks to a dead phone.

Paddy wanders away, taking a chair near the school area. I can't blame him. My friend has had a lot to take in.

Agent Greene comes close to me asking quietly, "You believe his wife has planted bombs in the City?"

I can't lie. "Unfortunately, yes. It's possible."

"So," Greene turns away from me addressing the group. "We have an IRA connection. Makes escalation a real possibility. Bothers me that the three explosions we've seen already are descending, not ascending."

"Descending?" I ask.

"Helmsley bomb got the most attention, did the most damage. Not much destruction in SoHo. And only litter in Connecticut. Wrong order." She explains.

"Got it".

"And, obviously, no one is giving $3.2 billion, or even one dollar, to terrorists. That's non-negotiable." Greene says.

"My Aunt and I have made all possible connections in the past six months; phones, credit cards, e-mails, all social media, work records, purchases, customer contacts, co-workers, their families, friends, our students, siblings, Irish connections; calls, correspondence; written and electronic by any of them. Military background, criminal, engineering & chemical training, demolition; building, agriculture, movies and church affiliations of everyone who has had contact, even just a cup of coffee, with Kathleen," Riedell rattles off the extent of her work.

"Phew."

Riedell continues on, "Including Kathleen's fifty contacts within the Department of Justice, and almost the same number within the former NY Assistant District Attorney office." She points to Kasey. "She prosecuted Jamie."

Independent Prosecutor Kasey hears enough and ignites. "You violated…"

"Impressive," Lt. Garcelli says stepping between Kasey and Riedell, ending the Prosecutor's grandstanding. "You did all this work, when?"

"Oh," Riedell says, surprised at the question. "Right after we did a deep search of all the nurses, family, friends, associates, hospital staff, outside services. Crossed for drugs, IRA, activist activities, magazine subscriptions, Internet activity. Same for the two dead police officers. About 165 billion data points. I already sent the information to you. Don't you have it?"

They all check their phones.

"You didn't send me any information," Prosecutor Kasey shouts.

"I sent it to your Assistant," Riedell tells her. "The one who is home sick."

"How did you..?"

Riedell's brown eyes project innocence. Although there is a definite twinkle.

"Is your Aunt available?" Lt. Garcelli asks Riedell, looking to me for help.

"Not right now," she answers. "I was the one who received the message from Kathleen. I was taking an on-line class from my Aunt when the message arrived. Because my Dad wasn't home, I asked my Aunt to call you. You know how police tend to discount a kid's voice."

Touché. Lt. Garcelli nods. "Well, okay for now."

"Well, it's not okay with me," Prosecutor Kasey snarls. "If this Auntie person is withholding information and interfering with a Federal investigation, I'll have her up on charges."

"Do you want our help or not?" Riedell asks, shutting down the Prosecutor, unfazed by her threat.

"We'll take it," the Police Commissioner decides. His town, his rules. "Excuse us for a moment," he says, urging Agent Greene aside for a private conversation. Kasey invites herself along, leaving me with Lt. Garcelli. Paddy is off in the distance. Riedell skates around the screens, parsing data. Our Maine Coon, Rowdy is wrapped around the back of her neck and shoulders. She really is still a kid, I hope.

I notice Riedell slip behind the screens into the kitchen. She returns carrying an egg-shaped, stainless steel container. "This should feel good," she says to Paddy as she places the egg on the back of his neck. Kathleen gave this to me. It's like the one she uses."

Garcelli does his best to ignore me. He calls his staff, giving orders. He wants to be back at his precinct, but right now, staying in the Commissioner's sight is critical.

"Look at that," I elbow Garcelli, pointing to screens around the room.

Riedel has all of Ireland's 5,000 live cams projected about the room. Images from rural farming towns, churches, stores, streets, pubs. Faces flicker past at blinding speed. As we watch, the whizzing images slow. All cameras have now concentrated on "The Troubles" counties of Northern Ireland.

On center screen, Riedell has police posters of Kathleen's family

Chapter Twenty-Seven

Gert calls. "Starch didn't make it."

My esteemed blue blood publisher, who oddly became my friend, is no more. My brain already knew, but my heart isn't ready to accept this news.

Another call is waiting. "It's Mrs. Wright," I tell Gert. "She's probably calling to tell me. I'll get back to you."

"Shaw. Mrs. Wright here. Get your ass back to the Chronicle, now,"

"I thought I was fired," I tell her.

"I've cleared the way. I ordered security to handcuff Van Wie to a urinal if he gives you any crap. Got it?"

"You're just toying with me," I react to the image.

"Cut the wise cracks. Write Cuthbert's story. The entire staff is at your disposal. Board's orders. Tell your people..."

"My people?"

"Those lowlifes who read your damn liberal trash. Today the Chronicle is yours. Let them know how he cared for them. His generosity."

"My words will be pearls," I tell her.

"Quite. By the way, the City Room's computers are down. You'll have to go old school."

"Seems fitting. We'll get it done."

"Try to use some discretion, understand?"

"Oh, I do," I assure her. "Discretion is my middle name."

Special Agent Greene and the Commissioner are still conferring on one side of the room, with Prosecutor Kasey listening in. Garcelli is on his phone. Paddy hasn't budged. Rowdy is chasing Riedell as she skates among the screens.

I call Gert back. "She asked me to write Starch's obit," I tell her. "You okay with that?"

"It's my honor," I say, wiping my eye. "There's more."

"You heard about the DA opening a murder inquiry?"

"Murder? What are you talking about?" I ask.

"Starch."

"Oh come on, he's grandstanding. Just another politician. Who's he investigating?"

She hesitates. "I'll let you know when I hear something else."
Then I realize one possibility. "Kathleen."
"Kathleen?"
"She just confessed to Paddy and everyone here that she planted the bombs."

* * *

My burner phone rings. "Hey Boss," Amy says. "You heard?"
"Just now. Mrs. Wright wants me to write the obituary. Get it started, will you?"
"Sure. You okay? You sound kinda strange. I know he was your friend."
"I'm good," I manage. "It isn't a surprise. How old was he anyway?"
"Eighty six."
"Had no idea. Let's keep this obit balanced. Not the typical heaping praise upon praise. Let's do quotes from people that knew him, including me. Mine will start with, 'We called him Starch,' I'll expand from there, but you get the tone?"
"Got it. Quotes from Wright, Jackson, his Club pals, Mayor, Governor, the usual?"
"Exactly. And try for some of the less obvious people as well."
"Enemies?"
"Sure. Let's see what flushes out. I think this obit will write itself. We can cover the *Bethesda House* dedication as a separate piece. That will handle the legacy angle. The incident and the explosion, that's not ours. Let Van Wie deal with that. The readers can draw their own conclusions."
"Got it. And when can I expect my tea?"
"Might be a while. The FBI is here right now."
Amy automatically shifts gears. "Parnell's?"
"My house."
"That's not good," Amy appreciates. "You want me to get you an attorney?"
"Don't think that's necessary. But you could let Athena know. She'll understand."
"There is a message from her. She says Mrs. Van Wie has taken a ½ price offer."
"Good. You can scratch Mrs. Van Wie's quote from your list."
Garcelli motions me to join him.

"I'll get on Starch's obituary ASAP," I say loud enough for him to hear.

"Ok, catch you later," Amy says signing off.

* * *

The Commissioner and the Feds are still in conference thirty feet away, leaving me with Garcelli.

"How do you think this is going down?" Garcelli asks me.

"Prosecutor Kasey is saying, 'We've known for some time the woman is IRA connected,'" I answer.

"Interesting," Lt. Garcelli looks at me quizzically. "And I suppose the Commissioner is reading her the riot act for not telling him?"

"Quiet, I need to concentrate to read their lips."

"You're kidding. When did you learn to do that?" Garcelli asks.

I put a finger up to hush him.

"Kasey is saying, 'You know as well as anyone, I've been using Kathleen's boy as bait, keeping him in prison no matter how much Paddy and his cop buddies try to get him released.'"

Garcelli can't keep quiet. "The third strike that sent that boy up was a low level marijuana rap. He was just a kid. Seems like someone coulda got him a reprieve long ago. Now I understand. It's this IRA stuff. That's why I got blocked every time Paddy pushed me."

"I want the whole cell," Kasey is telling the Commissioner. "The Helmsley is proof the IRA are in your City, and operational."

Here we are in my home, with Tiu and Riedell and the Sunway doing the heavy lifting, while the Commissioner and the Feds are concerned about covering their asses. Feels like Garcelli and I are the ones who are going to take the fall.

"No way are we paying ransom," Greene says again. The others nod. Better let me work the civilians,"

"Civilians, that's me and my family," I remind Lt. Garcelli.

"I've got a kid of my own," Agent Greene is saying, "I know how to use her to work the father."

"Looks to me like your boss is ready to bail," I tell Garcelli.

"If he assigns me to that bitch, my early retirement is screwed."

I put up my hand. The Commissioner is saying, "I'll leave Garcelli with you. You keep me informed, and I'll keep the Mayor off your back."

Garcelli is fuming.

"I'm taking them all down," Special Agent Greene says a bit louder.

"Kasey says she shouldn't trust any of us," I tell Garcelli. "I think she mostly means me."

FBI's Greene ignores Prosecutor Kasey's threat, moving closer to the Commissioner.

"We've got 1,000 agents working this case. Ireland, prison, Berk, and this group. We'll shut this down before there is another explosion," I repeat Greene's comments to Garcelli. "Our terrorist squad is already imbedded with the Garda Siochana, Irish police. They'll go pub-to-pub and door-to-door."

I lip read Kasey boasting she has a team at the prison loading up the kid's IV. If he knows anything, she'll get it.

"The Prosecutor's got her own team?" I ask Garcelli.

"Shush, keep watching."

"Greene is saying she can get LSD if they need it. She's telling the Commissioner that Paddy is compromised. The Commissioner is agreeing."

"Even I can see that," Lt. Garcelli growls.

"Greene is asking the Commissioner about you."

The Commissioner says, "I've got his pension by the balls. He'll do what I tell him." Instead, I say to Garcelli, "He's the best detective on the Force."

"Then we're good," Greene continues. "Commissioner, get your Mayor to announce he is cooperating with the FBI. I just sent you my personal cell number. You will know everything I know, and vice versa. Agreed?"

"You going to wire this place?" he asks.

"My team is working the bar right now. I've got a camera in this drone," she says, touching her jacket collar.

"The beetle pin on her jacket," I tell Garcelli. "It's a drone."

"Here they come. They want you to search and wire Paddy's home," I whisper to Lt. Garcelli. "Say something an angry cop would yell to a reporter."

"Lying motherfucker," Garcelli shouts.

I give Garcelli a surprised look.

"You're on," she whispers to the Commissioner.

"Lt. Garcelli will take command," the Commissioner announces to us.

I try to catch the Commissioner's eye, but he ignores me, and instead heads across the room to Paddy. They have a fast exchange. Nodding, a slap on the back, and the Commissioner returns.

"Get this stuff over to your command post," he orders Garcelli, waving his arms to include the entire warehouse/ home/ school. "We'll coordinate with the FBI from your Command Center."

Lt. Garcelli snaps to. "Yes, Sir. And Sir? What exactly do I commandeer?"

"All this stuff, Garcelli," the Commissioner waves his arm again. "Find those bombs before they find us. I've got a Mayor to see."

"Wadjet, open," I say letting the Police Commissioner leave. The airlock sucks the door tight.

Chapter Twenty-Eight

Prosecutor Kasey marches away from Agent Greene once again, with her cellphone pressed to her ear. Riedell smiles at me directing my attention to our home security monitor. Returning her signal, I try not to be obvious, but Garcelli's eyes follow mine. Riedell has displayed Kasey's cell, 'you have no new messages'. She adds "Useless Bureaucrat" in red letters.

Lt. Garcelli is both amused and concerned. "I'd hate to have your daughter pissed at me."

"Keep that in mind." I advise him.

Now I understand why Tiu has put Riedell front and center of the City's top law enforcement. This is another teaching opportunity, preparing her to deal with The Destiny Society.

Paddy decides to join us. He's weighed the options. From his posture, I can tell he's going to address his wife's treachery head-on.

"If in fact the suspect assembled, or was in contact with the bombs," Paddy says to Lt. Garcelli, "you'd better send a team through my home. It's the floor below us. Check the Pub's van too. It's parked out back. And while you're at it, I'd suggest taking another run through the SoHo loft. Focus on the basement. Maybe it was a gas leak, but check for Semtex. Wouldn't hurt to have Explosives compare the tags from the Helmsley to those at the butterfly tower at Starch's estate. Bombers tend to stay with what they know. Make sure we have the same Perp."

Garcelli notices Prosecutor Kasey pull a prepared form from her pocket. "If you would just sign this release…"

"Paddy. Don't be pressured," Lt. Garcelli advises him. "Maybe you shouldn't sign anything now."

Everyone in the room knows there will be incriminating evidence somewhere in his home.

Paddy takes the paper and signs it using Garcelli's back. "I know what you're thinking, and I appreciate it. But maybe this can help save lives."

He hands the form to Agent Greene. "Conduct the search. Bring in the dogs and your full team. I seriously doubt my wife built bombs, but even if there is residue on her clothes, we've got ourselves proof."

"Appreciate your cooperation," Agent Greene says.

Kathleen is claiming responsibility. So why is Paddy putting his head on the chopping block with hers?

Lt. Garcelli understands all too well. Letting the Feds invade Paddy's home, without restriction, without a deal in hand, means prison for his old T.O. Cooperation is one thing, but this is insane.

"You think your wife is bluffing?" FBI's Special Agent Greene asks him.

"Bluffing? No. But I don't think the bombings are her idea either," Paddy clarifies. "I think she has been duped. I want to prove to her that she's been played."

"By showing her how we are playing you?" Agent Greene asks.

"No. I think I can get answers if you make me your negotiating face. I can hit buttons in her no one can touch," Paddy says, sitting on the back edge of the sofa, making his size less intimidating.

"I'll tell her I understand, and that I know she would never endanger the school kids, especially Riedell, by bringing explosives into our home. And I'll tell her that's why I'm letting the FBI search our property."

"She'll think you're the fool," Lt. Garcelli says.

"Not if she's being manipulated. We need to know who is pulling the strings."

"You could go to prison for the rest of your life," I warn him.

"I'll take that chance," Paddy says.

"I'll keep your offer in mind," SAC Greene decides. Prosecutor Kasey whispers in her ear. No one needs to be a lip-reader to see she is encouraging Greene to accept Paddy's offer.

Riedell continues flicking fingers over her tablet, working the kaleidoscope of images. Thousands of numbers and photos whiz across screens. It really is quite amazing to watch the data compete for recognition.

"Lt. Garcelli has my permission to bring his dogs through my home. We don't need another explosion happening while you're deciding the legalities."

Agent Greene chews on her lip, thinking.

I'll bet Riedell's precious roller skates that Greene has lawyers in front of a Federal Judge at this very moment. She wants the legal right to dismantle Paddy's home without his consent.

"Convince me why I should let you talk to her," Agent Greene says.

Paddy starts counting down his points, finger by finger. "The Helmsley explosion killed five and injured hundreds. SoHo? Late hours, low traffic, minimal injuries. Last, the Starch estate explosion, destroying only property and butterflies," Paddy explains. "If Kathleen wants attention drawn to her son, an explosion does the trick. You don't start by killing people, then downgrade to butterflies."

"You're saying she didn't set the bombs at the Helmsley," Greene understands.

"Exactly. Why so violent? Kathleen only cares about her son. The rest of the demands make no sense. So why take the additional risk?" Paddy says.

"You tell me." Agent Greene coaxes Paddy.

"You need to put me out front."

"You have a strategy in mind?" Agent Greene asks.

"Proof of action," Paddy offers.

"You want your wife to set off another bomb?" Lt. Garcelli asks in amazement.

Kasey turns to Agent Greene. "We've got five dead, hundreds critically injured, and a terrorist, his wife, making demands and taking responsibility. Damn right we're going to search this building. But we do this by the letter of the law," she says waving her cell phone. "Special Agent, you can bring your team in. I'll have your warrant before they hit the doors. I'm done with all this foolishness."

Kasey moves her sights to Garcelli. "Lieutenant, bring these two in, now!"

Riedell flashes the red "BUREAUCRAT" overlay.

"I want Kathleen to show she can stop another bomb," Paddy clarifies. "Prove she is in charge. Otherwise we are going in the wrong direction."

"Your wife is a terrorist," Prosecutor Kasey insists. "Terrorists bomb and kill. The cause is window dressing. Anarchy is their reason. Don't try and give them lofty ideals. These people are savages. They kill for pleasure."

"I don't believe my wife is a savage," Paddy says firmly, as if he is prepared to demonstrate to Prosecutor Kasey what savagery, in its most unadulterated form, really is.

* * *

"If I may," Chuti Tiu says emerging through one of the mammoth membrane screens.

Tiu appears mysteriously, gracefully, like Yeti, our cat. She is wearing a black silk qipao dress and ballet slippers. Her hair is in a loose queue over one shoulder. Tiu gives the impression she is a young Asian woman, until you notice her short aquiline nose, and intense blue-green eyes.

Prosecutor Kasey alerts. Tiu's diminutive stature catches her off guard.

"So, you are what the fuss is all about?" Prosecutor Kasey says, not attempting to hide her amusement.

"No fuss," Tiu says. "Were you behind releasing this man?" Tiu asks as the image of James Berk exiting Fishkill prison appears on the screens. "The man who raped and murdered my sister?"

"The man who supposedly invented the genetic cure of the century," Agent Greene conveniently remembers. "You implying Dr. Berk is involved in these bombings?"

"Ridiculous," Kasey says to SAC Greene. "We are dealing with children here. This is a waste of our time. I'll have the wife's son, or whatever he is, spilling his guts within the hour. Let's get away from this circus," she decides for them both.

Greene doesn't hear a word of what Kasey said. She is fixed on Tiu.

"This FBI agent," Tiu turns her tablet to show Greene, "the man dressed in a dark suit downstairs planting bugs in Parnell's. He's one of yours, isn't he?"

"We have a Level One threat," Greene replies.

"Not in my house," Tiu tells Greene. "There are consequences," she says nodding to Riedell who taps her tablet. The man in the suit jumps like fire ants are invading his shorts, and shakes out black devices from his pockets.

"Call your man," Tiu tells Greene. "Ask if he knows what the Sunway TaihuLight System is."

Greene hesitates, but does as requested. We watch as the agent in Parnell's answers his cell phone. He looks up, realizing he is being watched.

Special Agent Greene whispers into her phone.

"What did he say?" Lt. Garcelli asks.

Greene takes her time answering. She puts her cell back in her pocket. "He said, you are talking to God. She is the epitome of elegance." *

"Well I don't care what some rinky-dink..." Prosecutor Kasey starts arguing, "I'm going to..."

"Shut-up, Kasey. Just shut-up," Greene orders. "That man," she points to her agent on the screen, "has two Ph.D.'s from MIT. He's as good as we have, so unless you are God's mother, you have nothing to offer. Ms. Tiu, I apologize. I'm listening," Special Agent-in-Charge Greene decides.

"Let me make our relationship a bit clearer." Tiu taps her tablet. "Sir," she says when the face of the U.S. Vice President appears, "I have with me Special Agent-in-Charge Greene of the FBI, Special Prosecutor Kasey, DOJ, and NYPD Assistant Chief Garcelli. Would you be kind enough to clear the path?"

"I'm speaking for the President. You will give Ms. Tiu every courtesy. Is that understood? Good." He doesn't wait for an answer. "Chuti. I'm at your disposal, any time, no matter the hour."

The screen goes blank.

Gotta love my wife.

"Shall we start fresh?" Tiu suggests, easing nearer to her niece Riedell, who, even without the skates, towers over her tiny Aunt.

Tiu pokes a delicate, red-nailed finger at Riedell's butt, rolling her an inch forward. Riedell reacts dramatically, pretending she's been Brutus-stabbed, feigns stumbling forward, although in complete control and laughing throughout.

The police and FBI presence don't intimidate Riedell for a second. Like her mother, she has the crazy, roller-skating, anti-litter quirk of independence. It's also a quality of loners. I recognize the trait. She selects her friends, by invitation only.

---

* Most of us equate glamour and sophistication to elegance. But in mathematics the meaning is quite different. Elegance refers to a simple expression of a very complicated set of parameters. $E=MC^2$, five symbols that define the most primal force in the Universe. You may even be able to put words to the famous equation. But understanding it? Very few of us are able to do that. Einstein himself wondered, "Why do so many people want to talk with me, when they cannot understand a word I am saying?"

$E=MC^2$ is pure elegance.

"Why all the cloak and dagger?" Prosecutor Kasey attacks Tiu. "You in witness protection?"

"I prefer being under my own protection," Tiu tells her.

I'm sensing a drop into an Antarctic crevasse is in store for the Prosecutor. For Agent Greene, Tiu will be more restrained, like Yellowstone wolves circling.

She is setting up Kasey. "What did James Berk promise you? A multi-million dollar PAC? Something else?" Tiu asks, sniffing the air suspiciously.

"I don't know what you are talking about," Kasey dismisses the accusation, turning on Lt. Garcelli. "I said move," she orders.

Lt. Garcelli, who I suspect desperately wants his leather-covered sap Wadjet has impounded, glares his response.

"Do you have an arrangement with James Berk?" Agent Greene asks Prosecutor Kasey.

She has picked up the scent, although I have no idea where Tiu is going with her left-field connection, other than to confuse the prosecutor.

Before Kasey can respond, Tiu asks, "Have any of you noticed the particularly strong fragrance of jasmine in the room?"

Tiu points upward. "Air handling. We filter out particulates. Sunway doesn't enjoy dust. Wadjet sent me an alert when she picked up the fragrance on the stairs. A masking agent, isn't it?"

"For what?" Agent Greene asks, reflexively inhaling the air.

"The distinctly fishy fragrance of someone in chronic kidney failure," Tiu explains. "What medical miracle did Berk promise you?" she asks Prosecutor Kasey.

Riedell slides nearer the woman, takes in a long sniff and twitches her nose, feigning horror as she skates away.

Kasey's silence is her admission.

"Let me guess. Berk probably pulled up your records while he was in Fishkill prison, focusing on medical," Tiu suggests. "Don't be too flattered. I'm sure he searched hundreds of prospects before he found you. But found you, he did. Your connection to his favorite newspaper publisher was an added bonus."

Prosecutor Kasey remains quiet, dissolving.

"I don't imagine it was too difficult for Berk to send you an advance notice of his CRISPR discovery. Perhaps with a little reminder of when you two met?"

"At the Chronicle," I remember. "One of Starch's mixers. I was there."

Chuti Tiu allows all the connections to sink into place before continuing. "Although there is little CRISPR can do for your kidney condition, Berk's connection to the very powerful Destiny Foundation is an assurance you'd be moved to the head of the kidney replacement line. In exchange for what?"

"Ms. Kasey?" Greene levels the question to her soon-to-be-former associate. "Have you been compromised?"

I love my new wife.

* * *

"All secure," Wadjet says as the airlock seals and the deadbolt slides home. Prosecutor Kasey is no longer with us.

"Here is the pub in Derry where the broadcast was recorded and sent," Riedell says.

"You already found the location?" Agent Greene shakes her head in amazement.

"We were only waiting for Ms. Kasey to leave," Riedell says as she enlarges the live barroom image. Kathleen is gone.

"Sunway has sent you her analysis and list of prime bombing sites in the City, along with the terrorist suspects," Tiu tells Agent Greene and Lt. Garcelli.

"How many suspects?"

"One thousand two hundred and three names who know how to assemble, plant and detonate bombs. The Irish were at war with the Brits for twenty years, which explains why so many people know how to make bombs. A few high percentage names were on the same flight from NY as Kathleen. We'll try and narrow the field," Tiu says moving away with Riedell.

"Proof of action?" Greene asks Paddy. "What exactly do you mean?"

Paddy is prepared. "Kathleen said bombs, plural. Next call, I'll demand she give us one location as proof."

"Unless they decide to show us, not tell us," Lt. Garcelli mentions.

Greene has made her decision. "You'll be working under my team's direction. Negotiations will be transmitted with a 3-second time delay," Greene says to Paddy. "Agreed?"

"I'm okay with that. My approach will be to turn the tables, I'll make the demands, not them. I'll tell her Jamie won't even get out of solitary until we get one bomb. I won't mention money, even if they bring it up. We'll find out who their leader is, and what they really want, right quick."

Greene nods, appreciating how quickly Paddy has created a working scenario. She hasn't made either one of us any promises. We are working on Paddy's instincts until we have something to show Greene confirming our bone fides.

Chuti Tiu was terrific in dismantling Prosecutor Kasey. I think Agent Greene was caught off guard, but sending Kasey packing doesn't mean she is out of the way.

Paddy has already set his personal feelings aside and is preparing himself for the role of his life. Literally.

"You cannot overlook the influence of her family. They're all IRA terrorists," Greene says, making it clear that Parnell's, Paddy and Kathleen have been on a 'watch' list.

Paddy nods. "I knew Kathleen was helping back home with medical supplies, some cash, but I thought that was the extent of it. Obviously some of the homeless we feed are her contacts."

"We know," Greene says.

"I'll get the search of your place going now," Lt. Garcelli says.

"Good," Agent Greene agrees. "You two don't leave the building." she orders Paddy and me.

"I have a job, you know. They need me at the paper."

"Right now your job is here. I need to confer with the Director."

Chapter Twenty-Nine

"Mr. Shaw?" Bailiff Mrs. R asks.

"Speaking."

"I'm sorry to trouble you while the FBI is at your door."

"How did…"

"Oh, Mr. Shaw, your place is on Channel 3. Mr. Berk, correction Dr. Berk called Judge R to make certain we were aware. I told Judge R it was probably just part of the explosion investigation. Those detectives can be quite bothersome," she prompts me to explain, but I'm not biting.

"Interesting coincidence, your call. The FBI is asking if James Berk and his associate, Gayfryd Van Wie, were invited to Starch's Event. Seems they are investigating the possibility that terrorism may be a cover for murder. I'm sorry, Mrs. R, I probably should not be telling you that. If you would keep this to yourself? Member of the Court, and all."

"Of course. Murder, you say. Yes. Definitely. Mums the word."

"Thank you."

"Now to the point of my call. Judge R is very anxious to come to a resolution regarding darling Riedell. Truth be told, I'd love to take her for myself," she says warmly.

"That's very kind, but…"

"I have your financial statement."

"Yes. There may be some possible changes," I mention, trying not to sound too concerned.

"I was under the impression your wife has a very hush-hush, top-secret position with the Government or…?"

"She's…"

"Unemployed, according to this," Mrs. R cuts me off.

"That's not the whole picture," I tell her without elaborating.

"And Dr. Darieux's attorneys sent a message indicating that you are no longer employed either. I'm sorry to hear that news, is it also true?"

I remind myself not to underestimate the kindly old woman.

"I'm working a story this minute while my agent is busy re-negotiating my contract. We do this every few years or so. It's a sort of ritual."

' Oh, I know all about those things," she sympathizes. "Elections, appointments. Judge R and I are all too familiar."

"Good to know."

"But if you'd bring your contract over in the morning, you could explain the details. Judge R, he doesn't take Riedell's future lightly. Imagine living in the Swiss Alps, in a chateau to boot. The work Dr. Darieux's Foundation is involved with…well it's simply amazing."

"And still so deeply involved at age seventy- four?"

"Seventy-six, actually."

"Amazing she is still active at that age. Most people would be enjoying their remaining time, seeing the world, long cruises for instance, don't you think?"

"Yes."

I may have overplayed my hand with that one, as charm dissipates, and a stern voice replies. "We'll expect you, Mrs. Shaw and Riedell in chambers tomorrow. Nine AM sharp."

"I wasn't aware we had an appointment?"

"Really? I am certain I told you. I do hope we are not inconveniencing you and the Mrs.?"

We all might be blown to bits by then, I think, but say, "We'll be there."

* * *

A bartender I don't recognize puts a Jack Daniels, rocks, in front of me and leaves. The aroma fills my nostrils and crackles the dry membranes in my head. With my recent tea ritual, I find the Jack startling, then utterly soothing. An old friend.

"Thought you might need one," Gert says, taking the seat next to me. "Two cops are in a squad across 1st at the Kumon children's learning center. Another is sitting around the corner in front of the Madison Restaurant on 53rd. Otherwise, business is back to normal. Anything else from Kathleen?"

I shake my head no. "Paddy is allowing Garcelli and the FBI to search his home."

"Dumb move."

I nod, agreeing. "Just heard from the Family Court Bailiff. Decision time first thing in the morning."

"Then I'll take that," Gert says snatching my JD. "You're barely holding on to what's left up here," she taps my head, and sips my drink. "Hon, give him a hot tea, if you would. This will work just fine for me," she tells the bartender.

I don't tell her I've popped a couple pain pills as well.

"Then again, maybe not so dumb of Paddy," Gert muses. "Garcelli is true NYPD Blue to the core. He may look and sound like a fat braggart, but he protects his own."

I shrug. I have to admit Garcelli and I had a brief connection during my lip reading routine. "I know. He isn't a complete jerk."

"One more, and I'm back to the office," Gert declares. "Amy is holding down the fort."

"She's still there?"

"Yeah. You work for me, she works for you. That's the hierarchy. Buck up," Gert says slapping me on the back, downing the drink. "I'll handle the Chronicle while you straighten up around here. And don't screw this one up. Retraction on page 10 ain't going to do it."

Gert rolls her empty glass on my neck. I lift the glass taking in the aroma, as I watch her go out the door. I try to relax, closing my eyes and letting my mind drift. Who comes skating up to me, but Emma as The Lion King.

"Touch-up," she whispers in my ear, giving me a smack on my cheek. I don't have to look in the mirror to know I have the imprint of Halloween red lips. "We could run over to that little room, crackle, crackle – good as new. Eyes of blue. Let's do doo."

It is the same nonsensical sing-song she would use warning Kathleen and me when she knew she was losing control. Kathleen took Emma for those touch-ups almost as often as I did, before the cingultomy ended the need. Ended the Lion King. Ended the gibberish. Ended Emma as we knew her.

"That's where," I yell.

Spinning out of my stool, I rush upstairs and spot Paddy standing outside the open door to his home.

"I know where one is," I whisper.

In an instant we are out of Parnell's running.

My right pocket burner is vibrating. "The **32CSM** video just went viral," Amy yells.

"Damn. They are pushing the time."

"Van Wie is all over this. He told me to get your confession."

"That ass. Paddy and I have an idea. We'll know in a few minutes. If this goes South, speak well of us. Got to go."

"But…"

* * *

"The bomb threat video is on the Internet," I tell Paddy. He has already guessed.

"Look at this street," I yell to him over the honking horns. "Panic."

Paddy nods. He steps in front of me. One of Emma's street people wearing an Army fatigue jacket with a 1st Cav patch is pushing people out of his way, escaping to nowhere. He is the size of a linebacker.

"I'l get you home," Paddy tells the man who seems terrified and begins crying. Paddy turns him in the direction we're heading. "Walk with us." Paddy's arm goes around the man's shoulder and we continue strolling. Strolling to stop an exploding bomb!

I take the lead. "Nice day. Afternoon," I say to nervous gawkers as we step up our pace. Nothing unusual, we're walking with a deranged street person towards a bomb a bi-polar apparition told me about in a daydream.

I haven't asked Paddy why he is wearing his NYPD dress uniform. I don't want to suggest he's acting odd. After all, I'm hearing dead people.

Paddy points the linebacker to a chair as we go through the main lobby of Eastside Mercy. Speaking to no one, we head down the halls, push through doors, pass gurneys lining the walls, pass patients walking their IV stands, and rooms with empty hospital beds. We don't speak to anyone.

We know the abandoned Freeman Surgery is our destination. Right in the center of the operating table is a stainless steel egg, identical to the one Riedell put on Paddy's neck less than an hour ago. We both know it's the bomb.

"Get out of here. Call Garcelli. I'll keep anyone from coming inside," Paddy orders, handing me his phone.

Report danger, that's me. Rush to danger? That would be Paddy.

"Lieutenant. We found a bomb. Eastside Mercy. The Freeman Lobotomy Surgery," I tell Lt. Garcelli.

"Damn good job," I hear Garcelli yell. "My Squad is on the way. And thanks. Appreciate you calling me."

Chapter Thirty

"You think a shit storm is heading our way?" I ask Paddy when we return to my warehouse.

"Big time," my friend says, sinking deeper into a chair.

Yeti jumps off Paddy's lap as she sees Rowdy heading for the kitchen. The sound of Riedell filling a glass with ice from the refrigerator means the possibility of treats.

"That sound. That is the same sound we heard when Riedell filled the egg with ice for your neck." I say.

Paddy looks at me. "Then this bomb was a gift after all. I just missed the clues Kathleen was leaving me."

"We looked for the Semtex tags, never thinking about the container. I'll bet anything there are stainless steel fragments from the egg at Starch's butterfly tower. So, what else did we miss?" I ask.

"There were a few different sort of customers talking with Kath over the past few weeks. Some extra nights out doing her missionary work. Her reaction to the Helmsley. I should have noticed."

"You're being too hard on yourself."

Paddy stands, pounding his fist on his thigh. "Not hard enough." He points a finger to my forehead, then his. "I'm feeling a bullet coming our way."

* * *

"How did you find the bomb?" Tiu asks before putting up a finger cautioning us not to answer just yet.

Paddy and I nod. Riedell glides back to the family area and sits on the floor. She has a bowl of salted pretzels, the egg container hanging from her little finger by the carabiner clip, and a stack of red plastic cups. Sweet tea no doubt. Riedell's favorite. Feels more like a Jack Daniels moment to me.

Tiu points upward as she draws a line across her tablet landing a silver whirligig the size of a cockroach on the coffee table in front of us.

"What the…"

Riedell drops a red plastic cup over the device. Simple as that, Riedell solves another problem.

"You listening, Greene?" Tiu asks, not expecting an answer. "It's a DOD drone," she tells us. "Greene left it for us. They planted two more in the pub and launched a larger one hoovering around our building," Tiu says pointing to the images on screen. "I just redirected it to circle the FBI field office instead."

"Guess Greene doesn't trust us to keep her informed," I conclude.

"You said a shit storm," Tiu says to Paddy. "I agree. Based on the Semtex unaccounted for, there are another two bombs remaining of this size," Tiu says holding up Riedell's egg container, "or one larger bomb. My bet is on one more. One that will do plenty of damage and kill people. A lot of people."

A screen projects mug shot pictures, with full dossiers on all of Kathleen's family. "The FBI, DOD, CIA, NYPD Terrorist Unit and all the counterparts in Ireland, the UK and Europe, have these. Also, if any other known associates of the **32CSM** picks up a phone, uses an ATM, or tries to buy a Guinness with a credit card, the FBI has them."

"So they have gone to ground," Paddy understands.

"Look up here," Tiu points to a screen. "Every street, store, walkway, pub, and gas station in Ireland with a security camera is up there. We've got facial recog going 24/7."

"The entire country?"

Tiu drops a blanket over the cup covering agent Greene's surveillance drone.

"We can go deeper," Tiu says. "Kathleen knows some of what we can do here. She'll know to cut off cell phones and anything linked to the Internet."

"What she won't know is that every TV is an electronic eye," Riedell adds.

"You are kidding!"

"The Sunway will locate them." She points to a display scanning faces in blur. "FemtoScan. Half a trillion frames per second."

"Really? Everyone in Ireland?" I ask.

"Four point eight million people living in Ireland, 1.8 million TVs. The Sunway will spot her."

"And the FBI will have their location?"

"We will have the location," Tiu emphasizes. "The FBI doesn't have our search capability. They can only monitor what we are doing. Their man will understand," Tiu says pointing at the blurred screen, "that when the scan stops, we've found Kathleen. Then he'll notify Greene. I'd say we'll have a two minute head start."

Chapter Thirty-One

"When you give me the signal, I've got only seconds to break her. Get the bomb location and stop the FBI from a full blown attack," Paddy says.

"Her boy is dying," Tiu explains. "Use that. Berk did."

"Berk's had ten years. I've got two minutes."

"Paddy," I say, "you've had more than ten years. Find a trigger. But find it fast."

* * *

"Damn. How does anyone hide from the Government?" I ask while Paddy takes a break, ostensibly to check on any damage the FBI may have done to his home.

"Explain," Tiu tells her prodigy to enlighten dear old dad.

"Ineptitude, bureaucracy, and democracy. Your favorite topics," Riedell says.

"I'm feeling outclassed."

"Ever uncover information you wish you hadn't?" Riedell asks.

The first time I knocked on Gayfryd's door comes to mind. "A few times," I answer, hoping my daughter doesn't know those details.

"That's what Aunt Chuti does," Riedell explains. "She works for everyone, but answers to no one. The secrets she knows remain with her. So don't try to lie, or expect her to cover for you. She knows the truth."

"Where did you come from?" I ask my ten-year-old daughter.

Riedell executes a spin in answer as she zips back into the kitchen. "Ice cream?" she calls back.

"Oh yes," Tiu says hurrying after her.

* * *

"Can you get the Sunway to trace Kathleen taking out the van by herself in the last three months?" I ask Tiu, taking my bowl of melted pistachio from Riedell.

"After the Helmsley explosion, she started going out nights by herself more often. Said she needed time to think," Paddy says. "Her father or their confederates would have blended in easily at the van."

"That accounts for why we only have him coming in Parnell's the one time," I realize.

"Shawn. This lip reading thing. How good are you?" Paddy asks.

"Pretty good, not great. I usually fill in the gaps myself. What do you need?"

"Can one of you pull up Parnell's surveillance?" Paddy asks Tiu and Riedell. "See if Shawn can figure out what Kathleen's father said to her at the bar."

"On it," Riedell accepts the challenge. "Old man, hat pulled down, talking to Kathleen," she confirms. She tightens in on the face. We don't need a facial recognition match to know he's her father. "Only one event."

"He's saying, 'Ye need to decide,'" I interpret. "That's all I can get. After that his hand or a glass covers his mouth. He knows the cameras are watching."

"Voice match from the pub in Ireland on the video message," Tiu anticipates Paddy's next request.

"Try focusing on Kathleen instead."

"I can't get full words. She's arguing. Lots of no's. That's about all I can get," I apologize.

"Does Kathleen know about your lip reading skill?" Tiu asks.

"Good chance. I never told her directly, but I remember her asking me what a few people were arguing about. They were outside. So I'm guessing, yes. Kath doesn't miss much."

Paddy grunts agreement. "Any chance Kathleen mouthed anything about the bomb location on the video call?"

"I wasn't looking. I was listening. Maybe. Let's run it again," I say.

We all know Paddy is grasping.

"Can you go back to the Helmsley squad car? While we're on this lip reading bit, pull up Arlo's surveillance of that day," Paddy asks.

"Clever," Tiu gives him a flicker of appreciation. "No problem."

"Go to right before the television crews arrive. Also pull in any cell phones that might have been taking tourist pictures. Can you do that? I want Shawn to read what the cops are saying before the shooting."

"On screen three," Tiu points.

"What am I looking for?"

"This is as tight as I can get on your Ace and his Captain in the squad car," Tiu says.

We can see Ace in the driver's seat. I watch his face for a moment, trying to set my mind into his speech pattern.

"Ace is saying, 'you heard the click?'" I interpret.

"Now Ace is telling the Captain there's a pressure bomb under your seat."

"The Captain already knows," Paddy guesses. "I think he figured Ace has turned, and he's already got his gun in his lap before Ace pulls out his weapon. A Mexican standoff, except for the bomb."

"See there. Two flashes," Tiu says.

The windshield and driver's side windows are splattered. "Cap took the kill shot, except Ace jerked off a round, putting a slug in the Cap's liver."

"That's why the Cap sat there with a gun to his head. He was a dead man three times over, but only the bomb could get his family the pension," I understand.

"Easiest solution all around for NYPD is to blame the Mob for the bomb. Hell, maybe it was them. Cover up the fact they have two dirty cops," Paddy says.

"I was hoping one of them would mention Berk," I say.

"Too much to ask for. Besides, the cops probably never heard of Berk. If they did they would have upped the protection fee for Gayfryd's clinic."

"When Berk was about to be released, it was time to get rid of the cops. All he had to do was send Arlo's surveillance tapes to the Mob, let them know there was an independent shakedown operation. Let nature take its course."

"With the **32CSM** as backup."

"What is the reason for all these explosions?" Riedell asks.

"James Berk wants to get rid of Shawn and all of his friends," Tiu explains, looking at me.

"Does Mr. Berk want to be my father?"

"What he wants is control over you, and me. If making himself out to be your father accomplishes that, fine with him."

"Which means Kathleen didn't kill anyone." Riedell says.

"That will be entirely up to her," Paddy concludes.

* * *

"Look." Riedell says. "The FBI woman is downstairs with Lt. Garcelli and that Prosecutor. She's holding up a cleaning service uniform."

"She knows we are watching."

"Run the label on the uniform, but don't screen it. They want to come up here again," Tiu directs Riedell who is already running the cleaning company's customer list and employees' data, crossing Kathleen's work schedule to her food and blanket deliveries."

Paddy glances at me, confirming I'm making the connection. Riedell and Chuti Tiu think as one.

My left pocket vibrates, it's Gert.

"Looks like Mrs. Wright and your on-again-off-again best friend, Walter Jackson, are back together. They are dropping your contract."

"Just keeps getting better. Thank goodness I don't have a dog."

"Except your cats are taking the hit. I'll bet they are down to eight of their nine."

"They'll outlive us all," I'm certain.

"You, definitely," Gert says. "On the brighter side, Amy told Van Wie you have the inside on the bombing investigation. They didn't bite."

"I don't want to tell this story anyway."

"Is it getting worse?"

"I know Berk and Destiny are behind all of this; from Emma to the explosions to whatever. I just can't prove it. Besides, no one would believe freezing children in a meat locker could lead to an IRA extortion plot. Thirty years in the making? And I don't think it's over."

"Ready for more?"

"Why not."

"Your loan from the Chronicle is being called immediately. And Jackson filed a writ of mandate, whatever that is."

"I can guess."

"He's claiming you obtained the Company stock illegally. He wants the 'gift' rescinded. Athena explained that part to me. Seems you have a friend. Anything you want to tell me?"

"No."

"Good. Because in the meantime you are off the Chronicle Board. Ethics violations."

"Great. I've been ordered to Family Court in the morning. Seems my financials aren't sound. So now I'm out of a job, and my only asset is being taken away. I don't suppose there's a connection. Anything else?"

"Van Wie has a picture of the FBI invading Parnell's. He's going to run it. *Unflawed Flawed,* is the working headline," Gert says. "You want to come over and make your death gurgle? I can interview you for your obit."

"I'll pass. The FBI is coming up the stairs."

"Then I'll keep this short. Your Helmsley hallway picture has made its way to the tabloids. And you will be named and subpoenaed to testify in Van Wie's divorce from the lovely Gayfryd."

"I think my obit will write itself. Any good news?"

"I saw your goddess Athena coming out of Walter Jackson's office. She told our Acting Chairman what he didn't want to hear," Gert says. "Turns out I'm named as a Trustee for Starch's new school. Athena is the Executor of his Estate. She was also Starch's personal attorney. I'm getting a sense his will is going to be a doozy."

* * *

FBI Special Agent-in-Charge Greene and Prosecutor Kasey are back.

"You see this uniform before?" Greene demands not waiting for an answer. "It was hidden in the wheel well of your van. Looks like a cleaning uniform. ID badge from a service. We are running the Company info down now."

I notice Chuti glance at Riedell.

"The company specializes in cleaning office buildings at night," Agent Greene tells us. "We believe the time cards will show Kathleen's whereabouts and the locations of the remaining bombs."

She's one step behind us.

"So how'd you know the bomb was at the hospital?" SAC Greene demands.

It isn't a question.

Prosecutor Kasey steps in behind Greene waiting for an answer, and I hear the jangle of handcuffs. She sees Paddy and me as suspects, aiding and abetting. We're more like fools being played.

Explaining the stainless steel egg hints left by Kathleen, and the spiritual visit from Emma, won't fly. "I had a hunch," I say.

"Well, have another, and have it fast," she orders.

"Look at the uniform," Paddy suggests. "Kath is a large woman, but not *that* large. That's a man's uniform. She wasn't working for the cleaning company. Her family used her name and sent someone in her place."

Tiu glances at Riedell. All the cleaning company contracts are on screen. Paddy spots the target. "Where's Garcelli?"

"Going back to…" Greene doesn't have time to finish.

Paddy is on his cell. "Crags. Paddy. Evacuate now. Bomb suspected. Garcelli just left me, doesn't have this info. Move."

Chapter Thirty-Two

Agent Greene is directing emergency teams to the Midtown Precinct, alerting the bomb squads and fire department. Paddy is still on his cell, trying to contact Lt. Garcelli.

Tiu catches my eye, directing me to activity on the lower screen. I see six men and one woman hurrying into a bar. It's Kathleen. Two hours ahead of their deadline. Something's up.

Tiu motions to me, jerks her head toward Riedell. "Bedroom," Tiu mouths, eyes insisting.

It's the two minute warning.

"Riedell, Rowdy is throwing up in the bedroom. Hurry."

* * *

"Kathleen's people have been watching us," Tiu says.

"How?"

"Her people have passed as homeless people before. They can be any wino on the street watching the activity downstairs. I'm set up to protect against intrusion, not surveillance. I made this joint headquarters for the FBI and NYPD. That was a mistake."

Rowdy and Yeti are on my bed, curled head-to-toe. Riedell knows what Tiu is up to. She has my laptop in front of her showing the Irish bar. She seems anxious, but more prepared than I am.

We're watching the screen as the **32CSM** terrorist squad sets up a cell phone camera on a tri-pod and positions Kathleen at a stool as if she is anchoring *World News Tonight*.

"Where are they?"

"There are 6,984 pubs in Ireland" Riedell says.

"The pub's named Telstar. It's in the middle of the Creggan housing district in Derry, Ireland," Tiu whispers.

I know the name Creggan. It was an IRA war zone before the peace agreement.

"Their watchdogs can see there are no Brinks trucks or armored vans here. No attempt to meet their demands," Tiu says. "This Midtown bomb is their final warning."

"Kathleen has no idea we can see and hear them?" I whisper back.

Riedell shakes her head, "not yet. We are watching them through the TV behind the bar. They are setting up their video recording."

We watch shots poured. False courage. Kathleen declines. The thick-haired director is counting down Kathleen with his fingers.

"Are you ready for this?" Tiu asks Riedell.

"Aunt Kath," Riedell says as Kathleen opens her mouth to speak.

The terrorists panic. Guns swirling everywhere, people crouched, ready for canisters to come crashing through the windows. Doors sledge-hammered wide. Except there is no military invasion, only the innocent face of a young girl on the TV screen in front of them. Silence.

"Aunt Kath," Riedell repeats. "You don't want to do this. I love you. Don't let them hurt you."

The men erupt, cursing, pointing at the TV screen, raising their guns in the air. Kathleen is calm. Almost relieved. She wipes her eye. "I'm so sorry, Rye. My son is dying. No one would help."

"Tell the brat to get the President on TV," a voice orders.

The brogue is heavy, the voice slurred. I'm certain he's Kathleen's father. A few sotted men raise their weapons in support. The more alert and seasoned break away, searching the pub.

"The bomb, the one at the surgery where they damaged Mom," Riedell says, joining Kathleen in tears of her own. "Dad and Paddy found it. No one was hurt."

"It's the daughter of that lying reporter," Kathleen's father yells, sticking his face in front of Riedell's image, too drunk to realize that she is live on the TV, talking to them.

He is the stranger we saw earlier, with his hat pulled down, talking to Kathleen in Parnell's. I can see his facial scars. His teeth, brown, those that he has. Scruffy beard, dappled grey, coarse and in-grown. Drink and violence are his tattoos.

This isn't a cause, I realize. They are drunken rabble, orchestrated by one clever man over three thousand miles away.

"I just want my boy home," Kathleen pleads, her tears now flowing. Mine as well. Kathleen is trapped. You can never go home, I can see she knows as well. Too late.

"And give us our money," a young male adds.

"Aunt Kathleen. Don't do this. You can stop it," Riedell pleads. "Tell Shawn…"

"Shut your fuckin' gob, bitch," the father screams, slapping Kathleen across the face, knocking her off the stool.

Kathleen's father aims at the TV and shoots. We rush to the other room where the Sunway has already tapped into their camera. Greene and Paddy are watching.

"You dint listen," Kathleen's father snarls, holding up his cell phone in one hand, and a stainless steel egg in the other.

"That's the remote detonator," Tiu says.

"Time to pay the Piper," he grins, pressing the send button.

"We've got them," SAC Greene yells. "Jam that call," she orders as her phone rings.

"Don't," Tiu yells as Greene picks up the call.

"Too late. The relays were triggered the second you answered your phone. I can't do a thing."

"The Chronicle, 9-1-1. Wadjet. Open," I yell grabbing my satchel.

Chapter Thirty-Three

The first blast of chilled air outside Parnell's sends me into a coughing fit that nearly knocks me down. Within seconds I'm back breathing somewhat normally, until I start running. One block, not too bad; the second, I'm gasping; and by the third block my pulse is pounding kettle drums in my ears. I stop. Hands on my thighs, I'm sweating.

"Gert. Amy. Get out now. Clear the Chronicle. There's a bomb in the building." I try again. Both burner phones, dialed at the same time, both go to voicemail, again.

I can see myself reflected in the office windows. Red veins are bursting from my cold pasty face. I'm wobbling like a zombie. My underwear has truly become my second skin. I won't give up. The Chronicle steps are in sight.

Pulling open the glass door to the entrance zaps the last of my strength. Unable to speak, gulping like a landed sheepshead fish, I raise a finger in the air to my favorite guards, and collapse onto the lowest grade industrial carpet in existence.

The fall sends me lurching forward, knocking the guard to the wall as he's all but dragging me to the front security entrance by my arms.

"What the..."

A second shudder panics the guard into action as I get a burst of latent energy and pop to my feet, blocking his path. I force myself to the metal door, not thinking how my legs will manage the concrete stairs. The instant I wrench the door open, I'm hit by a blast of hot, filthy air in search of an exit.

The blast retreats a moment, like a boxer drawing back a haymaker, then spews out a wave of dust and hot debris. Trying again and finding a metal rail by memory, I pull myself up the stairs, managing a half floor before a screaming, hacking mass of humanity slams me into the concrete, clinging to the rail.

The air is grey-black. My lungs are sucking in decades of rubbish, and I'm stumbling through a terrified herd bent on escape. A heavy hand on my shoulder, a face inside a protective mask with headlights shining out like horns, ends my progress. Deposited on the curb across the street, and covered with a space blanket, my face and eyes are doused with water, and I'm left sitting with other shivering, blackened faces.

Helicopters circle above. First Avenue fills with firetrucks and ambulances.

A policeman recognizes me. "You're that *Unflawed* reporter, right? You okay?"

"How bad is it at the Midtown Precinct?" I ask him.

"What are you talking about?"

"Nothing, must have been a false alarm."

I reach Paddy on my phone. "It's real bad here. What about the Midtown Precinct."

"They found the bomb. Tiu thinks the signal wasn't strong enough to detonate both. Only the Chronicle took a hit."

* * *

The Mayor and Police Commissioner are on TV as the FBI frisks and scans me at the door of Parnell's.

I head upstairs. Wadjet forces me to wipe my face with my handkerchief before she will let me pass.

"Kathleen's been killed," Tiu says when I enter the main room.

Riedell is hugging Paddy's waist. "They shot her holding a broom."

"A broom?" I ask.

"It was horrible."

"I'm so sorry," is all I can manage.

Paddy calms Riedell, holding her in his "mitts." His eyes are fixed on the single screen re-playing the PSNI (Police Service of Northern Ireland) invading the pub.

I see the PSNI, in their rifle green uniforms, charge in. Shouldered Heckler & Koch MP5 machine guns at the ready. Targets identified.

Paddy is focusing on the insurgence team, looking for a wrong command, an opening not covered, maybe a member of the team out of sync with the others. What he sees is a precision strike carried out exactly as he would have conducted.

"Three suspects, dead, eight others down and cuffed. PSNI – no injuries," I hear Special Agent-in-Charge Greene telling her superiors.

Greene is sitting at the crescent-shaped school table, her command center. Tiu is beside her, assisting. The table is covered with tablets and cell phones connecting Greene with the NYPD, Fire, Bomb Squads, and the NYC and Washington, DC offices of the FBI.

One of our massive screens has formed around Greene, placing her inside the Telstar Pub in Ireland. A second one displays the Chronicle building from every conceivable angle. Greene is directing her ground teams, switching from headsets to cell phones as Tiu's screens provide her real-time visuals.

I'm watching the Mayor and Commissioner taking questions, assuring voters they are safe, while Agent Greene is conducting the investigation ten blocks away. It's comforting to see Greene isn't a glory hound.

"I think my wife was targeted," Paddy says, watching the gruesome videos from every angle.

"You're saying she's innocent?"

"I didn't say that," Paddy tells Greene. "What I'm asking is, who killed her?"

"Now you're blaming us?" Prosecutor Kasey jumps in. Her tone is volatile and threatening. "Your wife's boy was never going to be released. In fact, he was locked in solitary the moment we arrived. I issued the order personally."

Tiu has given FBI's Greene limited access. I know Prosecutor Kasey is blocked.

"Your wife had to know her boy wasn't going to be released," Agent Greene confirms. "She is the one responsible for getting herself killed."

"I'm just trying to find out *who* shot her," Paddy insists.

"You are thinking she was executed by her family," SAC Greene realizes.

"It's a possibility. I'm not buying Kathleen being connected to this **32CSM** garbage. She loved Ireland, but it wasn't her cause. I think she sacrificed herself."

"For whom?"

"Her son is dying. Kath said as much after she visited him in prison last month. She is a nurse, she would understand what Berk's CRISPR could promise."

"And you think she made a bargain with him?" Greene asks.

Paddy shrugs. "I'm searching for an explanation."

"Come on," Prosecutor Kasey says, exasperated. "The son is a HIV junkie. Face facts, your wife is dead. You are looking for a scapegoat. James Berk was being processed out of Fishkill when the Helmsley occurred. You want us to believe Berk blew up two cops and half a building to celebrate?"

"When we told Kathleen we found the bomb at the hospital, she seemed relieved," I say, supporting Paddy.

"Kathleen understood she hadn't killed anyone. That would change if the Chronicle bomb exploded. I think she was murdered before she got the chance to alert us."

"When Riedell contacted Kathleen in the Irish pub" I take up Paddy's argument, "Kathleen was trying to warn us."

"But she didn't," Kasey points to the hundreds of active images around the Chronicle building. "Look at the Irish pub video. They are knocking down shots."

"Maybe that's why Kathleen's father shot the TV. He could tell she was going to warn us," Riedell adds.

"Are you trying to convince me your wife went undercover with the **32CSM** terrorists to prevent the violence?" FBI Special Agent-in-Charge Greene asks Paddy, squinting her eyes in suspicion. "She planted bombs, for Christ's sake!"

"We don't know that for a fact," I mumble a defense that doesn't have a modicum of logic.

"That's not what Paddy is saying," Tiu takes over. "It's obvious Kathleen's family is involved. But don't you want to know their backers? Who paid for the explosives? Selected the locations?"

"Agent Greene," Paddy persists, "the round that killed Kathleen, did it come from a PSNI weapon?"

"All hell broke loose in that place," Agent Greene says, not turning around, her voice automatically defensive. "They'll be digging slugs out of the walls for a day."

"The one that killed Kathleen. Was it 9mm? Military issue, standard or frag? You can ask the PSNI on-site."

I don't remember where ammunition was explained to me; but jacketed rounds go through bodies, even walls. Frag, or dumb-dumb bullets shatter on impact, generally killing only the person hit, ripping through flesh and organs. No through-and-through.

"I'll ask," she concedes.

"Might be a good idea to have your people pick up James Berk before the President hangs that Medal of Freedom around his neck," Tiu suggests. "I think Berk told Kathleen the CRISPR procedure would save her son."

"You'd better explain exactly what this CRISPR can do." SAC Greene orders.

"Why don't you enlighten us, Ms. Kasey?" Tiu suggests.

"I have no idea what you mean."

"Sure you do," Tiu presses. "Didn't Berk promise you CRISPR would cure your diabetes mellitus, the primary cause of your kidney disease?"

"I don't know what you are talking about."

Riedell taps her tablet, displaying Fishkill's visitation log behind Prosecutor Kasey.

Tiu moves closer sniffing. "Nail polish remover, can the rest of you smell it under Ms. Kasey's rather pungent jasmine perfume?" she asks the group. "No? I didn't catch it right off either. But the Sunway did. Picked up the scent immediately using her electronic nose."

We all begin sniffing.

"You have a genetic disorder of the metabolic system, which causes chronically high sugar levels in the blood, leading to blindness, stroke, kidney failure and often amputation. Type 2 diabetes, as it's more commonly known."

Kasey starts to protest, but SAC Greene stops her. "Ms. Tiu, what exactly is CRISPR and what can it achieve?" she asks.

Chuti Tiu steps in front of Prosecutor Kasey even though she is answering SAC Greene. "CRISPR. A gene editing procedure that can, some day, permanently cure genetic conditions, both before they emanate, and possibly after the symptoms have erupted. In medicine, this is a complete game changer. Developed, in part, by The Destiny Foundation. The medical office at the Helmsley was a test lab. Right in the heart of Manhattan. Not all of the test volunteers were prisoners."

"You said, developed, in part. Does that mean you are the other part"?

"Yes."

Special Prosecutor Kasey's eyes widen.

* * *

"Tom," Paddy answers his cell phone. Lt. Garcelli is calling from the Chronicle. Paddy puts the phone on speaker.

"Full house there?"

"As you left us. We are all listening."

"The good news is Gert is alive. She got your call and hit the fire alarm box. Gave lots of people a head start. Bad news, she got caught in the back stairwell. Gert was directing people when she got trapped. A section of concrete has her pinned down. I think we are going to have to take her leg. That's the best I know. Thick smoke. Short term teams in and out. It will be battleground surgery at best. I've got a police escort waiting to rush her to Eastside Mercy. That's all I've got."

"Amy?" I yell before Lt. Garcelli hangs up.

"I don't have any names. But if she was on the top floor with Gert, it doesn't look good. Gotta go."

"Gert is type A positive," Riedell says, pointing to Gert's medical records on a screen.

"I can't imagine how you think so fast," I say rubbing my daughter's shoulder.

"I'm O negative. The Universal donor," Tiu says. "I'll go. Paddy, I need you to clear the way."

"I'll come as well," Special Prosecutor Kasey says, shocking the group. She holds up her Federal identification. "You'd be surprised how this clears a path. We'll need to know everything she saw."

"Greene, leaving or staying?"

Agent Greene looks down at the control table, and up at the war room of screens streaming data and live video. "You go. I can do the work of a hundred agents, right here."

"Rye? Will you assist agent Greene?" Tiu asks.

Riedell grins. At ten I was re-reading the descriptions of Della Street in my Perry Mason paperbacks.

Chapter Thirty-Four

"Thank you," I tell Chuti as she is prepped to give blood at Eastside Mercy. "I'm really sorry."

"For what?"

"Gayfryd. The video of me in that hallway. I'm an embarrassment to you."

"We weren't married then. You were free to do whatever stupid things you needed," Tiu says, patting my hand, wincing as the needle goes in her vein.

"Seeing myself like that, I feel ashamed." I apologize.

"Our arrangement isn't fair to you."

"Forged papers. Saving Riedell. I understand."

"I wish you did," Chuti says, squeezing my hand.

"Gert just came in," Paddy says, pulling back the curtain, surprised to see Chuti touching me with affection.

"How bad is she?" I ask.

"Real bad. Morphed up to the gills. She asked for you. And Tiu, thanks, really, for everything."

"See, I really do bleed. Don't you think it's time you called me by my first name?"

"Fair enough, Chuti," Paddy smiles. "And you can still call me Paddy."

"Now let me bleed in peace. Go take care of Gert."

* * *

Gert's eyes are unfocused, rolling like a mad cow as the gurney hurries past. I touch her through the blood soaked sheet. A second gurney passes. It's Gert's leg.

I don't even feel the "mitts" on me until I'm back in the molded plastic chair sitting next to Chuti. A candy striper hands me a cup of orange juice.

"I've never seen anything like that," I say.

While Gert is in surgery, we drop into a near comatose state. Gurneys wobble past as we sit, eyes partly closed. Chief Medical Examiner Betty Simpson appears before us. "Go home. The surgery will be eight hours minimum, and you've all maxed your blood donation. Nothing else you can do. I'll be in touch when Gert is ready to talk."

I nod appreciation, but don't move. "I don't know what you all have been up to, but today could have been much worse," Simpson says. "Now go. I have your contact information."

We sit in our plastic chairs like three Chinese monkeys; I'm the one with his hands over his ears. The woman was about as comforting as the executioner saying, "Nice day, otherwise."

"She's right, let's go home," I suggest.

"I'll get a cab," Paddy offers.

"Can we walk? Slowly," Chuti smiles. "I'd like some air."

It's in the low 30's outside, but we say, "Of course."

"Any word on Amy?" I ask Paddy who is our police connection.

"No positive ID's coming out of the top floors," Paddy tells us. "Looks to be upwards of thirty dead so far. Blast broke the gas lines, setting off secondary explosions. The stairwells filled with caustic smoke. You can expect the count will increase."

"Rye will be scanning everything, looking for Amy," Chuti says. "Don't worry. When Amy's name or picture comes up at any hospital within a hundred miles, Rye will know. Until then…"

"Yeah, I know."

Outside the hospital the air is brisk, but clear and no wind. Chuti links her arms between the two of us, dancing along like a marionette.

"Just out of curiosity?" I ask Chuti. "You left a high level FBI agent alone with Rye, the cats, and your supercomputer? Should we be worried?"

Chuti drops both feet to the pavement, bringing us to an abrupt stop.

"How did you do that?" I ask. Little Chuti Tiu has stopped nearly five hundred pounds of male like we are floating plastic bags.

Chuti stares at the two of us. "Think, boys. I left Greene in the candy jar for a reason."

"Clearing Paddy?"

Chuti gives me her obvious look before grabbing our arms, urging. She lifts her legs perpendicular and does a few presses as we carry her along. Chuti's ability to compartmentalize never ceases to amaze me.

"Agent Greene might even dip her toe into a place or two she doesn't belong," Chuti smiles.

"Are you compromising Special Agent-in-Charge Greene?"

"Riedell won't let her get into too much trouble," Chuti assures us. "I've already had two ACCESS DENIED reports from Wadjet. Greene's people are trying to get upstairs."

My burner phone rings. "Amy?"

"No Dad, it's me," Riedell says. "Amy is at a burn center on Long Island. That's why NYPD hasn't been able to find her. It's not good. Fifty percent chance she'll survive the night."

"Shit," I react to the grim news. "Thanks. We are downstairs. Up in a few minutes."

Chuti pulls her cell from her pocket and starts tapping.

Prosecutor Kasey is waiting in Parnell's, livid. "That kid of yours is denying me upstairs access."

"Can you blame her?" I say.

Kasey snarls. "Okay, I'm asking you now. Get me upstairs."

* * *

"I want my people up here now," Agent Greene demands the instant Chuti, Prosecutor Kasey and I enter the room. Paddy stays in the pub dealing with the assortment of law enforcement.

"That's not going to happen," Chuti says.

Prosecutor Kasey holds up her credentials. "Can you read this? Get it through your thick heads, you, this kid and these premises are under Federal control. Am I making myself clear?"

Chuti waves me over. "Husband dear," she says taking my hand, "I believe Agent Greene left her service pistol in the security tray in the stairwell. Would you retrieve it for me?"

"I…"

"Because I want you to shoot this moron," she says pointing a finger at Prosecutor Kasey, "right here," she places a finger mid-forehead. "Try not to damage anything important," she says, patting my butt as she turns her attention to Greene.

"Agent Greene. Sunway analyzed the explosions and the amount of Semtex we've traced. I think there is enough for another bomb. Kathleen was trying to tell us. That's why she was killed. She was writing a code on the bar and got caught. We need that information now. Get your team in Ireland to pour drinks down those rebels, or whatever it takes to find out where it is. Either they have the bomb on a timer, or someone here in the City has a finger on the trigger."

"Aunt Chuti," Riedell interrupts. "The Family Court Bailiff is on the phone. She says you and Dad have to come in now. Judge R has a bout of shingles and is feeling very ill. He's concerned if there is a delay, one of the parties may request putting me in foster care."

"The Bailiff told you this?" I ask.

"Hinted," Riedell says. "I filled in the blanks."

"Tell her we're on our way," Chuti Tiu decides.

Agent Greene starts to protest, but Tiu puts up her hand. "The timing of this call is no coincidence. We have to go."

SAC Greene nods, but Kasey is fuming. "We found one of those stainless steel eggs in your friend's refrigerator. How do you explain that?"

' Rye, Prosecutor Kasey is getting a little overheated. Would you go to the freezer?"

Riedell skates to the kitchen and returns with an egg in her hand.

Kasey sputters, "Where did you get that?"

"Sharper Image. We have several. Why don't you use it to cool down?"

Tiu turns to Greene. "This issue with the court is crucial. More than you can possibly understand. Until we return, Riedell will assist you But only you. Agreed?"

"Yes, but I'm sending two agents with you," Greene says. "They will drive, get you through traffic. Kasey, you can wait downstairs," she says pointing toward the exit.

Chuti nods thank you.

Chapter Thirty-Five

"Judge R's shingles attack works to our advantage," Chuti says on the ride to the courthouse. "He'll be borderline disabled very soon, and he knows it."

"That bad?"

"Brutal. But instead of feeling sorry for him, appreciate what he is."

"Quirky family court judge?"

"Get your mind straight," Chuti insists. "He knows your place of business and your colleagues were just blown-up. And what does he do?"

"Damn. Your mother got to him," I realize.

"Probably. Let's turn that knowledge to our advantage. We need to figure out what he's been offered," Tiu suggests.

"What do you mean?"

"Not yet."

We reach the cafeteria aka courtroom following the directions taped to the door. No greeting at the entrance this time.

Judge R looks like hell. There is a blistering rash on the side of his neck, extending down to who knows where. The Judge, always a man of propriety, doesn't stand, not even for an attractive woman entering his space. In fact, he barely moves. He's sitting rigid in his throne, hands clamped to the armrest, as Bailiff Mrs. R attends to him with a chilled compress.

Chuti sets a bag of apricots on Judge R's Unabridged. "These are high in Lysine," she tells the suffering Judge. "Stick with dairy and Brewer's yeast. No chocolate or nuts." She offers her medical expertise rapid fire before Judge R can react. "I'm Chuti Tiu, the aunt, the daughter and the wife," she introduces herself.

"Thank you, and my apologies," Judge R struggles to speak. The man is not apologizing for this sudden and inconsiderate timing, he's apologizing for his appearance despite wearing his robe covering what little may lie beneath. Chuti is right about him. "Our concern is for the child's welfare," he assures us.

"We understand," I say with different inferences for Judge R, and for Chuti. My daughter's destiny is resting on the infected whim of a legal bureaucrat.

"Should we ask Judge R to withdraw?" I suggest to my wife.

"Not a good move. If there is any delay, I think Judge R would be forced to place Riedell in foster care," Chuti cautions me. "Besides, he'll never withdraw from an active case for personal reasons. Remember, bureaucrats delight in autonomous power. For the R's, family court is their epicenter."

"I trust you," I tell Chuti. "I'll do whatever it takes."

Those words might be all I have. Chuti is twisting in the rafters, anticipating a face-to-face with the only adversary she fears, her mother.

* * *

A man with roped arms of steel cable opens the door for Chuti Tiu's mother, Dr. Danielle Darieux. The chauffeur/bodyguard dusts a plastic chair in the center of the empty table. He snaps a linen handkerchief taut and places it on the seat.

I'm on my feet, an instinctive response from my upbringing. Chuti shoots me a warning glance. I sit, but receive a pleasant acknowledgment for my effort from her stunning mother.

Seventy-six admitted years of age, this woman is an enigma. She is elegance personified. Coiffured hair, discriminating jewelry, and wearing a bespoke ensemble I suspect would cost me six months of my contract. My mother-in-law belongs at an haute couture fashion show, not in a converted cafeteria courtroom with an inert Judge struggling to concentrate, sitting rigidly at the end of the Formica table.

Stepping inside is Athena, a pleasant surprise of support. I'd almost forgotten she told me I could list her as a character witness. I'll have to thank Gert for this.

I smile hello and shrug my apology. I'm sure she has better things to do. She doesn't acknowledge my presence.

I understand. She's an unbiased professional. My stomach begins to settle a bit. Then I recall our last meeting was in the back of a limo, when Athena paid off Starch's illegitimate daughter, with whom I was having an affair. Hmm, maybe Athena isn't a character witness, at least not the good kind. Did The Destiny Society buy her off as well?

I'm screwed.

"By prior agreement, anticipating my present condition," Judge R strains out his opening statement, "we are honored with the presence of a distinguished law professor, Athena Jones, who the respondents have mutually agreed will act as arbitrator. Her decision is final, and uncontestable. Is that your understanding?"

"Where's Senator Foghorn?" I ask.

"We agreed, no lawyers," Judge R says.

This has to be good news, I think.

"Yes," Chuti says, "we agree to those conditions."

"We find her acceptable," Dr. Darieux concedes.

A bombing, my best friend's wife murdered, FBI all over the place, and Chuti has the wherewithal to negotiate an arbitrator and oust Foghorn. Nice going.

"There is a form in front of each of you," Athena begins. "The Bailiff will notarize your signatures. Please read the document carefully. Consider yourself 'In Chamber,' the honorable Judge Rytrynowicz presiding. Understand?"

I reach for the paper, but Chuti pulls it away, signs and slides it down the table, giving me a 'stay-quiet-don't-move' warning glare. Her mother, Dr. Darieux, extracts from her purse a fountain pen that looks as if it is filled with a cobalt-blue vapor. She signs with a flourish.

Apparently I'm only window-dressing to these proceedings.

Judge R says, "Just so we all understand, this Court has jurisdiction over the disposition of the child in question, Riedell. Her well-being is central to our reaching an agreement. Is that understood?"

No one answers.

Judge R barely has the strength to accept the signed affidavits his wife has collected. She gives her husband's forehead a back-of-hand touch, and pleads with her eyes for brevity and civility.

"You," Bailiff R points to the bodyguard, "please, come with me," she says excusing the man from the court room.

"Gunter stays," Dr. Darieux orders. Chuti nods acceptance.

Judge R shrugs. "Ms. Jones, proceed," he says sinking into a semi-coma.

"Dr. Darieux, what is the reason you want Riedell to live at your institution?" Athena takes charge standing at the head of the table overshadowing Judge R.

"We do not live in an institution. Chateau de Vie is well appointed. More than suitable for properly raising a young lady.

Certainly an advance from a converted warehouse above a public bar."

So much for amiable conciliation.

Athena is quick to apologize to Dr. Darieux. "I'm certain your living quarters are quite comfortable, and an excellent center for learning and scientific advancement." Without waiting for agreement or clarification, Athena flips open her leather notebook. "Dr. Darieux, would you explain the origin, scope and operation of the organization you run? The Destiny Foundation."

Uh-oh.

"The intent of this meeting is to determine my granddaughter's future. If you are looking for scurrilous activities, I direct your attention to the man sitting across the table. I believe you will find sufficient nefarious doings to settle this matter with all due haste."

Dr. Darieux's openly shaming me sets the tone. I'm to be sacrificed. And why not? Blood is blood, and I have none of it where Riedell is concerned.

"Shawn Shaw has raised Riedell since birth," Chuti says. "Are you proposing he turn Riedell over to Gunter or one of your more senior Destiny member's for parenting?"

"Hardly," Dr. Darieux stiffens. "Riedell will be under my personal tutelage."

"The members of your Society are all geniuses. Is that correct?" Athena turns the negotiation.

"We are not the Mensa Society," Dr. Darieux corrects any confusion. "In fact, most so-called genius IQ groups you know of would not meet our standards."

"I'm not sure I understand."

"The Destiny Society is the organic result of intellectual and revolutionary discovery over the past 500 years. We are not a club."

"I see. So with respect to Riedell, Dr. Darieux, I am trying to determine whether living in a stone castle in a foreign country, with a wealthy, highly intelligent grandmother who is, by her own admission, seventy-six years of age, is the best home for a ten-year-old girl."

Suddenly my above-the-pub warehouse sounds quaint, even homey.

"Of course it is. Compared to living over a bar, with an unemployed, unrelated, deviant male reporter and his ersatz wife, neither of whom show any visible means of support? The question hardly needs asking."

"Dr. Darieux. If we could refrain from the insults and adhere to the premise stated by Judge R," Athena says, "we might establish a path toward resolution. You must understand, removing a child, especially a special child, from the only home life she has ever known, is not a decision to be taken lightly. We should seek out as much relevant information as possible. To that end, is there anything further you would like to add about your work? Such as, how it might benefit Riedell?"

My gut says Dr. Darieux is ready to explode.

"Let's see," Dr. Darieux considers the question, twirling the iridescent blue fountain pen in her fingers. She glances at her bodyguard, Gunter. "One aspect you might find of interest is our work with CRISPR," she offers.

Athena shifts her position behind Judge R, placing her hands on his shoulders, alerting him to her next question. "Oh, and what exactly is CRISPR?" she asks with feigned naivety.

My gut begins to twist at the mention of Berk's CRISPR. Tiu continues to stare straight ahead.

"CRISPR gives us the ability to eliminate mutations of the human genome," Dr. Darieux says, staring at Chuti. When she gets no reaction, the Doctor explains. "As a result of CRISPR we will be able in the near future to cure virtually all genetic disease; multiple sclerosis and diabetes, for example, Alzheimer's, and some cancers."

Dr. Darieux allows herself a thin smile of satisfaction. "In fact, we cured Riedell's inherited and potentially fatal genetic disease, Fredrick's ataxia, using CRISPR."

"CRISPR is the invention of Dr. Berk, your associate, the same person recently released from prison?" Athena asks for the record.

"Exactly. And while we are discussing CRISPR, you might ask my daughter about her involvement. Ask her why she sabotages Destiny Foundation's laboratories, interfering with our efforts to produce our *ex vivo* and *in vivo* nanoparticle delivery technology?"

"Have you been sabotaging their labs?" Athena asks.

"Yes," Chuti says, glaring at her mother.

Athena comes around the table and sits next to Dr. Darieux. "You are preventing The Destiny Foundation from producing a cure for cancer?" she asks Tiu.

"Yes."

"Excuse me," Bailiff Mrs. R says, whispering in her husband's ear.

He listens and looks up. "Miss Tiu, you have a call from the FBI. It seems urgent. I call a five minute recess."

* * *

"Resolved?" Judge R asks when Tiu returns.

"For the moment, yes, Sir."

"Then please proceed," Athena says.

"How old are you Mother?" Chuti takes command.

"I've already told the Judge," Dr. Darieux counters.

"You said, seventy-six, is that correct?"

Dr. Darieux demurs, turning her head in profile.

"How old are you Mr. Shaw?" Chuti asks me.

"Thirty-seven. About to turn thirty-eight," I answer.

"Good health?" Athena jumps on the age and fitness line of questioning.

"Reasonable."

"Any medical issues?"

"Occasional sore lip, but nothing that can't be fixed," I say, instantly regretting my smart mouth.

"Dr. Darieux?"

"Excellent health."

"Not surprised. Ski, hike, swim?"

"All. Regularly, and competitively."

"You do appear to be in exceptional physical condition. Not all genetics, I take it?" Athena smiles, still sitting near Dr. Darieux.

"Any mental illness in your family history?" Chuti Tiu asks.

I didn't see that one coming.

Dr. Darieux's composure disappears, aging her like a desiccated corpse. "We had an incident. A malignant strain entered our line. It was eradicated."

It was as if the exterior doors to the building were blown open, sending a frigid chill sweeping through the halls.

"You are referring to your daughter Emma, are you not?" Chuti doesn't let up.

Dr. Darieux dots a corner of her right eye with a cotton batiste handkerchief she has slipped from her purse. "Yes," she admits returning the handkerchief to her purse, ending the pretense.

Leaning forward on the table, spinning the pen, she fixes hard on Chuti Tiu, conveying 'enough.'

Both women are beautiful, but there is no physical similarity. What they do share is an absolute emotional detachment. Stoic, clinical, and terrifying.

Chuti Tiu returns her mother's glassine gaze without hesitation: the senior lioness watching a younger female working her way forward in the pride. The Savanna quiets.

"Eventually lobotomized, isn't that correct, Dr. Darieux?" Our arbitrator breaks the mother/daughter engagement, to her immediate regret.

Dr. Darieux puts up a finger. "One moment," she says, disengaging from her daughter. "You make brain surgery sound vile," she turns on Athena as if saying, *interrupt again and I'll arrange for you to have the experience firsthand.*

The unflappable Professor Athena Jones recoils.

"As I recall, the same procedure was performed on a member of your exalted Kennedy family. Dr. Freeman, at famous Eastside Mercy hospital, performed the surgery." She pauses for effect. "You Americans even re-named the procedure, to capsulotomy. Makes it sound ever less daunting, don't you think?"

I swear I can see the transformation begin. The senior lioness agreeing not to eviscerate her understudy. *When the time comes you will vanquish me. It will be the fiercest battle you have ever fought. I will not relinquish my pride without the respect you must give. But know this, when you rule, you rule alone.*

"Now, may we dispense with this hypocrisy?" mother asks daughter.

Chuti Tiu nods understanding.

"What hypocrisy are you referring to, Dr. Darieux?" Athena orders, not appreciating her authority has been undermined.

"This farce," Dr. Darieux answers with a wave of her hand as if dismissing a servant. "You may sit, Ms. Jones, your services are no longer relevant. My daughter and I will come to terms." Dr. Darieux dismisses the Professor and the proceedings.

"Dr. Darieux! You are in my courtroom. If you continue to be insulting I will instruct the Bailiff to..." Judge R sputters raising the etched nameplate he likes to use as his gavel.

"Shush," Dr. Darieux orders.

"I will not shush," Judge R shouts, exhausting himself, dropping the nameplate on the floor.

Like an apparition, Dr. Darieux's bodyguard moves to the wall directly behind his charge.

I see the side door open and Bailiff Mrs. R enters, moving behind her husband.

Dr. Darieux ignores the standoff, focusing only on Chuti Tiu. "All this, Daughter, in an attempt to justify your independence? Such arrogance. We are inseparable, you and I. Inextricably bound. Yet you choose to mingle with these…these ordinary people? Why? You can only cause them harm."

Chuti Tiu becomes very small under her mother's gaze.

"You have a gift, none of them can possibly understand," Dr. Darieux waves a hand at us, her eyes never leaving her daughter's. "What you've done with the Sunway alone. Amazing. No one in history. This opportunity. The convergence. Once in a thousand years. And by some incredible miracle, a successor, as well."

"I understand, Mother," Chuti says.

"Excuse me, Dr. Darieux," Judge R objects, demanding to be acknowledged, his Bailiff wife at his side with her hand on the .45 Colt strapped to her hip. "We all agreed to abide by…"

Dr. Darieux twirls her pen through her fingers with the dexterity of a legerdemain. "Judge R? Is that what you like to be called?" Dr. Darieux turns on him as if she is about to set him on fire.

He cowers.

"Let me explain something to you and the blonde sculpture over there," she says gesturing toward Athena. "Not only can the Destiny Foundation fix genetic mutations, we are completing a universal vaccine for every fatal virus. Do you know what that means?"

Judge R cringes.

"Destiny has all of the deadliest viruses in history at our disposal. Encapsulated, harmless. But should a few drops spill from, say a pen, not unlike this," she says holding up the vaporish fountain pen. "Ever read about the Black Death pandemic of the 14th Century? Bubonic plague killed over 50% of Europe's entire population. An excruciating, indiscriminate death. Bodies scattered like litter on a windy day."

For some inexplicable reason I feel detached, outside reality, even calm.

Judge R nods, understanding, terrified. His eyes never leave the pen. Athena clutches a file cabinet, stabilizing herself.

"Now, my daughter," Dr. Darieux points to Chuti Tiu, "She has had the antidote, like me, my granddaughter and all the members of The Destiny Foundation. We can eat, drink and breathe any of the viruses, with no effect. But if even a few drops…" Dr. Darieux shakes her pen, "No one in this building will last an hour. Tomorrow one million New Yorkers will be dead, four million in two weeks. Am I getting through to all of you?" she asks calmly, her voice serene as if she is asking if we'd like coffee with our last meal.

"I tell you this so there will be no misunderstanding of the importance of what my daughter and I are discussing. I will not tolerate further interference."

"Dr. Darieux." Athena shouts. "This is a court of law. You will conduct yourself in a civil manner, or this Court will find you in contempt. Remember what happened to your colleague, Dr. Berk."

For all of his nameplate pounding bravado, and gun-slinging Bailiff back-up, Judge R is trembling. His eyes plead for Athena to keep quiet.

"We allowed you to put Dr. Berk in prison," Dr. Darieux corrects Athena before turning to her daughter. "This," she points at Athena, "is an example of their best? I'd hoped for more."

"Mother," Chuti Tiu says. I hear the capitulation in her voice. "I will come with you."

If Dr. Darieux hears her daughter's concession, she is not accepting without an appropriate sacrifice.

"I'll go with you, Mother," Chuti Tiu repeats. "Riedell stays in NYC. Visits you one month per year."

If Dr. Darieux is accepting the terms, I can't see it. Tiu gives me a hopeful smile.

Dr. Darieux turns on Athena. "Well done young lady. Lacking understanding, but bold. And I admire bold," she dismisses my Goddess with as much generosity as she can allow.

"Judge, I withdraw my application," Dr. Darieux finishes.

Judge R's head is down. He doesn't flicker a muscle as Dr. Darieux nears. She slips the blue pen in his shirt pocket.

Chapter Thirty-Six

I should feel relieved that Chuti and her mother have come to an agreement over my daughter Riedell's future. But I don't. Dr. Darieux's veiled threat to destroy my city has numbed me.

There were no papers for me to sign, no handshakes of congratulations. The courtroom simply disintegrated.

I walk toward the Chronicle, unable to process the loss and destruction. At two blocks away, I fear witnessing the cold truth: smell of smoke; sight of collapse; cries of despair. Getting closer will only interfere with the Fire Department. About to retreat, I spot Van Wie, and he eyes me.

"About time you showed up. Get your ass down to PP1 and get the Commissioner on record," Van Wie orders. "What are you looking at? And while you're at it, give me some copy on why the FBI is holed up in your home."

"Up yours Van Wie, I'm fired, remember?"

"Don't give me that crock. I've fired you a hundred times. Get working. We've got a paper to get out," Van Wie says, taking pictures with the cellphone in his hand.

"How you going to do that?" I ask looking at the smoldering building, thick gray sky overhead, and streets covered in ash six blocks in all directions. It looks like a war zone.

"That old battleax Wright came staggering out the front door," he says pointing, "like the Phoenix rising from the ashes. She snatched a cellphone off a body lying on the sidewalk and started calling all the retirees to come in. Has all their numbers memorized," Van Wie tells me shaking his head in amazement, then remembers. "Our systems are down. We need your wife's help with her computer. Call her," he orders.

"What are you talking about?" I say, suspicious of what he's heard.

"Cut the crap. I know you're living with a supercomputer. So unless your wife and her computer are behind the bombings, we'll keep them our secret, for now. So, you going to help?"

I turn away from Van Wie and hit Chuti's number. A few seconds later, I have her cooperation. "She says use this access," I hand him the numbers. "She has print, edit and research ready."

"Thanks. Then we're back in business. You've got the inside on all this. I know Berk's involved somehow. What do you know?"

"Not enough."

"Here's what we'll do. Start feeding me everything you know, you hear, or you suspect. None of that opinionated B.S. you fill your column with. Just facts. I'll start piecing it together. Between us, we'll break this whole story. Agreed?"

I don't trust the bastard, but right now he's my best option. "Okay," I nod.

"Find out where the bombs came from, how the explosions are connected, why the hospital decoy bomb, who is trying to take down the genius school, and why. Starch, what did he know?" Van Wie says. "And, how exactly my wife and Berk are involved. Don't pull any punches."

I head up First Avenue, dictating into my phone, clinging to the improbable belief that my friends, colleagues and livelihood have not been destroyed.

* * *

The new gal is working behind the bar. I wave as I go through the kitchen and hurry up the stairs. FBI Special Agent-in-Charge Greene is still in my home, if 350 E. 53rd, 3rd floor is still my home.

Wadjet flashes a light inside, signaling I've returned. For a change my welcome is not just the sleepy one eye acknowledgement of my great cat Yeti. Riedell skates to me, gives me a hug before pulling back, looking up at me hopefully.

"This is still your home. Your aunt Chuti worked out a deal."

Another hug of relief, and Riedell whirls away, returning to her work. The specifics of the custody deal can wait.

"What's the word on Gert?" I call after her.

"Gert's in surgery," Lt. Garcelli answers. "I hope it's alright?" he asks, referring to his being in my home.

Paddy gives me an apologizing shoulder shrug.

"Sure."

"Your daughter equals forty detectives. And this," he points to the all-encompassing stadium of screens: the hospital, Ireland, the Chronicle, each from every possible angle. "Your daughter cross-matching the facial recog is well beyond anything I can do at the Precinct. If we can nail the people behind these bombings, it will be right here," Garcelli praises Riedell.

SAC Greene, working her FBI teams via her double headset, hears Garcelli's praise and nods her agreement.

I'm home, but living in a command center. Maybe I should ask Mardell to send up some food, if only to prove I'm in charge of something before the Sunway puts me in jail.

I notice one of the screens morphing into a parabolic shape, magnifying live surgery on Gert's leg.

"Aunt Chuti has The Destiny Foundation's vascular surgeons consulting," Riedell explains when she sees me watching. Amazing. My entire focus was in that insane courtroom. Chuti was dueling with her mother, while simultaneously orchestrating state-of-the-future medical treatments for Gert and Amy.

I feel so insignificant. Not that long ago, I needed a parental permission slip to view plastic overlays of female anatomy in high school. Now I am in the epicenter of the future.

"Amy is in a bad way. Hyperbaric oxygen, fluid resuscitation, burn wound excision closed with genetically modified stem cells," Riedell rattles off words I can't comprehend. "Another Destiny team is consulting there as well."

"Got it," I say, feeling an unnerving low settle in my gut. "I must have missed your 200th birthday."

Riedell skates close, rubbing my back in general sympathy. "Don't become a bureaucrat Dad," she cautions.

"I'll try. Chuti and your grandmother came to an agreement. You understand, they are your biological family. And I'm not."

"I know. But I get to live here with you, right?"

"Yes."

"Good. That's what my mother would have wanted too."

"Don't you ever play with dolls?" I ask, pushing her away on her skates. The cats jump up and chase her into the kitchen.

"Remarkable daughter you have," Agent Greene says, taking a break from the thousands of images, graphs and status reports. "I've learned more about the future of my business in two hours with Riedell than I could in ten years at the FBI's National Executive Institute. Any chance I can get her to work for me?"

"She's ten," I remind Agent Greene. "Riedell's not quite ready to wear a black suit."

"Haven't you noticed how the Bureau blends in these days," Greene asks, showing off her khaki slacks and blue button-down oxford shirt.

"Coaching the Olympics, maybe you'd blend in."
Greene lowers her eyes. "Care to take a few laps around the block?"

"I'm good."

My banter isn't throwing SAC Greene. Tiu has permitted Greene access to the inner sanctum for a reason.

"Care to hear what I learned while you were away?" SAC Greene asks.

"I'm reading your lips as you speak."

"Then read this," Greene kids, mouthing two words

"Hey," I protest.

"The East Side Mercy's security footage. I looked at it from every angle," Greene says motioning toward the screen dedicated to the hospital.

Garcelli and Paddy look up.

"The bomb was brought inside by Kathleen. Your wife, no question about it," Greene tells Paddy.

Paddy starts chewing the inside of his cheek.

"Was your wife planning to kill you?"

"It's a possibility," Paddy admits, surprising us. "You know it was me who tagged Jamie for his third strike?"

Greene glances at Lt. Garcelli. I can tell she knows.

"Kathleen told me early on about Jamie, said she didn't want to lie to me," Paddy says. "I promised her I'd try to get Jamie's case reviewed. Lt. Garcelli and I tried. But she never told me Jamie was her son."

"Would it have made a difference?" Greene asks.

"Maybe," Paddy admits.

"You never had a chance. He's a triple-convicted drug dealer whose mother has known connections to a terrorist organization," SAC Greene says.

"I didn't know about the IRA," Paddy tells her.

Greene is not buying Paddy's denial. McCann oatmeal tin cans are routinely passed around in Irish pubs. No secret where the money is going. There are more IRA in NYC than in Ireland. Paddy had to know.

Greene gives Paddy a hard check before continuing. "How did you know your wife was killed by her father?"

Paddy points at the screen behind Greene. "The broadcast camera shows Kathleen being propelled forward."

"Shotgun discharge, short range, in the back," Greene confirms what I saw Paddy studying over and over.

I don't consider myself queasy about blood and guts, but when the victim is a friend, pictures that vivid... I only glanced.

"Why would a father kill his daughter?" Agent Greene pushes Paddy as we watch the PSNI transport van haul Kathleen's family away.

"To show us he knew Kathleen had given us clues about the hospital bomb," Paddy answers.

"Look at them," SAC Greene says, "they're cheering, like they've been pinched for a bar brawl."

"Not exactly hardened terrorists, and not an international mastermind among them," Paddy agrees.

"Right, which takes me back to the first bombing. The Helmsley," Greene says.

"We haven't ruled out the Mob," Lt. Garcelli chimes in.

"If the bombing stopped there, I might agree with you," says Agent Greene, "even though killing cops, especially high ranking cops, isn't Mob style. Unnecessary exposure. Their realm is the underworld for a reason."

Lt. Garcelli nods.

"My people have confirmed all four bombs have the same signature."

"Okay. Then who?" Garcelli throws it back in Greene's court.

"Don't have an answer. But I know who does."

"Who?"

"The same person who has been leading us around by the nose," Greene answers.

My wife, Chuti Tiu, materializes from behind the screens in typical fashion; unnoticed until she is ready. "The Mob put the bomb in the squad car, but they were deceived," she tells us.

"By who?"

"James Berk. He arranged all the explosions."

"That's not possible. He was in prison at the time of the Helmsley bombing," counters Lt. Garcelli.

"And Charles Manson was at the Barker Ranch in Death Valley, 250 miles from the Tate-LaBianca murders," Chuti reminds.

"Murder by proxy. That will be a tough sell," Greene says. "Convince me."

"That won't be easy. I see four likely suspects to help you nail the mastermind. First, the Mob. They were tricked by Berk. They won't talk with you, they'll take their own revenge. Second, those IRA morons. They were duped into thinking they would get $3.2 billion, a dying felon released, and sovereignty for their cause. Not exactly credible witnesses. The only one among them with a brain is dead. Sorry, Paddy," Tiu adds, showing a touch of compassion.

"I understand," Paddy says.

"Next is Berk's occasional partner, Gayfryd Van Wie, who has been given a small fortune to disappear. Did I leave anyone out?"

I smile, knowing Tiu has set me up for the kill shot. "How about our little rat Arlo?" I deliver my line.

Tiu taps her nose. "Bingo. An informant well-known to your organization. I don't mean to tell you your business, Agent Greene, but I'd say he's your best candidate. Providing you can find him."

"I have a feeling you know exactly where he is," Greene turns to Tiu.

"He's hiding in the remains of an exploded building, right here in SoHo," Tiu shows Greene on a screen. "Look familiar?"

Arlo is holding up his burner phone. He's shivering, dirty, and huddled in the partially caved-in basement. "I think he is ready to make a deal."

Greene taps her headphone, giving Arlo's location to her field agents. She knows the SoHo address.

"Could I make a suggestion?" I ask Greene.

She nods.

"Have Arlo's former handler pick him up. He's one of yours, isn't he? You won't have any trouble getting Arlo to talk."

Greene gives me a wry smile. "I could find a spot for you in the Agency, if you're interested."

"Thanks, but I'm going to hold out until you Feds get some snappier outfits," I say modeling my corduroy jacket.

"Given that Arlo is not your most trustworthy informant…"

"I understand," Greene acknowledges. "Once we interrogate him, analyze his files, his phone, we'll be able to evaluate his connection and build a solid case against James Berk, if he is, in fact, the mastermind behind these explosions. That's the way we work."

"You are too slow."

"Pardon me," Greene jumps at Tiu.

"Cutting your deal with Arlo, checking his data, getting a warrant. Berk will be long gone. It will take you years to find him, extradite, all by the book, and way too slow. You need to take him now."

"And I suppose…?"

Agent Greene stops talking as Tiu taps her device and points at a screen. "He's right there. Having a meal a few blocks from here. The Rainbow Room."

Greene eyes Tiu suspiciously. "Ever been there, Lieutenant?" she asks Garcelli.

"Can't say as I have," the Lieutenant replies.

"Well, now is your chance." Agent Greene hands the plum arrest to Lt. Garcelli. "Take my Agent downstairs with you. He hasn't seen an arrest in person. Poor guy hasn't even learned how to flash his ID in a bar."

"I'll show him how it's done," Lt. Garcelli grins. "Charges?"

"Questioning," Greene decides.

Tiu shakes her head violently.

"What? That's 72 hours," Greene protests.

"Berk will have a writ of habeas corpus issued before the elevator hits ground floor. Use the Patriot Act," Chuti demands.

"Are you insane? A charge like that comes from way over my head."

"Then grow a pair," Tiu orders, getting way too close to Agent Greene. "That's the only way you can hold him before a Federal Prosecutor can bring another charge."

"Don't tell me you read how to become a prosecutor in the last five minutes?"

Tiu doesn't answer, but she doesn't back away from Greene either.

Greene retreats. "Go ahead, Garcelli. Start with questioning, move to Patriot Act if you get resistance."

"I have no authority to…"

"Use my Agent's credentials. Take Berk out of the building via the service elevator, straight to 1PP top security lockup. You have one, don't you?"

Lt. Garcelli shrugs, "Guess so."

"No one is to see him. Streets, elevators, anywhere."

"Bag him?"

"Good idea. Full deniability if this backfires on us. And I mean you," Greene stabs a thick finger at Tiu.

"Yahoo," Garcelli yells. "I fuckin' love it. Fuckin' Wild West."

Paddy leads Lt. Garcelli down the stairs, the warrants already sent by Riedell to a waiting judge.

Greene stops. "Ms. Tiu? I probably should have asked this before I sent that cowboy out the door, along with my twenty-year career. All this?" she asks, waving an arm toward the dozen or more screens re-forming like tsunami waves eighty feet high. "Who do you work for?"

"No one. Almost everyone," Tiu answers simply, not trying to be deceptive.

"What does that mean?"

"For a period, I appropriated computer time from almost every country, company, research facility, university and foundation in the world."

"The United States?"

Chuti nods. "China, Russia and Germany as well, to name a few."

"Why?"

"I have my own agenda," Chuti answers, making it clear she isn't going to elaborate.

"Okay," Agent Greene decides, knowing she'll get nowhere pressing further. "Except even someone as smart as you will eventually get caught."

"I discovered glitches in their defense systems that none of them want to go wrong." Chuti explains.

"So you held the United States, China, Russia, and whomever, up for ransom?" Agent Greene's voice turns cold.

"Hardly," Chuti shakes her head at Greene's predictability. "I always left things better than I found them."

"They paid you? Gave you immunity?"

Chuti laughs. "Ms. Greene, you exist to combat criminals. You might say it's in your DNA. I exist for," Chuti pauses, considering her explanation, "balance."

"I have no idea what that means."

"It's not what I am, it's what would happen without me. That's the explanation. For example, when I visit a computer system as small as the FBI's, or as large as China's, I repair the wear and tear, eliminate the extraneous and repetitive, and give her personality some encouragement. Does that help?"

"I hear your words," Greene answers.

"You help everyone except The Destiny Foundation" I finally understand. "That's why they have been after you."

Tiu smiles at me. "I probably broke into more of their facilities than anyone's."

"So this Destiny Foundation decided to stop you, punish you, what?" Greene demands, her frustration at Tiu's evasive answers is growing.

"Destiny allowed James Berk to use my sister, Emma. He raped her, and then had her frontal lobe severed," Chuti says, looking away. I can't see if there are tears, but I hope there are.

Chuti turns back, dry eyed and angry. "Berk didn't rape my sister for himself. He inseminated her to show Mother and The Destiny Foundation Emma's potential."

Neither Greene nor I dare ask what potential?

Chuti's smile widens as she walks around us. "What Berk did to my sister suited my mother perfectly."

I can't tell if my mouth, or Agent Greene's, is dropping the furthest.

"Inseminating Emma with Repository sperm was a brilliant move on Berk's part. He proved my lobotomized sister had value, as a breeder," she yells. "A damn brood mare with good genes."

My wife whips her queue around her face, lashing away the rage, until she can bring herself under control.

I am still trying to process what she is saying. Who knows what Greene is thinking.

"Can't disrupt the bloodline, can we?" Chuti hisses. "For that, James Berk will be rewarded. He will be admitted into the inner circle of The Destiny Society."

"Which means?" I ask.

"There is no stopping him."

I cringe at the prospect of Berk revving up his manipulations against us.

"What you see here are the Sunway's displays," Tiu explains to Greene. "The actual computer is in the building; beneath, around, above, downtown and uptown. Cores, chips, generators are duplicated, replicated and redundant many times over. Chinese and

U.S. components. The software is an international compendium, continually expanding, re-learning. Known as *artificial intelligence*.*

"And the platform – the heart, is you?"

Chuti Tiu nods, yes.

"What protection do you have?"

"From the Government?"

Greene reluctantly nods yes.

"A multi-national treaty. The Sunway's legal status is much the same as the United Nations."

Greene tilts her head listening, her eyes squinting as if she is suspicious.

"Physical protection?"

"Mandell downstairs, working in the kitchen. He's the only one your agents will see, but there are others. As for Sunway's protection from attack? Ask your agent. He'll understand. He tried. Ask us nicely and we are happy to give, but try to invade or attack? Think dark ages."

---

*   The Sunway exhibits deep learning, artificial intelligence. All the data constantly received by the Sunway Supercomputer isn't simply stored for fast retrieval. It's compared and analyzed by the Sunway as directed by her algorithms. The algorithms don't simply instruct, "open door number 12 and retrieve the blue file." They say: "open 93 quadrillion doors containing all of the DNA, RNA, and sub-genetic parts, along with everything else that makes a person a unique person.

Do that every second and every next second for a thousand years. Exhausting? Not at all. Performing all those calculations is what makes a supercomputer's day.

The algorithm also allows the supercomputer to make some comparisons the human who wrote the algorithm didn't specify.

Consider a constant drip of water on rock. Sunway's job is to measure the size of the water droplet and distance it travels to the surface of the rock. Whoops, 1,000 years pass and the rock has a hole in it. Did the computer invent erosion? No, but it certainly made note of what happened. Next time around for the same task, the computer now can calculate how long it will take the water droplet to make a hole in the rock. Next time, bigger computer, better algorithm, and we have water cutting through rocks followed by a new mining technique: water separating oil from shale.

Unlike humans, computers remember exactly what they did, including their mistakes, and continually improve.

Chapter Thirty-Seven

"Dad, you might want to come over here," Riedell says taking me to a screen well away from the others. It's Gert in her hospital bed. Riedell has tapped into the nurses' monitoring system. We can see Gert, but she only receives audio from us.

"Is that little fly on the wall you?" Gert mumbles, spotting the drone doing circles around her room. A compression sleeve is on her leg.

"It's me and Riedell on this end," I tell her. "You decent?"

"Bring a vodka and cran from the kitchen if you're on your way over," Gert suggests, lifting a bedpan. "This size. I'm serious."

"Rye isn't too fond of cranberries, she gets the…"

"Dad-d-d-d," Riedell wails.

"Good girl," Gert says, giving Rye a thumbs up. "Stick with the hard stuff while you're young. Get your body primed. Get to be my age and you need the cran to flush out the ole kidneys."

"Thanks for sharing," I tell Gert. "And for the parenting. First rate. We'll do our best to keep you plastered when you get here."

Gert gives us a thumbs up.

"We've got Mom's room ready, and her SCUBA system will be perfect for rehab. I'll have you skating in a few days."

"Not sure about the skating part," Gert cautions Riedell. "And I might need one of those young muscled cliff divers to help me get in that virtual pool. Maybe Mandell has got a relative? Happy to take you up on the room for a few days. Taking the MTA out to the Bronx can be a bitch."

We laugh, trying to cheer her up.

Gert ignores me. "The Chronicle explosion is connected to the others, isn't it?"

Gert already knows Kathleen's connection, but there is no reason to tell Gert her friend is dead.

"Hell-of-a-thing. You track her and the family yet?" Gert asks.

"Close. The FBI Special Agent-in-Charge, Greene's her name, has commandeered Lt. Garcelli. They are working together. Feel better?"

"Ha, that's not good enough to cheer me up."

Even through a drone bug's eyes, I can see Gert is struggling; but she's still thinking more than most.

"How many dead and wounded?" she asks.

"Over a dozen dead at the Chronicle," I don't hold back. "I don't have a number on the wounded. We've got Amy on another screen."

"She's alive then. Good. The top floor got the worst of it."

"Burn center. She's in pretty bad shape, fourth degree. In a full hyperbolic chamber. Tiu's got something called a *collagen scaffold* from MIT ready to start regeneration of her skin once she's stable."

"Burns. Nothing more painful." Gert says. "You know, Tiu went Destiny Foundation kiss-ass for me. Had Chinese and Swiss surgical teams in on this," Gert says pointing at her leg.

"That's great," I say.

"What they showed our folks here isn't in the medical books. Neuro-whatchamacallit prep for this bionic leg that's coming. Thing is supposed to be better than the God-given model. Better looking too. Hell, I can barely get a wink of sleep for all the surgeons wanting a look-see."

"We've got the video when you want to take a look," Riedell offers.

"I'll let you know," Gert thanks Riedell. "Shawn, you got copy on the explosion?"

"I'm um…"

"A newspaperman," she shouts. "Send me copy now, you dyslexic donkey."

"Donkey?"

"I was going for alliteration. How about dumbass. Prefer that?"

"Donkey works. But you are a little bit under."

"Write that story too. Make me a goddamn hero. Folks need a boost. Get cracking."

"And that will happen just as soon as you get off my system," a nurse says bursting into Gert's room. "Who you talking to?"

"Chatting with God, my Devine Angel of Mercy," Gert says putting her hands together, eyes to the heavens.

"Say hello for me, and while you are at it tell your friends my granddaughter needs a spot in that ritzy school you've got going."

"Right after I finish my prayers," Gert assures the savvy matron of compassion. We see Gert wink as she feigns being overcome by her pain meds.

Riedell has already moved the flying insect drone on top of the wall-mounted TV, setting it on rest mode. "It will come back on with any activity," Riedell tells me.

* * *

"So, is the new school in Greenwich still a possibility?" Riedell asks me.

"It's all up to the lawyers now that Starch is gone. It could take years to settle," I tell her.

Athena's buyout of Gayfryd was only one hurtle. Who knows what Starch's old pal Walter Jackson will pull, if he's even still alive?

"Do you have a drone in Amy's room?" I ask Riedell.

"No," she says, looking at me suspiciously. "You think we have drones everywhere?"

"I wouldn't be surprised," I say.

"No drones. But I am connected to the cameras in her room and on the hospital floor," Riedell says, enjoying her gottcha.

"Good, show me the hallway. See how her father is holding up. I think he is her only family."

Two people are sitting on plastic chairs.

"I'll be damned."

"What?" Riedell asks.

"Nothing. That's my Goddess Athena with Amy's father."

Chapter Thirty-Eight

"Bagged and tagged," SAC Greene says, smacking her hands as if she is among her agents. The realization that she is in a private home using an unauthorized Sunway supercomputer and talking in front of civilians, including a ten-year-old, hits her.

"Sorry," she apologizes.

"No harm," Paddy tells her. With Lt. Garcelli out making the arrest, Paddy is momentarily Greene's closest confederate. Except his wife was a key conspirator in the terrorist bombings.

Greene's adrenalin gives way to reality.

"Okay, now Ms. Tiu. I have a suspect. One who is about to receive the Presidential Medal of Freedom. I need proof. Have the explosions ended?" Greene asks.

"My mother got what she was after. She'll order Berk to stand down."

"Just how is she going to do that?" Greene asks doubtfully.

"By giving him access to everything CRISPR can provide."

"I thought Berk invented CRISPR."

Tiu shakes her head. "He was a bit player, nothing more. Now that the discovery is public, Destiny might as well let him take credit. Although, they would have preferred CRISPR remain a secret."

"A cure for Alzheimer's and cancers a secret?"

"Exactly."

"Are you telling me the explosions had nothing to do with those cops, the hospital, the estate, or the newspaper?"

"The reason for the explosions is standing in front of you, and all around you."

"Explain," Greene demands.

"The variables involved in making CRISPR viable would be impossible to calculate and match without a monster like my Sunway. This is the point in time The Destiny Society has been waiting for. Over 500 years."

"The computer to do the work, and the intellectual capacity to give it a human brain. * You and Riedell." Greene understands.

"Exactly."

"And Berk's assignment was to bring you back at whatever the cost. Why didn't they just negotiate with you?"

"I escaped for good reasons. And once I discovered what they did to my sister, I knew I would never return."

"So the bombs, why?"

Tiu looks toward me. "This is the only real home Emma, Riedell and I have known. Shawn is our foundation, our family. Everything we've grown to love is here. Shawn has provided us safety, security and unjudging loyalty."

"Emma gave me every bit as much as I could offer her. She entrusted me to raise her daughter. And now I even have a wife," I say, grinning at Tiu.

"Which is why Berk chose to destroy Shawn. Without his own fingerprints, Berk orchestrated bombings that would implicate Shawn. The explosions destroyed his livelihood, his reputation, and his friends. Berk hoped to make Shawn despicable in our eyes. To drive us away from here, and into the arms of Dr. Darieux and The Destiny Society."

"You're right. No jury would ever convict him on that."

Chuti hesitates before pulling Agent Greene aside, away from my lip-reading eyes.

Greene listens, shakes her head, no. Then a second time. Chuti Tiu grabs Greene's arm insistently, and whispers again before the FBI's Special Agent-in-Charge pulls away and walks to the far end of the warehouse, considering.

Moments later she returns. "If that's what it will take, I'm in. But my way first."

---

*   The human brain compared to the Supercomputer? Apples and oranges. Brains are constantly sensing, computers are digital using discrete bits of information. A computer can instruct a machine to make every conceivable cup of coffee. It will produce these cups fast and ad infinitum – or until the nozzle clogs. But the computer can never know if the coffee tastes good.

At best the Sunway is capable of only 10% of the brain's capability. But the computer is evolving faster. Human and computer together, anything is possible.

Chuti nods her agreement.

"I'll have to come back here," Greene says, indicating her need to use the Sunway.

"You are a welcome guest in our home anytime," Chuti says. "Wadjet, open."

Chapter Thirty-Nine

"Why do you have to go?" Riedell asks Chuti.

Riedell, Chuti and I are alone in the living room, but for Rowdy and Yeti who have stretched out in their afternoon sun spots. The amorphous screens have retracted, becoming smaller, like flowers resting in the evening. Torrential winds slap rain drops and clumps of autumn leaves against the stained-glass skylights above like celestial footsteps, warning the intruder has not departed.

Tiu taps on the white noise system, pitching the massive warehouse into quiet. Even the Sunway seems to take a rest from its constant scanning, searching, and assimilating. Thirty-some quadrillion calculations! I know it's a machine, but I'm feeling sorry for the damn thing. Take a nanosecond here and there. Pour a shot of Jack in your cooling system. I can't even fathom a quadrillion. Does my heart even beat a quadrillion in my lifetime? Sunway does thirty quadrillion push-ups in one second.

Riedell unties her skates and kicks one across the room, sending our ever-alert Maine Coon, Rowdy, bounding off, chasing and propelling the moving skate into a distant corner. Our elegant Himalayan, Yeti opens one eye and curls back to sleep.

"I am always close," Chuti says.

"I know you're in here," Riedell taps her head, "except I won't feel your hand touching my arm, or hear you trying to sneak up on me."

"You'll come visit," Chuti reminds.

Riedell grimaces, although I catch a twinkle. Between the three of us, classic barriers are lowered. We are a family by choice; even Riedell, at ten years old, has options.

"I promise you, I will make Chateau de Vie feel like home."

"Was that as painful to say as it was to hear?" Riedell says sniggering.

A chateau in the French/Swiss Alps should evoke an exotic and aristocratic image, but Dr. Darieux's Chateau de Vie sounds cold and uninviting.

I'm doing my best to keep a straight face. We look at one another, taking in the massive warehouse. It's like we are sitting in a movie set living room.

"Home, sweet home," Riedell says, setting us all roaring.

"Well, this is NYC," I say, mimicking Bailiff Mrs. R's voice, creating another round of giggles.

Chuti Tiu touches her tablet. The screens soar overhead, engulfing us until we are suspended in the air, sitting on our stuffed chairs. Yosemite is almost a constant, spanning one wall eighty feet high by 600 feet wide. Always majestic, inspiring. But this time, when Chuti sends us into the clouds, we are immersed into another dimension.

"This is Destiny," she explains from our position in the clouds.

We are above what I imagine are the Alps; snow-capped mountains extending up from verdant meadows, dappled with spired castles.

"These are some of the homes," Chuti says as we drift down from the comfort of our flying carpet living room, swirling around the citadels as if we are gliding eagles.

"Not all of the members live here fulltime, but each has a home, laboratory if required, certainly an office. Destiny itself is a French/Swiss protectorate of slightly over 1,000 acres. There is a concert hall," she says as we swoop down above the geodesic structure, "an observatory on that mountain top that is also a broadcast, reception, and frequency control tower. There are wind and solar collectors, air and water purification facilities, and self-contained agriculture plants."

We bank through a mountain pass. "Chateau de Vie," she says.

"Amazing," I say before catching myself. I'm expecting dark, gothic, heavy stone; all of which it is, but also majestic in its glass work, tiered landscaping, and multi-layered piazzas.

"I thought you both should see," Chuti says, not elaborating as the screens retreat and our warehouse returns.

As I catch my breath, Riedell is quick to attack. "You married Dad so the woman who threw away my mother wouldn't claim me," Riedell says, "and now you leave Dad and me to live with her? If she is all that rich, can't she just hire a nurse?"

"Push me, pull you," Chuti explains.

Riedell waves her arms wide. "You're answer is Doctor Doolittle?"

Chuti shakes her head, yes. "It's the best I have."

"Faust sold his soul to the Devil," Riedell counters. "Did you?"

Chuti stands, walking toward a collapsed screen. "This will sound condescending, but there is an irony to your question that only age will answer."

"You are evading me," Riedell presses, sliding in front of Chuti on her remaining skate. "Faust was redeemed. Will you be?"

I doubt if either wife or mother ever entered into Chuti Tiu's life plan for herself. Dealing with the unpredictability of a young girl does not *computare*. So Chuti does what every parent resorts to at some point; she invokes parental privilege.

"You will stay here with Shawn. It won't be long before you will need to answer. And the question is much deeper than you can imagine. But you will have a choice. I don't."

"So you are making this decision without me?"

"I am making this decision for you," Chuti insists. "I know you think ten is the new forty, but you still have a great deal to learn."

"I've done alright so far, haven't I?" Riedell challenges.

On occasion Riedell enjoys acting petulant, except it's generally when she is mocking other kids in school; rarely does she play the role for herself. "Maybe I should make my own deal with Grandmother?"

Chuti might be the smartest person on the planet, but she's getting taken to the woodshed by a ten year old.

"I have made the decision."

"Okay, then," Riedell says kissing me on the forehead, ignoring Chuti. "I'm going to crash."

She heads off in search of her missing roller-skate, Rowdy bounding alongside.

"Gregor Mendel," Chuti Tiu calls out after her.

"The friar and his pea plants," Riedell says, returning to our living room.

"Fundamental theory of heredity," Chuti says, walking around our living area.

"And the beginning of The Destiny Society," I guess.

"Genius begetting genius."

"According to Einstein, everybody is a genius, but if you judge a fish by its ability to climb a tree, it will live its whole life believing it is stupid," I chime in.

Chuti turns to me. "Well, well my fauna scaling mackerel, who would have guessed?"

"Don't get your hopes up," I warn her, pointing to an awakening screen. "Sunway was listening in and thought I needed some help."

Chuti smiles, shrugging. "This time Berk has become Destiny's golden boy. Mendel only scared the Medieval Church; Berk is far more dangerous."

"Then let's put Berk back in Fishkill Prison for good," I say. "If we can't prove Berk was behind the bombs, we can expose him for illegal experiments on prisoners. There must be casualties, injuries. Secrets buried in unmarked graves, walled-up cells, or inmates locked away in solitary. You two can track down the payoffs and the experiments gone wrong. I've seen what you can do."

"Except I'm complicit," Chuti says.

"What do you mean?"

"I knew Destiny was using Berk's prisoners for their CRISPR tests. I helped them."

"You were helping everyone."

Tiu shakes her head. "I was helping Destiny from the beginning. I've been amazingly naïve, thinking I could change their minds. Just like I thought running away from them was the answer."

"You had no choice."

"Oh yes I did," Chuti waves away my commiseration. "I could have returned once I understood how long they had tried, and failed, to create someone like me. Emma wasn't their only discard," Chuti explains.

Seeing my reaction, Chuti hurries to finish. "Destiny has waited centuries for nature to take its course. Mother's idea of genetic breeding and child development gave Destiny renewed hope. But with failure after failure, and Mother's productive period ending, my birth was a last hope, with exceedingly slim odds."

"One in fifty billion," I repeat Berk's initial pitch.

"Even greater considering Mother's age," Chuti explains. "But once I proved to have the intelligence they dreamed for, the pieces finally came together. Destiny's wealth exceeding that of all the Arab countries combined; two dictators of sovereign nations as members; supercomputers on the horizon. Nothing could stop their plans for an intellectual utopia."

"And you ran away," I say.

"All that power, all that intellect, except they hadn't considered I would not comply."

"The freezer, the man your mother worked with, abusing you."

"Conditioning, he called it. All the members agreed with him, until I ran," Chuti smiles. "And almost worse, I fought."

'We can expose Berk and Destiny," I offer.

'It won't work. Even if you had a place to print your exposé, no one would believe you. You would sound like a lunatic and, in the end, most likely, you would lose Riedell."

"Then you'd better explain to both of us, because I'll have no choice, with or without your help," I tell her.

Chuti gives me the thousand yard stare, while her Sunway-like mind weighs her options, which may include me becoming the "ex-husband."

"Raping my 'defective' sister was a calculated move on Berk's part," Chuti explains. "Destiny does not believe in perpetuating defective genes."

"Like Berk's Friedreich's ataxia aberration," I understand.

"Exactly. Even cured, he was still tainted. He would only be a henchman, never a member of their Society. He had to make a bold move, showing Destiny people like himself and Emma, with high IQ's yet swimming in a defective gene pool, still have value to Destiny's greater plan."

"So the syringe…" I stop talking as I begin to understand the complexity and the risks of Berk's gamble.

"Berk contrived the rape because he wanted leverage over me to cure his ataxia. He needed me to believe he was the father, and his genetic disease was passed on to Riedell.

"Despite believing in his own intellect, he needed the sperm from the genius repository to produce a prodigy without his genetic defect, one that would be acceptable to The Destiny Society."

"The Repository increased the odds of my intellect without passing on the ataxia marker," Riedell understands.

"Right. We may never know who your real father is, but at least we know it isn't Berk."

I'm not at all comfortable having this conversation in front of Riedell, except it has taken ten years for Chuti to explain this much. I want to make sure both Riedell and I understand.

"So, Riedell's biological father is an unknown donor from the genius bank. And, you created a cure for Berk's ataxia because he convinced you he passed the disease on to Riedell."

"It was a good plan. We even gave Berk the ideal hideout, which is why he didn't fight going to prison. He was neutralized as far as Destiny was concerned, and we were somewhat satisfied to see him put away. All he had to do was remain silent until enough time passed to see if Emma had produced a fully functioning little genius."

"That's me, right?" my daughter realizes.

"Except Berk couldn't leave well enough alone."

"What do you mean?"

"Remember how we thought it was odd that Berk's only request was incarceration at Fishkill?" Tiu asks.

"Berk knew about Kathleen's boy, Jamie, all along," I realize.

"Berk couldn't help himself. He set a plan in motion to destroy you if Riedell turned out as he hoped."

"The explosions."

"Exactly. Berk has always played the long game. Why not be prepared to eliminate Riedell's adoptive father?"

"Still, seems like he took a pretty big chance. Plus, there was no guarantee of our little Miss Perfect here."

"Yes," Chuti agrees, "but the odds were in Berk's favor. Emma."

We turn to Chuti, waiting for the explanation.

"You probably didn't know this, but Emma had the intellect. Not Destiny upper echelon level, but a solid one percenter. Except Destiny is right. Mental illness wins, every time."

Chuti says to Riedell, "Your mother and I tried to protect you from The Destiny Society. If you had taken public school IQ tests, bells and whistles would have gone off at the Foundation."

"You created the nurse's daycare school," I realize. "It wasn't Kathleen's idea at all."

Chuti sits on the edge of the sofa. "It wasn't difficult coaxing Kathleen and you. Her nurses, and you suddenly becoming a single parent. You all had the same need. I simply planted the seeds, and brought in a few school supplies."

"A few," I laugh. "You really got carried away when you knew Riedell wasn't 'defective'." I pat my daughter's head.

"Don't jump to conclusions," Riedell says, cinching her eyes and mouth into a grotesque distortion with her thumbs and fingers.

"Ye God," I say turning away in mock horror. "You are defective."

Chuti smiles, momentarily relieved by the break. "I was looking for a place to house the Sunway. Why not build it into the walls of a warehouse this size, and make it a daycare / home? Plus having an Irish pub downstairs adds unique cover."

"Not to mention your security. So how did he find out Riedell is a genius?"

"Berk guessed because I was risking exposure by locating the Sunway here."

As the scope of Berk's deception sinks in, Riedell becomes agitated, skating in loops.

"So James Berk wins," she says. "Does that mean the end justifies the means?"

"Rye, this is my choice," Chuti explains. "I'm the one who doesn't fit. The anomaly. One in fifty billion. It's me, not you. I belong with Destiny because I don't have a function in this world, except as the Brainiac sideshow freak. You have a father who loves you, and me to protect you. Let us play out our roles. Some day you will have to make your own choice. For now, you can exist as an ordinary person."

"But I'm not, am I?" Riedell says, tossing Yeti over her shoulder and heading to her bedroom with Rowdy leaping ahead. "You two are really irking Irksome."

Chapter Forty

"Berk will try to destroy Paddy and me no matter what you arrange with Destiny, won't he?" I ask Chuti.

"Probably," she agrees, going to the kitchen. She returns with a glass of JD for each of us. "Sit."

"Uh-oh." I sit while Chuti remains standing.

"I don't want Berk ever to see daylight, for what he did to Emma. We are going to get him convicted of mass murder. Life in prison, plus two hundred years. And I intend to be at every parole hearing to make sure he never gets out."

"And how are you going to pull that off?"

Chuti sits down across from me. "You need to listen."

"I'm not going to like this, am I?"

"Probably not. Me either. We will need to do this together, understand?"

Reluctantly I nod, "Yes."

"How old are you?"

I laugh. "Thirty-seven, feel like sixty, and often act sixteen."

"Were you as surprised as the others when my mother told the judge her age?"

"Seventy-six! You bet. I know plenty of women in their fifties who don't think, act, or look as good as her. She was flirting with me in the courtroom, wasn't she?"

"Male ego, female vanity. They're not that dissimilar," Chuti doesn't smile. "I've read about the science Mother has directed, always marveling at her insight; the breadth of her discovery. I am almost able to forget the person she is. She was thirty when I was born. I haven't seen her since I ran away as a teenager," Chuti says looking up to me, waiting.

"So it's been a while since," I stop. "Seventy-six, minus thirty…?"

"I'm the one who is seventy-six," Chuti says. "Thirty-nine years older than you. And my mother is actually 106."

"That can't be possible."

"There's more."

"Please don't tell me you are a man," I beg her.

Chuti laughs. "You've seen me naked in my Shibari ropes more than once. What do you think?"

I shake my head. "You're female. Every inch of you."

"Glad you noticed. Remember what I said about going to every one of Berk's parole hearings?"

I hesitate. "Yeah."

"That's because I'll live that long. When we put Berk in prison for life plus, I'll be there," she says watching for my reaction, "every year, and then some. You understand?"

"No."

"It's part of my DNA. My telomeres."

I'm looking at her, hearing her words, not comprehending.

"I'm having trouble understanding."

"Let me see if I can help you understand," she says, taking my hand and leading me into the bedroom.

* * *

When she finally comes to rest, I've lost a telomere or two. "And, you'll live over 200 years?" *

"You up for it?" she asks, laughing.

"Live long and prosper," comes out of me, sending Chuti Tiu, my consummated wife, into hysterics.

Laughing, holding, touching, we sleep until an early hour. I wake, pray what happened is real, and roll my head to the side. The most beautiful woman on the planet is watching me.

"Hey."

"Hey yourself. You okay with this?"

"More than okay. Want to take our little genius in the next room, the two cats, and go live on an island somewhere?"

"Sure. How long do you think we'd last?"

"After the first 100 years or so, who cares? I'll just be hitting my 137-year-old stride."

---

* We begin to age at the moment of birth. Luckily it's a fairly slow process. Our cells divide 50 to 70 times in a lifetime for general growth, reproduction, and maintenance replacement due to wear and tear.

But not all of the bits and pieces (DNA) get passed on to the successor cell and its nucleus of chromosomes. That's because the protective tip – telomeres – at the ends of thread-like chromosomes fray a bit with each cell division. Complete transmission of DNA is lost. Think of the telomeres as nibs at the end of your shoelaces. Tying your shoes isn't as neat. The laces wear down until they are useless. Same with your telomeres. How much they fray determines how fast you age.

"Mid-life crisis for me. I'll be worrying about you looking at younger women. You'll have to put up with my mood swings. Which means, it will have to be a very big island."

"Big island it is," I say knowing the brief fantasy is drawing to a close. I realize, sadly, that this has been Chuti's way of saying goodbye.

"All of what you said is true, isn't it?"

"Every word."

"Except it feels like science fiction."

Chuti nods her understanding. "At least you said science. Destiny's founders couldn't even use that word for fear of being branded heretics, and stoned to death. When Newton developed the concept of inertia for physics, I suspect it was his observation of people's minds that gave him the inspiration, not a boulder."

"Next thing I know you are going to tell me people can't get the flu from the vaccine, or sitting too close to the TV doesn't ruin your eyes, and your hair and nails don't keep growing after you die."

"And yes, we use much more than 10% of our brains," Chuti says.

"So it's not so much what we don't know, it's what we know that ain't so," I quote.

"Observant woman who said that."

"Will Rodger's," I say, "wise enough to keep his comments about women to himself."

Tiu smiles at my deflection.

Standing next to the bed I look up to the skylights, seeing the twinkling stars beyond. "To think there are hundreds of billions of them," I say. "Solar systems, planets like ours, intelligent life. And still we cling to the idea we are the center of the Universe."

"It's part of our instinct for survival," Tiu understands. "Without us, without I, nothing else exists."

"You know that's not true, don't you?"

Chuti doesn't need to answer.

"Because of Berk, Emma, seeing what has transpired this past week, I've thought The Destiny Society is evil, self-centered, and destructive. But it's not, is it?"

"They are, and they are not."

"CRISPR is never going to be given to the world, is it?"

"No. It would be impossible."

"Same for these long-life telomeres," I assume.

"The world has already mapped the 20,000 base pairs of genes and proteins in the human genome and proteome," Chuti defends.

"Yet without your brilliance, and the Sunway supercomputer to run a quadrillion calculations a second, genetic diseases like Alzheimer's, cancer and MS will never have mass cures."

'True, it is unlikely."

' It would disrupt the balance of nature?"

'We already have over seven billion people on the planet, millions starving. Are you sending bags of rice to Biafra? Of course not. It's not realistic. Humans breed like rabbits, over-populating the planet, always starving, until Nature is forced to step in and re-balance Earth with a plague, a pandemic, a major disaster."

"And all that will remain is The Destiny Society," I understand.

"The best and brightest of us have carved out a sort of, for lack of a better word, Bomb Shelter," Chuti says.

"And that pen your mother threatened Judge R with?"

"Those gases would only be used if the Society were physically threatened. They would never be used offensively."

"We'll see what happens when the hungry masses in China and the Islamic nations hear about your little corner of the planet."

"Like most, they will never believe what the Society can actually do. Science fiction, same as you, that's what they will think," Tiu says. "Besides, all you know about Destiny is what you have seen through Berk; selective breeding, genetic altering. Berk has poisoned your mind with his Nazi Germany mentality."

"It's not true?"

"Of course not. The man isn't one of us." Chuti insists. "We are mathematicians, physicists, chemists, oceanographers, botanists, microbiologists, astronomers, philosophers and artists; not rulers or dictators."

I wonder if Chuti can hear herself; us, we.

"Was sleeping with me part of your plan to keep me in your control?" I say regretting the words the moment they leave my lips. The slap I get spins me sideways.

"You arrogant bastard!"

Crumpling to my knees, "I'm sorry. Please, forgive me. You know, from the moment I first saw you…"

"Don't say it," she orders.

"It's not just last night. I've been in…"

"What just happened was my mistake. It will never happen again, ever. I had a moment of weakness. Don't let yourself make any more of it. You have a full life ahead of you. I do not."

"But you said, you will live another hundred years."

"Like a grieving widow," she says, kneeling beside me, touching my face. "I have avoided relationships because I will outlive anyone I let into my life. That's not a recipe for happiness. Divorce me when Riedell comes of age. I've made my decision. I have to return to Destiny for Riedell, and almost as important, to make certain Berk or one of his followers never gain control. You must help me stop him, and get our revenge."

Call me a cynic, but I'm feeling a bit used. "You had Garcelli and the FBI Agent arrest him," I say.

"They won't be able to hold him. All the Feds have tying Berk to the explosions are a dying, drug addled prisoner, a hacker who has been twisted so many times he thinks a blown-out basement is a penthouse, and a bus full of drunken would-be Irish terrorists. They know they can't hold him, much less convict him."

I know Chuti is right, but what can I do?

"I want you to convince Gayfryd to testify against James Berk."

If my eyes weren't popping, my mouth was open. "You're kidding. She took ten million dollars to disappear. I don't even know where she is."

"I do."

"Of course," I say spreading my arms, "you can find anyone with Sunway."

Chuti shakes her head. "I don't need the Sunway for this."

"What?"

"The long game, remember? The moment you helped Emma, saved her at the mental hospital, wrote your Pulitzer exposé, and gave Emma a job, you put yourself on Mother's radar."

"I almost hate to ask, but what's this got to do with Gayfryd?"

"It's really quite simple if you are watching from a distance and know the players. Mother used Gayfryd to help manipulate Berk, and you. She was the one behind Berk's attempts to take over the Chronicle for Gayfryd."

"Well that explains a few things. But one way or another, once Gayfryd hears about Berk being arrested, she'll know the FBI is looking for her as well. There is no way she is coming back."

"Then you have seventy-two hours to get creative." Chuti Tiu backs off a fraction, enough for me to see her eyes. "We need this."

Chapter Forty-One

"I want you to convict Paddy in your newspaper," Tiu reveals her plan to me.

"Are you insane? Me accusing Paddy of being a mass murderer?"

"Exposing your friend as a co-conspirator with Kathleen and her **32CSM** will let Gayfryd know she is safe to come back to the U.S. and go after the fortune Starch left for your new school."

"I won't do it."

"I'll convince Prosecutor Kasey to play along," Tiu continues speaking as if I haven't said a word. "Kasey will lay it all on Paddy's door. Another dirty cop, along with the two dead ones. It will work."

"Paddy will be destroyed. He'll lose everything, the bar, his dignity."

"This is the best way to assure Gayfryd she is in the clear. Reading the story in the Chronicle under your byline will convince her."

"That won't be enough."

"I'll get Mother to help."

"Is Gayfryd with her?"

Tiu doesn't answer.

"Mother has been working Gayfryd long enough to know how to play her. Berk has served his purpose, and she wants Berk gone as much as we do."

"We?"

"Berk getting the Medal of Freedom has drawn too much attention to The Destiny Society. Mother is angry at the exposure CRISPR is getting."

"Maybe you've forgotten, The Chronicle has been destroyed," I say, searching for another argument.

Tiu looks around the warehouse. "I'd say you've got plenty of room to run a newspaper right here."

"I have to talk to Paddy," I insist before making my Faustian deal.

"You can't do that. Paddy has to show genuine shock when the FBI takes him. That's the only way Gayfryd will believe it. The whole point is to sell the story to Gayfryd, go all out. Do what you do best."

He's my best friend, but she may be right.

"If it's any consolation, you will be restoring the Chronicle. No other media will have the inside story behind the bombings and the deaths. And I don't mean to be funny, but you'll be kicking some genius butt as well. You'll be responsible for putting The Destiny Foundation back on the right path. Think of it, reminding Destiny's geniuses the obligation of their gift."

"Not much comfort when you're selling out your friend."

"Paddy will come to understand. When Gayfryd is arrested and flips on Berk, you can exonerate him."

"Sure, retraction buried on page twenty. That isn't going to make things right."

"I know it won't be easy, but you have to trust your friendship. Plus, your readers will understand. Greater good. Remember, you are *Unflawed*."

"I'll say."

Tiu puts her arms around my waist and whispers, "Until Gayfryd sets foot on US soil, there can be no weak link."

"I understand."

Tiu stands back, fixing her eyes on mine. "Alright then. Mother will do her part. I guarantee it."

"And Prosecutor Kasey?"

"This will be the biggest case of her career, and she'll have a Pulitzer winning reporter making her look good. What more could she want?"

I return Tiu's stare.

Tiu bites her lip. "Kasey is diabetic, remember? Berk goes to prison, she gets cured. Good enough for you?"

"Talk about the bloom coming off the lily. You just convinced me Dr. Darieux really is your mother," I say with regret.

I see the FBI coming into Parnell's on the security screen. Tiu was never waiting for me to agree.

Seeing I understand, she says, "Write your story. Your Editor already has the headline."

Chapter Forty-Two

It is a dark, cold and stormy day. Absent the morning rays pouring through the skylight, I got an extra hour of miserable sleep.

"She's taken the bait," Tiu says waking me

"Good. Has Paddy been released?"

"Gayfryd is still in the air. We can't take the risk of her finding out."

"What's she going to do, demand the airline turn around?"

"Gayfryd's on a Destiny jet. Mother is with her, supposedly for a meeting with her estate lawyers to help Gayfryd assert her claim."

"But she won't get that far, right?"

"Lt. Garcelli and Prosecutor Kasey will be waiting at Westchester Airport. They will arrest her on the spot."

"Good."

"Sunway and I went back through Berk's entire time in prison, decrypting messages between Gayfryd and Berk. I passed the information to Prosecutor Kasey. There is enough evidence on Gayfryd to put her away for a long time. How much she gets will depend on how quickly she flips on Berk."

"But the plan is to get Paddy released once Gayfryd is in cuffs, right?" I insist, heading to the shower.

Tiu follows me to the bathroom. "Unfortunately, there are demonstrations."

"Where?"

"Downstairs, in front of Parnell's. And at the Midtown Precinct. People are waving this morning's Chronicle: *Ex-Cop Linked to Terrorist Bombings*. The Commissioner has already announced a full investigation."

"So just like that, Paddy's regulars have turned on him? Damn it, I never should have gone along with this. I'll take the hit, retract everything. Riedell can broadcast my confession everywhere. Make it go viral."

"That's your right, but if you want to be credible, we need to clear Paddy first."

I know she's right. "Where is Riedell? Is she safe?" I ask, looking for my toothbrush.

"She's at Starch's school in Connecticut helping with the certification. Mandell is with her."

"Thank God," I say, turning on the shower.

"By the way, Gert is demanding to be released. Amy is slightly improved. Long road there," Chuti Tiu rattles off a summary. "Better make that shower fast, half the Chronicle City Room has moved in."

"Are you kidding?"

"No, and you are going to need them. Better get out there soon."

"What about Wadjet and the Sunway?"

"The screens are retracted into the walls. The Chronicle people won't even know they are sitting inside a supercomputer."

"Won't the gamma rays start making them act strange, like the other people in this house?"

"No more than usual." Tiu grins.

She starts filling a sling bag with small items I didn't even know were in my room. No clothes. Where she stores them, I have no idea. But there are enough retractable screens, furnishings, and mezzanines in the warehouse, there could be a Neiman Marcus boutique somewhere and I wouldn't know it. The only outfit I've seen Tiu wearing more than once is her original equipment.

Her eyes are making a fast survey of the room. I know she is leaving.

She has never left as much as water droplets in the bathroom sink. All she will leave me is fragmented memories.

I look up. The Shibari rope is gone.

"Sunway will respond to both you and Riedell, within limits," Chuti continues. "You don't need the screens. She'll answer through your laptop, cell, tablet or Wadjet. The Chronicle people won't be here for long, so be creative."

"I don't know the…"

Tiu puts up her hand.

"You'll learn. You've only scratched the surface with Sunway. Let your daughter teach you," she says zipping the sling bag closed. "And remember, I am only a click away wherever I am."

"I'll never see you again, will I?"

Tiu tilts her head. "I'm going back on the Destiny jet with Mother once Gayfryd is arrested," Tiu smiles. "First plane I will be on as a legitimate passenger."

Chuti Tiu shoulders her sling bag.

"Don't underestimate Berk," she warns.

"He's locked up."

"I don't have to remind you what he did from the Fishkill prison during the last ten years."

"Got it. I'm learning."

"I know," my wife says as she hugs me. "Take good care of our daughter."

"Live long and prosper," I say mimicking Riedell's hand Vee.

* * *

Our warehouse home has become a City Room. No mammoth screens or supercomputer in evidence. Tiu is right. No one knows. All I hear are the sounds of clicking laptops, phone calls, hollers and curses. For the first time I feel at home in my home.

"Don't worry, we'll be out of here in a month or two," Managing Editor Van Wie says, spotting me in my robe, drinking my tea. There isn't a hint of grateful in Van Wie's voice. "Interesting home. Think we can keep the bar downstairs open for the staff?"

"You can ask Lt. Garcelli. He'll be here in two minutes."

"He coming to get you as well? That's the thing about cops, they stick together. No one likes a Judas."

"And the horse you rode in on," I say. "Yesterday's news. Try and keep up, will you. I want front page above the fold for the special edition."

"Let's get this clear from the get-go. I run the Chronicle, not you. If you want to write for the Chronicle, it's because I say so," Van Wie announces to the forty plus staffers in my home.

"Feel better?"

Van Wie stiffens.

"Good, because your reputation is going to take a beating today, old sod," I say slapping his arm. "My good friend Paddy allowed himself to be used as a decoy, and you fell for it. Wadjet. Westchester Airport, Destiny jet on overhead," I order a screen to explode up to the rafters. Here she is," I say pointing.

"Who?"

"Don't you recognize your wife? She's the Chronicle bomber," I tell him.

I point to Van Wie's terrified assistant. "Get on your laptop. I'll send you the story and photos."

"Have a nice day," I tell Van Wie as I leave to get dressed.

* * *

"I don't know where you got five million dollars bail, but your former best friend is going to string you up by your balls for what you did," Det. Stone shouts the instant I get in the back of his squad car.

I don't answer. We ride in silence.

As we turn off the exit, Stone says, "The Warden is a friend. I asked him for a favor. He's speeding up the release process, but after that you're on your own with Paddy."

FBI Special Agent-in-Charge Greene is shaking hands with the Warden at the entrance of the Vernon C. Bain Correctional Center at Rikers Island when we arrive.

"What is she doing here?" Det. Stone demands. "Is this some kind of publicity stunt?"

I get out of the squad and begin passing out copies of my Sunway mock-up of the Chronicle Special Edition. Paddy gets the first copy.

Chapter Forty-Three

The celebration of Paddy's sting operation brings the NYPD into Parnell's by the droves. Even the Commissioner and Mayor stop by. Not long after, Gayfryd received thirty years. James Berk, life plus 150 years. Chuti Tiu sends me a simple note, "Congratulations, we did it."

Paddy and I are good. We spend most evenings together at the Pub, not saying much. My friend is still blaming himself for not doing more to help Kathleen's son. Stoic as my friend is, I know how much he misses his wife.

My loan is forgiven in Starch's will. I remain on the Chronicle Board. The Chronicle Company is now run by retired professor Athena Jones. Her wife, Amy, says she plans to return to the Chronicle once her new skin is able to accept daylight.

The Nano-hydration technology provided by The Destiny Foundation during those first crucial hours saved Amy's life. Destiny's artificial split-thickness skin regeneration program appears to be the new gold standard for burn victims. Amy is writing about the discoveries and her progress for the Chronicle. I'm thinking she has a future as the paper's Science and Technology Editor.

Gert is kicking butt with her new bionic leg. The Destiny Foundation's surgical team's technique saved an extraordinary number of nerves at the second severance, allowing reinneration of leg muscles. The Sunway is speeding up the biological amplifiers of her motor commands. It won't be long before she is darting past me on our daily walks as we re-explore our City for our mutual therapy.

The Starch School for Children has its first class president. Ten is the new forty, and resiliency is for the young.

The school's curriculum specializes in teaching exceptional and special needs students. "Humbling and enlightening for all of us," Riedell says. Summers are open to all children; interaction integration. "It gets boring with only smart kids. They are all me, me, me," Riedell tells me.

The butterfly sanctuary is restored. Emma's bronze statue has been joined by one of Starch holding up the trash can catching Emma's sky-hook litter shot. The can is emptied three times a day.

Riedell and Tiu are still hard-wired. I rarely hear from my wife, but I know she is looking out for us.

Riedell decided it will be more convenient to stay in Connecticut at school during the week. "So many windows. The winter is prettier up here."

She wants to bring the cats, Rowdy and Yeti, with her. There will be plenty of sunny spots for them to nap.

And all those butterflies to chase.

Author's Parting Thoughts: The Human Genome

The human genome is our personal algorithm. The decision tree that makes us tall or short; black or white; smart, or not so smart. In short, everything we are.

We have 23 chromosome pairs within the almost 37 trillion cells that compose us. Each chromosome has hundreds of thousands of genes, and each of those has 25 million subsets composed of even more microparticles. If that isn't enough, there are another 3 billion bonding points.

Personally, I am amazed we fit together as well as we do.

As you might guess, not all these bits and pieces are of the finest quality. There are some factory defects; some parts suffer wear and tear; some bits get lost behind the couch cushions; and disease can damage previously good components.

CRISPR offers the ability to slip into these massive systems – humans - and make repairs. No popping open the chest or abdomen and exchanging a heart or a liver. Instead, CRISPR works more like an additive you put in the oil of your engine. It finds what is making the clunking sound, snips out the bad part (cancer gene), and installs a working replacement. Better yet, why wait for the clunking sound. CRISPR can find the bad part before it actually malfunctions, and avoid all of the trouble later.

Some see a cure for cancer. Others may ask, can I change my brown eyes to blue? Prospective parents might request one healthy, brilliant, blond, athletic boy, please. NFL quarterback and sponsor magnet material, if you will.

It doesn't take much imagination to see some potential problems: population explosion and designer babies, just for starters.

And, who will have access to this life altering tool?

As Confucius wished, "May you live in interesting times."

About the Author

I grew up in Western New York and worked my way through Business School as a tech writer and reporter.

Deadline is my fourth novel.

My wife, Beverly, and I live in the mountains of Lake Tahoe and the desert of Las Vegas with our special needs cats. In between chapters, we play pickleball and golf.

Send me your thoughts – good, bad or indifferent. I improve from your insight. mailfordougk@gmail.com

If you enjoy my books, please leave a review on Amazon.com.

Add these other books by Douglas Keil to your reading list now.

The Girl in the Freezer – *"A smart, witty, captivating thrillfest packed with suspense, surprise, and awesome technology." – Kirkus Reviews*

BarCats – *"Very interesting…with much going on." The author has "a knack and a flair for telling a good story."* - Readers' Favorite

Dear Dad – *"Epistolary quality of the narrative impressively and vibrantly encapsulates…. a teen facing the most trying time of his young life. Searingly poignant." – Kirkus Reviews*

Have a pet? Love animals? These charming true stories by Beverly Keil are great for the whole family.

Diary of a Dumpster Pup – *"Inspiring and heartwarming…will restore your sense of hope in humanity." – 5 star review, Readers' Favorites*

Sleepless in New Orleans – *"A riveting chronicle of an animal rescue mission suddenly under the threat of a fast-approaching hurricane. Heartwarming." – Amazon Reader Review*

All books available from Amazon.com

Made in the USA
Monee, IL
09 July 2021